Witches
on the
Road Tonight

Also by Sheri Holman

A Stolen Tongue
The Dress Lodger
The Mammoth Cheese

Witches
on the
Road Tonight

Sheri Holman

Atlantic Monthly Press
New York

Copyright © 2011 by Sheri Holman

Published simultaneously in Canada
Printed in the United States of America

FIRST EDITION

ISBN-13: 978-0-8021-1943-8

Atlantic Monthly Press
an imprint of Grove/Atlantic, Inc.
841 Broadway
New York, NY 10003

Distributed by Publishers Group West

www.groveatlantic.com

11 12 13 14   10 9 8 7 6 5 4 3 2 1

For those of us who went to the woods
and found our way out again

And with enormous gratitude to the
American Academy of Arts and Letters,
the Ragdale Foundation, and the PEN Emergency Fund,
whose support meant so much

Witches
on the
Road Tonight

Eddie

NEW YORK CITY

MIDNIGHT

Of all the props I saved, only the coffin remains. Packed in boxes or tossed in the closet were the skulls and rubber rats, the cape folded with the care of a fallen American flag, my black spandex unitard, white at the seams where I'd stretched out the armpits, sweat-stained and pilled. I saved the squeezed-out tubes of greasepaint, the black shadow for under the eyes, the porcelain fangs. Of the gifts fans sent, I kept that bleached arc of a cat's skeleton, the one you used to call Fluffy and hang your necklaces from, and a dead bird preserved with antifreeze. I kept maybe a hundred of the many thousands of drawings and letters from preteen boys and girls. There were some from adults, too, confessions of the sort they should be writing their shrinks or the police, and not a man who plays a vampire on TV. "Dear Captain Casket, Fangs for the memories."

But in the move up to Manhattan, in the successive apartments Charles and I shared, everything has been lost or thrown away. Coming to me late in life, Charles has been pitiless in tossing my prehistory, usually while I am off at one of the twice-yearly conventions I attend as if having an affair we both tacitly refuse to discuss. Now everything has been scrapped but the coffin, too big not to be missed, too great a conversation piece even for Charles, a bit of memorabilia that you might send off to a regional horror movie museum or sell to some

theme restaurant as the base of a fixin's bar to defray a small portion
of the funeral cost. We've been using it as a coffee table, pushed in
front of the big picture window that overlooks the Chrysler Building,
a view that accounts for three-quarters of the ridiculous price we paid
for this apartment. It has held up well over the years, made of wormy
chestnut, hand-planed and smooth as a wooden Indian. I used to keep
it in the carport between Saturday shows, and you played in it as a girl.
Sometimes when we couldn't find you, your mother and I would look
outside and you'd be curled up inside it, asleep, your hand bookmark-
ing the eternally youthful and nosy Nancy Drew, your mouth brushed
with cookie crumbs.

I have made it as comfortable as possible. It is lined with an old
down comforter tucked inside one of Charles's more elegant duvet
covers, a dusky rose shot with gold thread. I have a pillow for my head
and a scarlet throw to keep me warm. You might think I'd like to go
out in full costume, but camp comes too easily these days. I'm wearing,
instead, my most comfortable pajamas, the ones with the pug dogs you
bought me for my birthday last year. They are about the only ones my
chemo-blistered skin can bear. Before I put them on, I took a shower
and washed what's left of my hair. Maybe it was cowardly to wait to
do this until Charles was out of town. His mother, who is only a few
years older than I, is ill, too, and poor Charles hasn't known whom to
nurse more dutifully. He refuses to discuss my death, pulling, instead,
all sorts of prophylactic voodoo like purchasing cruise tickets for next
spring, or placing a down payment on a purebred mastiff puppy, if you
can imagine, as if he can mortgage me back to life, keeping me on the
ventilator of increasingly onerous financial obligation. I know he will
be furious when he gets back from Philadelphia, but maybe he'll take
his mother with him on that cruise through the Cyclades.

My only real regret is not seeing you one last time. I left you a message before you went on the air, something light and innocuous, and I
hope you're not too shocked to hear it after you get the news. I want
this good-bye to set the tone for all the memories that follow it. When
people approach me about my show, they never want to talk about the
cut-rate monster movies. Most can barely remember the titles. No,
it is the irreverence of the interruption they cherish, the silliness and

explosions. I made it my career for decades, but only now do I begin to understand the need to terrify, followed by the even greater need to puncture the fear we've called into being. It is a surrender and recovery that feels suspiciously like love.

The tea kettle whistles and I reach for my mayapple and burdock—those holistic Manhattan cancer quackeries that always bring me full circle back to the mountain—when I remember I don't need them anymore and pour myself a whiskey instead. Yet that, too, reminds me of the mountain. I have come a long way from ghost stories and digging roots. Here at the door to the balcony, I can look out over the huddled city, as underdressed for the weather as I on this miserably frigid August night. I don't like to think the weather has made my decision for me, but at my age, it's difficult to face inclemency in any form—you can't help but feel the world has given up, and yourself a bit with it. It has been the coldest, wettest summer on record, hasn't it? At least that's what you keep telling us down at your news network where you are always searching out new ways to panic us. Something to add to the wars and the stock market and the Depressions. Your twenty-four-hour cycle has grown more hysterical each year, that creepy crawl across the bottom constantly breaking nonnews. And now, with every inch of the screen filled and moving left to right, with no more hours left in the day, I wouldn't be surprised if your people weren't working on a particle gun to beam bad news directly into our dreams, stealing that last refuge where nightmares might still be personal. You've given us all sleep impotence, Wallis. But lucky for us, there's a small blue non-habit-forming pill for that. Don't think I haven't noticed who sponsors your broadcast.

The fog over Manhattan tonight hangs like the fog in the hollow where I grew up, and maybe that is what has me stitching together memories of my own first horror movie—a grainy, convulsive thing projected onto the bedroom wall of our dogtrot cabin. I was in bed where Tucker's car had put me. The sun had set but no lamp was yet lit and it was moving toward the shadow darkness that allows terror free play in the minds of suggestible young boys. He sat next to me on the counterpane with his hand-cranked projector steadied on our family Bible and fed the celluloid onto the reel. It's nearly seventy years ago

now, but I remember it like it was yesterday. Every work of art has its
own cadence, he said, slowly turning the wheel, working into a rhythm
that jerked the movie along with it. Too slow, too fast, until he got it
right. He was spinning a copy of *Frankenstein,* not the Boris Karloff clas-
sic, but a thirteen-minute Edison short, shot in 1910, the first horror
movie ever made, he told me, though there was nothing so horrific
about it—at least not to a modern boy in 1940 who'd been listening
to *Lights Out* on the radio for years. It was clumsy and old-fashioned
and the man playing Frankenstein's monster shambled about like an
oversized Christmas elf. And yet I remember being as afraid as I'd ever
been that night, sitting in the dark, watching this odd series of pictures
twitching to life on my bedroom wall. I had never seen a movie, you
see, living where we did, just as I had never ridden in a car until Tucker
Hayes, the man who brought the movie, struck me with his. And it was
possibility that thrilled and scared me that night. A movie. A car.

Wallis, where are you tonight? Forgive an old man. I am afraid.

Fear has a dialect for every occasion, doesn't it, dearest? The anxious
lyric patter of fresh love where every sentence has the potential to reveal
the unlovable self, the Atlas groan of a parent bent under the weight of
his own immaturity; there is the fear of failure and nuclear annihilation
and snakes, of getting up in the morning, and then, of course, there is
the fear of the dark, which is, as they all are, the fear of Death, which
we dare not examine too closely while in life, lest it ruin all the more
pleasurable fears of living and loving; for why else fall in love or marry
or have children except to trail our fingers along the deliciously dark
hallways and blind corners of What Comes Next? What comes next
for me? Well, if I can believe the empty bottle of sleeping pills on the
kitchen counter, it is that which stands in the center of my living room.
I am loyal to the end. Of course I asked my doctor to prescribe your
sponsor's brand.

Here we are, another Saturday at midnight, but this time, instead
of the slow creak of hinges, the bloodless white hand reaching through
a veil of dry ice and the zombielike mug for the camera, it is a climbing
up, a lying down, a settling in.

I called you, Wallis, and left a message. Something light and funny.
Remember that, won't you?

I

Panther Gap

October 1940

They are playing a game called Firsts that Tucker had made up to pass the time in the car that first week when he and Sonia barely knew each other, in the days before their first time, which should have imparted intimate knowledge, but had, in some indefinable way, made them feel even more like strangers than they were before.

"First word?" Tucker asks.

"My mother tells me it was 'baby,'" Sonia says. "Yours?"

"Tipi. She was our nurse. Been with the family since Mother was a girl."

"First book?" Sonia asks.

"That I remember? Our family Bible. It was big and red and I never saw it open. Yours?"

"Same. Only ours was big and black and open all the time."

It is hot for October and they ride with the windows of the '35 Ford rolled down, blinking against the dust from the ungraded road. The wind whips Sonia's platinum hair across her eyes; she pushes it back to read their Esso map. The paper has given out at the creases from their folding and unfolding of it, and the route is covered in Tucker's notes about churches and courthouses, the populations of cemeteries, the number of oysters shucked in an hour by a single Negro man in Hampton

Roads. They are somewhere along the spine of the Blue Ridge, coming into the Alleghenies, as best she can tell.

"First house?" Tucker asks.

"Was not a house," she responds. "It was a fifth floor walk-up on Rivington Street." She doesn't ask him about his first house but he volunteers it anyway.

"Mine was Folly Farm, fifteen miles north of Richmond. Like Tipi, it came with Mother. Of course Father lost it along with everything else. First assignment?" he asks.

"'Gloves Make the Girl.' *Ladies' Home Journal*, October 1920."

"A piece on shell shock for my college paper. My father was diagnosed in '23, but Mother says he thought he could talk to animals long before he ever set foot in the Marne."

He takes the switchbacks of the mountain fast, choosing dirt roads over anything paved. She is supposed to be logging their mileage but it has been hours since Sonia has seen a marker. She wrestles the map as it flaps in the wind.

"I've lost us," she says.

"Put it away. We should drive as we would divine for water."

"They'll be angry if we get it wrong."

"Oh, how the tourists shall whine," Tucker says. "We're doing them a favor."

Their assignment was to chart a driving tour of this region for the Virginia Writers' Project. Tucker was to describe landmarks and local history; Sonia was to photograph it all. Hundreds more, just like them, were mapping the other forty-seven states, one more public works project like the Civilian Conservation Corps whittling picnic areas on the Skyline Drive. Until now, no one had thought to sell America to Americans. *Everyone's sick of the dust bowl and raggedy babies*, their field officer in Charlottesville told them. *It's time for this country to love itself again.*

"Peel me an egg, would you, Mrs. Hayes?" Tucker says. Sonia takes a hard-boiled egg from their paper lunch bag and rolls it between her palms, flicking chips of shell out of the window. Her fingernails are permanently stained black from the chemicals she uses to get the cool, strong contrast she wants in her work. She holds out the egg for Tucker to bite.

"I've been proposing all my life," he says, grabbing her hand and kissing each black nail. "There was Cousin Flora of the skinned knees and slipped hair ribbons. Cruel Bette, who broke my heart with her Matryoshka-doll figure and diminishing affections to match. But at last I've found the ideal wife, who forsakes the common obsession with matrimony for the more sacred institution of honeymoon."

He bites the egg in half. "And she cooks, too!"

Sonia smiles and eats what's left over.

The car has drifted and Tucker corrects the wheel, hugging the narrow shoulder nearest the rock. On Sonia's side, the mountain drops away beneath a wide case-hardened sky. Lifting the Rolleiflex she wears on a strap around her neck, she points it out of her open window. She is notorious at *Wealth* magazine, where she works, for wasting film. Some of her colleagues say she doesn't trust herself and so takes ten shots for every one she keeps; some say she's voracious in the moment and her pictures are the photographic equivalent of owl pellets, just the bones and feathers of an experience. She doesn't care what they think—she's shot more covers than any of the men. Tucker fixes his attention on the hazy ridgeline.

"First love?" he asks.

They have been sleeping as man and wife since the third week of their assignment. It took him longer than most of the writers she's traveled with. With the others, after a few days, two rooms were awfully expensive, weren't they? We could sure save a buck if we were modern enough to share. They'd buy the tin rings at Woolworth's and sign the register Mr. and Mrs., then over cigarettes and whatever bottle they could get cheap, they'd stay up late talking until at last his head would end up in her lap. *God, you are so gorgeous. Why hasn't some man made an honest woman out of you? What a beautiful mother you'd make.* His finger would trace her calf and she would close her eyes at his idea of a compliment, remembering the sunken-eyed schoolboy in Berlin staring down at the kitten he'd finished off with a brick, or the little girl from Rivington Street, her first printing failure, who had emerged from the stop bath so poorly contrasted she was barely distinguishable from the tenement rubble behind her.

With Tucker it had not been words or whiskey offered up as seduction but, instead, a movie, projected on the cinderblock wall of a roadside motel in Harpers Ferry. For their six-week trip he had packed, along with his notebooks and clothes, a hand-cranked Pathé iron projector that had belonged to his father, and every night he showed her films, odd bits and pieces he'd collected, old Edison shorts, newsreels of famine, and scenes of the war in Europe. She sat in the crook of his arm as he cranked the handle, the bulb flickering to life and the dim blue picture jittery against the wall. He chose a newsreel piece on the work of Käthe Kollwitz, whose etchings of mothers cradling their starving children Hitler had labeled as degenerate. *I love these old films,* he said. *We have a hand in the speed of creation.* Then, without breaking cadence, he leaned down and placed his mouth on hers. With his free hand he untucked her shirt and eased his palm along her ribs to the curve of her breast. His mouth moved down her throat, over her pillowed stomach then farther, never breaking rhythm, and she continued to watch—the children reaching up, wordlessly crying out for bread, mothers hunkered over dying sons—until the film spun through and battered against the reel. *Could you ever love a wretched sinner like me?* he whispered, covering her with himself. But none of these men knew the first thing about sinning, Sonia thought, they only desperately wished to, as they wished to know all the dark rooms of the world.

"First love?" she repeats, her camera trained out the window. "Why you, of course."

She knows Tucker is Southern before he opens his mouth, by the way he spends the evening saying good-bye without ever leaving. He is already at the door when she arrives at Bennett's party, pressed in on all sides by the actors and antique dealers and men Bennett meets in bus lines. Tucker stands with his jacket over his arm, his eyes cast down, nodding as the woman next to him shouts close to his ear. Normally, Sonia isn't attracted to blond men, there is something pink and infantile about them, and their light eyes are always watering, but Tucker is blond like sandstone, softly eroded and a little abrasive. He wears a beige linen suit in a room full of black and brown jackets, and he slouches with his hands thrust deep in his pockets. The woman finishes talking and he speaks a few words in reply and kisses her on the cheek, moving even closer to the door, where another woman grabs him by the arm and draws her own concentrated nods. Bennett catches her watching them. *There's a lucky bastard,* he shouts over Artie Shaw on the record player. *His play flopped on Broadway so he signed on with the WPA back home. Now he's gotten drafted. He'll be swimming in peach till the day he leaves.* Tucker takes his hands from his pockets and holds them palm up for the second woman as if to say, See, there is nothing left. No man is so appealing, Sonia thinks, as one who apologizes for himself in advance. Then, *Speech, speech,* someone shouts and he lets himself be pulled back into the room and passed a fresh drink, and he is convinced to drawl a little drunkenly, *God bless this country where a man might so easily be transferred from one teat of Lady Liberty to another.* Much later, when Sonia goes to retrieve her scarf and purse, she finds him drinking alone on their host's bed, staring out the window onto Washington Square Park below. The cars race up Fifth Avenue and turn sharply when they reach the white triumphal arch. In the glass above him she catches a glimpse of her own tired face, she has talked and drunk away all but a red smudge of her lipstick. She takes a seat on the bed beside him and they sit in comfortable silence for such a long time that Sonia thinks she just might be asleep. But then he catches her off guard. *What scares you?* he asks, and she answers without thought, *The Nazis have taken Paris, London is flattened. I'm scared everything exciting is happening somewhere else.* She pauses and asks what is expected—*What scares you?*—knowing before he even suggests it that she will be leaving with him. *Dying,* he says. *And women like you.*

"Mrs. Hayes," Tucker commands.

"What?"

"I spy with my little eye—Sider and Apples Sold by the Pound, Bushel, or Truckload."

They are cresting a hill and Sonia doesn't have time to read the misspelled, hand-painted sign before they have reached a clearing and a slapped-together wooden stand. The structure's sloping roof is shingled with apple slices drying in the sun and behind it sits an elderly man working a mechanical peeler like a pencil sharpener. He shakes his denim jacket free of skins when Tucker excuses the car to a stop.

"Look at that ancient specimen," Tucker says to her as the man ducks beneath the shed's awning and rises to his full height. "We could saw him in half and count his rings."

Tucker and Sonia sit in the front seat letting the old man appraise them through the windshield. He has a fifth-button white beard that Sonia guesses he's been growing longer than she's been alive. He has halved his Model T and fitted it with a flatbed. On it, wooden crates of more apples are stacked three high.

"We need one of him," Tucker says.

Tucker swings open the car door as Sonia adjusts the aperture of her camera. There's good light and a panoramic view of the valley, and she thinks, yes, Tucker is right, this is what they want to see of this place, a roadside Sider Man with his apples and his time. She watches Tucker approach him, loose-limbed and casual, holding out his hand as if for a wary dog to sniff. The Sider Man shakes it stiffly.

"Mighty fine fruit you have here," Tucker says, picking up a dull green apple from a basket at his feet.

"Mountain pippins what's ripe now," says the old man. "A few Fousts."

"Some venerable orchards up this way, I'd imagine."

"Yup," says the old man, eying Sonia, who has found her settings and stepped out of the car to join them. He traces her figure through her linen shirt and plum-colored trousers. Then his eyes go to the dark roots of her platinum hair and linger disapprovingly.

"Where I grew up," Tucker is saying, "we had an Apple Blossom Festival. Y'all have anything like that up here?"

"In the spring."

"I love those festivals," Tucker says. "Pride of place."

The Sider Man nods. His face is deeply lined from sun and tobacco. He rocks back on his cracked naked heels and waits for Tucker to get to the point. Sonia wants to get the truck in the shot, too, and circles around him, looking for her angle.

"Y'all just passing through?" the Sider Man asks at last.

"Me and the missus are out and about on behalf of Mr. Roosevelt," Tucker says. "Works Progress Administration. They're writing up travel guides to the forty-eight states to give artist types like us something to do. We're on good terms with the battles and business of this common-wealth, but they want us to send back some flavor. You know, stories, legends, anything that makes this mountain special."

The Sider Man stares at him blankly.

"I don't suppose you know any legends?"

"Can't say I do," the Sider Man answers.

"What about local features?" Tucker asks kindly. "Caves or springs? Twice a year when I was a boy, we'd drive these mountains so my father could sit in the hot springs. Met veterans who fought at Bull Run."

Sonia can see him casting around for that thing they share. Tucker is always able to find something, she's seen him get lumbermen and merchant marines, cigarette rollers and seamstresses to talk for hours. But the Sider Man stands mute.

"Now's your chance," Tucker says bluffly. "You're going in a guide book. People will drive from all over to find you, and you'll be selling apples faster than you can pick 'em. My wife here will even take your picture."

Sonia smiles politely. "It would be an honor," she says.

The Sider Man turns back to his stand. "WPA took my photograph years ago. Some Jew from New York City. You vampires gonna come back for a man's soul, you might buy something first."

They are back in the car with a bushel of pippins and a jug of applejack between them. The Sider Man fits another apple to his peeler, unwinds his long russet ribbon. Sonia turns in the front seat to steal a shot as they pull away.

"Don't," says Tucker gruffly. "You can't take a picture of rejection without deserving it."

The stand is gone, they are headed down the other side of the moun-tain through a granite pass. Laurel bushes cling to the cliff while rain-swelled springs flow in channels beside the road like running boards on a car. In a month, this way will be impassable, she thinks. Tucker is taking the turns too fast; three empty Coke bottles roll lazily across the floorboards and clink together, back and forth down the hill.

Using one hand to drive, he uncorks the applejack with his teeth and takes a deep draw.

"First lie?" he asks.

"I don't lie," she answers.

"I asked for your first, not an example," he says.

Sonia turns away in annoyance. She has been told *no* so often she doesn't hear the word anymore. Someone has always arrived before her wherever she's been and she has learned simply to shoot from a different angle.

"He's right, you know," Tucker says. "Who are we to turn a person's life into a stop along the way?"

His hands are trembling lightly on the steering wheel, his face rudderless and resigned, just as it was the night of Bennett's party, as he watched the cars along Fifth Avenue. As if the trip out here is more than the trip inside, and the forward motion alone might prove him courageous. She knows because her body becomes the journey as much as anything else, the unfolded map upon which all of these men lose and refind themselves. They speak of marriage and wanting to give her a child to show that this is *real* and she plays along, going so far as to give their imaginary child a name, calling him Pa when he calls her Ma, feeding each other waffles in the brown and olive crypts of one-star hotel dining rooms. Then, later, with quiescent Juliette or Angela or Veronica (they always want a girl, these men) sanctifying the union, he is free to fold her legs up to her ears and weep away his guilt on her breasts, telling her how beautiful they will look swollen with milk. It's the same thing, she thinks. Before. After they just have to somehow make it okay. All these men with their hats in their hands and their pained, expectant faces.

"Stop the car," she says with enough force that he obeys her. He stops on a blind curve, parking the Ford as close to the cliff as he dares. Below them on the other side, a gorge of grapevine and waxy rhododendron spills down to white water. Sonia picks up her Rolleiflex and steps out, slipping down the embankment.

"Where are you going?" he calls. A tinny, gimcrack blue jay answers loud above the water.

Caves and rivers and natural bridges. Their assignment is to send back anything other than the orderly intersections of towns, or why else would a family feel the need to purchase a car and pay for gasoline and overspend themselves to leave home? Sonia points her camera into the gap, trying to capture the dizziness of plunging into the forest. Forget the Sider Man. It's all an intrusion, where they've been, where he's headed next, the fat black line of Fort Dix that underscores the end of their trip, and from there into whichever European woods or field or intersection of streets they'll send him to fight. If you're going to feel guilty about one trespass, you might as well feel guilty about them all.

Sonia has slid halfway down the embankment and stops to catch her breath. Now that she's put enough distance between them, she feels sorry for Tucker Hayes. She is the last woman he'll be with before he leaves. She is old enough to remember the soldiers returning from the last war and how their women understood, dropping the barricades of bustles and corsets. Here boys, you've crawled through enough mud. Here is a shoulder, a knee, a field of flesh. Sonia's fingers hover over the buttons of her damp linen shirt. Ahead is the roar of water deep in the gorge. Here, she thinks, as one by one she loosens the buttons, leaving her shirt draped over the low-hanging branch of a black gum. Take it. The shade is damp and her Rolleiflex is cool next to the sweat between her breasts. Sonia unbuckles her belt and steps out of her trousers, walking deeper into the woods.

Tucker will be impatient when she doesn't return to the car. Come and find me, she thinks. He leaves the road, his pride twisted up over not being the Sider Man's first, but she can imagine the tug in his groin the instant he spots her shirt hanging like a surrender. Up the hill, she hears him call her name. Beyond the shirt, he finds her trousers, ahead a stiff wire brassiere, a pair of perfectly white cotton panties—the only part of her untouched by road dust—that she washes out and hangs to dry in every hotel sink. He is moving forward, away from sadness, one discovery at a time. I am alive, he thinks. Here is life to be touched and tasted, a woman who makes herself a maze for me. She is waiting for him at the bottom of the gorge, stretched out on a blanket of moss.

He is breathing heavily when at last he finds her, holding her discarded clothes in one hand and the crock jug of applejack in the other. What would she have done had he not come? But she knew he would come, and for a moment she sees he hates her presumption.

"Refresh me with apples," she laughs, teasing him out of the mood. "For I am faint with love."

He drops her trousers and shirt and bra at her feet, and tips the jug to let an amber stream of brandy spill down over her naked body. She twists her hips away. She's played this game before and knows how it can burn.

Tucker kicks off his shoes and tears at his belt, stepping out of his crushed linen trousers. He falls upon her and licks her clean like a mother cat. Sonia closes her eyes and arches her back. In the ravine behind her, the white water rages over stone as he puts himself inside. She is here and at the same time she is sitting by a stream in Potsdam outside of Berlin, the sun falling through the branches of a willow onto the page of her book. The scientist has no proof, still he writes that all the continents once were one, the Appalachians and the Atlases part of a long, contiguous chain. Now they are two halves of a broken heart, separated by an ocean, each eroding in its own time. She wraps her arms around Tucker and holds him close, even as he tries to pull away and not leave anything inside.

"Don't go," she whispers against his ear. "You just got here."

Does she know what she's saying? his eyes are asking her. She knows. But her body is not hers anymore. It belongs to this bed of moss and its black ants tickling the monument of her thighs. It belongs to the wind in the trees and it belongs to him.

He groans, thrusting deeper still. She loves him, she must love him, not to send him away.

When it is all over, he lies inside her for a very long time. She moves in and out of sleep.

"We'll bring our daughter back here when she is five years old," he whispers, licking her nipple still wet with applejack. "We'll bring her to this spot where we first imagined her. We'll hold a little ceremony in the woods like the Druids used to, and you will be naked and I will be naked and she will be naked and we'll daub ourselves with mud in all the right places and have the sparrows and grazing deer and grizzly cubs resanctify our union. Then we'll get drunk on elderberry wine and she'll sip nectar from a tulip cup."

Sonia nods against his strong shoulder and lets him kiss her deeply. Her clothes are tangled between their ankles. Her bra, her limp white shirt. She had meant for him to come get her, hadn't she? So why does he taste like the bread crumbs she dropped to find her own way home?

In the gleaned sorghum field behind the school, a dozen kids form a circle around Eddie. There's Frank, whose daddy has him chopping wood so his fingers are nothing but knots and sinew. Ray, pushing two hundred pounds at ten years old. The hands of DumbDon are weak as fresh butter, but Eddie could never break through on DumbDon because he has water on the brain and it would be shameful. The brothers, Monty and Jim and Calamus, are playing. Calamus has been left back three times and Jim twice, so that they are all bunched up in their youngest brother's fourth grade class at school, which is also Eddie's class. It's rare they all show up on a given day, but the crops are in, so their mama sent them to school to get them out from underfoot. The two bad girls from sixth grade, Lou and Rosaleen, usually lead their own circle games—How Many Kisses Do.You. Get? They don't count. Eddie steps up to Ray and Frank.

"Is the door locked?" he asks.

The two boys tighten their grip and chant. "Yes, child, yes."

"Can I get out of here?" Eddie asks.

"No, child, no."

Eddie walks a few paces toward the other side of the circle then spins, running at the clenched hands of the two boys. Their fists land in his gut and send him flying backward onto his eight-year-old ass. No one smiles but DumbDon. DumbDon laughs at dogfights.

Eddie picks himself up and brushes away the sorghum lint. His jeans are turned up three times at the cuff but he has grown this year and his mama needs to let them down. He's stalling, retying the rags around the unstitched flap of his old shoe. Eyeing the feet of the other boys, he's looking for whose are planted wide and strong, who seems off balance. He sees the mean black boots of the other Jim, who taught them all how to play this game. He'd learned it from his uncle, who learned it from some other boy when he was a kid, who got it from his big sister, and so on and so on. The other Jim is fourteen and even though he is holding the hand of his six-year-old cousin, Ferris, it will be like trying to blow down a house built of bricks.

Eddie approaches the big and little boy. To hold hands, Ferris has to reach high like he's flying a kite. "Is the door locked?" Eddie asks.

"Yes, child, yes," say the boys.

"Can I get out of here?"

"No, child, no."

Eddie squares his shoulder and rams the two. The other Jim is so tall he has only to swing his fist and it connects hard with Eddie's grinder teeth. Eddie falls to the ground and grabs his cheek. It will be purple tomorrow and his mama will ask about it.

Leaping up, Eddie flings himself from side to side, thrown back each time as from the ropes of a boxing ring. The kids of the ring stand firm, their calls fast and wild. *Is the door locked? Yes, child, yes. Can I get out of here? No, child, NO!*

The sky tilts blue against what yellow the birds have left in the field. An hour ago he was in the woods with his mama. She always keeps him home during ginseng season, there's too much money to be made digging roots. I'll go this way, you go that way, boy, she said, and he'd walked for miles finding nothing until he reached the clearing and his friends. He'll only stay a little while, he tells himself, then he'll hunt some more.

Eddie is flying inside the circle, tossed from one set of hands to the next. His mama said: Don't come home empty-handed. You'll have no school clothes this year if there's nothing to trade. Beyond the boys, a cloud of dust whips down the dirt road and for a second he thinks he hears her calling from the whirlwind. *No, child, no.* Then the others turn to look—it is not a car they recognize. Eddie feels their distraction and takes his chance, charging hard into the two biggest boys. Their fingers fly apart, he stumbles to the ground, then is up and racing away.

"Escape!" DumbDon shouts from his big head and the chase is on. Whoever lays hands on him is the winner and gets to be prisoner next.

Everyone wants to be the prisoner. He's the one with all the action. Eddie runs like a rooster from the ax, leaping away from Monty, whose legs have grown so fast he trips all over them. His red shirt open and flying behind him, Eddie sprints the distance of the sorghum field, leaping the broken stalks, jumping his own shadow. Poor, fat Ray, doubled over and panting. He's only a year older than Eddie but he's big enough to be a man. He'll never be a prisoner, though, because he's too slow and fat to catch anyone.

"I've got you!" Eddie hears a scream up close, sees a flash of braid. The girl, Rosaleen, is on him. How Many Kisses Do. You. Get? He can't be caught by a girl, it would be worse than being kissed and counted. He doubles his speed, running blindly toward the road. Behind him the children shout—*Watch!*—when he is tossed once more, this time high into the air before hitting the ground. Through a haze of sudden dust, he watches plaid and navy shirts scatter across the field, disappearing into the woods. He watches Rosaleen race off to catch her bad friend, and Ferris, the littlest boy, cowering behind the schoolhouse, begin to bawl. Their teacher has long gone home.

Eddie licks flecks of stone and dirt from his lips. He has landed in the ditch by the side of the road. A woman with silver hair is kneeling over him. She looks nothing like his mother. Where is his mother? He hears a man's angry voice shouting.

"What the hell, kid? Didn't you see the car?"

"Can you move?" the woman asks.

"Sure," says Eddie, struggling to sit up. His blood feels stuck in his chest but he tastes it in his mouth. How is that possible?

"He needs a doctor," the lady says. "Did we pass a hospital?"

"No hospital," Eddie insists, struggling harder. Then the angry man is kneeling over him, too, though now he looks more worried than mad. He wears a suit but he needs a haircut. His hair is gold and the lady's is silver. They are like money.

"How are you feeling?" the man asks.

"Okay," he lies.

"Do you know where you live?"

Eddie nods. The man waits.

"Where?" he asks at last. Eddie tries to remember.

"Up the mountain. Toward Panther Gap."

"Can you show me how to get to it?"

"I think."

"I'm going to pick you up now," the man says. "We're going to drive you there."

"Be careful," the lady says. "His neck."

The man scoops him under his shoulders and knees and Eddie cries out without meaning to. Little Ferris has inched around the old clap-board schoolhouse and is making a break for the woods, where Eddie sees plaid shirts behind trees.

"Are those your friends?" the lady asks.

"The prison," mumbles Eddie. He is sagging in the man's arms and now his head hurts very bad. The lady runs ahead while the man carries him to the road and stops before a big black car. She is already in the backseat and Eddie is passed through the door and onto her lap. On the floor he sees cloudy glass Coke bottles; the car smells like syrup in the sun. The man appears in the front and turns the ignition.

"You know my daddy had fourteen pieces of shrapnel in him," he says, turning around to address him. "He told me when the bomb went off, it felt like someone standing a few feet away driving baseballs into his ribs."

The stranger's voice sounds distant and crackling, like a voice over the radio. Cradling his head, the lady traces Eddie's cheek with black-tipped fingers. She is so gentle, he never wants her to stop. She is looking at him and the man is looking at him. They want him to say something, but his brain is a blank, blooming with pain, petal upon petal opening out and dropping to the ground. He says the only thing that comes to mind, the last thing he remembers thinking before he ran against the car and the car tossed him back.

"Is the door locked?" he asks.

Tucker leans over and presses down the latch.

"It is now," he says.

Over the boulders and down the ravine, hand over fist up grapevines, Eddie follows the muddy hemline of her housedress. He hears the boys and girls whisper. When Cora Alley is mad, milk sours in the pail. Storms blow in from the east. And they don't even know what Eddie knows. The men she keeps buried in the woods. Or how she slips out of her skin from time to time, leaving it hanging on a peg in her bedroom while she disappears through the keyhole. Still, is it proof enough? A boy never wants to believe ill of his own mother.

They are saying, "He doesn't want his mother to know."

He follows the thick gray braid that she wears in a cobweb spine down her back. At eight years old, Eddie is still young enough to find his mother the most beautiful and terrifying woman in the world. He can stare at her for hours and see nothing remarkable, but then, just as he starts to look away, to clear a dish or milk the cow, the light will hit at exactly the right angle or she will smile in some knowing way, and suddenly her features rearrange themselves, and he can see that second self, like the Mother Mary appearing in the crazing of a rock face or the dew on a screen door. It is that second self he wonders about now, that hint of nonmother caught from the corner of the eye. Is that the part of her they call witch?

"They pay most for the roots that look like men," she says, startling him with that Daniel-in-the-Lions'-Den voice of hers, thrown up from some flinty chasm deep inside her. "Listen close and you might hear them scream when you tug them from the ground."

His head aches from listening to her, his neck aches scanning the understory for telltale golden leaves of sang. They never gather or collect the sang, but hunt it, like a wild and sentient creature.

"You might think you know her habits, where she holes up," his mama says. You might be thinking she's sweet on you, even, that she wants to give herself to you. One year you know just where to look for her, she lets herself be gathered unto you; the next year she's vanished, though you've made yourself a map and know her woods like you know your family Bible. For two years, three, she'll go underground, sucking from the soil all that makes it strong. Then on the fourth year, fifth one maybe, she'll stretch her stalk through that packed earth and show her blushing berries once again, with a little come-and-get-me. "Ginseng, she's faithless," his mama says. "She's a plant what looks out for herself."

Where do you go at night, Mama? Eddie asks the muddy hem of her dress as it switches across the road ahead, on its way with the feline rest of her, naked calves and raw red ankles rising from his father's work boots, crossing into Panther Gap. Where do you go when you slip through the keyhole?

"I'll go this way, you go that," she says. "Don't come back empty-handed."

"He's dead, isn't he?" Tucker asks.

"He's not dead," Sonia replies. "He's resting."

Supporting his neck, Sonia tests each of his joints to make sure nothing is broken. Tucker hunches forward over the steering wheel, scanning the woods for something else to race across his path. There is nothing, but he feels it again, the jolt like the involuntary jerk his body gives when falling asleep. Tucker watches them in the rearview mirror. Does she blame him? The kid came out of nowhere.

"We've gone too far," Tucker says.

"There," Eddie whispers, pointing to the woods.

"Where?" Sonia asks. "There's nothing there."

Tucker steers the car into a small clearing at the edge of the woods. He cuts the motor and the swell of cicadas presses in. A footpath leads deeper into the forest and up the mountain, but even leaning out the window, Tucker can see no house. Feeling the car slow to a stop, the boy in back rouses himself as if from any lazy summertime nap.

"I'm feeling much better," Eddie manages, struggling to lift his head.

Tucker looks back doubtfully. "What're you called, son?"

"Eddie Alley," the boy replies.

"Can you walk, Eddie?" Tucker asks.

"Yes, sir," he says. "But can I sit here just a little longer?"

"Of course," says Tucker, surprised. "Take your time."

Sonia helps the boy up to sitting and his dirty hand sneaks out to stroke the velvet seat cushion. Maybe he's not hurt that bad, Tucker thinks, maybe it will all be okay. He tries not to be too obvious looking at the boy's pupils. They are of equal size and not too big. No concussion.

"This is a nice car," says Eddie.

"You're riding in a 1935 Ford, son," Tucker says out loud, "and the comfort you feel is Centerpoise. *Backseat passengers receive a front seat ride.*" Tucker rotates a red dial in the dashboard to reveal an ashtray.

"Now you see it, now you don't."

The boy grins, showing his stair-step teeth, and the pounding in Tucker's chest begins to ease. Yes, they'll all be okay. He just has to face the parents and explain. Your kid ran right out in front of me. No. I didn't see your kid when I came around the corner. No. I'd been drinking applejack and my mind was back in the moss by the river gorge.

Eddie leans over and cranks the window open and shut. After a few dozen rounds of this, Sonia gently pats his knee, which means it's time to go now. Tucker helps the boy out of the car.

"It's hot," Eddie says, running his hand over the flank of the wheel well. Had he been a second or two quicker Tucker would have missed him altogether, a second or two slower, he would have struck him head on and killed him. The math sets Tucker trembling again. Sonia is out of the car now and watching him.

"Let's get you home," he says to the boy.

Eddie is unsteady on his feet, but leaning against Tucker he starts up the footpath that leads uphill through virgin hardwood and younger scrub. Running patches of oak seedlings and shoulder-high saplings, their few leaves already yellow against the deep green of pines and hemlock. Sonia walks ahead, waiting every few yards for them to catch up. They scale a near vertical dry creek bed before the way jags to the right, running along the rim of a gully filled with broken bluestone, fern, banks of lacy vine. Tucker worries a single misstep will take them both down.

Eddie says, "When my mama had me, the snow was so deep, the doctor couldn't get up the path. Daddy took the legs off the kitchen table and roped her to it so he could drag her down to the road. She near died."

Sonia meets Tucker's eyes over the boy's head. "She's okay now?" she asks. Eddie shrugs.

"I guess," he says.

Together the three trudge upward past a clearing planted with tobacco, where a wooden rack holds drying leaves. A few yards on and the woods close in once more, tree roots wrap like the tentacles of a giant squid around granite slabs overhead. Tucker passes through a rampart of white birch and then, without warning, they are there. Eddie's home, a hand-hewn dogtrot cabin, built of chestnut planks and divided by a breezeway, teeters at the edge of another drop-off. Tucker has seen a lot of miserable dwellings in his travels, but this isolated shack, roofed with flattened Pennzoil cans, the chinks of its windows stuffed with dirty rags, is among the poorest. Behind the cabin, a springhouse is fit into the ledge of rock, and beyond that sits the barn, its planks gapping like the space between milk teeth. Half a dozen black Silkie hens pecking in the dust rise up when they approach.

"Tucker, catch him," Sonia says. The climb has been too hard and Eddie sits heavily at the edge of his yard. Tucker lifts him once more and carries him up the broken front steps of the cabin and down the breezeway. The house is silent and empty, only the lowing of an unrelieved cow echoes off the rock.

"Hello," Tucker calls. "Anyone home?"

"Eddie, do you know where your parents are?" Sonia asks. "Do they go out to work?"

Eddie's eyes are closed but he mumbles. "Mama's hunting the sang."

Sonia shakes her head, not understanding. "She's hunting?"

He says, "Maybe I could lie down?"

Across from the kitchen, the door to the bedroom is open. The room is barely large enough to hold a bedstead and dresser with space to turn around. Tucker lays the boy on a neatly made bed that smells of mint. Tugging Eddie's knotted bootlaces through their eyelets, Sonia plucks away a tick crawling across the ribbed neck of one filthy sock. All the while, Eddie lies ashen and tight-lipped, holding in a moan.

"You rest up," she says, drawing a quilt over him. "We're going to get something to help you feel better. Your mother will be home in no time."

"Chin up," Tucker says, joining Sonia in the breezeway.

"He really should see a doctor," she says, lowering her voice. "What if he has internal injuries?"

"The car just glanced him. Nothing's broken."

"Jesus, Tucker," she says, and now she is shaking as he was before, and that gives him the strength to hold her. He presses her tight, until he feels her start to stiffen, her need for comfort fleeting. She detaches herself, stepping into the kitchen.

"Do you suppose his mother keeps morphine?" she asks.

The kitchen is another raw box with a window and a second door onto the back porch. To keep out the drafts, its walls are papered with overlapping newsprint and comic strips. The war in Europe. In the center of the room stands the family's dinner table, its legs restored, covered in red-checked oilcloth. They still eat on that? The potbellied cooking stove rests on a slab of fieldstone by the back door; beside it is a porcelain sink whose faucet is a bent lead pipe channeling water from the spring down a hole back into the ground. The kitchen has none of the homey touches of Tucker's own childhood kitchen; there are no Seasons of the Year figurines on the windowsill or bud vases purchased at church bazaars, no electric wall clock with its sunny daisy face and cloth cord trailing down the wall. There are instead four mended cane-back chairs, a mismatched crockery set on open shelves, and two portraits on the wall, tanned and blurred by cooking grease. One is FDR in a wooden frame. The other is of Jesus Christ, titled "The Unseen Guest," and underneath are the words, "Christ is the head of this house, the unseen guest at every meal, the silent listener to every conversation."

Tucker draws back a gingham curtain that partitions off the pantry shelves. Looking for morphine, he finds instead a cloth sack of graham flour and a nearly empty sack of sugar. The shelves are stocked with jars of canned beans and tomatoes, damson preserves, a leathery haunch of deep red ham. Or maybe it is dried venison. Ropes of herbs hang from the ceiling. A furry line of boric acid runs along the baseboard to keep away the ants and cockroaches.

Sonia has taken down a wooden cask from the ledge above the stove. She sets it on the table and looks around before opening it. I don't want to be here, her look says. It's only because we nearly killed your boy, ma'am, that I am pawing through your things. Sonia lifts out an unlabeled brown glass bottle.

"This may be something," she says. "Or maybe I'd poison him."

"Keep looking," Tucker says. "His mother has to be home soon."

He leaves her in the kitchen and steps across to the bedroom. Eddie has rolled over on his side, anxiously watching the door. Tucker feels a little impatience rise up, not knowing how long he'll have to stay here, keeping this strange boy company.

"Hey chum," he says, taking a seat on the bed. "You sure know how to get a person's attention."

Eddie's lips tremble. "I'm sorry I ran in front of your car."

"We'll send you a bill," Tucker says.

Eddie has been fighting hard not to cry and he wipes his runny nose on the back of his sleeve. The pattern of his shirt is the same as the red-checked flour sack in the pantry. Hanging on wooden pegs along the wall Tucker sees only carefully mended dresses, but no overalls or greasy work shirts.

"Your daddy's not at home?" he asks.

"He's off with the CCC."

"So you're the man of the house?"

"I guess," Eddie says.

Tucker says, "That's rough. My daddy was away when I was a boy."

"Where to?" asks Eddie.

"Belgium. France. Hospitals."

"My daddy's on the Skyline Drive."

"You miss him?"

The tears that Eddie has been holding back begin to flow. He rubs his face against the pillow.

"When he's home he takes me fishing sometimes," Eddie says.

"My father used to take me fishing when I was just about your age," Tucker says, reaching over to wipe the boy's nose with the untucked bedsheet. "He used to say that fishing gave him a good excuse not to talk. So every few weeks or so when he needed very badly not to talk, we'd roll our cuffs and skim ourselves some minnows and carry them in a bucket up to a stream not far from our house. We'd set up on a flat rock and I'd reach into the bucket and take a minnow flip-flapping in my fist and sink my hook just behind its head, like this," he says, demonstrating with his fingernail on the back of Eddie's hand. "You ever do that?"

"Mostly we use bloodworms," Eddie says, brightening a little. "And crickets."

"One afternoon," Tucker continues, "we got to the stream and a wicked old mama water moccasin had nested under our rock. My father rolled up his cuffs and cast his minnow; I remember that silver fish flying overhead in a great arc against the blue sky. He sat down on the rock and let his naked white feet dangle in the water, but that water moccasin did not understand his peaceful intentions. She thought he was after her babies, and she sank her fangs into his ankle so deep I thought she'd snap clean through the bone. Do you know what my father said, Eddie?"

"What?" asks Eddie.

"He pulled up on his line and he turned to me and said—so calmly—'Tucker, son, I believe I have a bite.'"

Eddie is unsure whether or not the story is supposed to be funny.

"My daddy would've grabbed her by the tail and bashed her brains out," he says.

"As he should," Tucker replies. He looks across to the kitchen where Sonia is still searching the wooden box. He thinks of the jug of applejack down in the car. Maybe that would help the pain?

"What time you think your mama'll be back?" he asks.

"When she goes hunting she's mostly home by supper. I'm mostly with her though. She might think I'm lost."

"You worried she's out looking for you?" Tucker asks gently. Eddie's tears threaten once more.

"She'll be mad I came home empty-handed."

"But you're not empty-handed," Tucker chides. "You found us."

Eddie smiles weakly. He half hides his face behind the covers. "Can I ask you a question?"

"I'll reserve my right to evoke the Fifth."

"Is that your name? Tucker?"

This poor kid, thinks Tucker. Hit and carried and preached at by a complete stranger. He never thought to introduce himself.

"My name is Tucker Hayes," he says. "And I am profoundly sorry I didn't tell you sooner."

Eddie sinks back into his pillow and Tucker sees him turn over the name. It is not a mountain name but it is a nearby name and Tucker thinks it comforts the boy that the stranger is not even stranger.

"Is there anything else you'd like to know?" Tucker asks.

"The lady's name?"

"Her name is Sonia. She's a photographer and a goddess."

"Where're you from?"

"That's a tougher question," Tucker says. "Virginia via New York City then back to Virginia. Sonia? I do believe she sprang fully grown from the head of Mr. Franklin Delano Roosevelt. He was suffering a violent headache on behalf of our dolorous country when Eleanor lifted a mallet and split his skull. Out leaped our dear Sonia, eyes flashing, camera ready to document all the world's ills."

"Tucker," says Sonia, joining them. "This boy needs his rest."

"Do you need your rest, Eddie?"

"No, sir."

Sonia has brought a wet rag from the kitchen and uses it to wipe Eddie's face and hands. He squirms at the attention; he's not a little kid anymore. Tucker hated his mother washing behind his ears, too.

"Did Mrs. Roosevelt really crack Mr. Roosevelt's skull?" Eddie asks.

"Don't listen to a word Tucker says," Sonia instructs, gently washing between each of his fingers. "Your daddy's building parks and we're writing the book that tells people where to find them. That's how we came to be on your part of the mountain."

"You're writing a book?" Eddie asks, blushing deeply. Tucker can tell he wants to say something.

"What is it?"

"I thought you might be movie stars."

"Why?" asks Tucker, with a laugh. "Because we're so damned good-looking?"

Eddie hides his face. "You're different from anyone here," he says.

"You like movies, Eddie?" Tucker asks. The boy shrugs, even more embarrassed.

"You've never seen one, have you?"

He shrugs again.

"I have something I think will fix you right up," Tucker says, rising from the bed. "If you'll excuse me."

"Where are you going?" Sonia asks in surprise.

"Down to the car," he says.

"You can't leave, Tucker," she says. "What will I say if Eddie's mother comes while you're gone?"

Tucker is already out on the porch, filled with the excitement of having something concrete, at last, to offer this kid.

"Tell her you were driving," he says over his shoulder. "Don't worry. I'll be right back."

Of course he isn't right back. She knew he wouldn't be. Sonia tries to remember how long it took them to walk up, then doubles it in her head. She tells herself he isn't lost or injured in the woods, she won't be left to raise this orphaned child. She glances over to where Eddie is finally sleeping. In the first fifteen minutes, she made all the conversation she knew how to make with him. What grade are you in at school? How do you like your teacher? What do you want to be when you grow up? Eddie wanted to see the camera around her neck and she took it off and showed him how it worked; he peered through the viewfinder but she wouldn't let him take a picture. *That film belongs to the government,* she said. When he was done with the camera, Eddie wanted to know more about New York, so she told him about the Cyclone at Coney Island and how in the middle of the most crowded spot in the city, a place called Times Square, a boy could sit in Chock Full o' Nuts, eating cream cheese on date bread that had been untouched by human hands. Eddie thought Chock Full o' Nuts was a funny name and she had to agree, and then she said, *Okay, no more talking, you need to rest.* His eyes drooped even as he struggled to stay awake to see what Tucker would bring. Sonia leaned her head against the iron bed frame, slowing her breathing to show him how it was done. In a matter of minutes he was asleep and at last she was free to orient herself in this strange house, to see where this collision had brought her.

It is a spartan, clean-swept room. Plank walls nailed to plank floors and a plank ceiling. On three pegs beside the door to the breezeway hang three changes of Mrs. Alley's clothes: a summer cotton shift with snaps up the front and a deep pocket patched with a cloth cabbage rose; next to it hangs the Sunday dress of charcoal bombazine, funeral respectable, remade from last century, with mended lace at the cuffs and collar; then there is the nightgown, hung on the peg closest to the bed. Washed thin as cobweb, Sonia can still make out every stain not quite removed—brown at the armpits and watermarked by old breast milk, the dark freckles of dried menstrual blood low at the hem from where she slept with it bunched between her legs. Sonia takes up her camera from where it lies on the bed and peers down the finder. It's dark in the bedroom and she left her flashgun and light meter in the car. Glancing at the sleeping boy, she eases herself off the bed and reaches up to open wide the shutters, letting the late afternoon sunlight flood in. Under his covers, Eddie does not stir.

Like Tucker fretting over the Sider Man, Sonia used to care who was on the other end of her lens. Then, in October '29 she was early for a shoot with socialite Sarah Churchill's husband, Winston, a comer in British politics. Setting up to take an exterior of the Savoy Plaza where they were staying, she heard a shout directly above Winston's room on the fourteenth floor and, instinctively, she swung her camera around. Taking the picture had been like throwing her arm up against a punch, she remembered, she didn't even know if she'd gotten it until later, when she developed the negative, but there he was—the anonymous businessman in his suit-and-vested free fall, his legs peddling, his arms wrapped around his body as if embracing a lover. Her grainy, blurred exclusive, the only confirmed suicide of those early days, was her first cover for *Wealth.* "Crash," read the headline. And inside were the more carefully composed snapshots of his broken body where it landed on the hotel's bank of Aucuba hedges.

Tucker had asked her about that photo, which had made her an instant celebrity. They were lying in one of their first motels and the headlights from the road outside swept through the loose weave of curtain, casting a net of shadow over their naked bodies. She didn't know why he brought up the suicide as they lay with their legs entwined, sharing a last cigarette, except that with each drag, she'd felt herself slipping away again and maybe he sensed death was the only thing more intimate than what they'd just shared. *How did you feel about it?* he asked her. *Getting that on film?* It had taken her a long time to answer. He waited. *Just lucky,* she'd said at last. *Just lucky, I guess.*

She points the lens at the clothes on their pegs and pauses, listening for steps along the breezeway. Nothing.

Click.

On her dresser, Mrs. Alley has grouped her personal possessions so as to hide old water rings on the dark wood. A butterscotch Bakelite vessel for loose powder and a furry, store-bought puff for applying it. A man's comb with a spine of white, compressed dandruff. Her leather-bound Bible with gilt edging, bloated from humid weather. A chipped bubble-ware dish holding four black bobby pins and a long curling hair. Gray. How old is Mrs. Alley?

Powder and puff don't belong, Sonia decides. They look too expensive. Other photographers have been accused of socialism and worse for altering a shot. Congress came down hard on Rothstein for moving a bleached cow's skull in the Badlands ten feet to more dramatically cracked earth. But Sonia knows the New Deal depends on how it's framed. Poverty. Want. Fortitude. In order for the world to change, first it must see what it has overlooked. It will be the same with war.

She removes the powder and puff and opens the Bible to 2 Corinthians. *We are troubled on every side, yet not distressed; we are perplexed, but not in despair.*

Click.

She listens again before turning to the only thing left in the room. Eddie sleeps under the amber blanket of the setting sun through his window. Too delicate for this place, he looks like a changeling from Botticelli, with soft, downy cheeks and full red lips. Sonia has never been able to appreciate children for the age they are, but always finds herself measuring them against the golden mean of adulthood, a third there, half there, three-quarters there, so she finds Eddie to be most beautiful asleep, when she might, in his repose, look for the man in him.

Sonia may shoot any part of him to give whatever impression she likes—his soft cheek to suggest vulnerability, his shorn hair that makes him look both stupid and mad, the full length of him under the covers that will grow to become that which covers another in a bed just like this. And any part of him she shoots will be true and anything she leaves out will be truth left out and it is the most burdensome responsibility, this, the art of documentation, because people expect objectivity when in fact all that word can promise is the devolution of what is human and myriad into a jack, a cube of frictionless ice. It's what she couldn't get across to Tucker that night when he asked her how she felt about the captured suicide. Lucky, she'd thought, for the accident of it. Lucky, for being absolved of the responsibility of choice.

Eddie moans in his sleep. Is he in pain? Having a nightmare? She advances her film, ready to capture the wide dilated pupil beneath the blink as confusion gives way to waking life. This instant might say as much about the state of the world as a thousand war photos, she thinks, for what better sums up man than the thousand-mile journey contained in that split second between sleep and waking? She waits and the tension builds in her wrist and neck. Wake up, she wills. Wake up. But as if to spite her, he sinks deeper into his dreams, deferring the pain of consciousness just a little longer. After a minute, Sonia lowers her camera. As a picture it would be interesting, but she's kidding herself if she thinks it's important. Everything important is elsewhere, and once again the impatience of getting there wells up in her.

Where is Tucker? she wonders flatly, moving to the bedroom door. The boy lies exactly as she found him, she has returned everything to its place on Cora Alley's dresser. She takes a last look around and decides it's impossible to tell she's been in the room at all.

Eddie opens his eyes to a word thrown against his wall.

Frankenstein.

"Wake up," the man's voice says close to his ear. "I have something to show you."

Eddie struggles up to sitting, forgetting the pain in his shoulder and ribs, mesmerized by the flickering light on the rough chestnut planks. Tucker sits beside him on the bed, an iron film projector balanced on the family Bible. Delicate as a birdcage, it has two flywheels on the back and a graceful wooden handle arching from the side. As Tucker cranks, the word on the wall gives way to a man and a woman in a parlor, dressed in old-fashioned fancy clothes. Is he dreaming?

"This isn't the Frankenstein every other punk kid has seen," Tucker says. "This is Edison 1910. The first horror movie ever made."

Eddie thinks of Rosaleen. Calamus. Jimmy. DumbDon. He remembers their names and then he remembers the game they were playing.

Still half asleep, he looks for his mother. He sees a lady cooking over a pot on the kitchen stove. The lamp has been lit and her hair shines in the shadows. She would not be there if his mother were home.

Tucker reads the title cards. I'm not stupid Eddie wants to say, but it is so startling to have words on his wall, he worries he would say all the wrong things. *Frankenstein Leaves for College.* It might come out *Stranger Chock Full o' Nuts.*

"My father bought this projector off a traveling showman who used to crank stag films at the lodge," Tucker says. "Got the lot cheap when the feds caught up with him."

"What's a stag film?" Eddie asks.

"All in good time, son, all in good time."

Two Years Later, Frankenstein Discovers the Mysteries of Life. A student's room, now, and a skeleton sits at the table as if it had been invited to dinner. The man is pouring a potion into a big brass pot.

"What's he doing?" Eddie asks.

"Making his monster," Tucker explains. "The girl who wrote this story never says how it's done."

"Girl?" Eddie asks, disappointed.

"Girls can be very scary," smiles Tucker. "You'll learn."

Eddie's mother tells ghost stories sometimes when she wants to make him mind. His dreams are haunted by avenging beasts and murdered children, women hanging themselves from trees over lost lovers. But those stories have never moved inside his bedroom, close enough for him to touch. Eddie wiggles his fingers before the bulb to make a looming shadow hand.

"Look," says Tucker. "Here's the good bit."

Rising from the cauldron is a hint of creature. As Eddie watches, charred flesh attracts more charred flesh, it's like his daddy at butchering time, tossing chops and ribs into a pail, rebuilding a hog in section slices. Suddenly an arm jerks up in salute and a misshapen head appears through the fog.

Instead of a Perfect Human Being, the Evil in Frankenstein's Mind Creates a Monster.

"Eddie?" He hears his name over the rattle of the projector. "You're not scared are you?"

He doesn't understand. There was nothing to show Frankenstein was a bad man. He went to college, he got a wife. Yet here is proof, just as his mother says, that wicked thoughts take on a life of their own. Why are you showing me this monster? Now it will always be hiding under the bed or lurking by the path. Waiting for him as soon as he's forgotten about it. The monster moves through its master's house and catches a glimpse of itself in the mirror. It draws back.

Eddie looks to Tucker for help, but Tucker is looking across the breezeway to where Sonia stands over her pot, and there is something in his face that mirrors the mirror, that Eddie sees and recognizes. *Set down your spoon and join us,* he can almost hear Tucker's thoughts.

There is no point watching movies alone or with children. Movies exist, like music or poetry, only to explain oneself to women, to infiltrate women and call forth women. And the women are always too busy moving and pouring and chopping in the kitchen to want to be a part of him and so more movies must be made and poems and plays and novels written and songs composed to lure them away from work and into ecstasy or one will be left sitting with boys on beds in darkened rooms and worrying that one has by accident called forth a boy in place of a woman and now has him permanently attached like a shadow or a specter waiting for What Comes Next. She must have noticed because she steps across the breezeway to stand just inside the bedroom door, her arms crossed over her chest.

"Dinner's almost ready," she says softly.

Tucker's face relaxes; that waiting, anxious look leaves him, and now he can smile reassuringly at Eddie.

"You want to crank it?" he asks.

"Can I?"

"Sure thing."

Eddie moves forward on the bed, kneeling next to Tucker and the projector propped on the Bible. The picture bounces up the wall—the monster is terrorizing Frankenstein's bride on the ceiling, until Tucker readjusts himself to give Eddie room. They bring the frame back down to eye level.

"Put your hand over mine," Tucker says, "and crank like this. It's called the silent speed, the rhythm a film wants to go."

Eddie places his hand over Tucker's. His daddy's is horned and hard but Tucker's is soft from driving and writing books and showing movies. Tucker slips his out from under and Eddie is gripping the wooden handle all by himself. The film slows and almost stops.

"Keep cranking," Tucker warns, "or it'll burn through."

Eddie cranks fast, jerking the monster through the rooms, into the arms of his master, wrestling in double time. It's funny and he wants to laugh, but more than that, he wants to get it right, and so he cranks a little slower, finding his pace. He's doing it, he thinks with pride. Under his hand Frankenstein saves his bride; the monster finds himself back before the mirror and then, in some marvelous special effect, trapped inside it. For a brief second Frankenstein and his monster are locked on either side—reflections of one another—before the final title of the movie makes all things right again.

The Creation of an Evil Mind, Overcome by Love, Disappears.

Eddie keeps cranking but the film's run through, the wall is now an unfocused square of bright white light. Tucker has moved to stand by Sonia, his arm around her shoulder. They are snug and smiling—at him, but secretly for each other, like two children playing house. They cannot see the figure coming up behind them, her shadow long and thin along the breezeway.

"Whaddya think?" Tucker asks.

Eddie wants to answer but he cannot. Her face is dark and angry and then he knows she has been walking the woods searching for him even as he has been in bed watching a movie. He stops cranking and the room falls dark, but she is lit by the kitchen lamp she's picked up. Behind her, he sees the flames of her stove where someone else has been cooking her food. Tucker and Sonia sense his fear.

"I think someone best say who's in my house," says his mama.

If she hadn't come upon them like that—silently, in shadow, at the end of a monster movie—would he have formed the impression he did? Tucker asks himself. She startled them, that's all. Yet his heart is pounding like a kid's. He looks to Eddie for protection, but Eddie is cowering under the covers. What can he expect from her? Mountain people keep loaded guns, she must have one.

"Come out of the bedroom," she says. "It's not proper."

She moves like a woman who has been walking all day as she lights them into the kitchen. She sets the lamp back on the table and crosses to the sink, leaning against the cool, white porcelain. Tucker thinks she might be a few years on the other side of thirty, though she may be younger. She wears a deep green dress that once fit a rounder self; the sleeves are rolled and her collarbones show sharply below the neckline. With her hollow cheeks and freckled, parched lips, Tucker thinks someone has found Mrs. Alley's bunghole and let her juice drain out. Her skin has the dusty look of flattened snakes he has seen along the road.

"You must accept our sincerest apologies," Tucker begins. He had thought himself prepared for this moment, but this poor woman's evident exhaustion and discomfort fills him with embarrassment. Once he'd determined Eddie was not gravely injured, he'd half-convinced himself they would all have a laugh over it, that his mother might even welcome the novelty of company.

"What did he do?" she asks. Her voice is low so that they must lean in to hear her.

"It was all our fault," Tucker says swiftly. "I didn't see him on the road."

Eddie watches his mother nervously. Over her dress, she wears a lumpy burlap satchel. She lifts it over her head and silently hands it to her son.

"I'm sorry, Mama," he says. "I was looking but I didn't find——"

She cuts him off.

"You hurt?"

"Not much."

"You say sorry?"

"Yes, ma'am."

"Then don't just stand there, you can hear the cow needs milking."

Eddie ducks away and Tucker can tell he's relieved to be given familiar chores. With Eddie gone, the discomfort in the room is even greater. The soup boils over the lid of the pot. Cora steps to the stove, covers her bare hands with the hem of her dress, and slides the pot to the back where the iron is cooler.

"Eddie hadn't eaten all day," Sonia explains. "We weren't sure when you'd be back. I found a few potatoes in your pantry. Some ham——."

"Thank you for tending him," Cora says politely. "Will you stay to supper?"

Over just a few hours Tucker had come to think of this as Eddie's house. He felt comfortable in Eddie's house, as if it could have been his own. But Mrs. Alley's formality knocks him back to intruder. He wishes he hadn't brought the suitcase and applejack up with the projector. He was worried they wouldn't be safe in the car, but now they feel presumptuous sitting outside in the breezeway.

"That would be too kind," he says.

"What can I do to help?" Sonia asks.

"Maybe I could know your names?"

Hasty introductions are made and the story told of how they came to be here. As if she might doubt him, Tucker reaches into his satchel and pulls out their Esso map with his notes and distances. They are legitimate. They are with the government.

For her part, Cora Alley is unconcerned about their credentials. She washes her hands at the running sink and begins the supper preparations, measuring flour and lard enough for four biscuits, rolling and slicing the dough. After a while, Eddie returns, struggling with a metal bucket of milk, which Cora skims and sets on the table. Without being told, Sonia takes plates from the shelf and sets out the knives and forks. She is like a soldier in the field, fitting herself to the work as if born to it. Tucker feels extraneous and awkward, waiting to be fed.

"Will you take a drop of brandy, Mrs. Alley?" he asks, uncorking the jug. "We bought it up the way."

"Don't touch the stuff," she says. "But feel free."

He pours himself a coffee mug and starts to pour for Sonia, but she places her hand over her cup in solidarity with Cora. So he will be the only alcoholic at the table, is that it? He considers adding Sonia's portion to his own mug but lets not doing so be his concession.

He says, "This is a fine place you have here."

Cora looks around at the chipped china, the busted chair, the empty corners. In the uncomfortable silence, Sonia checks the biscuits.

"You'll have to excuse my saying it's beautiful," Tucker smiles. "I've been a slave to the city for so long, I am starved for nature."

"Have your fill," says Cora. "Don't cost you."

"Oh, but it does," he says. "It costs me peace of mind, wanting to be in two places at once. Don't you ever feel that, Mrs. Alley?"

Cora Alley cocks her head as if to say, Mr. Hayes, who doesn't feel that way? Some of us are adults. Eddie slides into the chair across from Tucker. He is holding his side but doesn't want his mother to see. Cora clears her throat and he pops up again, passing out the bowls of soup that she has ladled.

"Mr. and Mrs. Hayes are from New York City," he tells his mother.

"They're pretty lost then," Cora says.

"They're writing a book about us," Eddie says.

"It's a book about places," Tucker corrects. "A big, fat book of interesting places to visit. How else are we to make Henry Ford a little richer?"

Cora sets the biscuits on the table with a crock of butter and another of sorghum molasses. She takes her seat and holds out her hands for grace. Tucker takes Cora's in one and Sonia's in the other. Eddie completes the circle. Tucker hasn't said grace in years and hopes Mrs. Alley doesn't offer him the honor. She nods to Eddie and closes her eyes.

"God is great, God is good, let us thank him for our food . . ."

The soup is thin but flavorful, with ham and potatoes and some dried thyme Sonia found in the pantry. The low lamplight brings them all a little closer over their bowls and the kitchen is filled with the sound of scraping spoons.

"I never would have thought to season a soup like that," says Cora.

"I hope you like it," Sonia offers.

"It's different," says Cora.

Tucker takes a biscuit and slathers it with butter and syrup. He's eaten nothing since the hard-boiled egg and he's drunk a little too much applejack. He's never known a woman to bake less than a dozen biscuits. He longs for another.

"When do you return to New York?" Cora asks politely.

"Maybe next year, maybe never. I've been drafted, ma'am."

"Your number got picked?" Eddie asks excitedly.

"It did."

"My daddy's didn't get picked," he says.

"A lot of men up this way was hoping to get drafted," Cora says in her quiet voice. "The pay is good."

"They are welcome to my spot," says Tucker.

"You don't believe in serving your country?" she asks. She is surprised not that a man would feel it, but that he would admit it.

"It's hell what's going on over there, but no one has attacked us," Tucker says. "Our country has never had a peacetime draft. If the president feels entitled to pluck men out of their lives over a war we're not even fighting yet, and pay them less than they were being paid in their old jobs, why not draft them for the munitions plants? And for the utility services? Why not draft men to be firemen and policemen, and just assign them jobs like Stalin does, or Hitler?"

"But they've seen U-boats off Virginia Beach," Cora says.

"Have they? They scare us when it suits them. They spent the last miserable decade trying to calm us down and now everything is a great emergency. I don't want to die because the rich bastards of the world weren't happy with how things got divided up after the last war."

Eddie's eyes are wide. Cora doesn't know where to look. Sonia is suddenly very somber, as if this conversation in this little kitchen has the power to affect the larger world.

"I've lived in Berlin," she says. "Hitler won't stop unless someone makes him stop."

"Hitler is a bully. He's not the first and he won't be the last, he's just the punch line of a bad joke that sooner or later we'll be telling here."

Cora pushes back her chair, rising from the table. Tucker and Eddie rise, too.

"Let me get your bed ready," she says.

"Oh no, we can't impose—" Tucker begins. She interrupts him.

"You won't get far this time of night," she says, cutting through the pretense. "Besides, you brought up your suitcase."

Tucker blushes but says nothing. Cora nods to her son. "Eddie, you clear the table."

Excusing herself, Cora steps across the breezeway. Eddie collects the bowls, pouring Cora's remaining soup back into the pot. He covers it with a towel to save for tomorrow. Tucker's shame creeps higher at how much he ate. He lowers his voice so that Eddie won't hear.

"I wish I had some money to leave," he says.

"She wouldn't take it."

"I'm not a coward, Sonia," he says.

"I know you're not a coward," she replies. "You'd be happier if you were."

"First death?" he says a little louder, challenging her.

"Tucker—" she warns, glancing back at Eddie. He is not going to back down, and so she answers. "My great-aunt Miriam. She was ninety-two."

"My father," Tucker retorts. "Only his body didn't have the good grace to follow for another twenty years. Women don't know the first thing about war. You're never called on to kill."

Eddie rinses the bowls under the lead pipe, trying to make as little noise as possible. Tucker can see he doesn't want to miss a word. He drains the rest of his mug and crosses to the sink.

"Let me do that," he says, taking over. "You've had a long day."

"Do you think the war'll still be going on when I'm old enough to go?" Eddie asks. Tucker frowns as he takes the still greasy bowl and wipes it dry.

"I'm sure of it," he says. "I tell you what, Eddie. I'll make you a deal. Get yourself grown, find your way to the city, and if the world is still standing, I'll introduce you to the New York Yankees."

"You know players for the Yankees?" Eddie asks in awe.

"Only the ones I've hit with my car. But that's a good ten or fifteen of them."

The boy looks down, embarrassed, and Tucker regrets the joke.

"Really, kid," he says, as serious as he can manage. "I don't hit and run. I'm yours for life."

*   *   *

In the front parlor, Cora has removed the seat cushion from the divan, wrapped it tightly in a patched sheet, and put it on the floor. She has taken the pillows from her own bed and laid over them a square of embroidered linen that looks to be a tablecloth. Together it is a makeshift mattress. On the wooden mantle above the fireplace, she has placed a hurricane lamp to light the room.

"I'm sorry but you'll have to use the outhouse in back," she says. "There's a bucket here by the door for washing. And a little bit of soap."

"We'll be fine, Mrs. Alley," Sonia says. "Please don't trouble yourself."

"We don't get many guests," Cora apologizes.

"You've been such a gracious host," Tucker adds. "Far more than we've deserved."

Cora nods and looks shyly away. She is almost pretty when she is softened up in blushes, he thinks.

"We'll try not to disturb you in the morning," she says.

"No special treatment, please," Tucker says. "We do as you do."

When the door is shut, Sonia takes one look at the sheet, pinpricked with blood, and begins adding layers. Her trousers and shirt, socks, Tucker's oversized jacket, a red and tan Hermès scarf she sometimes wears over her hair but now tucks tight around her neck, protecting her bare skin as much as possible.

"We should get an early start in the morning," she says, pulling a book from the side table and dropping it on the bare floor to use as a pillow. He is embarrassed at the precautions she takes and strips to his underwear before blowing out the lamp and lying down beside her. On the other side of the wall they share with the back bedroom, he hears Cora Alley preparing for bed, feels the give and creak of their common floorboards as the springs settle under her weight. The thin yellow light leaking between her wall and theirs is extinguished and he becomes even more aware of all their bodies, discrete and in space—his, Sonia's, the mother and son together in a shared bed—and the flow of air and night between them. He pulls Sonia tight, craving the feel of her against him, a yielding woman's body full of the unspoken, shared complaints of minor deprivations.

"Eddie's a special kid," Tucker says, feeling generous and fatherly in the dark. "I'll send him something from Fort Dix."

"What's so special about him?"

Tucker is surprised at her. "I've met lots of country kids. He's a cut above."

"Of course," she says. "You wouldn't have hit an unspecial kid."

"What's eating you?" he asks, trying to sound light. He moves aside the scarf and kisses the back of her neck. "Besides me?"

"Why do you make promises you have no intention of keeping?"

"What are you talking about?"

"What will you do if Eddie shows up at your door one day?"

"He won't," says Tucker. "And if he did, I'd help him."

"How?"

"You're taking this all very seriously. I'm just trying to give the kid some encouragement."

"You're lying to him. Kids get mean when they're disappointed."

"Darling," he sighs. He is as aroused by her added clothes as he was by her striptease. His fingers slide into her trousers, reaching between her legs for that soft warm enveloping space, but she clamps her legs together tightly.

"Jesus, Tucker," she says. "Bedbugs."

They are too new for *no,* and his hand burrows deeper. He pulls her even closer and lets her feel how much he needs her.

"We could stand up?" he whispers.

Sonia rolls over so that his fingers lose their way and he is left with only the stiff evidence of his own desire, as tight and determined as she. Goddamn it, he thinks. He had Sonia all to himself before the accident. Now he feels the boy between them, and her own loss of confidence in him. Fumbling in the dark, he finds his pants and pulls them on, wishing they made the sound of a door slamming or a glass breaking instead of the soft, womanish whoosh of a tugged zipper.

"I'm going out for a smoke," he says.

He walks out to the edge of the breezeway and releases his half-stiff cock for a pee. The moon is nearly full, rising through the break in the trees. From his front pocket he fishes out his pouch of tobacco and rolling papers, strikes a match against the wooden railing. The hens are asleep in the barn, their beaks tucked beneath their wings. He steps out and walks toward the spring plashing from the rock into the stone basin of the family's bathing hole. They wash there in warm weather, and he envies them their freedom to stand naked in the sun.

The yard is too small to contain his restlessness and Tucker starts into the woods, finding the path down to the road. He walked it with Eddie and again with the projector and suitcase, and it, too, is becoming familiar to him. Just a week before he took the assignment, Tucker had stood in a line of men stripped nude like himself. Trembling behind the screen in the recruitment center, some shielded their penises with their hands, some stood tall and proud. When it was his turn, the draftee in line ahead of Tucker froze. He was a farm boy with wide shoulders and a faded scar across his buttocks. *I won't go. I'm against all war,* he said to the confused functionary who sat at his desk doling out white induction cards. His objection triggered no surprise or wrath, but was merely absorbed by the bespectacled man, stamping cards 1-A, 4-F. The farm boy moved on as if he hadn't spoken and it was Tucker's turn and he wanted to repeat everything just said, *I cannot kill another human being. I don't want to die.* But looking at the same blank face, he had answered instead, *No, I have never had gonorrhea. No, I have never had syphilis. Yes, I am heterosexual. I am unmarried. Yes, I am fit to serve.*

He could never tell this to Sonia. No woman could possibly understand the need to act against everything one believed or be called a coward. She has no idea, even, the comfort her body might provide at a time like this. If she knew, she would never withhold it.

Yes, the car. He just needs to rest his head against something plush and soft. He half-slides down the unanchored stone of the dry creek bed and comes to a large boulder formation he remembers. It is shaped like a calf bending down to drink, runoff water left in the creek bed pools there. From the calf's left fetlock, the path veers into the denser forest; he can see the shadowy, parted entrance to it and beyond, deeper, the alien green glow of jack-o'-lantern mushrooms thriving on rotted logs. Tucker hesitates. I should go back, he thinks. It's wrong to leave Sonia there alone. He thinks of her cheek against the sharp corner of a book, sleeping in a house with strangers, and he is swiftly ashamed of forcing himself on her, for not taking into account the stress of the circumstances, and her exhaustion, and, of course, the goddamned bugs. He squats down by the boulder and splashes cool green water on his face. Let it go, Tucker, he says to himself. Let her go. It feels good to be outside alone. Soon enough he will be crammed into a stifling barracks and made to march, to drop, to clean, to parade, to aim, to pivot, to shoot, to dig a grave in concert with men, and he, Tucker, a man who might get up in the middle of the night and take a walk in the woods, and let a woman go, will be lost.

The moon floats blowsy and fat in the rippled green pool as if he could scoop it up, a worm in a bottle of tequila, and swallow it. He is so thirsty. Tucker drinks, the flinty water cold on his lips. He looks more like an animal, he decides, than a man. A milky beast with flaring nostrils and the rolling eyes of a horse, white like the moon, a creature of the full moon and the glowing mushrooms. Where do other men find the belief in their own righteousness, he wonders, when all he wants to do is run away? Reflected back, he looks to himself like Pegasus sprung from the blood of that which turns men to stone and he feels like he could actually be a beast, rising up and running, and then Tucker realizes that he *is* running, just by virtue of wanting to. He hears his feet on the forest path, the gallop of hooves. The wind is in his hair as he makes straight for the dark wood, which opens, just a slit for him. Tucker feels weightless almost, leaping tree roots and stammering gullies, a hobo jumping trains, an atom fissioning into starlight, letting go of thought, he thinks, and then thought is snuffed. And as his thoughts go, he is almost imperceptibly aware of a weight upon his back, a gentle pressure, then a hand in his hair. The pressure doesn't slow him, it is not heavy, just present, and revives him like a second wind, lengthening his stride, stretching out. Against his flanks, he feels the press of thighs solid and muscular commanding him forward, he is not imagining it, he feels it skin to skin, smells it on the cold mist around him, fresh, empty shelled beans, fresh dug earth. He thought he was running before, but now, under the spell of this new weight, he sees his previous steps were slow and stumbling, still a man's steps, the motion of a man's thoughts. Under her hand—he knows it is a her, he feels the lean and the touch of her—he works himself into a rocking, rhythmic canter which is itself flesh breaking like a wave, and soon those tortured human associations are no more than the wind behind him and Tucker surrenders to the pleasure of being ridden, feeling the fluidity of horse and rider, savoring the weight as if it were all that kept him earthbound and connected to life itself.

She urges him on with her bare heels and he matches his breathing to hers, letting her push him faster and faster, over fallen trees, scrambling up stones. She kicks him once, a little hard, and he leaps forward, abandoning the lazy, romantic rhythm they'd found, working now, struggling uphill, his heart slamming against his chest. He lunges higher up this new path, through a tall stand of sourwood, crashing through the underbrush of dying laurel, brown and crisp on the vine. Her body feels like a challenge—are you the man I think you are? Can you keep up? He can taste the slaver in his mouth, the boiled egg of the afternoon, the applejack, the ham soup and biscuit, fresh milk with butterfat. He is lost but cannot slow down, weak with sweat and fear now, for as she goads him, Tucker no longer feels like a partner but like a creature made to serve, the slow ecstasy pushed too far into punishment.

He still cannot see her but her growingly oppressive weight bears down on him. He must stop or surely he will drop and die, he has lost all strength, his mind a blank but with no peace, no moving toward the light. Pain and humiliation and darkness. They have come to a fell of ghostly cankered trees, stripped of their bark and toppled over, stumps jutting sharp as dragons' teeth. He feels something slash his side and in the sickly moonlight sees blood on his white linen shirt. They race up the mountain and down into the next hollow, along the lip of a ravine so narrow his back leg slips and he nearly takes them down, falling in dream time with legs peddling the sky.

But she is too expert a horsewoman to let them fall. She pulls him up sharply at the chasm's edge and he hears pebbles skitter but not reach bottom. Suddenly, he is relieved of his burden, and he sees the thing he carried. She moves behind him, leans over and marks the ground with an X. Unbraided, her hair falls over her face, but he knows her instantly. It is Cora Alley, a vision of blood and sinew, standing raw against the moon.

This is not real, thinks Tucker, shutting his eyes. Our car went over a cliff. I died and have gone to hell.

Hours or maybe seconds later he opens his eyes again. Sprawled on the back porch, he stares up at the tin oilcan roof. The moon has dropped behind the mountain, he has no memory of how he got here, got back, if he ever left. Maybe he fell, had a stroke, maybe he did die and was returned to life. He breathes heavily like an animal stunned by an electric prod, unable to move, only to blink. Nothing stirs around him. No one rolls over in bed, no hen shivers in her straw. *What happened?* he thinks, and marvels that he can recall human speech. With great effort, Tucker draws himself onto his hands and knees and crawls down the breezeway to her shut bedroom door. He puts his eye against her keyhole.

There, Cora Alley, freshly dismounted, is wriggling back into the soft folds of empty arms and legs; she, too, returning to her human skin.

"Tucker, wake up," Sonia says, opening the shutters. Tangled in a sweat-soaked sheet on the parlor floor, he winces at the sun through the window.

"What time is it?" he asks.

"Nearly eight."

"How did I get here?"

"You don't remember?"

He shakes his head.

"You don't remember passing out? Or my waking you up?"

He shakes his head.

"Then you were drunker than I thought."

The crock of brandy sits in the corner, half full. He doesn't remember drinking it.

Sonia is dressed, or undressed rather, having taken off the scarf and his jacket, wearing nothing but the shirt and trousers from yesterday. Her suitcase is neatly packed and standing upright by the door. She wears her Rolleiflex around her neck and looks around the room as if she's shown up an hour early for a train and is trying to decide what to do with herself.

Tucker is ravenous and thirsty but when he rises his body gives under its own weight. His legs shake and his head is pounding with the magnitude of his worst hangover. He steps around Sonia and limps down the breezeway to the kitchen. Through the screen door, he sees a plate left for him on the kitchen table: flies lifting from a fried egg, a slab of country ham, fried, curled, and nearly black. If he steps inside, everything in him will come up, so he keeps walking, off the back porch and across the yard to the spring, where he forces himself to drink.

He splashes his face and runs his finger over his mossy teeth, waiting for his balance to return. What the hell happened to him? He has never dreamed so wildly in his life. From the barn, he sees Cora Alley approaching with the morning's milk. She wears the same green dress as yesterday and the same ugly men's work shoes. He is mortified at the sight of her, wincing to remember the lashing he took at her hand.

"Good morning, Mr. Hayes," she says. "Sleep well?"

He searches her face for any sign she is playing with him, but she wears the same weary, slightly embarrassed look of yesterday. Her skin fits tight around her body, no sag or gap. Stop it, he tells himself.

"I left some breakfast for you in the kitchen," she says.

"I saw, thank you," he gets out.

"Are you feeling ill?"

"Just didn't get much sleep last night," he says. "I'll be fine."

She looks troubled. "I hope the bed was comfortable."

"It was perfect," he reassures her. "I have always been a miserable sleeper."

Cora nods to him and starts toward the springhouse where she will leave the milk to cool. He watches her go, the muscles jumping in her strong calves. He can still feel them pressed tight against his flanks, and against his will, finds himself growing hard. She turns and speaks to him over her shoulder.

"When I finish with chores, I'm going back out to hunt the sang," she says. "You can come if it'll help your book."

"I would love to," he says, without hesitation.

Returning to the kitchen, he takes his place at the table where the flies hunker down possessively on his food. The fork by his plate has been used to stir eggs and the raw, dark orange yolk has dried between the tines, but he digs in anyway, and eats hungrily, feeling strength slowly return. Every bite is more intense than what he eats in the city—the ham gamier, the milk oily and tasting faintly of onions. His appetite rushes back and he eats with the gusto of a dog after a day's rabbit hunt, as if in six urgent gulps he could replace all the flesh he'd melted in the chase. Truly, he marvels at the properties of sleep that can wire mind to body so that a reflexive jerk upon nodding off might spawn a dream of tripping off a curb, or dreaming of a mountain woman on his back might make a man feel he's run a marathon. He wipes the last trace of egg from the plate with a biscuit and looks up to see Sonia in the doorway holding an enameled mug. She walks to the stove and fills it with some overpercolated chicory concoction that mountain people substitute for coffee during hard times. She adds a bit of cream and a touch of molasses from a small pitcher on the table.

"Eddie asked for some coffee," she says. "He's in more pain today."

"You always feel it worse the next day," Tucker agrees.

She sips and frowns, adds another dollop of molasses, stirs it with her finger, sips again. "I think he'll be fine with a little rest," she says. Tucker can feel her waiting for him to respond. "I'm all packed," she prompts. "We can leave whenever you're ready."

"I'd hate to chance anything," he says at last. "I was thinking we should stay and help out for a day or two."

Sonia is surprised. "Yesterday you were in such a hurry to leave."

"I was," he says. "But Eddie—"

"We have less than a week left before we have to turn in our notes, and you have to—"

"What's more important?" he cuts her off. "A person or a book?"

He speaks more sharply to her than he ever has before. She pauses, stung.

"Why did you take this job," Sonia asks quietly, "if you didn't believe in it?"

"Same reason as everyone else," Tucker says. "Less messy than suicide."

"You ready?" Cora Alley's voice interrupts them. He hadn't heard her come back from the springhouse. She has tied the feed sack across her shoulder and carries a small spadelike hoe.

"Ready for what?" Sonia asks.

"Mrs. Alley invited me to hunt sang with her today." Tucker feels the blood rise in his face, and busies himself with his notebook and pencil. A dream is a dream. He hasn't lied to anyone. There is no reason to feel ashamed. Sonia is speechless, holding Eddie's mug of coffee.

"You can come, too, if you'd like," Cora says.

Sonia is waiting for him to look up. He stuffs his notebook inside his satchel and drops the bag across his shoulder in imitation of Cora's feed sack.

"Of course you can," he echoes. "If you want."

"Someone should stay with Eddie," Sonia says coldly. "I'd hate to chance anything."

"You are so good," Tucker whispers, stepping up to plant a kiss beneath her ear. "Our kids will be lucky to have you."

Following Cora down the breezeway, he peeks into the open bedroom door where Eddie lies huddled under the covers.

"Take care of my lady, chum," he says. "I expect to find her as I left her."

Cora has her hoe and Tucker has fashioned himself a walking stick from a branch. Together they hike the steeper slopes of the western face, clambering over rocks slick with gray-green lichen. Light filters through the canopy of scarlet black gums, staining their hands and faces until they are absolved by an open field and blue sky above them. She reads the signposts of the mountain as he would the city streets. Indian Branch with its iron-brown water, Mad Sheep Branch where a flock of rabid animals came to drown themselves, Blowing Rock, Snakekill Rock. She doesn't talk much but takes him quickly through this harvested part of the woods, knowing she'll find little or nothing of value so close to home. He hadn't noticed yesterday, but Cora Alley walks with a limp. What caused it? Polio as a child? A nail in her hoof?

Is it his imagination that Cora looks rounder and softer and a little more satisfied than she did at dinner last night? Yes, it is his imagination. Yet, after walking only a mile or so, he is winded and sore as if something vital had been stolen from him. When he slammed on the brakes to avoid killing Eddie, his body hit the steering wheel. A mild case of whiplash? Perhaps that explains the muscle ache.

"What am I looking for?" Tucker asks.

"Palest gold," she says. "Look for five leaves in sets of three or four. If you find a two- or three-prong, look up. Seeds roll downhill so there's like to be even bigger plants up above."

"I've only ever seen ginseng hanging in the windows of Chinatown. Never knew what it was for."

"Sang's the cure for everything," Cora says. "It'll bring down your high blood pressure or pick up your low. It cures sugar diabetes, and some men say, well—" she trails off.

Tucker helps her. "It picks up other things, too?" Cora looks down and doesn't answer.

"The man I sell it to sells it to a Chinaman in New York who takes it all the way back to China," she says. "Over there, he says they call it Essence of Man in the Earth."

Tucker likes the sound of that. He likes the sound of Cora Alley talking. He feels an intimacy between them, as if the dream did change something. He has surprised himself coming to the woods with her. He doesn't usually let himself be alone with women, aware of what alone can bring. But he's in love with Sonia, so he is safe. Maybe that's why he takes the risk.

As they walk, he's conscious of trees fallen across their path, and he finds himself climbing their trunks like stair steps, planting a foot and pushing up, pausing at the rise for the brief, slightly higher vantage, before dropping lightly down to the other side. Up ahead, Cora balances on a stump; beyond her is an unnatural horizon of leafless and fallen trees, as though the forest has been blown over by a giant.

"What happened?" he asks. "Was there a fire?"

"We're coming into the chestnut graveyard," she says. "Blight's taken them all since I was just a girl."

He knows he's never been here but the devastation looks familiar, stretching as far as he can see, broken only by patches of opportunistic understory. He scales another splintered trunk as he walks through the dry tatters of last year's litter. Amid the ash-gray and brown, he spies a stand of yellow leaves. At least a dozen hidden plants.

"I found something!" Tucker cries, flushing at the excitement in his voice. He waits for Cora to come over and together they squat down before it, their shoulders just touching. She reaches out and teases the soil around the root. It comes out of the ground long and fingerlike.

"Sorry, Mr. Hayes," she says, "but you found yourself some Fool's Sang. This is just plain old sarsaparilla. Makes a nice root beer."

"You're sure?" he asks. "It looks right."

"Looking's not being," she says, and rises, wiping the root on the hem of her dress and handing it down to him. He takes the stiff, skinny root and sticks it between his teeth like FDR's cigarette holder, tilts his chin, and squints up at her.

"We have nothing to feeeeear," he drawls, "but feeeeeear itself."

It was worth the embarrassment to make Cora Alley smile.

Suddenly, she puts her hand on his shoulder and points to a snag ahead. "Look there," she says.

"What? Is that it?"

"Not the plant, the bird."

Perched upon briar, a bird about the size of a chickadee preens its feathers. Its wings are crimson and its belly white. Cora stands motionless a long time, until Tucker speaks. He is still down on his haunches and his knees are beginning to ache.

"What are we waiting for?" he whispers.

"To see which way it'll go."

He waits another few minutes as the bird zips its tail through its beak, shakes itself, looks around with a bright, black eye. "Why?"

"It's a ginseng bird. It'll lead us to the sang."

"How does it know?"

"Its wings are the color of berries," she explains, as if it should be obvious to him. "Don't scare it, or the way won't be true."

Tucker is growing impatient. Cora strains to remain still, her narrow green eyes fixed on the bird. She *does* look different this morning, he decides. Unlike him, she got a good night's rest. Her plait is not so tight and her face is scrubbed clean and rosy. He'd put her a few years over thirty, but now he's guessing she might be a few before. Closer to him.

"How long've you been married?" she whispers.

"Not long," he replies, surprised and a little thrilled at the question.

"If you don't mind my saying, you don't seem suited."

"How so?" he asks, keeping his voice low.

"She's coiled up like a snake and you're a plump little mouse ready to be swallowed whole."

"I'm glad you think so highly of me on such short acquaintance," he says, not bothering to whisper any longer. The bird on the twig takes notice.

"Don't move," she commands.

"And what of Mr. Alley," Tucker asks. "Is he a man or a mouse?"

"It's not proper to ask a lady about an absent husband," she says.

"Of course it isn't, which is why I'm asking," he says, but the bird chooses that moment to take off. It is gone before he can tell which way it went.

"It headed toward Panther Gap," Cora says, moving forward, all business now. Tucker rises and tosses away the root.

"Panther Gap? Sounds like a story behind that."

"There's one if I choose to tell it."

"Mrs. Alley. You mustn't lead a man to woods just to tease him."

Cora shakes her head. "This way," she says. "We can't lose the bird."

Tucker is stubborn. "Tell me as we go," he says. "I'll put it in my book."

Cora frowns at him and keeps walking, faster now, headed farther west. Tucker leaps the fallen chestnut trunks to catch up, and together they walk briskly, Cora searching the sky for the crimson bird. Her voice is so low it takes him a moment to realize she's begun her story, and then he has to strain to hear.

"Once there was a girl in our family who had the bad luck of falling for a boy from the valley," Cora says.

"This is a story about your family?" Tucker asks in surprise.

"This story is our burden, Mr. Hayes," Cora says, somber and self-importantly. She is still shy of talking at length, and they walk a little ways in silence before she begins again.

"The boy of her desire was fine-looking but vain. His mama spoilt him with fancy clothes she sewed out of magazines, and put it in his head he was destined for great things."

"I know quite a few boys such as he," Tucker says.

"I'm sure you do," says Cora, fixing him with the sort of look his mother gave when he was especially impertinent. "Well, this boy had been paying attention to this girl of our family for months, walking her home from church, taking her to parties. You see, she was expecting a proposal, and so one afternoon, when her parents had gone into town for Court Day, she gave into his whisperings. It didn't make her bad; preachers came by so seldom that a man's word was his bond. And yet, stupid girl, she should have known better, 'cause everyone knows any country boy in a suit spells trouble, and he, stupid boy, should have known better, 'cause it was understood by all within a hundred miles that this girl was a witch."

"A witch?" asks Tucker. "In your family?"

"Once witches slip in," Cora replies, "they're hard to get rid of."

Tucker laughs delightedly, but she looks injured. This is more than Cora Alley has spoken since he met her; he never would have guessed so many words were trapped inside. "Please," he says. "I didn't mean to interrupt."

"Well, the deed was done, and when it was all over, as often happens, they opened their eyes and saw each other clearly for the first time. As the boy rose to put back on his mama-made suit, the girl thought, surely he will speak to the future. Surely he will invite me to come live at his mother's house. And as the boy pulled on his clothes, he thought, surely that was tasty, but I am destined for greater things. Maybe I am mistaken, she thought, as he slipped on his jacket and socks and shoes. Maybe he will speak now. But when he had fully suited up, kissed her forehead, and started for the door, she had her answer. This girl, pretending nothing was wrong, rose and packed her young lover a nice supper for his long journey home."

"I suppose that boy gets what he deserves?" asks Tucker.

"Oh, Mr. Hayes," says Cora. "You know how these stories go."

Her hair has slipped its plait, falling loose around her cheeks. It's habit, he sees, how she gathers it back, rebraiding as she goes. He finds himself looking for that dream creature in her, as if it were not something of his own creation.

"See, this girl had given herself over to the Devil years before, in despair over another boy she'd loved till this one come along to take his place," she continues. "Back then, she'd swore in with the Dark Man, and he gave her the power to hex people's cattle and sour their milk in the churn. She mixed witch balls of hair and fingernail clippings and earwax for paying customers, and now, used and messed, she called upon her first love, the Devil, to avenge her."

Cora takes the fallen chestnut trunks as a hurdler might, up and over each one gracefully, while Tucker struggles to keep up. There is almost no clear ground between the felled trees now, they are walking across acres of extinction, as if across the bones of a mass burial pit. The ginseng bird has disappeared but Cora walks as if she knows where she's going.

"The hollow that night was a kettle of fog," she continues, opening her arms as if to conjure it. "That boy'd got about two miles along, thinking thoughts of city girls and smoothing the wrinkles from his suit, when behind, just off in the woods he heard something shriek. It sounded like a woman screaming with child, but it weren't no woman. The boy trotted along, he still had a good mile to go before he reached his mama's house. As he walked, he heard a rustling behind him in the woods—SNAP—a twig. CRACK—a broke branch. Now he was troubled 'cause in his letch for the girl of my family he'd forgot to bring along his gun. All he had was the supper she'd packed him."

Cora is pushing them to walk faster though her voice is no more urgent. She doesn't look at him, but keeps her sharp eyes fixed on the way forward. I have been here before, Tucker thinks, trying to keep up. I know this place. When he was a boy coming through these mountains the chestnuts had been tall and healthy, but now the few standing are scored with deep orange marks as if raked by angry claws. Every grown thing is dead, and the saplings pushing into the empty space are themselves showing cankers of the blight that had taken their parents.

"Then suddenly," she says, "he heard a low growl like a bar threat in his ear. The boy spun and there, glowing out of the fog, were the two green eyes of a hollow-bellied panther. He froze, not knowing what to do. Now the Devil might be evil, but like all sinners, he's easy to distract, and this girl was a good cook. So the boy flung his supper at that witch cat. When the panther stopped to gobble up the boiled egg and cornbread and salt pork she'd packed, the boy ran as fast as his long shapely legs had ever carried him. He was just ready to congratulate himself on a close escape when, sure enough, he heard the gallop behind him, crashing through the brush and howling with rage. This time when he felt that cat's hot breath, he ripped off his jacket and flung it as hard as he could off the path behind him. The panther turned and fell on that jacket, tearing it to shreds. Again the boy ran, but soon enough, the panther had caught up. This time the boy peeled off his vest, flinging it in the opposite direction, and again the panther went for that. Off comes his shirt, his shoes, his suspenders, till, at last, to his huge relief, the boy saw through the clearing, the light in his mother's window. He saw his mama through the glass, her foot working the treadle of the spinning wheel upon which she'd spun the thread to weave the fine suit he'd worn to bewitch the witch of my family. *Mama!* he cried. But she didn't hear. She was too busy spinning for him. With the lamp just ahead and the cat just behind, he peeled off his underdrawers, jumping on one leg, so ridiculous, so close to home, just at the clearing of his mother's yard. But do you know anyone who's ever outrun the Devil? His legs got tangled up and down he went. In an instant, the panther was all over him, and they say that faithless boy's widowed mother found nothing but a bloodstained rag the next morning when she went outside to milk her cow."

They have reached a drop-off, down into which spills a vortex of inverted grapevine. The gray loops froth with a false bottom of leaves, Tucker knows. If they fell, they'd keep on falling, forever and ever, amen. He looks back and the graveyard is behind them.

"That's quite a story," he says, breathing hard. "You know the Greeks had one very similar, about a man who wanted to win a woman who was a mighty runner. Every time she'd be set to pass him, he'd fling a golden apple into the bushes to distract her. He turned her off course enough times she had to marry him."

"But mine is not a love story," says Cora simply. "Nobody wins. And that's how you can tell it's the truth."

She stands looking down over the edge without the least sign of fear. This is her terrain and it makes her, for a blinding instant, beautiful. Not city beautiful like Sonia, but in the way a cracked blue patent medicine bottle found in a trash heap is beautiful or a tin can rusted down to tetanus lace.

"Do you see the bird?" Tucker asks, to have something to say. He feels giddy from the story and the walk. He's come unmoored again, with no idea where they are or how he would get back. He's getting used to this feeling.

"He may have gone deeper," she says. "There's a hollow below this hollow. A part of the mountain that's just mine."

"A private part?" Tucker grins. "Then surely we must go."

Cora grasps a trunk of vine growing on the edge of the gorge and swings herself down into the leaves. He watches her hang, suspended over the deep green pit before she lets go. The tangle swallows her, he hears the tearing of leaves stripped away, and then the sound of her finding solid ground below. It's his turn and Tucker grasps another loop, giving a holler, and he's swinging out, too, pushing off from the rock face. He squeezes his eyes shut and drops, absorbing the shock through his knees, and then he's there beside her, on the ledge of a deeper fissure. Once his heart stops pounding in his ears, he can hear rushing water somewhere far off, or maybe it's close by, the chasm sends up plumes of mist and sound.

"This way," Cora says, heading toward another dry creek bed. She will keep going and going, he thinks. They will never come to rest.

"Cora, stop," he says.

She turns back, impatient, but it's too bad. Taking his pouch of tobacco and his papers from his satchel, he rolls himself a cigarette. He is too lost for comfort.

"Like one?" he asks. Cora shakes her head.

"No brandy, no cigarettes? Have you any pleasures at all, Mrs. Alley, besides scaring grown men half to death?"

Tucker makes a seat for himself and leans back against the wall of the drop-off. He has fallen down a well, and looking up he can see clear blue sky and hawks wheeling on the updraft. Juniper grows along the rock face opposite. He recognizes the silvery berries and wafting familiar smell of gin. The other side of the pass lies deep in emerald shadow, but the sun on their side is hot on his face; he'd sell his mother for a cold gin and tonic right about now.

"Won't you sit down?" he asks, because her pacing is making him nervous, but she shakes her head no to that as well. So be it, he thinks. Holding his cigarette between his lips, he fishes out his notebook and fountain pen from his satchel to record what he can remember of her panther story. It's an archetypal legend, nearly every culture in the world has its avenging furies and its striptease. He thinks of Medea and Jason fleeing with the Golden Fleece, and how Medea hacked her brother to bits, casting his pieces into the wake of their ship, compelling her father to stop and retrieve the remains.

"What do you have in there?" she asks, as he flips the pages to find a blank.

"Genies in a bottle," he answers.

"You going to cork me up, too?"

"Something tells me it would take a good deal to contain you, Mrs. Alley."

Cora paces slowly while he smokes, walking the edge of the ravine. She could go over at any minute, and she's aware she's disturbing his rest.

"I like the quiet of this place," she says. "Other parts of the mountain can get so crowded and up in your business."

"What exactly is your business?"

"I'd like to be a hairdresser," she says. "If I could get my license."

Well, thinks Tucker. That's what he gets for trying to flirt. He takes a deep drag of his cigarette and exhales. If she goes over, she goes over, he tells himself. He can't keep holding his breath on her behalf. "How did that one survive?" he asks.

"What?"

"That tree, across the divide?"

On the other side of the ravine a single chestnut is standing. Even from this far away, he can see the spiny pods among the flat leaves, it's one of the trees he knows because, before his mother sold their farm and moved them into town, a chestnut grew outside his bedroom window, and on a certain morning every autumn, a storm of nuts would wake him, raining down on the red tin roof. He would rise and pull on his boots so the pods would not cut his feet and fight the foraging pigs for the sweet meat inside. The air is crisp and the smoke of his cigarette looks like autumn breath. He can hear the rolling deluge on the roof, and he feels mournful out of proportion.

"The trees infect each other," Cora says. "Can't say exactly how. All we know is their roots are still alive, underground. A chestnut can live just so long as it never pushes up. I suppose that one is far enough away from the others."

"Is that a house back there?" Tucker asks. Beyond the tree, through a thicket of underbrush, he can just make out the outline of a shack. The planks are light and dark, of wattle and daub; it looks to be very old. To his surprise, Cora is blushing deeply.

"That's my old homeplace," she says. "Where I was born."

"This is where the witch slipped in?" Tucker asks.

Cora Alley stares off over the chasm. There are no roads for miles around. Why would anyone choose to live here?

"Do you believe in witches, Mr. Hayes?" she asks.

"Of course not," he answers, shortly. "Do you?"

Wordlessly, she kneels beside him where he sits on the ground, dirty and sweating from their walk. With tender fingers, she lifts his shirt. Tucker tenses, not knowing what to expect. Across his ribs runs a long lash mark, lightly raised and scabbed like a march of aphids. He feels that old hunger dread that led him to follow Sonia's trail of clothes rising in his groin. Cora lets his shirt fall.

"You got hurt, too," Cora says, standing. "Just like Eddie."

Tucker looks down at his wound. Had it gone unnoticed from the accident? No, it wasn't there before this morning. Her face is so close to his, he feels the panic of his dream rise up in him.

"Why did you bring me here?" he whispers. She shakes her head.

"I don't know," she says. "I just wanted to show you someplace different. For your map."

Her face is so close, and he knows if he kissed her now, she would never tell anyone. Neither would he. It would just be a lovely thing between them, like an acorn dropping to the ground or a flower opening in the sun. Something natural and expected and out of time. He could get back in the car with Sonia tomorrow and kiss her and not feel bad about either one, because both were honest and offered. And yet the dream hangs between them, that grotesque red and raw creature he knew her to be. Was it her plan all along to bring him back to the place he dreamed, is he being led once more?

"I am not bringing you good luck on your hunt," Tucker says gruffly. "I'd like to go back. I don't like leaving Sonia alone so long."

She nods and rises without another word. The way back up and out is steep, without the thrill of the leap down. Cora pauses uphill ahead of him and reaches around to tug the elastic from her braid, digging her fingers deep underneath her white-shot hair, letting it spill over her shoulders before she blindly replaits it. He finishes off his cigarette and drops it to the ground, crushing it with his shoe. A flap of crimson wings and a streak of white, the startled bird lifts up and whips across the chasm, faltering at the edge before coming to light on the chestnut across the way. And there, at Tucker's feet, where he flushed out the bird, he spies the X drawn in the loose dirt. A whorl of golden leaves and a spray of bloody berries. Of course it's there in plain sight, where it's been hiding all along. He had been sitting right beside it. If it had been a snake, as his mother used to say, it've bit him.

"Cora!" he calls. "Come back."

Cora turns and gazes down at him from her perch a little higher up. "Well, look at that," she says, without surprise. "The wily sang."

Eddie

NEW YORK CITY

1:00 a.m.

The other day I asked my oncologist how I could remember the smell of seventy-year-old chestnuts when I couldn't remember what I ate for lunch. I think it was my oncologist I asked. It might have been my butcher.

He told me there was no past. Or should I say, that the past is always on and waiting. Memories coded on a billion chemical loops playing in the background like a movie with the sound turned down, until we reach back for that day in time. That face. That kiss. He said, Oh, our marvelous, mysterious little brains. Evolved from the single-celled bacteria we once were, huddling together for survival, and we still communicate as those colonies once did, one impulse colliding with the next impulse, in lightning strikes of fight or flight, leaping the gaps of synapse; and the memories we retrieve most frequently carve the deepest neural pathways, like water eroding a mountain gorge, and become our truth. Walking and rewalking our hauntings, our family story evolved from our human family story.

Or maybe he said, Want me to trim the fat off that, Mr. Alley?

It's dark inside this box.

Wallis, you haven't called me back. I know your show is over. I couldn't watch it tonight. An interview with a failed suicide bomber?

Did you think that was funny? A fitting tribute? Did the irony even cross your mind? You have not forgotten what night this is.

Yes, the past is always on. I've been remembering Tucker Hayes but it is Jasper who haunts us tonight, isn't it, sweetheart? And the path between those two is carved the deepest in me. So far, Jasper is the only one of us who has succeeded in getting it right. You, Wallis, have always been more subtle in your suicide attempts. I remember the day of your last try, yet another path that winds through time, returning to tonight.

I was out grocery shopping for the week. Your mother had always been so on top of things when we were married that we were all surprised by how competent I was. It's really not that hard to know what you need when your cabinets finally belong to you. I came home that afternoon with my Roma tomatoes and wedge of Parmesan, my olives and capers, all my greens and the to-be-refrigerated jar of salad dressing, but by that time Charles had already accepted the overseas charges, spoken to you, and hung up. Between the two of you, you'd decided the emergency was over, there was no point alarming me. Charles is always so scrupulous about keeping other people's secrets that I didn't suspect a thing, though how he got through that dinner, I'll never understand. Secrets are always hardest at the beginning. After a while they settle in, like the cavities in your teeth, and you only think about them when they hurt. I probably never would have learned what happened, except about a year later, I made that exact meal again, but this time Charles couldn't eat it. *This puttanesca tastes like burned flesh,* he said, and when I threw a fit and accused him of not appreciating all the things I did for him, I got the real story. With you safely home, it felt less like a betrayal. But I was angry with you for telling him before you told me.

In between phone calls and letters, we killed each other off, you and I. You couldn't have been thinking much of us, to put yourself in the situations you did, leaving us to rehearse your death a dozen times a day. Or maybe you knew we enjoyed it, too, being able to talk about you with pride and trade on your war stories. You were doing something important while we were back home cooking spaghetti sauce and slicing bread. I told myself your rudimentary Arabic and press pass were shield

and armor enough, that being a woman—which made you vulnerable
over there—also kept you safe; for a strong woman, no matter where she
lives, still has the power to shame men, and maybe that would be enough
to get you through. But knowing all that, I still had to kill you off to get
through every day. Here's how it would go: we'd get one of your long,
hysterical letters about the gum under the school desk where you hid in
Chechnya, or about being blindfolded and led through mountain passes
to the birthday banquet of a warlord. You would spend pages trying to
capture the precise gaminess of the stewed goat and mare's milk, while
the drones overhead merited no more mention than a passing hawk.
Charles and I would sit up in bed and take turns reading your pages. He
did your voice perfectly, so lilting and melodious for the ferocious girl
you've always been. We'd get to your signature on the last page. Love,
W., and then Charles would pass the letter to me and I'd fold it up carefully and stick it in the drawer of my bedside table. When I closed the
drawer it was like sliding your body into a crypt. I couldn't think about
you until the next time, because that letter had brought you so directly
into my bedroom and made me love you all over again. And then all I
could think about was the loss of you, of a stray sniper's bullet in your
temple or a land mine beneath the wheel of your jeep. Sometimes, when
the news was especially grim over there, your mother would call and
beg me to do something, but what could I do? You were an adult and
you were becoming more famous with every broadcast.

It wasn't until you wrote that you were coming back to take the
anchor position that I began to worry. A straightforward suicidal impulse, that I could understand, its directness suited you—but this new
turn of events? You were getting married, you wanted to start a family?
Finally, Charles confessed what happened and it all made sense. Your
friendship with that woman whose brother was killed in the city square.
The powerless, powerful prayer meetings and long, anguished talks of
revenge. The trip into town, both of you dressed in full burqa, and the
explosion, as Charles told me you described it—so close you couldn't
tell if it was her or yourself shattered to bits. Jasper was long dead, but
you had fallen in love with another bomb waiting to go off. You could
have won a Pulitzer but the story hit too close to home. The suicide
bombing became one of a hundred random, unreported attacks.

The first weekend you were to anchor the news, Charles and I settled on the living room couch; Charles put his hand on my knee and said, *Isn't it nice to have her back?* The commercial ended, the music swelled, you were so pretty and bright sitting next to that asshole with the plastic hair—not too distant, not too familiar. I thought to myself, Maybe this will work out. Maybe I don't need to be afraid for her anymore. Then you read your first story. It was about missing uranium rods and their suspected links to weapons of mass destruction. Next came bird flu. The missing blond child, the deadly bacteria in our kitchen sponges. I pictured you in the editing room, choosing which truths to include, which ones just confused the story. Mixing in your anxiety music, conjuring your bold and commanding graphics. You had claimed your full Alley family inheritance. A ghost story in the mountains, a monster movie on TV—mere local, minor terrors. But you—you have the influence to back the whole world into a corner until it lashes out from pure survival instinct. Would you have become this creature had Jasper lived? Would any of us be here had Tucker Hayes not shown me my first horror movie before he disappeared? Do you believe in witches?

I know you haven't forgotten what tonight is. And knowing that and knowing you, Wallis, I would wager, wherever you are, you are not alone.

Wallis

NEW YORK CITY

MIDNIGHT

She saw the message from her father as she was finishing makeup. It was just like him to call when she was about to go on air. Dying had only made him needier. Charles deserved a halo and gold cock ring in Gay Heaven for putting up with him.

"I know a secret about you." The new cameraman pops his head into the dressing room, interrupting her. MaryAnn presses powder into her cheeks. Wallis's face is always too tight until she loosens it with talk.

"What's that?" she asks.

"Find me when the show's over," he says.

"Tell me now," she says. "I have to leave when the show's over."

MaryAnn gestures for her to look up, powders under her chin. Wallis checks him out through lowered lids. His brown hair curls over his forehead in a reassuring, sensible way. He has the firm and reliable body of a fireman, a good Irish, union-contract body.

"No, I want to show you something," he says with a grin and saunters off. How cheeky of him to flirt with her just as she's about to go on. This is his first week with them; he came from that horrible morning talk show Wallis catches only if she's home sick or hungover. MaryAnn shields Wallis's eyes with her hand and sprays her hair.

"He's cute," MaryAnn says.

"He's a kid," says Wallis. "What's his name?"

"Jeff, I think," MaryAnn answers, dabbing on her lipstick. "He's older than he looks."

"Then he should have a better job than this," says Wallis.

In the mirror she sees herself looking good. Calm and together. Her highlighted and lowlighted shoulder-length hair lies perfectly, her pores are closed. She scans for flaws. That woman in the mirror has none.

MaryAnn removes the cape from her neck and brushes stray powder from around the collar of her pink tweed suit. Tweed in August. But it has been raining nearly every day for a month and the temperature has not broken sixty. Has it been forty days and forty nights? Global warming? She had experts lined up on both sides. And next week: experts to refute the experts of the week before.

Tonight though, she'll be interviewing via satellite and with a translator. She needs to concentrate.

I want to show you something, he'd said.

"We're having trouble with the feed," Lou says as she walks to the set. "We haven't been able to get him yet."

"Is it us or them?" Wallis asks.

"I think it's them. Could be us."

"Make sure the others are ready to go. Jesus," she swears. "He's the one we're here for."

It had taken her weeks to get the interview, working all her old contacts. The boy was supposed to be dead. He did everything right but his bomb failed to explode. *I am my own ghost,* they said he cried when the feds caught him and whisked him away. They didn't have to torture him; he was so humiliated he immediately began naming names. What does it matter, he said, when I am already damned.

"I don't know how people do shit like that," Lou says.

"You don't?" asks Wallis.

She goes on air in under three minutes. Alone at the table on the set, she looks into the monitor and sees the other guests, in other studios, fumbling with their mikes, licking their lips, looking off into space. They lined up an Australian backpacker who had been ordering a falafel when the second bomb went off. A talking head from Whatever-the-Fuck Middle East Think Tank, and a shrink with theories on learned helplessness. The fourth feed was supposed to be him, live, from where he was being held. It is nothing but gray static and the time signature.

Jeff, the cameraman, is smiling at her. What's his problem? She lets Lou clip on her mike. She goes over her hard copy quickly, making sure she knows how to pronounce all the names. She remembers her cell phone in the dressing room and the waiting message from her dad. They all feel entitled to interrupt her whenever it suits them. She thinks of Olivia at home with an ear infection and wonders if Laurence has remembered to give her the antibiotic. She imagines Ollie screaming herself to sleep.

Jeff counts them down. The heads in the other monitors stop fumbling and licking. They intently watch their feed of her, the one who will ask the questions and redirect them if they ramble and keep them from looking stupid. They watch her take three deep breaths and they feel calmer in their own bodies. Wallis Alley, their host, is in control. Even when she glances over at the fourth monitor, empty of its guest, her eyes betray nothing. She's an expert at working around what should have been.

Her phone is ringing and this time she picks up. Hold on, she mouths to Jeff, who is leaning against her at the bar. It is after one in the morning and they've all gone across the street, as usual.

"I told you," she says into the phone. "Neil's going-away party. The Paris bureau."

Ollie woke up and was crying for her. Over the laughter and music in the bar, she can't hear a thing Laurence is saying about it. Putting her hand on Jeff's arm, she gestures, Save my place.

Even with the traffic on Columbus Circle, it is quieter outside. She pulls a broken black umbrella from the corner trash can and opens it to stand under. "Can't you get her back down?" she asks. "Did you give her Tylenol?"

The lights are shining on the steel globe across Broadway, the traffic lights smudged red and green down the wet street. *Do you want to talk to Mommy?* Laurence is asking. Wallis stares into the dark entrance of Central Park, where all the horse and carriages have gone home. Once, she saw a driverless horse racing down Ninth Avenue with its buggy careening after it. A woman was inside screaming, her husband and the horse's driver chasing behind. The horse kept pace with the green lights for blocks and blocks, until it finally ran a red. Wallis caught up and saw the overturned carriage, the lady sobbing on the curb. The horse was making for its stable, for rest and food.

"Hi sweetheart," she says when the two-year-old gets on the line. "How are you feeling?"

An hour ago she was on a set talking to strangers. Now she is in the low light of Ollie's bedroom where Laurence is rocking their daughter in his lap, holding the phone to her good ear. Wallis sees the stuffed turtle on the floor, the blanket pulled out of the crib, a half drunk sippy cup of apple juice on the dresser. She hears her daughter's ragged breathing over the line and she says, "You don't have to talk. I'll sit with you until you fall back asleep."

She leans against the exterior plate window of the bar. The music throbs against her back and the rain rolls off the sagging fabric of her umbrella. She is floating from the two whiskeys she's already had plus the beer chaser. Wallis rarely drinks whiskey in the summer but she is pretending to be in Ireland tonight. It's so cold.

Laurence has her on speakerphone to make sure she can hear him breathing, too, and the rhythmic creak of the rocking chair where she should be. He only calls when he wants her to feel bad, and it always works. He has the power to pull her through the phone line, across the river, into the bedroom lit only by light from the cracked closet door. Ollie is whimpering in his lap, softly speaking her name. Mommy. Mommy. Wallis will stand outside all night if she has to.

"I'm here. Just go back to sleep," she says.

"When are you coming home?" Laurence asks. His voice is hollow and suspended over the speaker.

"Soon."

She turns her head to look back through the window. Her staff is there, young and unmarried; Lou who fancies himself the Apollinaire of cell phone apps, always showing off his clever programming to bored girls in bars. MaryAnn who knits and bakes and is too kind to keep any boyfriend more than a few months. The interns are here, too, and a bunch of strangers crowding the long wooden bar and grouped around the jukebox with its deep list of blues and bluegrass. You are here, late at night, attracting each other to make sure you will never spend late nights here again, she thinks. Jeff sits next to an empty stool, holding her place.

You handled that really well, he'd said before she stepped out. Their guest never showed, or maybe he was there on the other end of the disconnect, but who could say? She had to throw out half her questions and let the shrink and backpacker talk longer. Several times during the broadcast she had paused to ask aloud, *Do we have him yet?* The answer was always no.

I have some experience with suicidal boys, she told Jeff. *I had some questions I really wanted answered.*

You were in Baghdad, weren't you?

And Syria and Sierra Leone. But I wanted a family. So I came home.

"Mommy?" Ollie asks.

"Yes, sweetheart?"

There is no question, just the need to know she's there, which Wallis supposes is the only question. Her daughter's voice is softer and less anxious and Wallis feels the letting go in her whole body. She remembers the early days before she went back to work, when time stood still for them both. I am teaching you not to need me, she thinks. Even as I need not to need you.

After her first whiskey she said she had to go home, the car was waiting. *Do you live in the city?* she asked Jeff, who shook his head. *Willets Point, on the 7 train,* he said. *It's the end of the line.*

I know, she said. *I used to ride to the end of all the lines just to see what was out there. Willets Point is an auto body shantytown. No one lives there.*

I do, he said, leaning in. *Don't you want to see?*

Ollie's breath evens out on the other end of the line. Wallis hears the rocking chair slow and Laurence rise. He has the phone tucked between his shoulder and chin, and he carries their daughter back to her crib. Wallis hears the soft sigh of real sleep and knows Ollie will be okay for now. She has tomorrow off and will take her to the doctor. There is no emergency, she reminds herself. It's just an ear infection. Like she had a million times as a kid herself.

Laurence says, "Your father called. I was with her and didn't pick up."

Wallis remembers the message she never retrieved. "I need to call him back," she says.

"Tell Neil I said bon voyage," Laurence says.

Wallis looks back through the window where one of the interchangeable interns with the long straight hair and a spring break tan is approaching Jeff. She is sipping a Rolling Rock and easing herself onto Wallis's stool.

"I will," she says. "Get some rest yourself."

Wallis ends the call and looks at the time. It's too late to call her father. She tosses the broken umbrella back into the trash and steps into the bar. Ignoring the girl in her seat, she strides up to Jeff.

"So what was it you wanted to show me?" she asks.

The card, when he pulls it out of his wallet, is creased and worn almost to lint. It has been through the washer and dryer more than once but, even faded, she recognizes it immediately. Pale and blue, the size of a social security card, it has the exaggerated cartoon head of her father on one side. On the other it says, Jeffrey Walton Reece: Official Casketeer.

"No fucking way," Wallis swears.

Jeff hums the tune that is too much of a rip-off of the Mickey Mouse theme to ever be legal today.

> Who's the digger of the grave,
> For you, and you, and me?
> C-A-P
> T-A-N
> C-A-S-K-T

"He ruined spelling for an entire generation of children," says Wallis. "Where did you get that?"

"My father was in the navy and we were stationed in Norfolk when I was in fifth grade. I am a card-carrying fellow traveler."

MaryAnn was right. *Captain Casket* was canceled in 1980, so to have this, Jeff must be about her own age. He is grinning as if he's given her the best gift. It's not a secret Wallis is the daughter of a campy, former horror show host. He was regional and one of many, but people re-member him. It used to bother her; now she just rolls her eyes.

"Your dad was my hero," he tells her.

The intern has moved on. Lou and MaryAnn are saying their goodbyes, looking forward to sleeping in tomorrow. Wallis perches on her stool with her face close to Jeff's as they read over the card's fine print. THIS ENTITLES THE OWNER TO ONE KIDNEY, HALF A BRAIN, AND A SCREAM TRANSFUSION. TO BE REDEEMED AT ANY CITY MORGUE BETWEEN THE HOURS OF MIDNIGHT AND HALF PAST MIDNIGHT, NIGHTS OF THE FULL MOON ONLY. VOID IN CANADA.

"It was so stupid," says Wallis.

"It was great," Jeff says. "It gave boys like me something to do while our older brothers were out getting laid."

Wallis smiles halfheartedly and reaches for his beer. The intrusion of her father on this night is not what she wanted. She shouldn't have let her car go after the second whiskey, she thinks. The thrill has worn off Jeff and she wishes she were already home in bed.

"You want another?" Jeff asks.

"I'll finish yours."

"I remember everything about that show," he says. "I remember the coffin and the saw he played. He had that skeleton cat, and toward the end there, I remember some creepy redheaded kid who would do skits with him. I was so jealous."

"That boy was Jasper," Wallis says. "He lived with us for a while."

"Lucky bastard," Jeff says.

Wallis is suddenly feeling the nausea of too many drinks. She doesn't want to think about her father or Jasper. She is irrationally angry at Jeff for bringing them up and she hears in her head, like an echo, the Australian backpacker she interviewed an hour ago. He was telling her that the suicide bomber, the boy who stood her up, was young and handsome and spoke perfect English. *Your leaders are liars! Your women are whores!* he screamed just before he malfunctioned. *You are afraid of all the wrong things!*

"We could transfer to the 7 at Forty-second Street," she says.

He holds her gaze for a long minute and slowly puts the card away. He pulls out a $20 bill and leaves it on the bar.

"Sure," he says.

"My dad is dying, you know," Wallis tells him, standing up. She rebuttons her pink tweed jacket like she does in between commercial breaks.

"I didn't know that," Jeff says. "I guess I thought he was already dead."

"Let's walk downtown," she says. "I need some air."

She kissed him somewhere over the East River in a subway car that had an advertisement for her show. It was months old and someone had erased her pupils and redrawn them cross-eyed. They had given her a scar across her forehead and a speech bubble with a phallus inside.

"Wow," said Jeff when he saw it. "You want to move to another car?"

"Why?" she asked. "It looks just like me."

A dark-skinned man in a janitor's uniform stepped in and then out when he saw them. Jeff's hand was up her skirt, her hand was on him. They were laughing. It was a long ride out to Queens.

She doesn't know exactly how she got to the illegal loft above the Mexican coffee shop. She remembers a walk over an iron bridge and corrugated Quonset huts and the updraft of pigeons along Roosevelt Avenue. She remembers his mouth all over her and reaching back to lead him along a dark footpath. There were no streets or sidewalks in Willets Point, there was no infrastructure at all. Every mayor from the time she moved to the city threatened to clear it away, but the scrappers and chop shops held on. Through the fog, the neon lights of Shea Stadium glowed red like a flashlight shone through the palm of a hand. Jeff told her he moved here to see games from his roof, but could only see what took place between third base and home plate.

"Wow," says Jeff now as he rolls off of her. "Wow."

Where she lives, in her much more established Brooklyn neighborhood, someone had spray-painted that word on all the lampposts along her avenue. Wow. And underneath it, its mirror: Mom. WowMom. WowMom. Strolling Ollie down the street to the playground or to go shopping, she would find herself chanting it like a mantra. Wow. Mom. Wow.

A knotted sheet is tacked up for a curtain over the window beside his bed. The floodlights of the scrap yard next door blind her when she sits up. Wallis looks down at the pale silver stretch marks across her belly from Ollie and the ropy veins of her hands that halfheartedly cover a clipped patch of pubic hair. No point in hiding it now. He'd fucked her forty-year-old body and still said, Wow.

"Would you like something to drink? I have some beer in the fridge," he says, raising up on his arm.

Wallis glances at the clock. "Sure," she says. "A beer would be great."

He walks naked to the other side of the room where a stainless sink and two burners constitute a kitchen. To her surprise, his refrigerator is not the forlorn bachelor cliché of a six-pack and carton of Chinese takeout, but neatly arranged milk and carrots and Tupperware containers of what looks to be soup and actual meals. She is suddenly ravenous.

"Would you mind if I had something to eat?" she asks before she can stop herself. "I haven't had anything since lunch."

The thought of feeding her seems to delight him, and he reaches into the sink for a saucepan and pours into it something from one of the containers. He turns a knob and calls up the spiny blue flame of a tenant's stove.

"So now you've defiled the daughter of Captain Casket," she says. "How does it feel?"

"Like every Casketeer's dream come true," he answers.

She looks around the loft with its unpainted plywood floor, the exposed I beams and conduits. The absence of furniture is something other than poverty, for poverty, out of pride if nothing else, gluts itself with *stuff*. She wonders why Jeff has chosen to live so far away with so little. Across the street, a crane swings a load of scrap metal from one pile to another like a giant metal insect building and unbuilding a nest.

"Do they work all night?" she asks.

"You get used to it."

In the kitchen, Jeff dumps stew into a bowl for her and a plastic Mets cup for himself.

"Smells good," she says.

"It's lentil and tofu. I'm a vegetarian. I hope that's okay."

He climbs back into bed, passing her the bowl and a beer. They eat in silence, watching as the crane parts the rain, sluicing a waterfall of aluminum. "Who taught you how to cook?" she asks.

"My girlfriend. She's upstate at the Culinary Institute."

Wallis looks at him with new respect and lets the comforter fall away from her chest. She'd been working too hard to nurse Ollie for long, and her breasts still sit high and firm. The rain has washed away the shellac of hairspray and her hair falls naturally around her shoulders. She feels pretty enough to compete with anyone at the Culinary Institute, for chrissakes.

"When's she due back?" Wallis asks.

"Day after tomorrow," he says.

Wallis remembers why she stopped riding the subway to the end— what she found when she arrived was never all that interesting. She drains her beer and scrapes the last lentily carrot from her bowl.

"Well, I hate to fuck and run, but I should get going," she says, surrendering the warmth of the comforter. "I'm assuming you don't get many taxis out here. Would you be a sweetheart and call me a car?"

Her lined pink tweed skirt and jacket are damp and flaccid when she pulls them on, and she shoves her bra and panties into her pocketbook. Laurence will be asleep when she gets home and she can step straight into the shower. She gave up a night with Ollie for this, and she suddenly feels very old and tired. Wordlessly, Jeff climbs out of bed after her, pulling on his own boxers. He finds his cell phone, gives the car service his address, repeating it twice, and quotes her the price as if it makes a difference. Then the long standoff begins. In this rain, in this neighborhood, it could take half an hour for the car to arrive and Wallis can't bear another minute here now that she has her clothes on. He is watching her with that searching, expectant look she gets from men she shouldn't be sleeping with, men she works with who, like herself, are married with children, whom she goes out with and jokes with and drinks with. It's the same look Ollie gives after an especially good push on a swing, a grateful yet still needy look, and Wallis realizes she is expected to stand there bored and pushing for hours. Jeff leans against the window and she shivers at his nakedness touching the cold glass. He's not sure what he's done wrong.

"Maybe we could find the opportunity to do this again sometime?" he says.

Wallis smiles warmly, the smile she flashes for the camera to signal the transition between a double homicide and a puppy trapped in an elevator shaft. Standing in the oversize window with his tousled hair and square jaw, he is quite handsome, but more than anything else, she wants out of the playground.

"Maybe," she says.

Jeff turns his back to her and looks out at the claw in the scrap yard chewing another load of damaged metal. He sets his shoulders like he doesn't care.

Good, she thinks. He hates me. Now I can go.

She has been waiting under the awning outside his apartment for close to twenty minutes. The neighborhood cesspool has overflowed in the rain; it smells like the streets of Damascus. She could be in any third world country, she thinks. The door to the Mexican coffee shop is locked, the glass cases holding *aguas frescas* and open cartons of milk are dark. Beyond is nothing but glass replacement and auto body shops where racks of multicolored car doors are stacked tight as library books. Water and brake fluid flow over the rutted pavement; somewhere behind a chain-link fence several blocks away, a guard dog barks a warning. They call this neighborhood the Iron Triangle and, standing in the rain, Wallis feels she could rust in place, never to move again.

I want to show you something. She still falls for it. Ever since Jeff uttered those words at the station, she's been thinking of the boy who used to say it all the time. Then to have him pull out his card and talk of the redheaded kid who showed up toward the end. Wallis is a woman with a profound respect for the conventions of stories. In the ghost stories her father told, things never happened on any night, they happened on *this very night*. It was tonight, thirty years ago. Somehow Jeff knew, that's why he approached her. Why she's here in this crotch of Queens. She chides herself, stop being stupid. He couldn't have known.

Overhead a plane banks low and loud, its landing lights shining into her eyes, flashing her reflection blue and bright into the flooded road. The dog barks again. Is it her imagination or is it closer than it was before? Maybe it wasn't a guard dog, maybe it was part of a pack. Wild dogs prowl the Iron Triangle, she knows, they've even been spotted on the subway. Wild dogs haunted the back lanes of Baghdad, but they never barked. Considered unclean, they had to learn the art of silence or would be routinely shot. While she was on assignment there, she'd adopted a pup she'd found behind Al Kadhimain mosque and, back home, the poor thing hid under the bed whenever it heard the call to prayer, even in a teaser spot on TV.

Wallis pulls out her phone to check the time again—2:45. Her car is not going to come. No one lives here, they think they're being set up for a robbery. She'll give them ten more minutes and then she'll have to find her way back to the train. It's not that far away, she can see the purple 7 glowing through the fog as it rounds the elevated bend, but it seems a world and a lifetime stands between her and the way back home. She sees the old voicemail message from her father, still unretrieved, but she knows now why she has avoided listening to it all night long. *Wallis, it's Dad.*

"I might be out of touch for a while, darling," he slurs, though he's given up booze for the chemo. "I'm going on a ginseng hunt." That's all, but she knows what he means.

A troubled boy we tried to help, a damn bright kid. We thought we were getting through to him. Sonofabitch. We thought he was learning to trust us. That's what he told the police the night they stood in the doorway of their Cape Cod, her dad's elastic face flashing red/blue/red/blue in the patrol-car light. Dad, Mom, Wallis huddled in her pajamas, shaking from the adrenaline rush of being awakened mid-dream by sirens to learn they'd found his body in the swamp, his flesh teased to rope by snapping turtles, his stomach full of pills. Her father stood there and lied to the police while Mom reached for the appropriate tears she kept on reserve for every occasion, including Sudden Death of Foster Child, and Wallis stood between them, twelve years old and vibrating with rage—rage she hasn't put down since, just spent decades finding different excuses for—and saw in her mind's eye the primitive carving she had made of Jasper's face on the swamp oak and the nail she'd driven dead center between his eyes.

A ginseng hunt, his message said. It was the phrase they used for any unexpected adventure, walking into the dark woods without knowing what they'd find. She hears the click of nails coming closer, the heated breath nearby. She hears a soft, low growl.

"You motherfucker!" Wallis screams and throws her phone hard into the night. "You cannot leave me alone with this!"

"Wallis!" Jeff shouts from his open window. "Are you still down there?"

"Jeff?" she pleads, not caring who hears, as if there were anyone here to hear. "No one's come for me."

He is down the steps and opening the front door and then she is in his arms, sobbing like a child. She clutches him tight, breathing in his clean skin, the reassuring vegetarian absolution of him. You are one of us, she thinks. I can talk to you.

"What's wrong?" he asks in shock.

"That creepy redheaded kid. Jasper. My father and I killed him. Thirty years ago tonight."

Wallis

August 1980

Her arm is stretched in front of her, the black plastic comb quivering on the back of her fist. She's got Jasper fixed, holding his eyes steadily, waiting for any flicker of movement to give him away. He's a heavy-lidded foe, drowsy, a genius of this game, dissociated from his body, his hand able to grab the comb and rake the teeth across her knuckles before she can jerk it away. They sit cross-legged on her pink, little-kid bedspread faced off: Wallis the brown-bobbed girl with gray eyes, reflected back as a pale, freckled boy with a carroty afro.

The goal is to draw first blood, not to flinch but to retaliate, the goal is to take it. Why they play the game, she doesn't know. He suggests it. She goes along. He's a guest in her house.

She's lost three times in a row, but this time she'll be quicker. Though her muscles are screaming, she can outlast this boy. A minute passes, two. The curtains are drawn and the window unit, set to high, blasts cold air across her bare arm. A grudging respect settles on his face, the shadow of a smile. He has underestimated her. His gaze softens a bit, he flinches; she flinches but does not give. Her arm is not part of her, it belongs to someone else. He is lazy, his hands in his lap; she has all the power because she can endure. He must feel that.

As though he has read her mind, he opens his eyes wider, naked and raw. In them there is confusion, desire, need. This is what making love must be like, she thinks. At twelve years old, she understands little more than that it will begin with loss—the loss of virginity, the loss of innocence—but that at some point there stands to be a gain. She knows he has lost everything in his short life, his parents, his home. They are perfectly balanced. Help me, his lips part slightly. I need you.

She blinks. The comb comes down savagely over her already swollen knuckles. She bleeds, four weeping drops.

"Bloody knuckles," Jasper says, standing up. "Come on. I want to show you something."

She hates this boy who has invaded her house and stolen her summer, who finds her wherever she goes to escape him, proposes to her, I want to show you something. What he shows her always hurts. He is mean and trailerish in the thin gray and green baseball shirt he wears, the ragged fringe of his cutoff jeans, the tip of his black comb peeking out of his back pocket. I hate you. She rises and follows.

Outside of her darkened bedroom, the day is bleached flat. He walks across the yard, grasshoppers corkscrewing from the grass clippings bounce off his shins. It is her yard but he leads as if he's lived here all his life. Across their neighbor's soybean field, into the stand of woods behind the house, he guides her down a path he's tramped himself to where he has hidden the gasoline and Styrofoam. He's found the packaging from a stereo she got for Christmas; the inserts she turned into doll beds when she was a kid only a few months ago, before she became this new, awkward thing. He found them with the trash in the garage along with the red gas can for the lawn mower, and brought them here hidden inside a garbage bag. He slit the bag and spread it like a picnic blanket, set out a metal bucket, a paint stirrer, a pair of work gloves. He squats down and begins tearing rough squeaking chunks of Styrofoam and dropping them into the bucket.

"What are you doing?"

"You'll see."

He shakes the gasoline like the sputtering end of a great long piss, and melts the chunks to glue. More Styrofoam, more gas, he stirs. It's hard to breathe, as if someone has pulled the plug on the day's oxygen. When he arrived, besides the two changes of clothes and a photograph of his dead parents in his duffle bag, he had brought hydrochloric acid and hydrogen peroxide and Methyl salicylate (which was nothing but wintergreen oil) and naphthalene pounded from mothballs. He had flash powder mixed from potassium perchlorate that he kept in a mason jar and aluminum he ground up from the bottom of a soda can. Later, after he'd initiated her into the mysteries of combustion, he'd smacked his scrawny ass like an underfed porn star and said, "The finer the ingredients, the more unstable the mix."

Jasper is done stirring the Styrofoam and gasoline, and now he pulls the comb from his back pocket, dips the tip in the sludge, and strikes a match. The color is up in his face. His Adam's apple is a gooseflesh knot.

"I love the smell of napalm in the morning," he says, grinning.

A flick of his finger and the fireball scuds across dead leaves. She leaps forward to stamp it out but he moves quickly and has her pinned, his elbows digging into the sides of her sore, pathetic breasts. She can't breathe.

The napalm burns for half an hour, but after about five minutes, it's pointless to struggle. She gives in and he lets go and, together, they stand and watch.

Mom is calling them in for lunch. She stands at the patio door in her blue oxford shirtwaist dress, her frosted hair pulled back in a patrician ponytail, her lips and nails frosted pink. Wallis suspects Mom rose fully formed from the foam wearing a pair of espadrilles and clutching a Brooks Brothers charge card. Because Eddie is home today, she's made his favorite, tuna-fish sandwiches with sweet pickle that seeps like little green mold spores into the Wonder bread. She spears each sandwich with a pimentoed olive on a toothpick.

"Wash your hands, kids," she says brightly.

Wallis ignores her, walking deeper into the dark house and flopping down in the den where Eddie is reading the newspaper, tilted back in his recliner like an astronaut at ignition. Her father looks crisp in his plaid Bermuda shorts and a kelly green polo shirt. His thinning hair is damp from a shower and crazed on top of his head from toweling it. Tonight he'll shellac it with black shoe polish, but now it stands up soft and fine like babies' hair. The wall behind his chair is a shrine to Captain Casket. Captain Casket with Zacherley. Captain Casket with Ghoulardi. Captain Casket with M.T. Graves. With Sammy Terry. Bowman Body.

Sivad. Morgus. Jeepers Creepers. Chilly Billy. Svengoolie. Count Gore
De Vol. Dr. Paul Bearer. Asmodeus, and a recent one of him leering
at Elvira's cleavage. She has nothing on Vampira, the original, he told
Wallis. Maila Nurmi. Rumor had it she wore out James Dean.

"What have you kids been up to?" he asks.

"Mischief and mayhem," Jasper answers.

"Marvelous," he drawls, turning back to his paper.

Jasper heads to her dad's collection of *Famous Monsters of Filmland,*
two bookshelves of issues carefully preserved in plastic. He's working
his way through every original her dad has collected since 1958, the
pointed teeth and saddlebag eyes of Lon Chaney in *London After Midnight,* the sexy space women invaded by tentacles of the green slime,
all the monsters and aliens that hid behind her shower curtain as a girl.

"That's mine," Wallis says when he pulls out September 1967. On
the cover a beefcake Wolfman rips his shirt to tatters, though the main
headline reads "Vampire of the Opera."

"Sorry." He tosses it at her. "Didn't know you were so possessive."

"I mean I'm in it," she says, flipping to page thirty-four. There is
the picture of Eddie in whiteface and his same black cape and unitard,
holding a baby swaddled in fake cobwebs. The caption reads: Daughter
of Captain Casket. Horror Host Spawns Baby Ghoul, 6 lb. 5 oz.

"She made a great prop," Eddie says.

Jasper studies the picture. "You were an ugly baby."

She wants to argue, but he's right—she was born premature and
spindly with bulgy puggish eyes. In the picture, her father holds her
like a mongrel puppy, supporting her bottom with one hand, the other
behind her neck, while Mom stands behind him in a sequined strapless
gown, her frosted hair worn in a sleek French twist. She leans over
Dad's shoulder, slim and glamorous, as though he and not she had
given birth. They made a gorgeous interracial couple—monster and
debutante—and her dad knew it.

"What happened to your parents?" she asks Jasper. He has a snapshot
of them in his bedroom. A fat, gray-faced man with a crew cut and an
extremely skinny woman with drawn-on eyebrows, wearing what Mom
would say was obviously a wig. And not a very expensive one.

"Don't you know you're not supposed to ask an orphan that question?" Jasper says. He barely moves his lips when he speaks, like a ventriloquist, she thinks. She wonders if he practiced that.

"Why? Did you murder them?"

"I poisoned their Metamucil," Jasper replies, and her dad stops reading his paper, waiting to see if it's gone too far.

"They cut off her first tit when she was fifty," he says. "A few years later they cut off the other, then a few years after that, she died. My dad lasted another year. He couldn't handle me so he drove his car into a tree. They tried to sugarcoat it, said something about spinning out, losing control, but it was seventy-five and sunny that day and he left all his bank records out on his desk so I wouldn't have to look for them."

"That sucks," she says.

"They were old," says Jasper.

She catches a brief glance that passes between Jasper and her dad. Eddie's face is round and soft with no strong nose or chin to distinguish it. His is a face of expressions rather than features, and it is rare she catches, through the mugging, a look of tenderness. Something this close to human is unsettling.

"We're happy you're here with us," he says.

"Kids. Eddie," Mom calls, more annoyed. "Lunch is on the table."

"I'm washing my hands," shouts Wallis. "Like you said."

Wallis hoists herself up and walks to the half bath. This is one of the few concessions her parents made when Jasper moved in. She didn't want to share her bathroom so they let him take over this one. Except for the damp towels, it would be impossible to say he lived here, in this house. He cleans up after himself meticulously, as if he wants to leave no incriminating evidence. If he fixes a sandwich, he sweeps away the crumbs and returns the mayonnaise to the refrigerator. There is never a smelly tennis shoe left under the sofa. Unless Mom forces them to play a board game or watch television together, he mostly stays in his room, emerging only to *show her something*. Yet even when his door is closed, Wallis feels his eyes on her. Nothing feels normal since he moved in, and she walks through her days as if she's in a movie, playing the role of herself. Before he came, she took her life for granted but now, through his eyes, she is conscious of her place in the Happy Family and how lucky she is supposed to feel to have one.

Wallis squirts some of her mother's new gardenia scented hand soap into her palm and rubs. She doesn't look any different in the bathroom mirror. The same chin-length chestnut bob (*If you're not going to take care of it, I'm getting it cut short*). The same pale skin and faint freckles across the bridge of her nose. She is one of the few girls at school without big hair, but Mom says it's cheap and, anyway, Wallis doesn't like to stick out. She likes that the other girls are vaguely afraid of the big, fat *No* of her, which comes with being the daughter of Captain Casket. She rinses her hands and holds her mouth under the bathroom faucet. A single frizzed strand of red clings to the pearl-pink basin of the sink. Here in the bathroom, he's let down his guard. Now that she's noticed the hair she sees, looking down at the nap of the rug, a brittle triangle of fingernail paring. And another. And another. In all, five forgotten snippets left for her to step on, and without knowing what she'll do with them or why she wants them, Wallis picks the fingernail clippings from the rug and pushes them, along with the strand of hair, deep into her front pocket. Boys should be careful what they leave behind for girls, she thinks, and is startled by a sharp rap on the door.

"Hurry up," her father says.

Jasper is already there when she takes her seat at the round Formica table. She sits more easily now, knowing that she has something of his. Mom asks him to pour the lemonade, giving him a chore to show she trusts him with responsibility. Mom is still uneasy having him in the house, though it was her idea that he come live with them in the first place. Later, Wallis would wonder if it had all been an elaborate trick, if Eddie had planned it all along, knowing Mom was incapable of turning away a stray, knowing once the idea had been mentioned she would have to pursue it, to show that anything was possible, that, as always, he gave up too easily. They were sitting at this very table the first time her dad spoke of the boy who hung out at the station, who took any job thrown his way, took it gratefully and did it well, seemingly having no place else to go. It was a Sunday in May, Mother's Day, and later she would wonder if that, too, hadn't been carefully worked into the plot, playing that particular day on Mom's sadness about not having given her husband another child, a son, even though he acted perfectly content with Wallis (Mom: *Oh, my poor daughter saddled with a boy's name for life. God, I should have put my foot down*). The three of them were sitting around the table and Wallis said grace and Eddie sliced a ham and he'd mentioned the boy so casually, *too casually*, saying, *You know, he reminds me of myself at that age*. Where are his parents? Mom had asked, and Eddie had shrugged, as if such a thing were unimportant. *I don't know if he has any. He's been sleeping in the hall outside the control room*.

Her mother set down her fork as if she'd been slapped. How could he possibly think she would allow a fifteen-year-old boy to sleep in a hall when they had all this extra room (*When did she ever even go into the upstairs sewing room? Who sewed anymore?*) and plenty of money. What sort of monster did he take her for? He never would have brought it up if he didn't expect her to *do* something about it.

And then Mom had taken off, researching in her secretive Mom-ish way, the methods by which they might legally take him in, because they could not be so casual as Eddie would have it, he always assumed things would just work out. If the boy was an orphan, he should be reported to the state and they could offer themselves as a foster family. If he was a runaway, his parents should be notified that he'd like to declare himself emancipated. Mom would have prayed he was an orphan, because if he were a runaway, she'd always wonder why he couldn't get along with his parents—if the fault lay with him or them. She would have gone to the library and thumbed the card catalog and phoned the right agencies, all the while telling herself she was just collecting information, not committing herself to anything, and while Eddie was at work and Wallis was at school, she would have listed her sewing machine in the *Trading Post* and driven to Sears and bought an aqua blue bedspread and orange pillows and worried a bit that she had inadvertently bought the colors of some sports team he hated, but then she would have chided herself with worrying about nothing—*for goodness' sakes, I can't know everything!*—but still looked up orange and blue so that she might apologize if he didn't like the Miami Dolphins. Mom would have thought she'd wait until the end of the school year before she told them that everything was taken care of, that Eddie could invite the boy to live with them. But then one night she would have decided that Eddie seemed especially distant and she just couldn't take it anymore, his being angry with her, and that's exactly how Wallis found out a foster brother was being test-driven for the summer. Her mother had led them both upstairs and flung open the door to the newly transformed sewing room and said, *It would mean so much to me if we could take in that boy from your station,* and her father had seemed really confused for a minute, as if the thought had never occurred to him, and had said, *You mean Jasper?* And Mom, having spent over a month surreptitiously decorating his room, replied, *Jasper? That's his name?*

Waiting for Eddie to join them, they sit with their hands in their laps. Jasper stares at the tray of carrots and celery floating in ice on the lazy Susan at the center of the table, puzzled as to whether it is food or decoration. Everything Mom makes feels like a ladies' luncheon.

"What's the movie tonight?" she asks.

"Something about an alien," Wallis answers.

"So, I spoke to Cary and we're all set," Mom says, abruptly lowering her voice conspiratorially. "He'll have a table waiting for you at seven on Friday. You need to keep your dad there until at least eight-thirty so that everyone has a chance to get here. But make sure he's home by nine at the very latest."

Mom had begun planning the surprise party for Eddie as soon as she was done planning the surprise of Jasper. The party was the following week, and she had assigned Wallis and Jasper the job of keeping him away while the caterers set up so that he might return home to be surprised and delighted by the prop coffin full of beer, the novelty canapés, the coworkers dressed as vampires and madmen (Their wives: *Where are we supposed to get costumes in August? Why does she always make things so hard?*).

"I don't want to sit through another dinner at Cary's," Wallis protests. "Couldn't we do something else?"

Mom presses her lips tightly together. "Have you thought of something?" she asks.

Wallis looks to Jasper but he just shrugs. "You'll have to ask him," Wallis says. "He'll never believe I want to go."

"Thank you, kids," Mom says, relieved. "I knew I could count on you." Then, because she is done scheming and can give way to her exasperation, she shouts over her shoulder, "Eddie! We're all waiting for you."

"Tuna. Crudités. Ann, as always, our appreciation for this bounteous feast."

Eddie is standing in the archway, surveying the table. Mom gives her half smile of acknowledgment and defensiveness.

"It has sweet pickle," she offers. He sits and her apology for trying to please him is accepted. Wallis plucks the toothpick from her sandwich and licks the mayonnaise from the tip.

"Wallis tells me the movie tonight is something about an alien," Mom says.

"An alien, yes," Dad replies. "It's about a quivering blob that oozes across the manicured side lawns of a neighborhood much like this one you found for us, imbibing koi ponds and belching out the bones of cement birdbaths, swallowing up any and all who stand in its way, until it finds its bottomless, tyrannical appetite finally sated with the unholy sustenance of tuna fish and sweet pickle."

Mom sets down her napkin, pushing back her chair.

"Would you care for something else?" she asks acidly.

"Sit down, Ann," he laughs. "You need to lighten up."

She does, but the meal belongs to Eddie; he's taken his shit on the ladies' luncheon and now they can all relax. Jasper wolfs down his sandwich, Wallis spins the lazy Susan until it is a green and orange blur. Mom sips her lemonade while they joke about people down at the station that she doesn't know, and her dad tells Jasper the story about how once, back in the early days of the show, when things were live and much more unpredictable, he set off a smoke bomb and almost got himself fired. "The kids loved that stuff," he says. "Didn't they, Ann?"

Mom replies, "Yes, Eddie, they did, the kids loved that stuff."

"What are you going to show for the anniversary?" Jasper asks. Wallis kicks him under the table. Don't get him started or we'll be stuck here all afternoon.

"*Frankenstein*," he replies. "It was the first movie I showed."

"I know," Jasper says. "It's the first movie in the Shock! package."

"Ann's father bought the Shock! package very early on," Eddie says. "It had all the classics—*Dracula, The Wolfman, The Mummy,* along with a bunch of crap—'beware the gypsy' and 'don't walk about on the moors' sorts of things. Ann, you remember that, don't you?"

"Of course I do," she says.

"Your mother is very modest," he says to Wallis, "but Captain Casket was really her idea. Your granddad owned the station back then. When he bought the Shock! package, Ann insisted I host it. I hadn't really thought about it. We had our own show, your mother and I, and, of course, I did the weather, but she thought it would be good for my career, it would advance me, you know. I wanted to call myself Bela LeGhostly, but she thought that was too obscure, by which she meant European. Something American and strong, she said. Something manly, that's what you need. And then she sewed my tights and unitard and little cape. She designed my makeup and painted my set. Ann has always taken such good care of me."

Eddie collects the plates and takes them to the dishwasher. He leans over Jasper and reaches across him for his glass.

"The love of a good woman shows us who we are," he says. "Let those words be my gift to you, son."

Jasper glances up and again Wallis sees something pass between them. It looks as close to pity as his last glance approached tenderness.

"Let's hit the road, kids," he says. "We still need to load the coffin."

Wallis glances over at Mom, who will spend Saturday night here, alone, while the three of them go to the station. When she was very young she used to wake to the grind of the blender on Saturday nights, Mom making herself a half pitcher of frozen daiquiris. She would smell the invitation of strawberries and popcorn, and stumble to the kitchen where Mom would smile innocently—*What are you doing awake?*—and instead of leading her back to bed as she did on the nights Eddie was home, would pour her a shot glass of ruby slush and together they would sit nestled on the sofa in the darkened den, eating popcorn and watching Dad. Wallis was never sure whether she was awake or dreaming, the images came and went as the night wore on, shadowy faces on the screen, her mother's still, lovely profile, Captain Casket's manic patter bracketing commercials for furniture liquidators and used-car lots. All she remembered was the floating feeling of sleep and rum and safety.

Jasper stands at the patio door, her dad is already headed to the carport where he parks his long black Miller-Meteor hearse.

"Wait up," she says.

The fog of the graveyard weaves between tombstones. The full moon hangs heavy in a jaggedly painted sky. The coffin, center stage, and the pale hand reaching up, opening the lid from inside. The deep groan, the rattle of chains. The bloodcurdling shriek. Mom, almost twenty years ago. They still haven't found a scarier scream.

You do my makeup better than anyone in the world, he'd said to Wallis in the dressing room after he finished the weather, as the Soul Train feed ran, brought to them by the mysterious elixirs of Afro Sheen and Ultra Sheen. And it was true. This was something that was theirs alone. She took her time, as people do when making up someone else. She slicked his hair with the black shoe polish and drew in a widow's peak. She stippled on the white greasepaint, feathering it into his hairline and over his eyelids and sweeping it down into the hollow of his throat; they wanted no trace of healthy human flesh peeking through. With her fingers she ran the greasepaint over his ears, where it blurred gray with the shoe polish, and then she shaded in dark shadows under his eyes, following the outline of the dark shadows already there. She drew his lips deeply red and sinister and left it up to his jokes to soften them. The more she put on, the more she erased, and soon the white moonscape of Captain Casket had reached its gibbous state and Eddie was nearly gone, and she had the fleeting wish that they were not her fingers moving on his slack cheeks, that she could be like other girls and just gaze up at her father's face shining down over her bed as he tucked her in. And maybe her father could read her mind, because he caught her eye in the mirror and flashed her that reassuring Captain Casket grin, and she thought they were both a little relieved to see his reflection there and to know that, yes, he still had a soul.

The sirens go off and the noosed skeletons drop from the rafters, gyrating like go-go dancers. The disco ball, the blare of music, kids singing off-key—his first Casketeers. All her life she's sung along:

Who's the digger of the grave,
For you, and you, and me?
C-A-P
T-A-N
C-A-S-K-T

Come and squirm with all the worms,
And set your spirit free.
C-A-P
T-A-N
C-A-S-K-T

And her father, complete in his transformation, tumbling violently out of the coffin into a tight somersault, springing up in quick recovery, manic, alive, as spry tonight as he was in 1967. She stands just offstage in the wings with her toes on the glow tape for *Quiz Kids,* which shoots on Monday nights, entranced. Jasper holds a pitcher of water he's poured on the pan of dry ice to create the fog. John and Jack, the cameramen who love Eddie, who have worked with him for twenty years now and are incorporated into his gags, playing offstage voices—Corporal Bones, Cemetery Sam—all the characters he's cooked up over the years to keep Captain Casket company, grin and nod. They're game enough to ad-lib some bad lines if he swings toward them, get spiders down their shirts, fake blood on the camera lens. They love her father because when the movie is running, in between bits, he'll play gin with them, comfortable in that guy's world of cameras and cables. He is his best self here; for two hours he is completely free. It's why all the kids love him. Even her. The camera pans in.

"I have a treat for you tonight, guys and ghouls," Captain Casket purrs. "A film so perfectly dreadful, so agonizingly boring, it's been held directly responsible for the deaths of sixteen middle school students up and down the Eastern seaboard. It's a cyanide pill of a film, it's so bad it will take you directly to your father's bathroom sink for that rusty razor blade sitting in the pool of soap scum, or your mother's underwear drawer for that little orange bottle of pills Dr. Whatzizfeld prescribed for when she wants to float away and forget all about you and your monstrous little siblings."

"Here's your cat," Jasper whispers, handing her the wired-together feline skeleton she named Fluffy. "When Eddie laughs for the third time, after the cauldron has been brought in, toss it to him. Not too hard; underhand, like this."

"I know what to do," she says.

He is wearing thick work gloves and reaches into the red-rimmed canister for another triangle of dry ice. He places it in a metal pan just offstage and douses it with water. Wallis shivers as the cold wings get even colder.

"Would you rather freeze to death or burn to death?" he asks.

"I don't want to do either," she says.

"But if you had to?"

"I would freeze to death," she says.

"Why?"

"Because it would be uncomfortable for a while but then I would start to feel warm and go to sleep and let my soul blow away like snow."

"Freezing to death is for pussies," he says. "I'd go out fast and fiery and get it over with."

"Boys always want to get it over with," she says. "Getting it over with is for pussies."

He hits her hard in the arm with his middle finger bent and protruding through his glove. Without thinking, she swiftly turns and hits him back.

"The movie is called *The Beginning of the End*," Captain Casket is saying. He has climbed onto his coffin and straddles it like a kid balancing on the rim of a bathtub. "And you'll want it to end before it even begins, guys and ghouls. Giant grasshoppers munch, munch, munching the Empire State Building. Is it a government experiment gone awry? What might you find, little ones, wriggling under your covers tonight, or lurking beneath your pillow, waiting to gnaw the roots of your hair and lay their eggs in your ear while you're dreaming your sweet, sweet dreams . . .?"

"What's your problem with me?" Jasper asks.

"I'm just sick of you bossing me around. How did you get a job here anyway?"

"I sucked up to Captain Casket."

"I know what you suck," she says.

"Jealous?"

"You're disgusting," she says. "I don't know why I bother being nice to you."

"You're not nice to me," he says. "You've been a cunt ever since I moved into your house. A spoiled little cunt."

"And here's a little lullaby to get your nightmares flowing . . ." Captain Casket says, reaching back into his coffin for his signature saw and bow. Jasper tugs on a length of fishing line and a chair placed off in the wings magically glides across the stage. The Captain takes his seat, pressing the saw handle between his knees, and lightly bends the blade. He draws the bow and high-pitched eerie notes float over the stage, mingling with the fog. Sweetly, he chants:

> *Now I lay me down to sleep,*
> *Across my scalp the bugs will creep.*
> *If I should die before I wake,*
> *I trust the bugs my crumbs will take . . .*

"When my mother was in the hospital the last time, I couldn't sleep," Jasper is saying. "My dad had already checked out by then and he didn't care what I did. I used to stay up and watch the *Creepshow*. I didn't care about the movie. I wanted to see what shit would come out of the Captain's mouth."

"You think my dad is really like that?"

"He says what we're all thinking. What everyone else is too chickenshit to say."

She laughs out loud then stops herself because the microphones might pick her up.

"Captain Casket might be. But *Eddie* is a middle-aged weatherman in a bad costume. He's a *dad*, for chrissakes."

Jasper shoots her a look of pity. "You're so blind. Give him half the chance and he's just like me, both of us out there on a rampage, ready to saw the pretty girls to bits then go out and wreck the city."

"You're both so lame," Wallis says. "Everyone wants to be the bad guy. It's easy to be bad."

"Easy for you, maybe. You're already a cunt."

"Will you stop it with that word," she says. "You think it makes you sound cool? Why don't you smoke? Or go get drunk and wreck your car? Oh wait, your dad did that already."

He walks away. Good, she thinks. Onstage, Captain Casket cues the movie.

She has only one job to do. Eddie laughs three times and she tosses him the cat. He plays mad scientist after the first commercial break; they wheel in the cauldron after the second. He adds the ingredients one by one for his family recipe, Captain Casket's Primordial Stew. Old oxford shoe. Jug of moonshine. Finger twist of earwax. Seasoned with a sprinkling of straight pins. And then it's her cue. She leans against the back wall offstage right, wrapped in his weatherman's sports jacket against the chill, and she hugs the cat to her chest. She has only to stay awake for this one thing, but the movie is so long. A pretty man and a pretty woman with knitted brows. Was it the Russians or could their own government be keeping secrets from them? And the grasshoppers multiply and grow. She has an itch on the back of her leg. And another one on the back of her neck. Offstage left, Jasper and Eddie huddle with the stagehands, talking through the tech cues for the next commercial break. They don't need her, they turn their backs even, and who cares, it's just a stupid movie and a recycled skit he's done in one version or another for years. She slides down the wall. It is so cold and her eyes are so heavy and she would give anything to just close them right now. She shuts them, just for a tiny rest, it feels so good, and there is Mom in the living room sitting up watching on their red gingham sofa, *Here's a blanket darling, come snuggle up beside me.* Her party lists are spread before her. In two even columns, Mom's handwriting is small and precise; she gave Wallis a fountain pen when Wallis was ten and Wallis used to practice making her letters flow like her mother's, the thick loops and the thin connections. Mom is going over the list of hors d'oeuvres for the party, calculating how many she'll need based on a complex algorithm of men to women to dropped on the ground to pinched by children who shouldn't be allowed so near a buffet when

there are obviously bowls of chips for them out on the patio. She told
the caterer not to bring toothpicks because she had bought an entire
case from a seafood restaurant that was going out of business. They're
just adorable, sporting skulls and crossbones. Pirate flags, really, but
she hopes no one will notice. She found black napkins and black paper
plates, and a man who is willing to do an ice sculpture of Captain Casket
based on an old photograph from back before he looked so dissipated.

Even when she's so tired she'd like to crawl in bed without doing
the dinner dishes, Mom makes herself stay up on Saturday night. She
glances up often enough so that she can say something nice about Eddie's
skits when he comes home, to let him know his work is important to
her. She gets every third sentence or so. *We're back, guys and ghouls . . . The
mysteries of creation . . . Don't try this at home . . .* As if "home" were some
frozen sanctuary where nothing interesting should ever happen. Still,
she winces at the Bunsen burner, an open flame on set, it would be so
easy to burn the whole place down. And, of course, she knows. Before
Captain Casket, back when they had their own cooking show, she was
flipping an omelet for the kids, something she'd done dozens of times
at home, when the edge of her apron brushed the open flame of the
camp stove they were using and caught fire. She knows it couldn't have
been the case, but in her memory she burned for a full thirty seconds,
dropping the skillet, slapping at her dress with her dry pink palms. She
remembers thinking, *Where is Eddie? Why isn't he helping?* And then suddenly, she was soaked. He'd pitched the pan of water where the hard-
boiled eggs were cooling, and it was like being stoned in the center of
the town square, all those hard, white things coming at her and rolling
under the table, across the set, away. Eddie was laughing and the cameramen were laughing, and Eddie lifted the hen puppet Ann had sewn
and clucked it at her, saying, "Whenever you're using the stove, boys
and girls, be sure to ask *Mom* for help." She was furious he went for a
sight gag when she could have gone up in flames. But she couldn't let
on. Not when everything was live.

If she's perfectly honest, she has to admit she doesn't much care for
horror movies. There, she's said it. She doesn't understand why people
would want to put themselves through something so unpleasant. It's
not that she's squeamish; no, she used to pore over *Butler's Lives of the*

Saints in the library at school and wish she'd been born Catholic so that she might so much as light a candle, even at the dinner table, without feeling like a character in a play. Breasts on a plate and a body pierced by arrows; she didn't turn away from violence, she just felt it shouldn't be purely recreational. They'd tried to keep their cooking act together once the Captain Casket job offered itself, but this philosophical difference kept coming between them. When Eddie wanted her to play his mother, a body in a rocking chair he might dismember every Saturday night, she balked. *The great thing is, you'll be resurrected every week. Doesn't that appeal to you, darling? I would think it would.*

A hundred and twenty people will be coming to the party next Friday night and she has work to do. Eddie has so many friends. She's never heard him utter a single unpleasant word to anyone except family, but, after all, we're hardest on those we're closest to. This tedious movie, Mom closes her eyes. When will it ever end? Whenever a story becomes too scary, he's there with a joke to keep you from hiding under the covers; and when it's like this, banal and grinding, he adds just enough darkness to keep you awake. He is the perfect balance, this husband of hers, a little bit of antidote and poison in a single pill. She wishes others appreciated him as much as she, and didn't find him silly. One shouldn't have to take up one's husband as a cause. It certainly would be easier to be married to a dentist or an orthopedic surgeon. Which reminds her—she reaches for her guest list—Dr. and Mrs. Neumark.

Wallis opens her eyes. It is after one in the morning and Captain Casket is juggling test tubes. The flame onstage is leaping blue with sparks of orange around the tip. Jasper stands in the wings on the other side of the soundstage, in the purple gel of the kleig lights, his hair glows as if painted on black velvet. She hasn't missed her cue. She shuts her eyes again.

Mom is telling her about the first show she did with Dad.

"It was *Frankenstein,* you know," she whispers. "The poor thing. He didn't know what he was doing, just got in front of the camera and sputtered. He didn't have a costume, he was trying to say something serious about the movie, like he was a film critic. He talked about the novel and a ghost story contest with Lord Byron, and he almost put everyone to sleep before the movie even started. Other men in other markets were becoming big stars with these packages. Zacherley was on the cover of *TV Guide*. And here was dear Dad, trying to be an expert on something he knew nothing about. It was just too sad.

"*Frankenstein,*" Mom sighs. "I've had to sit through that movie over a dozen times." Her lists are forgotten, they're on the couch in the sunken living room, across from a fire guttering in the fireplace. Mom cradles Wallis in her lap, running her fingers through her hair. "And do you know who I always feel for? Not that awful scientist or his stupid monster, but poor Elizabeth. Elizabeth, his fiancée, pale and worried in her wedding dress, her veil so long it stretches across the room to the doorway and tugs her nearly off balance with every step she takes. All those guests outside feasting and making merry, waiting for her to appear and the wedding to begin. It was supposed to be Elizabeth's day, but instead there was a monster on the loose, and a dead and dripping child took center stage and all that planning and organizing and care was ruined. And when the movie's over and we see her through the doorway, nursing broken-down Henry, who really should have known better, she's still not married. That dress must be hanging in a closet somewhere, I suppose, out of sight. And she'll just have to put it on again, all stale and rumpled, and pretend it's good as new."

Wallis's eyes fly open at the boom of a loud prolonged explosion, clouds of smoke like the finale of July Fourth fireworks. Captain Casket is performing his last skit after the final commercial break of the night. His soup pot is stirred, dinner is ready. Through the clearing fog, the creature is born—a corona of red rises, then pale flesh, two narrow eyes, the long nose, the parted lips. The cauldron with the false bottom and Jasper's head swiveling, his eyes imploring—*Master*—a velvet rose between his teeth. She is still holding the skeleton cat, no one bothered to wake her. And here's her father's nighthoarse laugh echoing through the soundstage, the station, the dark dens and bedrooms beyond. *Oh, the spark. Oh, the glory. Mine! All mine!*

Eddie slathers his face with Vaseline until it is a soft gray slurry then, burying it in his towel, he gives it a violent rub and Captain Casket comes away in a single swipe. No matter how many hypoallergenic lotions and cotton balls Mom packs, he insists on doing it this way. His face is red and angry for several minutes before it settles again into just a face. Wallis leans her head against the file cabinet.

"*No way!*" She jumps at Jasper shouting down the hall. "*No mother-fucking way!*"

Eddie sticks his head out of the door in alarm. "*Cowards!*" Jasper is shouting. Now she hears another voice, too. Fat, bearded John the cameraman arguing with him. Jasper rounds the corner, his face red and mottled. Besides Captain Casket's weekly stack of fan mail, he's clutching a sheet of paper and a torn envelope. John follows close behind, holding an identical envelope.

"After twenty years, this is how they tell us?" Jasper demands. You're barely fifteen, Wallis is thinking. What are you talking about, twenty years?

"What's happened?" Eddie asks.

"I checked your box just now," Jasper says. "They waited until everyone else was gone. It's fucking disrespectful."

He passes the paper to Eddie, who begins to read.

"They've canceled us," Jasper says.

"It's not just us," John says. "Memo says they're looking for a buyer for the station."

"They can't do that," Jasper insists.

Eddie had pulled the top half of his unitard down to his waist and now steps out of his costume. Wallis is aware of Jasper and John both watching her dad for his reaction, waiting for him to tell them how to feel about it. Eddie is aware, too, and takes his time stuffing his unitard into his duffel bag for Ann to wash.

"Twenty years is a good run," Eddie says at last. "Now I can become that male prostitute I always wanted to be."

Jasper stares at him, incredulous. "I'm not hearing this."

John says, "Shit, Eddie. Used to be Ann's daddy's station. I bet she'll take it pretty hard."

Her father hadn't considered that. Wallis thinks of Mom at home with her lists and menus, unaware she's planning a wake. Eddie says, "We don't have to tell her right away."

Yes, let's put off the inevitable, Wallis thinks, turning away from her father's bare shoulders and graying chest hair and the tight white

briefs which seem too full to her. She's seen it all before, but she doesn't
want to have to see it now, not in front of Jasper and John, so she
leaves them in the dressing room and wanders back to the soundstage
where the ghost light sits on its solitary pole, casting a pale blue glow.
Captain Casket's laboratory has been put away, the news desk rolled
in, and the cheery orange a.m. sunrise flats have been lowered for the
morning broadcast. Only the old wooden coffin is left, awaiting its
return to their carport. She once asked her father where he got this
casket and he said his mother had sent it as a wedding present. *Will
you give it to me when I get married?* she'd asked him. It depends, he said,
on who's willing to marry you. She lifts herself into its hollow belly:
no splinters, but no real comfort either. If sex is bloody knuckles, this
is what marriage feels like. She lies back, staring into the rafters at
the PARs and Fresnel lamps on the beams overhead. The disco ball is
tucked out of sight and the skeletons rolled up in their nooses. Will
they really sell the station? What will six o'clock be without Eddie an-
nouncing the weather, and Sue and Adam reporting the daily shootings
and travesties of the school board? Adam has been hosting the local
news since before she was born. He gave her a ballpoint pen every
time she came onto the set. Sue had arrived ten years ago, swept in,
Mom said, with Women's Lib. Who would Wallis be if her father were
no longer Captain Casket, if he was just Eddie Alley? She tugs the lid
closed like pulling up a blanket on a cold winter night and the inside
of the coffin smells like greasepaint and sweat and the fried onions her
father always orders with his dinner.

Rest. It's so late and it's all she wants. Her heavy eyes adjust and
in the right-hand corner of the lid, she spies the raised head of a coffin nail that has worked loose. It's an old russet square head, narrow
and straight like a spike for a miniature railroad. It feels valuable and
important to her, at this late hour; this nail should be magnified by its
flake and decay if only because it has endured. The space is too tight
to raise her arm, but she hinges at the elbow and picks at it with her
fingernail until gradually she works it loose. It could have dropped at
any moment and put out her father's eye, she is doing him a favor. She
holds her breath, listening for the sound of footsteps. As she touches
the point to the lid and scores the initials, she tells herself there is a one

in twenty-six chance of what each might become, she can't be certain, and yet they are becoming exactly what she feared they might, a W plus a J. As soon as she sees them, she wants to scribble them out, but her hand and the nail trace a heart instead, a shallow little heart.

"Wallis!"

Eddie is calling from the hallway. He hates it when she runs off. "It's late. Let's go."

Wallis doesn't answer, hiding like she did when she was a little girl. Hide-and-seek was always over so fast in her house. There was only her to search for and she always hid in the same place. She shoves the nail deep in her pocket.

Her father knocks on the coffin lid. "I know you're in there."

"Carry me," she says, muffled.

"Stop playing around," Eddie says.

"Carry me. You're strong."

No one says a word, then, with a jerk, the foot of the coffin is lifted off the ground. Her head is brought even and she is weightless, bobbing through the soundstage and down the darkened hall.

"Okay, stop," she says. "You're going to drop me."

But her pallbearers keep walking, taking their rights and lefts, their feet shuffling along the granite floor. They are trying to scare her now, letting the coffin drop an inch or so, then bouncing it up again.

"Where are you taking me?" she asks. She lies with her arms folded across her chest, trying to stay dead center in the casket so that her shifting weight doesn't cause her to tip over.

"We're going to put you in the ground," her dad says. "And cover you with dirt."

"The worms crawl in, the worms crawl out," sings Jasper.

They are grunting and laughing as they heft her down the back steps and into the parking lot. The light from the transmitter tower blinks red through the air holes. She is getting used to the powerless feeling of floating in the dark.

"It's nice to be a corpse," she says. "I like the star treatment."

"Maybe another station would pick up the *Creepshow?*" Jasper is trying once again. "You can't just let them kill you off."

"You assume, dear boy," says Eddie, "that I want to live."

"Hey, what are you going to put on my tombstone?" Wallis asks, because for a minute they've forgotten who is center stage here. She hears the back gate of the hearse open and is jolted sharply as the casket hits the interior wheels and is rolled into place.

But no one answers. She's just freight now, alone in her box in the back. They've taken the joke up front.

She waited until Thursday, one day of the week for each of Jasper's fingernail clippings. In her left hand, she carries a candle, several straight pins, a box of matches, and the hair she stole from the bathroom sink. She grips the five fingernail parings so tightly that they cut into her as if they were the nails of her own clenched fist. None of her spells are planned, but come to her like snatches of poetry or a doodle on a napkin. She knows enough about how magic works to know they must be wrought at night and in secret. Better under a full moon. Better with fire. Fire is love but it is also revenge. She's not sure yet which way this spell will go. Either Jasper should love her or he should disappear. There is nothing in between.

Across the new-mown lawn the grass catches between her naked toes. She looks back at the house where everyone is sleeping. All week Mom has made her dust and vacuum and mop and sweep. *He's your father and you should care that he's been at something for twenty years, twenty years of anything is quite an accomplishment, you don't even know.* You don't even know, Wallis wants to snap back. Every night after dinner, Mom folded the laundry into four separate piles, watching Eddie draw the highs and lows on his weather map. And she would groan as the poor man blithely forecasted a 70 percent chance of his own surprise party getting rained out.

Wallis moves through the soybean field and grazes a handful of fuzzy pods in the dark. Her father told her not to pick those beans, they didn't belong to her, but they are fresh and green and she loves how they sheer in half between her teeth, like twin pebbles in her mouth. She comes out into the woods where the loosely planted trees suggest a dozen different paths, and she walks until she feels the soil beneath her feet change from pine needle to ash. The girls at school pay five dollars apiece for spells conjured by the daughter of Captain Casket. She takes their money and buys herself candy and watches the girls walk taller down the hallway, smile brighter for their secret knowledge. She feels the power in her own chest as they claim their own, and the boys feel it, and Wallis knows she put it there.

Wallis sets the nails and hair and candle and pins on a rock beside her and kneels to dig a shallow hole. With each handful of soil she creates an upheaval of earthworm, feels the singe-shut of pill bugs snapping tight. It's all words for the girls at school, incantations in red ink ripped from spiral notebooks. But Wallis has real pieces of Jasper, forgotten bits, vulnerable and hers. By the light of the moon, she lifts one of the bayberry candles Mom had stashed in the credenza. Through its woven wick, she fixes Jasper's hair with a straight pin. She strikes a match and allows herself to think his name. The flame jumps and in an instant, acrid puff, the hair is gone, leaving nothing but a carbon-black pin. Wallis sinks the candle in the dirt beside her and sows the five bits of nail in the trench she's dug. No other words are coming to her, this is beyond the work of words; she can't even remember what he looks like or why she wants what she wants. It comes to her then to lift the hem of her nightgown and pull aside her underwear and water what she's planted. The night air is a hand between her legs and this is what she's needed—to surrender to the quivering relief of all that power she's been holding in. She closes her eyes and the first few drops prime the soil, the shower makes things bloom. But gentle is not her way, and Wallis pees for forty days and forty nights until the earth is flooded and all who imperfectly worship her are wiped away. Rocking back on her haunches, she looks up through the veil of trees. The house was dark when she left, but now Jasper's bedroom window is a wide-awake yellow animal's eye, and she imagines him having heard her sneak past and pulling the cord of the lamp beside his bed at the first violent splash. She imagines him sitting in the window even now, confronting his own reflection, having forgotten that to see out into the dark, you must turn off the light behind you. Can you see me, so far away? No, she thinks. You cannot. She steps off and the last remaining drops soak through her panties and roll down her leg. The earth bowl is full of her and its surface is frothy and the little bits of Jasper float on top like bait tossed out at the end of a fishing trip. Wallis kicks dirt into the hole with her bare toes and stamps it down, leaving a flurry of footprints. It is well past midnight but she takes her time walking home, back through the verdant soybean field, stealing pods and splitting them as she goes. She moves toward the light in his window, knowing full well by the time she arrives, it will be extinguished, whether or not he has returned to sleep.

The phone has rung steadily all afternoon—the caterers with a half dozen substitutions, and now, closer to dinnertime, the last-minute cancellations of semi-acquaintances who had told themselves up until an hour ago they'd pull together a costume but had decided if they were going to pay a babysitter, they'd rather catch a movie instead. (Mom: *Well, tell him to please feel better, you know how heartbroken Eddie will be to miss him.*)

With the phone cord stretching from the wall to the refrigerator, Ann talks with the receiver between her shoulder and ear, emptying the shelves to make room for all the backup beer people were sure to bring, though she had told them specifically it wasn't necessary. Wallis watches her through the patio door. She has spent the last hour scrubbing the patio furniture of its purple bird droppings and now she turns the chairs upside down to dry as she hoses the suds from the flagstone. Mom will make her right them because if her dad drove up now he would instantly suspect something and sure enough, Ann, still talking on the phone, taps the window and makes the hand gesture, turn them over.

"I want you to get Jasper to help you," Mom says, replacing the receiver when Wallis walks in. "Tell him there's sand in the carport. I need you to fill the white paper bags and get the candles ready to line the driveway. Do it in the attic so your dad doesn't see."

"You ask him," Wallis says. "He doesn't like me."

"Of course he likes you, he just doesn't know how to show it," Mom responds, handing Wallis a thick stack of white lunch bags. "Men are oblivious, darling. Jasper is in the den right now answering mail because he doesn't know what to do and he doesn't understand he should ask."

"Maybe he's answering mail because he feels like it," Wallis says.

"Wallis, please," says Mom. "He's making me a nervous wreck. I just vacuumed in there."

The phone rings again and Wallis walks into the doorway of the den where Jasper has spread several dozen letters and eight-by-ten publicity stills of Captain Casket across the rug. It's a ten-year-old photo of Eddie stretched fetchingly on his coffin like a Playboy Bunny. With a black marker Jasper is signing each photo: *Don't let the bedbugs bite, C.C.*

"Mom says you need to go to the carport and bring some sand to the attic," Wallis announces.

"Why do I need to bring sand into the attic?" Jasper asks.

"To pour it into paper bags."

"What for?"

"To hold candles to light the driveway."

"I'm doing something important."

"My mom thinks putting candles in bags is more important."

Jasper has slit the envelopes carefully with a letter opener and unfolded all the letters and the crayon-on-loose-leaf-paper portraits of Eddie: in his coffin, floating in a graveyard, holding knives and assault rifles and cartoon bombs with lit fuses. Over the years his preteen fans have used Captain Casket to destroy school buildings and blow up the planet. She's seen it all. Jasper doles out Casketeer cards, fills in the names, and carefully forges Captain Casket's signature. He is as concentrated and serious as if he were counting money in a bank.

"That's so sad," she says.

"What?"

"All those dumb kids writing to a fake vampire."

"Eddie doesn't think they're dumb. They matter to him."

"Maybe they mattered in the beginning, but it gets old. The only people who really matter to him are me and Mom. We're family."

Jasper slides a photo and a Casketeer card into a self-addressed stamped envelope. He licks the seal and sets it aside.

"It meant a lot to me to get a signed photo," Jasper says.

"Check the signature," Wallis says. "Who do you think had this job before you?"

Wallis takes the steps to the upstairs hallway, where the trapdoor string dangles from the ceiling. A blast of hot air drops with the folding ladder and before her head is fully inside her neck is running with sweat. Yesterday Mom switched off the attic exhaust fan so that it wouldn't guillotine the helium balloons she bought for tonight and left to drift in the rafters. Up here, she has hidden papier-mâché sarcophagi and peanut cans of exploding snakes and all the other ephemera that she thinks makes the Captain casket-y. She collected and framed the congratulations of other horror hosts, among them a 45 of "Monster Mash" inscribed "Many Morbid Returns, Zacherley." Wallis can't remember her father ever throwing a party like this for her mother. She supposes he's never really had the chance. By the time the dishes are in the sink on this one, Mom will already be planning the next.

She has set up the last row of paper bags when Jasper returns with the thirty-pound sack of contractor sand Ann bought at the lumberyard. She knew he would come but she doesn't acknowledge it. Wordlessly, he rips a corner and pours while she squats to hold open the mouth of the first lunch bag. He tilts the sack and the cheap sand rushes out, exploding in a cloud of dust when it hits the bottom, making it even harder to breathe. Wallis wipes her eyes with the cleanest corner of her salty T-shirt. He moves to the next bag, letting the sand spill across the floor.

"Pay attention," she snaps.

"To what?" he asks. "Is your mother going to come up here with a ruler and measure each one to make sure I got them exactly equal?"

"We can't win with you, can we?" Wallis asks. "If we leave you alone, you think we don't care. If we ask you to do something you act all put out. Tell me how I'm supposed to treat you?"

"Why don't you tell me how I'm supposed to act?" he counters. "If I offer to do things, you think I'm sucking up and trying to weasel in. If I'm myself and relax for five minutes, I'm being ungrateful. I was fine sleeping at the station. I don't even know why I'm here."

"You're here because Mom thinks Dad needs a son."

"I don't want to be Eddie's son," Jasper says.

"Consider yourself lucky you have a roof over your head," Wallis says. "If you were sleeping at the station, where would you go when they sold it?"

That shuts him up. Jasper lifts the sand and begins pouring again, this time more carefully. She holds open a bag, he fills it three-quarters, moves to the next. She is conscious of her movements, graceful and balletic as she moves from bag to bag. If he is going to make her feel like she's performing, he should appreciate the show.

"I'm not some starstruck kid," Jasper says. He's still back at her father. She shrugs.

"You're inside now," she says. "Can't you see there's nothing special?"

"I see things in Eddie you can't see. Things you'd never understand."

"Like what?" she challenges. Jasper shakes his head and moves to the next bag. He won't give her anything.

"I thought so," she says. He wants to believe there is something more there than what her father lets on. He's trying to turn him into something larger than he is. "You're going to wake up one day and be really embarrassed."

He drops the bag of sand in frustration, sending up another plume of dust.

"Ask him why his mother killed someone."

His violet eyes are slits in his face and his jaw is clenched. The summer sun has darkened his caul of freckles until barely any pink flesh shows through. "That's right," he says. "Ask him what she was."

Eddie never speaks of his mother. Wallis only knows she died a long time ago. Her name was Cora, and she sent a coffin for a wedding present. Wallis has never seen a picture of her. Through the attic walls, she feels a tremor, a slight vibration to match the jumping in her stomach. The tremor becomes a heavy bass, shaking the floor; a few moments later, she can pick out a melody. She puts her face to the attic fan, peering out between the silver blades as Captain Casket's hearse pulls up. Her father coasts to a stop, drumming the beat on the steering wheel. He has changed out of his weatherman clothes and is wearing instead a bright yellow, wide-collared shirt she's never seen before, unbuttoned low enough to show his chest hair. The howl and sideswipe of guitar is music Mom would hate, but behind her, Jasper bangs the rhythm with his fists on the floorboards.

"That was a close one, kids!" Mom's bright blonde head pops up from the hole beside him. She is giddy with the thrill of having almost been caught. "Now aren't you glad I sent you up here? I always have to stay one step ahead of that man."

She disappears and Jasper walks away from the bags of sand, leaving Wallis to place the candles. He dangles over the hole where Mom just was, showing off with a few chin-ups, the kind men do in prison.

"Why would Dad tell you things he hasn't told me?" Wallis demands.

"Maybe I matter," Jasper says, letting go.

The hearse windows are up for the interstate but as soon as her dad pulls off the University exit, cruising the tight, one-way streets in the shadows of tall federal buildings, he cranks them down and dials the radio to an R & B station. It is nearly sunset and the mood is summer peaceful among the black men who stand in groups of four and five on the corners. In the years since Wallis was a kid, coming to the department store to sit on Santa's lap, downtown has become a ragged country crossroads where tree roots push up the pavement and men claim their squares of empty unmown lots like the front porches of feed stores. They shield their eyes against the low sun, raising paper bags to their lips. The glare is red on the windows of the check-cashing shop, swallowed by the drawn metal blinds of the Army Recruitment Center. The rest of the block is nailed tight with sheets of butter yellow plywood. Broken Christmas lights stretch between the streetlamps overhead, and at the center of each is a tinsel snowflake. Her father takes a right onto Plum Street.

"Some guys from school came down here one night and beat the shit out of a drag queen," Jasper says.

"Behind the post office?" he asks.

"I don't know," Jasper answers. "I just heard about it."

My grandmother has killed someone and I have pissed on the boy beside me. What have you done? she wants to ask the men on the street corners, who have surely done things they are not proud of yet cannot say they regret. They earned their peaceful laughter and lost their women, for there are never women out here drinking beer; the women are drinking and laughing inside somewhere, Wallis guesses, as manless as these men are without women. It's not how it's supposed to be, yet somehow everyone seems relieved it's how it is.

Her father pulls into a space down the block from Cary's, in front of the Biograph, the last surviving non-mall movie theater. Built in the twenties to suggest a mosque in a town that would safely never have one, it once showed first-run movies but now it screens mostly foreign films in the evenings and porn during the day. Wallis tries to see through the door as they pass by but the windows are painted deep purple.

"*The Cabinet of Dr. Caligari* is playing next week," Jasper says, reading the marquee. "We should see it."

"*Cesare,*" Eddie shouts. "*How long do I have to live?*"

"Never ask a somnambulist for a straight answer," Jasper replies.

"What's it about?" asks Wallis.

"You wouldn't like it," says Eddie. "It's old and weird."

Says Wallis, "Not like anyone else we know."

"Eddie you old ghoul!" Cary shouts from behind the bar when they step inside. The TV station is only blocks away on Main, and Cary's is the anchor's haunt. It's another building stuck in time, with round maple tables, round-backed chairs, and round red-parchment clip-on shades on all the low-hanging chandeliers. The divorcées crowd the bar laughing too loud and smoking. Last year Cary put in a salad bar, roofed with etched glass and a metal well that holds chilled plates; it glows like a Lucite spaceship in the middle of the room. Now every child's an Artful Dodger of crackers and butter packets, her father says, every woman a war bride heaping her plate for her husband as if they'll never eat again. Eddie always makes a point of ordering a Caesar salad mixed at the table. Let us politely converse over reasonable portions, he says, and let the waiters earn their money.

Cary pours bourbon into a highball. With his other hand, he wields the soda hose and fills a glass for her.

"Your table is ready. How are you, Wallis?" he asks, and turns to Jasper. "Dr. Pepper for you, right, young man?"

"Thanks," Jasper replies. They take up their glasses, weaving their way to the back table near the bathrooms, and heads turn to see who, on a busy Friday night, merits the little "Reserved" tent. Oh, it's Eddie from channel 8, and the grown-ups smile because old people love the weather, and the kids grab their napkins and beg pens off their moms.

"Can I have your autograph?" A boy about Wallis's age is at the table before they've even sat down. He wears braces, the rubber bands stretch at the back of his mouth like a cobra.

Eddie is gracious. "What's your name, son?"

"Clay," says the boy.

"Clay, are you O positive or A negative? I've ordered a Bloody Mary and the bartender needs to know."

The boy cackles and the rubber bands fill with spit. Eddie signs four more autographs while Jasper watches, slumped in his chair. He plays with the salt shaker, rolling it back and forth, showing off his unblemished knuckles. Wallis's are healing but she keeps them in her lap; the scabs feel as shameful out in public as a hickey. She never knows where to look when other kids are making idiots of themselves, so she turns her eyes to the bar, and the news channel playing on the TV. News twenty-four hours a day and it's all about the hostages in Iran. It's August 1980, but in the alternate news-dimension, it's Day 284 of the crisis. Jasper reaches for his Dr. Pepper and gulps until there's nothing but ice.

"How did Cary know what you drink?" she asks him.

"We're regulars," Jasper says.

Eddie overhears. "Before Jasper moved in, we'd come for lunch," he says. "We needed to fatten this boy up."

"Mom and I used to meet him here before the show. But Mom doesn't like driving downtown."

Cary arrives with the menus as Eddie signs his last autograph. Comparing napkins, the kids push past him back to their tables.

"Wallis always checked the price and ordered whatever was most expensive," Eddie says proudly. "When she was only seven, she'd order a sirloin and eat the whole thing."

"What'll it be, boss?" asks Cary. He's trying to catch Wallis's eye, but she doesn't want to play the game I-know-what-you-know. His name is on Mom's guest list. She's surprised he's still here.

"The usual," Eddie says.

"Sirloin well-done," says Jasper.

"I'll have the salad bar," says Wallis.

She's happy to have an excuse to get up. The kid with the braces is getting lectured by his father about interrupting other people's dinner. He looks up as she passes, wondering whether her autograph is also worthwhile, and decides it isn't. She waits in line for her chilled plate but most of the stuff on the salad bar is disgusting—three-bean salad and shredded carrots with raisins. Back at the table, Cary is gone. Jasper leans in, laughing with her father as if they are trading more secrets. He's dropped the sullen act now that he has Eddie all to himself. What he said about her grandmother is nothing more than napalm in the woods, she thinks, another way of seeing how much damage he can do. If her grandmother had killed someone, Wallis would know. Her mother would have let it slip, or she would feel it somehow. But then she realizes, she does feel it and always has—in how much further she is willing to go than other kids, at least until Jasper arrived. He makes her feel halfway normal by being so much further beyond her. Standing in line in the middle of the restaurant, Wallis is suddenly aware of a dozen different conversations taking place at a dozen different tables, but she is standing outside them all. She heaps her plate with romaine lettuce and croutons, then sprinkles on some Parmesan cheese.

"There's nothing older than *Caligari*," Jasper is insisting when she gets back. "It was the first."

"I tell you, Edison made *Frankenstein* in 1910; I saw it as a kid. If I still had it, it'd be worth a fortune. Every copy's been lost."

"That's convenient," says Jasper.

"You saw it as a kid?" Wallis interrupts. "Where?"

The sparring stops and Eddie looks over, annoyed. He hadn't meant to talk about being a kid. Now that Jasper has pointed it out, it seems to Wallis that Eddie not only hasn't spoken of his boyhood, he's gone out of his way to avoid it. Why had she never thought to ask?

Eddie looks around the restaurant, hoping to be rescued by food. An elderly lady with a walker knocks over her chair getting up to leave. The noise is swallowed by the worn green carpet.

"A man came through Panther Gap with a hand-cranked projector," Eddie says. "The movie had been his father's."

"Panther Gap?" Wallis asks. "That's where you lived? It sounds made up."

"It sometimes felt that way," Eddie says. Jasper is watching his face as if for clues.

"So what happened with the man?" Wallis asks.

"What makes you think something happened?" Eddie asks. He glances darkly at Jasper.

"Something did, right?" she pushes.

"As a matter of fact," Eddie continues, "he was supposed to report to Fort Dix but apparently he went AWOL."

Wallis can tell from the way Jasper is looking down that he has already heard this story. She doesn't know much about World War II but she knows everyone wanted to go. It was the one good war.

"Something must have happened to him," she says. "Everyone wanted to fight Hitler."

"This was before Pearl Harbor," Eddie explains. "No one had directly attacked us. It was hard to know what was real. But how do you ever know until it's too late?"

From the kitchen Cary appears with a rolling cart. On it is Jasper's gray steak and a bloody plate of prime rib for Eddie. Cary whisks together lemon and garlic and a splash of Worcestershire, tosses it with some lettuce, and cracks open a raw egg. Pietro, the maître d', follows with a covered plate.

"I've got somewhere I have to be tonight," Cary announces, with a wink at Wallis, "but I'm leaving you in good hands."

Pietro, with his dyed black hair and stained burgundy tuxedo, lifts away the silver dome to reveal a slice of cake and a lit candle. The guests at the tables nearby turn to look.

"Twenty years can't go uncelebrated, you old fiend," says Cary.

In his broken English, Pietro begins, "*Happy Birthday to you . . .*"

The old lady on her walker pauses by the door. Her husband smiles back with his squared-off dentures. The parents contemplating infanticide are grateful for the interruption, while their children sing just loudly and off-key enough to make them reconsider. Only at the bar, where the divorcées are ordering Stingrays, and flags are burning in Iran, are they disinterested. Now's your chance to tell them you're cancelled, Wallis thinks. That soon you'll be nobody. Or worse, you'll be the man who *used* to be somebody. Jasper has joined in—*Happy Birthday, dear Captain*—and Wallis imagines the cars pulling up at home, parking in neighbors' driveways so that Eddie won't suspect anything. Will he tell them tonight? Will they even care, and if they don't care that he's cancelled, why are they bothering to sing to him tonight?

"Make a wish, Eddie," says Jasper.

Her father smiles up at everyone and blows out the candle. The flame sputters and sparks and relights itself.

"Very funny," he says. Cary slaps him on the back and he indulges the joke three more times before dousing Captain Casket's trick birthday candle with his highball. Wallis glances at the watch on Cary's wrist. It's eight o'clock. Mom expects them home in half an hour.

"We should eat," Wallis says loudly. "It's getting late."

They don't return to the subject of *Frankenstein* or the man who showed it, but Eddie's mood has changed. When he picked them up, the night had the energy of a first date; now, with his third drink, Eddie is dull and quiet. This feels more like old times, when she and Mom came to join him on Saturday nights before the show, when Wallis would provide the only entertainment by ordering her large plates of meat. He pays the bill and they leave, walking past the Biograph again. A couple is buying tickets for something called *Die Blechtrommel*. They pass their money through a cage and the heavy Moorish doors swing open, but all Wallis can see is the marble floor and the blown-plaster pillars of the lobby. A tripod holds a poster of a shrieking blond boy beating a drum.

"We used to be afraid of monsters," says Eddie, "now it's children."

"What's the difference?" asks Wallis.

"None of those movies are scary," says Jasper. "I've never once been scared."

"Then why do you watch the *Creepshow*?" asks Eddie.

Jasper shrugs. "I keep hoping to feel that thing everyone talks about," he says.

Eddie unlocks the passenger door of the hearse and Wallis slides into the middle. Jasper follows, letting no part of his body touch hers, which means he's thinking about it. Soon they'll be home and she'll be passed along to entertain all the TV station brats while the grown-ups drink, all those little girls who will paw through her old Barbies and the boys who will camp out in front of her television. She's the oldest one now, not a kid at all anymore, and sometime around eleven, when the news comes on and the substitute weatherman lets them know the front passed to the north, she'll round them all up and lead them outside to the backyard, still awake but jittery, all strung out on soda and someone else's toys, up so far past their bedtimes, and it will finally be her turn. She'll take her stage, sitting on the picnic table as is her oldest girl's right, and softly, she'll tell them the one about the babysitter who is alone in the house, who gets the phone call, *Go check on the twins. Go check on the twins.* And Jasper will be among them, listening in the dark, leaning against the carapace of the oak tree, unaware of the pieces of him buried just beyond in the woods. *Get out now,* the operator will say. *We've traced the call. He's inside the house with you.*

"Where are we going?" she asks, suddenly realizing the hearse is hurtling in the opposite direction from home.

"I want to show you something," her dad replies. "It won't take long. Unless it takes all night."

"Dad, we need to go home," Wallis says, truly nervous now.

"It's your mother's fault for not asking me if I wanted a party," Eddie says low. "She should know by now how much I hate surprises."

The hearse's headlights rasp the dark as they speed along an unfamiliar road, scattering rabbits and turning the night-grazing deer to statuary. The windows are down, the radio off. They pass empty fields and glassy obsidian ponds that float upon their gauze of reflected clouds, repeating pearls of moon. They ride for miles in this hushed, rolling darkness, not talking, Wallis trying hard not to think about her mother greeting the guests—*You know Eddie, always unpredictable, that's what we love about him*—sucking the ice cubes of her third drink to delay pouring herself a fourth. Wallis has failed her mom but the paved road gives way to dirt and there is the music of cracked gravel and the night-sweet smell of honeysuckle. She lets her body relax until her shoulder brushes Jasper's. The ride has softened him, too, he doesn't lean into her but he doesn't flinch away.

About ten miles out of town, Eddie pulls the car onto the side of the road and cuts the engine. There is still the aroma of honeysuckle, but now it is accompanied by orange and brown trumpets, sweetly rotting into the decay of swamp. They've taken the back way, which is why she didn't know where they were. In front of them is a rusted NO TRESPASSING sign hung on a chain across a path. Her father cuts the headlights and they are plunged into darkness.

"The trains have always run by this swamp," he says, and his voice hangs disembodied. "Twice a day and twice a night, they've been coming by for years. Once, long ago, an old conductor rode this route, a bitter, gaunt old man. He had no wife, he had no child. His whole life was this trip, up and back, up and back, hauling freight. Nothing had ever happened to him—he'd lived a tight, ordered, solitary life, and now he was close to retirement. I suppose there are some men who can slip through life without a single tragedy, but mostly we don't like to hear about them. We like our stories to be full of bad luck and undeserved misfortune, don't we? So here's this old conductor, on the verge of retiring when, suddenly, late one night, he spies a bundle left right in the middle of the tracks. Oh no, he thinks. It can't be. Truly, it was too far away to know for sure, but then, as fate would have it, the bundle began to squirm.

"*Hit the brake!* he shouted, but you know how long it takes a train to slow to a stop. And this was a heavy, barreling old thing. The squeal was deafening. The conductor fell, the coal in the hopper slid to the ground, they shuddered to a long, aching stop. It was too late, they had passed the spot where the baby had lain. What kind of mother would have walked off and left her child on these cold metal rails? What monster would have made him—an old and blameless man—responsible for the death of a child? He put his head in his hands and sobbed, knowing his life was over. He could never live with the guilt. Just then, suddenly, in the dark, he heard a tiny desolate cry. He was saved—the baby lived!

"The conductor snatched up his lantern and leaped from his post, swinging his light all around. It flashed on the tall swamp grasses and glittering black eyes of bullfrogs. It flashed across the green scum of pollen and lily pad on the swamp below, the sickle heads of snapping turtles. He swung his lantern under the carriage of the heaving train. Was it there? He heard it crying louder. Was it there? He peered deep underneath, reaching along the rail, when—

"SNAP! The train rolled forward and off came his head."

Her father bolts from the hearse and leaps the NO TRESPASSING sign. Suddenly, it's all a game, and Jasper bounds off after him with Wallis close behind. She hops the chain herself, following the wake of them in the dark. This sign was here back then, Wallis knows from her father's telling and retelling of her parents' first kiss, before Captain Casket or the weather or Sailor Eddie or any of the characters he'd played over the years, back when he was just Edward Alley, an intern hailing from the mountains, judging by his flat-foot accent, who was determined to get a job at the new television station. Even then, he wooed with ghost stories, and her mother, the daughter of his boss, sat cross-legged and enraptured, not believing a word he told her, yet wanting to believe, and falling in love with this odd looking, not-tall, plastic-faced boy, who would not even tell her his age.

One evening when she was sitting in the station manager's office he'd brought her a cup of coffee like she liked it—black, which was charmingly pretentious in a schoolgirl of seventeen—and he had leaned against the gunmetal desk where she worked. Her yellow hair had been pulled back in a ponytail and her sleeves were rolled up. There was a story he'd heard, he told Ann, about a decapitated conductor who walked the railroad tracks of an old line just west of here. Ann had shivered and smiled up at him from underneath her bright hair and he had invited her to come with him to look for those lights and she had accepted without hesitation. The next night she had concocted a lie for her parents about sleeping over at a friend's house that came out so easily and well she wondered why she hadn't thought to tell one before; and then she was speeding down the same dark nothing that the three had just driven, hopping the same NO TRESPASSING gate that they just hopped, onto the same private property, already known as a make-out spot, for who wouldn't want to press tight together when faced with a decapitated conductor wandering a desolate track?

Jasper and Wallis scramble down the embankment to the tracks where Eddie waits, a shadow among shadows. That night, hand in hand, he and her mother had walked the line, talking softly about the lives they'd lived before this night, for both felt themselves to be in the midst of the most glorious reincarnation; they'd walked and talked for hours, despite a light drizzle that pulled at her mother's ponytail and brought out, like salt in a soup, the vegetal highlights of the nearby swamp. Then, wanting him to kiss her but not knowing how to make the request, Ann had stopped and, with eyes full of trust and complicity and something just a little challenging, asked Eddie the question Jasper now poses like a smart-ass, here, years later, in place of her whom they had left alone with guests, humiliated and drunk now, asking Cary once more what time he left, if Eddie had ordered dessert. Jasper asks the question Wallis knew had been her mother's part of the script that night, *Are we supposed to believe this?* and her father answers it in the same way he had answered her mother that night, as they stood in the center of the railroad tracks that disappeared in each direction off into the woods; he said, and he says: *Now, once a year, on this very night, the conductor walks these lonely tracks, swinging his lantern, searching for his missing head . . .*

As if on cue, far away, a point of light appears in the woods. And as her mother and father watched, as *they* watch, it advances slowly, flirtatiously, bobbing like a cork on water. Wallis has heard of will-o'-the-wisps and swamp lights, but nothing prepares her for this inexplicable thing coming straight toward her, growing larger with each bounce. It is a light like a rubber-band ball with no edge or ending, luminous, diffuse, just a brilliant exhalation of the night.

Sweat breaks out on Wallis's forehead and under her armpits. She tries to remember how the story of her parents' first date ended, but fear has erased memory and all she can see is her mother back home pulling her sweater around her, watching the children of her guests racing from tree to tree in their backyard playing Ghost in the Grave-yard—one o'clock, two o'clock, three o'clock, the children shout, on till midnight—her eyes scanning the road for Eddie's car. At Wallis's side, Jasper stiffens, trying to make sense of what he is seeing, willing himself to hold ground. It has passed through and swallowed her father. The light is mere feet from them now, taking up their entire world. It should be thrilling, but it is too real and she can't let it touch her, she doesn't know what it is, so she turns and runs like a little kid and remembers now how her mother had, too, that night, racing down the railroad tracks, leaping the wooden ties. It is not after her, it just *is,* but she can't help running. There is pounding close behind her, then beside her, then overtaking her, and then she is running after his shadow, Jasper the bold, and he's lit by the staccato flashes of moon on the worn metal tracks. She runs, not glancing back, running in a straight line as she always screamed at people in the movies never to do—*you can't outrun it, use your head, leave the path and lose it in the woods*—but she can't think, she can only try to keep up with Jasper, whose legs are twice as long. In the story, her father caught up with her mother and spun her around to face the conductor's lantern, the headless man himself, who dissolved into the mist like the light, which was coming, which had definitely been coming, but which no longer existed, if it had ever existed; and in its absence, he had kissed her, as the rain picked up, no longer a drizzle but fat, cold drops, and he kissed her for a very long time until her heart raced not from fear but from his kisses—though for the rest of her life, she would later tell Wallis, the two feelings would be too closely intertwined for her comfort.

Wallis slams into Jasper, who has stopped. She hits into him sharply and he grabs her to keep from falling over, holding her tight. Together they stare down the tracks to see if they've outrun it, whatever it was, but instead, like her mother, find themselves staring into a stretching darkness that holds only the vibrations of their footfalls. No light. No conductor. Nothing.

Jasper could let go but he doesn't. "What was it?" she whispers.

"Swamp gas, maybe," Jasper says, his eyes wide and black. "Lights from the highway. Where is Eddie?"

"You were afraid," she says. "You *are* afraid."

He tries to let her go then, but she doesn't move, because this night will get them in so much trouble already, why stop now? And so as it must be done, as they both finally know it must be done, he leans forward, and his lips are yeasty, his breath sweet.

He pulls back and she sees the look of dismay on his face. Still she doesn't move, but this time he pushes her, hard, and disappears into the funnel of trees toward the swamp and the conductor's lantern. She is alone with that kiss. The night is still and finished, everything is suspended in that kiss. Slowly she follows, making out in the moonlight a field, a pickup swallowed by kudzu, the wreckage of what had once been a farmhouse, its windows target practice for decades of boys who had brought their dates to this place. Beneath her feet, she feels the vibrations before she hears the whistle, high and plaintive. Into her open bedroom window, when the wind is just right, she sometimes hears this far-off whistle and, as a little girl, she used to imagine a brightly colored train carrying cars full of tigers and elephants off to tented circuses across the country. Now, she can think only of the conductor, and even as she imagines him swinging his light, looking for something that doesn't exist, the train's head beam blinds her. She steps out of its way, feeling the shock waves of crashing metal, melting into its own force and noise, oblivion, it's rackety freight and rattling gondola cars. She had thought to tell the ghost story tonight, but she should have known her father would not allow it. She could never compete with the master.

Ahead she sees her father in the laser of moth flutter down the tracks. He is waiting whole and unhurt on the embankment, knowing what he has set in motion by bringing them here. Jasper walks toward him, his face the carving of a lover's initials into a tree. Jasper was brought here to feel what he had never felt, and learn what must be feared, and now her father opens his arms; Captain Casket, who has spent the last twenty years of his life teasing young boys with ghost stories and whose idea of seduction is a ball of vanishing light.

Wallis

NEW YORK CITY

3:00 a.m.

Wallis talked as Jeff led her back upstairs. She talked as he stripped her naked and stood her in the crummy freestanding Plexiglas shower in the center of the loft, and continued talking when he climbed in beside her and lathered her hair, digging his fingers into the roots, letting large dollops of lather run down his elbows. She talked while he tilted her chin and rinsed her hair clean and wrapped her in a towel and led her back to the bed. She had never talked this long, naked, in her life. Now, she wonders why not. No one had ever let her, she supposes. That's not what naked had been about.

"What did your mother do when you got home?" he asks.

"We didn't get home until after midnight. A few people were still there, which made it worse, I think, because she had to listen to him apologize in that charming way of his and make everything okay."

Wallis rolls over. Her mother had let her father talk to the drunks who were still there while she excused herself, saying she needed to put Wallis to bed, even though she hadn't done that for years. She laid out her daughter's pajamas and Wallis pulled them on, wondering what her mother was going to say, wanting to explain that she had tried to make them come home, but what could she do, she was just a kid? What power did she have to make anyone do anything? She had crawled miserably into bed but her mother had still said nothing, only took down the red hard-shell Samsonite from Wallis's bedroom closet and began filling it with clothes. That's when she knew how serious it was and that Mom meant to leave Dad. She would have to spend the rest of her life with her mother alone. She wondered what would become of Jasper. If Mom would put him out like the garbage or if Dad would get him. She wanted to ask but her mouth was too full of having been kissed for the first time and wanting to cry because she knew if they left, it would never happen again. Then they sat in the dark in silence, the two of them, Mom looking out the window, Wallis strobing through the light and the chase and his mouth against hers. She wanted to tell her mother they'd been down at the railroad tracks, that she and her mother had shared something, and she wanted to ask if it had been complicated for her, too. But nothing about Mom invited conversation. It was after two in the morning when the last car pulled out of the driveway. Then her father burst in, in that state of drunk she always liked best but trusted least, past cynical but before morose, when he was just happy and expansive, and he flipped on the light, blinding her, and said, "Wallis, darling, wake up! We're going on a little ginseng hunt!" Her mother had been waiting until morning but, as usual, her father trumped her. *I've already packed her bag, Eddie,* said Mom, rising stiffly as though she had been waiting for him instead of for the sun to come up. *Have a nice trip.*

"How did you know?" she asks Jeff. "Why did you show me his card tonight?"

Jeff studies her with red, tired eyes. "I didn't know tonight was important to you. You have a reputation at the station. I just wanted to see if I could have you, too."

She's not mad. Stretched out beside him, she runs her hands along his body, slipping them between his thighs.

"I learned something in the years I spent among suicide bombers," she tells him. "The boys and girls who are willing to blow up their lives are not the true believers. They are the ones in agonies of doubt. There is always someone with nothing to prove who buckles the belt around them."

Jeff tilts his head back as she runs her tongue the length of him. "Living out here like this," she asks, "being with me. Do you believe in anything, Jeff?"

She knows they all want her because she creates the doubt, and doubt is where they all feel safest. She knows why they chose each other tonight and why he is listening to her and she doesn't feel guilty anymore for taking what she needs. He climbs onto her and bites her neck hard enough to leave a mark. Then he rolls her on top.

"Hold that thought," she whispers, reaching for his cell phone next to the bed. "I just need to make one quick call."

Eddie

NEW YORK CITY

3:00 a.m.

You would think by now I would feel something, wouldn't you, Wallis? Some numbness or tingling or drowsiness? You must have a word with your sponsor—I feel wide awake and more alert than I have in months. It's dark in here, and muffled, but through the air holes in my lid the smells still circulate. Diesel fuel on the rain, toasted horse chestnuts in Central Park, the blood metallic scent of the penny my neighbor tapes to his record needle to keep it from skipping over a Carmen Cavallaro 78 played on the 1960s console he rescued from the curb last Large Garbage Day. That is one of my favorite underappreciated New York institutions—the ultimate redistribution of wealth, when we might with impunity place on the curb for pickup all of our sluggish refrigerators and cat-clawed couches and hutches and such. Maybe Charles will come home tomorrow and instead of calling the funeral parlor, he'll get the doorman to help load my coffin onto the freight elevator and they'll just leave me out on the street for Large Garbage Day. I will end up scavenged for some dorm room at NYU.

I have a confession to make. Charles phoned about an hour ago. I thought it might be you and I opened the lid and climbed out and checked my caller ID. Since then I haven't been able to get it back, that feeling of wanting to die. I didn't pick up. I could have. I could have listened to the update on his mother and how he had to phone the insurance agency five times to get her preapproved for her surgery. I could have assured him I watered the plants and mailed the birthday card to Ollie and took my medicine when I was supposed to. Instead, I let him leave a message for a dead man. Better that than talking casually about those daily routines we took such comfort in. Which would be worse for him? Wondering if I was already gone when he phoned or having had our nightly conversation in which I forgot to mention this one small thing?

Have you checked your messages, Wallis? Are you on your own ginseng hunt tonight? I close my eyes and see our stories like two fronts passing somewhere over the Brooklyn Bridge, turbulent and electric, causing this rain to fall, this far-off thunder. I see them colliding, yet finding in each other some lovely marriage of sense and larger truth, so that I might with my final breath sigh, Ah, and know, after all this time, that finally we understand each other. But I suppose this is the real ghost story, Wallis. The lonely horror at never knowing if what we put out there for each other will be understood. Or recognized. Or even heard.

Am I just talking to myself? This life, this massive love. Has it all been in my head?

I've been thinking of the night of my surprise party—why is that? Remember, we drove all night long and reached the mountain at daybreak. Did you know your mother kicked me out of the house? I don't think I ever told you. She left me a note in the master bath where I'd find it when I brushed my teeth before bed. It said, *I think it might be wise for you to take the children on a holiday. I have some matters to attend to here and I need some time alone. If you ever intend to humiliate me like that again, don't bother coming back.* She signed it, *Yours, Ann.*

We stopped at the Waffle House at the foothills just as the sun was coming up. There was a woman in a flannel shirt pulling the arm of a slot machine and her baby in its car seat on the table by her ashtray. I remember you complained your neck was stiff from sleeping against the cold window. Jasper ordered orange juice and put two packets of sugar in it. Then we were back in the hearse taking the switchback turns that led along the ravine and beside the river up to Panther Gap, which transported me to the backseat of Tucker Hayes's car and the pain in my collarbone that aches right now, because of the dampness

I suppose. Or maybe because my bones are brussels sprout stalks of tumors these days. I always wondered if that crack allowed a certain malignancy to slip in.

When we finally arrived, the path to my mother's dogtrot was choked with sumac and briar, but I recognized the rock formation that looked like a calf bending to drink. You complained about having to carry your suitcase up the steep hill—why did we have to park so far away, you grumbled, and I'm tired, I didn't get any sleep. Jasper said nothing but walked close beside me. My mother's yard was barely distinguishable from the path, all blown soldier weed and sorrel with alopecia of anthill, but the house was still standing, listing and reproachful like it had been waiting for me all these years, resigned to the fact I'd never come.

The spare key was still hidden on top of the windowsill and I threw open the door to the front parlor to reveal a study in animal entropy: muddy footprints of vermin across downed drapes, spilled candle ends, cushions dragged into the beginning of some inhuman pattern. One by one we walked through the rooms, finding in each traces of interrupted industry, whether it was the half-spun spiderwebs at the ceiling corners or the red-checkered cookbook you found under the kitchen table, abandoned, on its way to who-knows-what nest when its weight overwhelmed its worth. You reached for the light switch but there was no electricity. The bent lead pipe still channeled water into the sink and with no faucet to turn it off, stars of green moss had filled the basin. In the pantry, we found a black raisin carpet of droppings, the flour bin knocked over, and the cursive mandala of trails of tails, years' worth of petty crime.

We can't stay here, kids, I said, or I should have said. It's too far gone.

With a little work, Jasper answered, we can bring it back.

You, Wallis, were your mother's child. You knew this place was unreclaimable, but you fell to work anyway. I handed you a bucket and a dry-rotted mop and you stepped across the breezeway to the bedroom. Inside I could see it was as it had always been. My mother's waist-high chestnut dresser stood against the interior wall, pegs along the exterior, and the iron bedstead, where I'd recuperated all those years ago, below the transom window. I thought of your girlhood and how, when you had a little flu, you would convalesce in your pink shag-carpeted, poster-hung bedroom. You'd been brought up with so much clutter and diffusion. Safer, if one dreams of movie stars, to hang their faces on a wall than to carry all your yearning on the inside, as we did. And yet there was something so spare and elemental about this room in which my mother and I had slept, as if it had been scoured with stone. I could breathe here. Why had I waited so long, I wondered, to return?

Jasper was shaking a rusted metal can of Bon Ami into the sink. He had taken off his shirt and his back ran with sweat as he scrubbed the green stains. You were more than halfway done, the floor in the bedroom where you mopped dark, like a phase of the moon. Standing in the breezeway, I was an eight-year-old boy again. Tucker Hayes and I were about to walk into the woods, leaving them all behind. He turned and asked, as if I might provide an answer, why God created a species that considered itself grown only when it left the place it most longed to be?

We had driven all night and I was home.

Wallis

Panther Gap

1980

The sun has set on a long day of work. Eddie will sleep on the sofa in the front parlor, Jasper will take the back porch in the open air. Wallis is given her grandmother's room and the bed. They dragged the mattress out back and beat it with branches until the dust flew out. Her father ripped a handful of spiky, purple pennyroyal from the overgrown garden and rubbed it front and back. This should kill any bedbugs, he said, but for God's sake if you get bit in the night, sleep on the floor. I don't want to hear it from your mother.

Wallis doesn't want to think about Mom. She tries not to picture Ann waking alone to a house full of dirty glasses and crumbs in the carpet. She is moving slowly, emptying ashtrays and half-full beer bottles into a bucket. By lunch she has discovered the scuffs in her grass and the snapped necks of peonies. Stooping in the late afternoon sun, she picks the cigarette butts from her mulch.

For dinner they ate what her father had shoveled into a cooler from the refrigerator before they left. They rolled slices of bologna, fished bread-and-butter pickles out of the jar, and dug their fingers into marshmallow spread. Eddie had brought two six-packs of beer from the party. Sitting on the back porch, he passed a can to Jasper without offering her one. Instead, he taught her how to dial up the wick of a lantern and light it. Now Wallis sits between them, sifting through an old dovetailed wooden box, Cora's first-aid kit, her father told her. Instead of Band-Aids and aspirin, it is full of dried burrs, spiny pods, and cork-stoppered glass bottles that conjure words like *tincture* and *unguent* and *salve*. By lantern light, Wallis carefully turns the brittle pages of Cora's herbal, trying to match the plants she finds inside. She had immediately searched out ginseng, but the entry showed only a simple line drawing of leaves and berries—nothing, from what she could see, worth riding all night for. Barely a day since Jasper taunted her with her grandmother and now they are in her house, lighting her lamps, reading her books, and watching her moon rise.

It wouldn't take much, Jasper is speaking excitedly with her dad about wiring the cabin for electricity. He sketches a diagram on the endpaper of the red-checkered cookbook, connecting the singular rooms to a fuse box outside the kitchen. Her father is skeptical but doesn't say no. *Tomorrow we'll drive into town for supplies,* Eddie says. How long will we be staying here? Wallis wonders. Why have we come?

Mom has cleaned the house and is sitting on the sofa in the dark, waiting for someone to call and tell her they're safe. Wallis wonders if she can consider herself kidnapped.

"I'm going to bed," she says, to test how far she's allowed to go. Her father looks up.

"Sleep tight."

She takes up her lamp, her box, and book, and walks the breezeway to her grandmother's bedroom. It is the only room in the house with relics of Cora's old age. A stained 1960's purple-and-green polyester quilt on the bed. Ben-Gay and Rose Milk next to the Bible on the dresser. A pair of translucent gray reading glasses, crusted with dust at the hinges. Her father had kept them moving all day; no sooner was Wallis finished mopping than he had them beneath the roof beam of the springhouse, lifting it back into the support grooves. They pulled down fallen curtains and washed them in the spring, spreading them on rocks to dry. They restacked firewood. Through it all, Wallis looked for signs of her grandmother's alleged crime, but she has found none. Now, with the privacy to explore the bedroom, she hopes for something more.

She sets the lamp on the dresser and tugs open the solid, heavy top drawer.

The first layer of her grandmother's wardrobe is polyester to match the bedspread. Zip-up-the-front paisley housedresses and elastic-waist slacks. Clothes she would see on any old lady comparing the prices of canned peas at the grocery store at home. This is not the grandmother Wallis wants to know, so she roots swiftly down to the garments below, older cotton and linen pieces that smell of cedar when she shakes them out. Even after they are washed, she suspects the discolored folds will show. She holds up a faded green dress that looks to be about her size, and a long white rag of nightgown. It is low at the collar with three bone buttons. The hem is stained gray from years of being dragged along the ground.

The woods are so dark. Where's Jason and his hockey mask?

Wallis freezes with the nightgown clutched to her chest. Jasper's voice is so loud and close, it could be in the room with her. They are talking on the back porch; she can hear them through the open window above the bed. She climbs up onto the mattress and peers out. Eddie is pointing to a white dot that smoothly transverses the sky. Is it ours or the Russians'? She no longer mistakes satellites for falling stars.

That's the problem with horror today, he says. *It's all anxiety and faceless slaughter. When I began, at least we knew the enemy.*

I'm sorry I told her, Jasper is saying. *You trusted me.*

It's not your fault, Eddie answers. *It was a long time ago.*

Wallis turns from the window and pulls off her sticky T-shirt. She drops the nightgown, soft and smelling of the woods, over her head. She thinks about her spell and the kiss, and glancing at the herbal book she dropped on the bed, Wallis wonders what sort of magic she can make with the tools of the larger forest.

Cora stored her linen in the second drawer. Wallis yanks away the garish bedspread and remakes the bed with a patched sheet and an unremarkable quilt. It's not like the ones she sometimes sees hanging in her friends' mothers' dens next to their macramé. This quilt has a drab gray stripe with random squares of color, but it fits her mood. If Mom were here, she'd tell Wallis to be respectful of other people's things, but Mom is not here and Cora is dead and these are Wallis's things now as the last living female Alley. She wonders if there is jewelry—a pocket watch or a ring? Her other grandmother died when her mother was only a teenager, but she left a strand of pearls in the event of a future granddaughter, which Mom has promised her when she's sixteen.

The bottom drawer is the deepest and heaviest yet. Wood scrapes against wood and she thinks—family silver. She drags forward a box about the size of a portable sewing machine. It's no jewelry box, she sees immediately, placing it on the newly made bed. Her fingers hover over its brass latches before she flips them up and lifts away the top.

She touches the burnished wood crank, the brass plate that reads Pathé. The film is still thread on its iron reel, unmarked, but what else could it be? She thinks immediately to call her father—*Your movie. It's not lost!*—but she stops. He and Jasper are walking the perimeter of the house and Jasper is explaining how the circuit would flow. They have just arrived and already the men want to change everything.

I want to show you something, she can hear herself say.

Wallis replaces the lid and returns the projector to the back of the bottom drawer. She fits the ugly bedspread around it and pushes the drawer closed. She has, at last, something he desires. Their footsteps are on the breezeway now, then someone knocks at her door.

"Sweet dreams," her father says.

It is difficult for her to answer. She has the tingling aftershock in her chest of having touched an ungrounded wire, feeling the danger only after she's let go.

"Sweet dreams," she replies.

The sheet is bunched under Jasper's cheek and twisted between his legs; his mouth hangs open against the arm he's used as a pillow. He's still asleep, drugged by the heat of the morning. Overnight a smudge has risen above his upper lip, a rustier red than his orange hair, and stubble creeps along his jaw toward his ears. Two days ago, Wallis thinks, we were enemies, but no more. We have kissed each other and now we are in love. I must be kinder to this face, she thinks, stepping over him to join her father in the kitchen.

Eddie has lit the potbellied stove and put a pan of water on to boil for coffee. He sits at the long, torn-oilcloth-covered table in his cut-off shorts and white T-shirt, his bare feet hooked in the chair rung. Before him is a growing list of provisions he wants to buy and things he's identified as in need of repair. He needs to buy shingles for the roof and a nail gun. Charcoal and potatoes and kerosene and paint. Up here, in this place, it is easy for Wallis to see her father as a capable man, cooking and cleaning and planning repairs, not needing to talk much about it. Without Mom, he seems younger and older at once.

"You shouldn't put ground beef next to caulk," she says, reading his list over his shoulder. "They don't go together."

"It's a list, not a grocery bag," Eddie replies. "Words will not contaminate each other."

Wallis spoons a mound of coffee crystals into a mug and adds water from the pan on the stove.

"You didn't pack the creamer?" she asks.

"It builds character to take it black," Eddie says, looking up. "What are you wearing?"

He is seeing her for the first time and is not pleased. Wallis has buttoned herself into the faded green dress and rolled up the sleeves. The hem is frayed and it has been patched in several places, but it fits as if it had been made for her.

"I found it in your mother's dresser," she says, "along with some other things. Can I have it?"

"You look like a bag lady," he says.

"Are you planning to wear it?" Wallis asks.

"It's not my color," Eddie answers.

"Good. Then it's mine."

She'd like to take her coffee out to the front porch where she can watch the mist rising from the hollow, but she doesn't want Jasper sleeping at her feet like a hound. Instead, she paces the room, reading the yellowed and peeling kitchen walls. Dunkirk Evacuated. Verdun Falls. Churchill to Commons: Prepare for Hard and Heavy Tidings.

"Why are all these newspapers pasted up?" she asks.

"Poor people used them to keep the drafts out," he says. "We were a little short on interior decorators up here."

Under the window near the sink, Queen Wilhelmina has fled to England. In the corner by the door, the Blitz has begun. What Wallis knows of World War II is mostly D-day and the Holocaust, but there is no mention of the Jews on these walls. "In this new system of force," she reads aloud from a longer column, "the mastery of the machine is not in the hands of mankind. It is in the control of infinitely small groups of individuals who rule without a single one of the democratic sanctions that we have known. The machine in hands of irresponsible conquerors becomes the master; mankind is not only the servant; it is the victim, too."

Eddie rises and reads over her shoulder.

"That's from Roosevelt's 'Stab in the Back' speech," he says. "Delivered right after Mussolini entered the war. Breaking news, circa 1940."

"Life must have sucked growing up without TV."

"Back then people could wait a few days to learn about all the things they couldn't control," Eddie answers, returning to the table and his lists. "Nowadays we're much more impatient for our impotence."

Wallis joins her father at the table. The checkered tablecloth has black burn holes from dropped matches. She can see down through the furry scorches to the wood below.

"Why haven't we ever come here?" she asks.

"There's been nothing to bring us," her father replies.

"Meeting my grandmother?"

"She died before you were born, while your mother was pregnant with you, actually."

Wallis takes a long sip of coffee, watching her father over the rim of the cup.

"Why won't you talk about your mother? Are you ashamed of her?"

"Why would I be ashamed?" he asks, surprised.

"Tell me something about her then."

Eddie sips his own coffee and considers.

"She believed in telling ghost stories at bedtime," he says at last. "I never knew until I met your mother that parents were supposed to comfort their children to sleep. I thought they were supposed to scare them into staying in bed."

"That's not what I mean," says Wallis. "Tell me real things."

"That's not real? That's the realest thing I can think of."

"I mean like—was she pretty?"

"Beautiful. I thought so, at least."

"Like Mom?"

"Nothing like your mother. More like you."

Wallis feels herself expanding under the comparison.

"Did she have enemies?"

"That's a strange thing to ask," Eddie says. "Why would she have enemies?"

"I don't know," Wallis replies. "Did she?"

"Quite a few. If you don't die with at least a handful of people hating you, you probably haven't lived a very honest life."

"Do you have a handful?" she counters.

"Nowhere close. But then again, I'm not dead yet."

Wallis looks around the papered room with its sieges and expired horoscopes. The water running in the sink sounds like a fountain into which she could toss coins. Mom never lets her make wishes at the fountain at the mall. It's a waste of pennies, she says.

"Let's leave this place exactly as it is," she says. "Don't change anything."

"You like it here?" Eddie asks.

"I love it."

"What do you love?" Jasper asks. He has come in behind her father and stretches, half-naked, in the doorway, lifting his ropey arms over his head to show his muscles and unmucked stall of armpit hair. Then he is beside her at the sink, shoveling Tang into a mug and running it under the open spigot.

"This house," she says, coloring.

"I had a dream about this house," he says, "but it wasn't this house. It was made of candy and we ate the whole thing."

"That's a nice dream," says Eddie.

"Was there a wicked witch to shove in the oven?" she asks.

"No, you weren't there," Jasper says flatly. He turns his attention to Eddie. "So, what's the plan for today?"

Wallis pushes her chair back and walks to the stove for more coffee. She doesn't want to look at either of them. Her father is watching her, even as he talks to Jasper.

"There are a few loose stones in the chimney, and the roof over the porch really needs to be patched," he answers.

"What about the wiring?"

"I'm having second thoughts," Eddie replies, glancing at Wallis. "I think we should get a real electrician."

"You don't trust me?" Jasper asks.

"It's not that," Eddie says swiftly. "I don't want you to fry yourself."

"I know what I'm doing," Jasper says.

"I know you do. It's just not worth dying over."

"Which means you don't think I can do it."

"I like this place just the way it is," Wallis turns to say. "I don't want the two of you to ruin it."

Eddie gathers his list. "Both of you—let me think about it. Right now I'm headed to town for supplies. I must fetch my daughter some cream for her coffee."

"Let me get my shoes," Jasper says.

"We worked all day yesterday," says Wallis. "Can't we go exploring?"

Eddie looks between them—Wallis with her coffee, Jasper with his Tang—each of them with false smiles at the corners of their mouths—brown and orange—still kids, so messy. He reaches out and wipes Wallis's mouth with the edge of his T-shirt like he used to do when she was a careless toddler. And because he doesn't want the foster boy to feel left out, with a melodramatic sigh, he reaches out and wipes Jasper's, too.

"Stay here," he says to Jasper. "You and Wallis start on the barn. Later, we'll figure out how to electrify this old place. We'll need heat if we're coming up this winter."

Wallis glances at Jasper, her soon-to-be brother. Jesus Christ, she thinks. *We.* They really plan to keep him.

None of the dozen keys on the old ring Wallis found fit the padlock to the barn door. She's tried each one, twice, while he's stood beside her, waiting. It's not her fault the lock won't open but after the third go-round, he grabs the ring from her and begins trying them all again himself. He is systematic, going around the ring, inserting and jiggling until all have been tested.

"So where did you learn about wiring?" she asks, needing to break the silence. Kissing him is beginning to feel like having kissed a mirror in a darkened room, the way girls do as practice for a real boy.

"At Eastlake," he says, naming the high school across town from hers.

"Are you going back there in the fall?"

"There's nobody to make me."

"School is important," she says. "I would go even if nobody made me."

"No, you wouldn't," Jasper says. "You just say that because you've been told to."

He tries a key that goes in easily, the same one she thought would work. He turns it so hard it starts to bend, but the lock doesn't budge. He moves on to the next.

"Don't you have any friends there?" she asks.

"Not really."

"Why not?"

"People around me die, Wallis," he says in frustration. "Kids don't really like to hang out with that."

"It's not like it's your fault," she says, but wonders if she believes that, if she would have chosen to hang out with him had he not shown up in her house.

"People don't know what to say to you. They look at you like a crack, you know, like you're this big hole that's opened up," he says, tossing the useless keys to the ground. By his foot is a broken piece of millstone, and he takes it up.

"Sometimes it feels like I'm living in some cartoon where all the carpets and drapes and floor lamps get sucked down and I'm Wile E. Coyote or some such fuck, hanging on to the mantel for dear life. It feels like everything, the whole world, has rushed in and keeps piling up, pressing down, tighter and tighter till—BAM—and Jesus it feels so good to just let go."

He brings the rock down hard on the old padlock and it goes flying across the yard. With both hands he pulls back on the heavy barn door, flooding the threshing floor with sun. Their shadows fall across it long and tall.

The barn is built of warped chestnut plank like the house, with a loft and a peaked roof that slopes away on either side like the top half of a drawn star. To the right of the double doors are the stalls for livestock. Eddie said his mother had kept a cow, but once there must have been a horse, too, for she finds, in a jumbled heap of farm equipment, an old leather saddle and a pair of stirrups. Metal milk cans lie on their sides and a three-legged stool is woven into the tines of a pitchfork. Above the corncrib hangs a sheaf of tobacco leaves, half-eaten by weevils. Wallis opens the lid of the corncrib to find hinges and oily car parts scavenged over the years. Crammed in around it all and drifting from the loft above is hay seasoned by decades of rain and snow that has worked through the gaps, mildewed and packed down with age. A ladder leads to the loft, and from it dangles a long winch rope tied off with a baling hook.

"I'll take this side," Jasper says. "You take that one."

He tugs the pitchfork from the pile and sets about clearing the floor of hay. He pitches it into a big stack that he'll then pitch out the sliding side door and into the woods behind. He hates being left behind and he works quickly and angrily to let her know, as if he can make time speed up and Eddie return with each ferocious thrust of the fork. He strips off his shirt to work, as he did yesterday, and she sees his back splotchily sunburned, threads of hay settle in his hair and cling to the nape of his neck.

Wallis falls to work sorting and categorizing the equipment and the bin. The heavy iron gears and pulleys are useless now, worth nothing more than scrap. Still, she loves the weight of them, each with its embossed patent number and named manufacturer. Reaching down into the corncrib, she comes up with a coffee tin of rusted, square-headed nails like the one she took from her father's casket. She pours them onto her flat palm, measuring them like money. Whose soul might a girl purchase with a handful of coffin nails? She retrieves the millstone Jasper dropped outside the door and uses it to hammer a long row of them into a beam along the wall. From the nails she hangs the hoe and shovel and saw she finds. And the long mowing scythe with its splintery handle and dulled sickle. Is this how her grandmother did it? With a quick swipe to the neck?

"I don't get what's wrong with Eddie," Jasper says as if talking to himself. "He's rolling over like a dog. Like twenty years is nothing."

It takes her a moment to realize he's talking about Captain Casket and the television station.

"He's been doing Captain Casket a long time," Wallis answers. "Maybe he's bored."

"All those letters he's gotten over all the years. All the people who have showed up wherever he goes. It's like they meant nothing to him."

Jasper has gathered a high pile of hay and climbs the ladder to the loft to pitch more down on top. He lifts the fork and tosses; pitch-toss, pitch-toss, as rhythmic as a spinning wheel. The air is golden with chaff and straw, she can think only of Rumpelstiltskin producing skein upon skein while the miller's daughter sleeps sound, trusting it will all come out right in the end. Jasper's pitching becomes the music of square-headed nails rolling against tin, of milk pails tipped and spilled, the old wagon wheel with its broken spokes, the memory of his mouth on hers in the conductor's ball of light. The sun fills the loft window and she squints to see him above her.

"You like to think some things are going to last, you know," he says, staring down at his growing pile. "Like you're not the only asshole who cares."

"I care," Wallis says.

"About what?" Jasper counters. "Name one thing in this world that really matters to you."

He challenges her from high above and she has a light-headed, queasy feeling of needing to make the right answer. *You,* she could say, *you matter,* but she would be saying it because it came to her like a line in a movie.

"Have you ever had a girlfriend?" she asks instead. He stutters, the fork poised midair, before finding his rhythm again.

"No," he says. "I don't like to be tied down."

"You planning on going somewhere?"

"Not yet."

"But one day?" she asks. "Do you see yourself going somewhere with someone one day?"

"I don't think about it."

"Really?" she asks.

"Really," he answers.

"Do you think about what it would mean to be in love with someone in your own house, who is supposed to be part of your family? To see them every day and not be able to touch them?"

"Shut up, Wallis," he says.

"That would be so romantic and tragic, I think."

Jasper tosses a hank of hay at her feet, making her take a step back. He hurls another one, more directly at her, hitting her in the chest.

"Stop it," she says, "you're getting my dress dirty."

"Why are you wearing that ugly thing anyway?" he practically shouts. He is pitching more hay, fast and furious now, hailing it down on her until she can't breathe, until her eyes and mouth are full of hay, until she drops to the ground with her arms over her head to protect herself, and then he flings the pitchfork itself, like a javelin. It strikes the threshing floor and skids to a stop.

"You could have killed me!" she shouts.

"Why do you have to ruin everything?" Jasper demands.

"Why can't you be like normal boys?" she hurls back. "Most boys would kill to be alone with a girl in a barn."

He grabs the rope beside him, fitting his sneaker into the hook of the winch, and swings wide over the edge of the loft. He dangles for a long moment and then he drops into a crouch, scattering most of what he raked. She is frozen, not sure if she should run, and then it's too late, his hand shoots out and grabs her ankle, knocking her to the ground and pulling her to him. He is on top of her, pinning her by the shoulders, his knee pressed into her skirt between her legs. He puts his mouth to the bodice of her grandmother's dress and sucks hard at her breast through the fabric. She feels a string plucked deep within her, almost painful, it is so intense.

"What is it," he asks, "that you like about me?"

His eyes are over her eyes, his nose, lips above hers. Why would he ask her such a thing? How is she supposed to answer a question like that?

"I want to fix all the things that are wrong," she whispers.

"Do you think I want to be the kind of person who needs to be fixed? Why would I like a girl who loves the parts of me I hate most?"

he asks, shoving her harder into the straw. Getting up, he hunts for the pitchfork, needing to clean up the mess he's made.

"I'm sorry," she says. "Maybe that's not what I meant. I meant I want to understand."

He is ignoring her now and she knows she can't call him back. Nothing she says comes out right. Maybe her parents won't keep him after all and then, if he was out of the house, they could just be boyfriend and girlfriend. Because how could she stand to live with him, watching him date other girls, listening to him call them on the telephone, their names in his mouth like food at the dinner table? She pushes herself up from the hay and returns to her work, hanging the stirrups and the bridle from the row of coffin nails. Tears roll down her cheeks and she swipes them away angrily.

Jasper reforks his yellow mountain, the top sliding to the bottom, resisting height. He keeps his back to her.

"Let's just forget it," he says as more hay comes slipping down. "Okay?"

She is silent, she doesn't trust her own voice.

"Okay?" he asks again. She nods. It's the best she can do.

"They didn't have any six-gauge wire," Eddie says. "I had to get number ten."

The hearse's back doors stand open and half a hardware store rests where the coffin should be. Buckets of paint and pallets of shingles. Staple gun, hammer, nails, fuse boxes. An iron hibachi with a bag of charcoal. Brown paper sacks of groceries. Take those first, Eddie tells them. We don't want the meat to spoil.

Jasper climbs into the back.

"Where's the white for the neutral?" he asks, looking at the five heavy spools of black cable Eddie purchased.

"They didn't have any white," Eddie answers. "Only black."

"I'll try not to electrocute myself."

Wallis has never heard Jasper be short with her father. Eddie, too, is surprised. He thought Jasper would be pleased he'd given in, but he's made a mistake. He has bought way too much of the wrong thing.

Wallis reaches in for a bag of groceries and another of charcoal. Jasper tugs out one of the ungainly spools and hefts it onto his shoulder. Eddie trails behind with another bag of tools and the heavy, squat grill. She hasn't spoken to Jasper since they finished cleaning the barn and sat waiting for her father on the porch. Now it is after four and her throat feels tight and her voice quilted to the roof of her mouth.

"Did you make yourselves some lunch?" her father asks.

"We were waiting for you," Jasper says.

"If you get hungry, you should eat," Eddie replies. "It's your house, too."

"Number ten won't carry as much current," Jasper says. "The smaller the gauge, the more it can handle. If they didn't have six, you should have gotten four."

"If it won't work, we'll take it back."

"I can get it to work," Jasper says. "It's just not right."

There is silence and Wallis steels herself for the retort and re-crimination. She finds herself thinking of Mom for the first time since yesterday and wonders if her father called while he was in town.

"If anyone can make it work, it's you," Eddie says kindly. "Around the station you can always make something out of nothing."

"It's not so difficult when nothing's all you've got."

Her father matches his steps to the boy's by way of apology. Halfway up, Jasper's body begins to relax, and by the time they've reached the cabin, she can tell Eddie is forgiven. She doesn't understand how silence between some people can be so comforting when, between others, it falls so heavy. She doesn't understand what she's doing wrong.

Ducking beneath the low doorway, Wallis takes the groceries to the springhouse behind the barn. Yesterday she had swept it clean but more debris from the roof has fallen and the dirt is even dirtier. She sets the meat and milk next to the beer in the shallow pool of black water where flakes of chipped whitewash float like melting snow. Outside, her dad and Jasper are talking. They sound more natural when she is around, they use her, she knows, as a conduit to each other, like a spring that goes underground to feed two bodies of shallow water. How long would she have to stay kneeling in this building before they lapsed into silence? She looks down to where she swims in the dark, Wallis Alley, a girl who has been kissed and now something more, though she doesn't know if that something more has added to or subtracted from what came before. Wallis touches her troubled reflection, puts her hand in the cold water to erase herself, wets the back of her neck, rises, walks outside.

"You can't let those bastards push you out," Jasper says. "You have to stay and fight."

"Fight what?" Eddie asks. "Late night belongs to the news now."

"She's right," Jasper mutters, glancing back at Wallis. "You are more comfortable in a suit."

Wallis looks to her father.

"I was picking tobacco and hunting roots when I was your age," Eddie says, trying to make light of Jasper's insult. "There are worse things than wearing a suit."

"I'd rather be hunting roots," Jasper says.

"Jasper says he's not going back to school," Wallis announces.

"Taking a year off is fine, after everything you've been through," Eddie says, serious now. "But you need to finish your education."

"Stop talking like a dad," Jasper retorts. "You're not my type."

They've reached the hearse once more, and Eddie slides out a ply-wood pallet of plastic-wrapped asphalt shingles. They are too heavy for one person and Jasper steps up to lift the other side. Wallis grabs two gallons of paint like milk pails. Back up the steep path, sometimes Jasper walks backward, sometimes her father, sometimes there is room for them to walk side-by-side. They are going so slow, inching along the drop-off by the overgrown tobacco field. Wallis wants to pass but there is no room on the narrow trail.

"If you changed jobs, would we have to move?" Wallis asks.

"I don't know, we might," Eddie answers, grunting under the weight.

"Would Jasper come with us?"

Jasper looks straight ahead, his jaw set, not wanting to hear his fate discussed. Her father is uncertain what he is supposed to say. Does Jasper belong to them now?

"I suppose that would be up to Jasper," he says at last.

What's the return policy on you, she wonders, and where would you go if we decided not to keep you? She swings the paint, carefree. Yes, she thinks, we are all at someone's mercy, and she was here first.

The thought gives a little extra momentum to her swing, she doesn't have to trail behind them, she knows the way up the path to her own grandmother's house.

"Watch—" cries Eddie, losing his grip as Jasper drops away. The single misplaced step, then the slide and fall, the boy's strangled cry swallowed by a crash of the shingles torn from Eddie's hands, hitting the ground and avalanching over the edge after him. Jasper's sneaker takes out stone and vine, a pine sapling in a ball of root. He is scrambling, trying to slow his slide, but gravity takes over and his body twists beneath him, flipping him headfirst. The pallet has torn apart and gray shingles slither past in an angular rivulet. Eddie is behind him, leaping down the gully and stopping just short of where Jasper comes to rest.

"Are you okay?" he shouts. It has all taken place in an instant, though the fall is still crashing in echo. Wallis stands clutching her paint cans. The thin metal hoops cut grooves in her palms.

"I'm okay," Jasper says, fighting tears.

"Don't move," Eddie says.

Instead of extending his hand to the boy, he runs diagonally up the drop, never letting the angle get steep enough to pull him back down. Wallis paces on the path above him, not knowing if she should stay and stand guard over Jasper. Even without the aid of her grandmother's herbal, she recognizes the twining pale-green leaves of three that fill the pit into which he's fallen. Poison ivy coiled around his wrists and ankles.

Her father comes up a few yards ahead and twists an armload of branches from a flowering orange bush. She has seen it growing all along the road and up the mountain path, its nodding orange slippers peeking out against the laurel and honeysuckle. She runs back to help Jasper but her father shouts again.

"Don't touch him. You'll get it all over yourself. Wait for me."

He drags a fallen branch behind him and returns along the same path as before. "Here, use this," he says, extending it to him.

Jasper does as he is told, grabbing hold and using the branch as a guide rail to come even with Eddie. Her father flings the branch away, grabbing Jasper tightly by the wrist to pull him the rest of the way up, scrubbing his arm violently with the orange blossoms. He pulls the boy's shirt over his head and tosses it aside, continuing to scrub his naked back and freckled chest, his neck, underarms, down into the waistband of his pants. Jasper pulls away like a startled animal but Eddie yanks him back fiercely, working fast to spread the sap of the plant across his infected skin before the blisters rise.

"Get some more of that jewelweed," he orders Wallis. "The bush with the little orange flowers."

She drops the paint and races back to the flowering shrub, breathing in the slightly sharp perfume of its break. She's not sure what part holds the medicine, so she tears roughly at whatever she can reach, spilling blossoms through her fingertips. Sharp, nutty seedpods skip away like crickets. Her hands are full and sticky when she turns to see her father helping Jasper the rest of the way up the hill, rubbing the boy's other arm as he pulls. He is stained saffron with crushed petals and scraped raw by the twigs. Her father takes the fresh green leaves from her and crushes them between his palms.

"Close your eyes," he says, working quickly to cover the boy's face with a sticky mask. "My mother always said God planted jewelweed close by poison ivy to act as its antidote. In my experience, though, you'll find acres of poison ivy growing without any jewelweed, but you'll never find jewelweed without poison ivy lurking nearby."

Jasper stands stunned and blind on the path, letting Eddie grind the leaves through his hair and into his scalp. Wallis looks down at the paint cans, the splintered pallet and few remaining shingles. She can still feel his mouth on her breast and has the uncomfortable feeling of wanting to laugh. Did she mean to cause this? Eddie nods to her again and she goes back to the bush for more, taking her time now, relieved to leave the emergency behind. This time she picks more carefully, breaking the stems off at the base as she would for a flower arrangement. How does nature arrange these pairings? she wonders. She turns back to where her father is concentrating as if sanding down an ornate piece of furniture, rubbing behind the boy's ear, inside its whorl, down the grain of his throat. Eddie has moved down to Jasper's pale legs when he looks up to find her waiting. His leaf-filled hands pause, gripped around the boy's thigh. Slowly, Jasper opens his eyes. Wallis stands hardly daring to breathe, clutching her astringent bouquet.

Eddie rises and takes it from her, passing it to Jasper so that he might finish rubbing himself down.

"I think we caught it in time," he says gruffly.

Eddie rubs his hands roughly on his own cutoffs and turns back to the hearse for the next load. Wallis watches him go, then slides carefully down the hill to see how many shingles might be salvaged.

"Your mother is going to haunt you," Wallis says to her father.

"It's not her house anymore," answers Eddie. He is drinking a beer while he washes his paint roller in the sink. It has taken them two coats to cover the kitchen newsprint and now Wallis finds the room falsely bright and cheerful. Her naked forearms are staticky with dried white paint. She can read herself like braille.

"If she wanted electricity she would have gotten it," Wallis says.

"Rural Electrification Administration came through after the war, wiring up all our neighbors," Eddie tells her, squeezing out his roller. "She said they only came to the country when they ran out of city people to sell appliances to. Power wasn't about us, if it suited their purposes, they'd keep us in the dark."

"Who is *they*?" Wallis asks.

"Factory owners, the government, the capitalists, the communists. Anyone with more power than her, which was pretty much everyone."

"She sounds paranoid," Wallis says.

"Paranoid was the least of it."

Eddie washes his hands and dries them, watching Jasper from the window. In the hours before it got too dark to see, Jasper set his drill bit against the surface of the wood and leaned his weight against it, cranking the old hand drill, opening a hole beneath the windowsill of her bedroom. The wood shavings rose around the bit like sparks from a Roman candle, falling in a soft pile on the porch boards below. He had drilled holes in all the other windows as well, feeding through the thick black cable, running it along the baseboard and up to the ceiling, where he screwed in a raw fixture with a hanging chain. Now he has wired everything but the kitchen where Wallis and Eddie were paint-ing, and the circuit snakes along the baseboards, across the breezeway to a new fuse box. It is ugly and exposed and, Wallis thinks, someone is sure to trip over it.

She tosses her roller into the sink, turning the water to milk, and steps out onto the porch. The wind picked up with the setting sun and tosses the treetops in the hollow. High purple thunderheads muster over the next mountain. Wallis hopes the rain holds off. Eddie told them tonight was the first night of the Perseid meteor shower. When he was a boy he would sometimes count twenty falling stars an hour. Earlier, Jasper rinsed off in the spring and changed into yet another baseball shirt and pair of cutoff shorts. He is a boy, she thinks, of very few options. He is casual here in a way he never is back home, leaving his dirty shorts in a ball by the porch stairs. Wallis steps over them so as not to infect herself.

"How is this supposed to work?" she calls to him. "It isn't connected to anything."

"There's enough cable to run it down to the road pole at the bottom of the path," he says. "I can hack into the transformer."

"You are not going to hack into a road pole," Eddie says, joining them outside. "When we get home, we'll call the power company and schedule a hookup."

"Why would you pay for it, when I can get it for you for free?" Jasper asks.

"Because I don't have insurance on this place," Eddie answers. "Or on you."

"You know the problem with you, Eddie," Jasper says, shoveling dirt over the cable as he unspools it across the ground. "You'll feel a girl up but you're too scared to fuck her."

"Excuse me," Wallis says, offended.

Her father takes a lazy sip of his beer, not protesting. "Dad?" she insists.

"What can I say?" Eddie answers, laughing. "He's right."

Eddie sets his beer on the railing and busies himself pouring charcoal into the hibachi. Dousing it with lighter fluid, he strikes a match and stands back as the grill explodes in flame.

"What will it be, kids?" he queries. "Shall we feast upon the rare burger? Or the well-done?"

"Raw," says Wallis.

"That's my girl," he says. "How about you, Jasper?"

"I'm not hungry," Jasper says, unwinding more of the spool and packing the dirt around it.

"Settle down, son," Eddie calls. "This doesn't all have to be done tonight."

"Settle down, settle down," Jasper mutters. "I'm not you, Eddie, I don't like to settle."

"Whoa," Eddie says, not ready to be bullied out of his good mood. "Where's this coming from?"

"Tonight is Saturday," Jasper says, not looking at him. "Who's doing your show while you're hiding out up here?"

"They'll put on a rerun, I won't even be missed," Eddie says, more seriously. "Except by you, my loyal henchman. And you're here."

It should be funny, Eddie meant it as a joke, but Jasper keeps digging, not looking at him.

"For now," he says.

Eddie claps his hands, for show, but also, it seems to Wallis, to keep from hitting something. Jasper's anger has them all on edge. "Come on, kids," he says. "If we're to look so funereal, we must at least stage a proper cremation."

He snatches up a stick and lifts the poison-ivy-contaminated shorts, pitching them onto the grill.

"Father, into Thy hands I commend my spirit," he intones, blasting the coals with another squeeze of lighter fluid by way of eulogy. The shorts go up in a sudden conflagration and a column of white smoke shoots up to the trees. Eddie watches it spiral overhead, fingering out to fog. Wallis worries the sparks will land on the roof and take the house along with it. At least he's gotten Jasper's attention.

"The other day, I saw a pattern on my weather radar that looked like thousands of tiny airplane contrails," Eddie says. "They call it *chaff*, and my Bible-quoting mother would have said that's what must be separated from the wheat, like the sheep from the goats. But this chaff was tiny little strips of aluminum-coated paper the military drops from its fighter jets to confuse an enemy's radar, so they can't know what to shoot at. They were running a training mission and the station's Doppler picked it up."

"The Germans used it during World War Two," Jasper says.

Wallis watches the fabric burn. The squat blue flames lick into the back pocket of the jean shorts where the studs glow red. The three of them stand over the grill as if they were roasting marshmallows.

"The allies used it first," says Eddie. "During Operation Gomorrah over Hamburg. And the poor bombed-out Hamburgers wandering through the rubble stared up and wondered at all those nothing little strips falling from the sky. Such an effectively simple distraction. A cardboard box slit open and tossed from the ass of a plane."

"My dad was 'Stand or Die' in Pusan," Jasper says. "He had stories like that."

"Mine didn't make it home from Normandy," Eddie says. "I'm glad I never had a son. I wouldn't know how to lie him off to war."

Jasper's shorts have burned through and the brass button at the fly drops into the coals, sending up a veil of sparks.

"Make a wish," Eddie says, passing Jasper the beer to finish.

"May you never have a son," Jasper says, finishing it.

Wallis has watched their exchange silently. Now she rises.

"I'm not hungry, either," she announces. "I'm taking my shower and tomorrow we're going on our ginseng hunt."

"Yes," says Eddie, nodding absently. "Tomorrow it's your turn."

She leaves them to their fire and their beer and walks across the yard, her body prickly as if the smoke had transferred the itch onto her skin. She heads toward the sound of the spring, needing to wash off this feeling that has resettled over her. Overhead, behind the smoke, clouds move across the moon. One by one the stars are extinguished.

Wallis walks away from them, into deeper darkness, before lifting off the green dress and reaching behind her back to unhook the bra she is still getting used to wearing. Stepping out of her underwear, she strides through the night free and invisible even to herself. Her foolish father, thinking he can make things right by striking a match. As if combustion led to anything but ashes. She reaches her arms in front of her, groping for the wall of rock, touching the water that foams between stones. She spreads the dress in the shape of herself over the rocks and steps under the cascade. The air is warm and the water cold, and she tilts her head back, letting the spring water smooth her hair from her face, which she lifts to catch the rain that has just begun to fall, neither one temperature nor the other, water in and around her. She feels for the bar of soap Jasper took out there earlier for his own shower, and lathers her hair, squeaking the strands between her fingers before the spring washes the suds away.

Without their audience, Jasper and Eddie have drifted apart. A lantern moves across the yard and then the belly of the barn is filled with yellow light. Back at the house, another lamp is lit in the kitchen, then more white steam on the porch, her father dousing the coals with water. Wallis is the absence of light, alone outside, naked where no one can see, and the falling rain divides them all. She washes away the bits of straw that have stuck to her breasts. She stretches her neck and lets the water plant its kiss, then bends over so that it may play along her rounded spine. There is no measure of time here, no hot water to run out. No one waiting a turn. She could stand under this spring all night and into the next day and month and year and this water would not stop running until it had flushed away every atom of her, sending her as a freshet down the mountainside. She could join up with other washed-away girls in the dark, making a larger black stream that fed into an invisible river that fed into an ocean that circumnavigated the world before evaporating and becoming the storm that starts it all, falling now, on the tiny house and her upturned face.

The rain falls harder, replacing the clean feeling with the clammy cold of falling leaves. Coming out here she hadn't thought how she might get back. She has no towel and so she wraps the wet dress around her body, covering most of herself.

The lantern is back, perched on the porch rail out of the rain; Jasper has brought from the barn a tall iron pipe and the millstone. As she passes, he lifts the rock and brings it down sharply on the flat edge of the pipe. It is sudden and violent and rings back over the hollow.

"What are you doing?" she whispers.

"Driving in the grounding rod," he says.

"In the rain?"

He answers with another blow and another. "The water softens up the earth."

There is no thunder, no flash of lightning, just an increasingly heavy downpour. He won't be electrocuted if that's what he's hoping for. She darts around him, leaving her wet footprints on the wood, and ducks inside her grandmother's bedroom where her father has left another lamp burning for her. She drops the wet dress to the floor, finds her brush on the dresser top, and tugs it through her matted hair. From books, she knows the games girls played on St. Agnes's Eve and Halloween, how to raise visions of their future husbands by sleeping with wedding cake under their pillows or combing their hair while looking over their shoulders into the mirror. She walks to the door, where a fragment of broken mirror hangs and, standing on tiptoe, she can just see her face as she pulls the brush through her hair, ten, twenty, thirty times. Her hair is drying, softening, her body, too, relaxing in the heat thrown off by the lantern. She draws the brush in time to his hammering outside her window, every blow another sweep from root to end. She watches herself in the flickering oil light until her large gray eyes cease to be her eyes, her lips curl slightly fuller and rounder. She holds her own gaze. Show me the future, she whispers to the face she has pinned there, herself but not herself, some fiction of herself that she can direct and release and let behave as it desires without being a part of her. It's a trick of the light, this shifting face. She sees herself young, older, very old, cycling in rapid succession. Wrinkled, prime, dewy soft. She blinks and as if he feels her, outside he pauses. Just a rest. As if listening for something. But there is only the sound of rain on the roof, water dripping down his hole, then he's back to driving his stake into the softened earth. She sets down her brush.

You don't know where you belong. Come out of the rain and sit with me. She moves to the bed and the box of Cora's roots next to the medicinal she's used to identify them. *Watch me brush my hair, watch me name these roots. Watch me.*

Wallis reaches for the peg with her grandmother's nightgown but decides to leave it hanging by its scruff tonight. She stretches long and lean. If Jasper could see her now in all her nakedness, he would be hers to command. She would shower him with seeds and petals and herbs to invite dreaming and she would tap him with her root wand and put him into a deep sleep. Then she could look at him and keep him forever without having to talk to him or fight. She could kiss him when she wanted and his lips would still be awake and warm. She could lie beside him and rest her cheek upon his smooth back and she could touch his torch of hair and not get burned. She could animate the parts that pleased her and keep napping the parts that did not.

Come lie on this bed and I'll show you a movie. You don't need Dad, I can show it to you. It can be only us, a boy and girl, with a movie and a bed. To the sound of falling rain. No one will even need to know. Just stop hammering.

She lies down in bed and curls up beside Cora's box of roots. There are many ways to call a person when words don't work and desire alone is not enough. Sometimes dreams are the only things to trust. The rain drumming on the old tin roof is deafening, yet even that can't drown out the methodical, maddening contact of stone on pipe. Lying still, she feels the dust invisibly suspended in this old room settling around her. She reaches for the lantern, brings it to her lips, and blows out the flame. The night breeze from the window instantly hardens a new skin in place. Rising and sleeping here, she thinks, she will begin to live in layers, with each night setting the last day.

He must be nearly finished, the blows fall faster and more furious. Something answers in her chest, a sharp pang that takes her breath away. Awkwardly in the dark, she fumbles for the cool mug of water that earlier she'd left on the bedside table. But the water is tepid from sitting out all day, the same temperature as her tongue, and going down it feels like she is swallowing a piece of herself.

They rise early in the morning to leave before the heat of the afternoon. It will be hard to spot, Eddie has warned her, the leaves will still be green and the berries barely ripe. We'll hunt the sang but we won't dig it. We'll come back in the fall when it's fully grown.

Her father remembers more than he thought; in the hours they've been walking, he has pointed out poisonous pokeweed and jack-in-the-pulpit; he's slit the throat of bloodroot, and pulled both blue cohosh and black cohosh—take some of that home for your mother, he told her. It's good for the Change.

"Every cliff and creek had a name and a story when I was growing up," he says. "I can remember the plants but I've forgotten the stories. You'd think it'd be the other way around."

"Every story I've ever heard about a cliff or a creek has an Indian maiden leaping or drowning," Wallis says.

"Another forest, another brokenhearted girl," he says.

Eddie lopes up the rudimentary path he refound, scanning the low growth between boulders and at the base of trees. Jasper straggles along behind, and Wallis brings up the rear in Cora's deep green dress. Eddie had presented her with his mother's ginseng hoe, a long-handled spade Wallis uses to help her up the slopes. More and more she is seeing the country boy in her father, this easy, barefoot way of walking, even in his penny loafers, as if his toes are digging into rock.

"Come look at this," Eddie says, kicking over a log spongy with bright orange mushrooms. "This is jack-o'-lantern."

He plucks a mushroom and makes a dark cavern with his palms, gesturing for Jasper to catch up. The boy sidles over and Eddie holds his hands to Jasper's eye.

"What am I looking for?" he asks.

"Stare at the gills underneath, let your eyes adjust."

Wallis pushes in. "Let me see," she says.

"Get your own," Jasper says. "There's no room."

Wallis bends and tugs off her own pumpkin-colored mushroom. In the shadow of her hands, its underbelly glows an almost imperceptible green.

"This is how my mother was beautiful," Eddie says, answering her earlier question. "You had to know what to look for."

Next to her Jasper shrugs and turns away, scouting the landscape, ready to move again. All morning her father has stopped to show them things and Jasper's impatience has restarted them. Eddie drops his mushroom and walks uphill to where a trickle of a spring bleeds from the rock. "Come wash your hands," he tells Wallis. "They're also poisonous."

It is noon, the day flayed out in either direction. Climbing up to join him at the spring, the heat is on her shoulders, washing down through the dark dress to where her legs might move free and cool beneath the skirt. Wallis never wears dresses at home and finds she loves carrying her own green shade. She pulls herself up the slope behind Eddie. Bald ravines fall away around her; somewhere in a farmer's field not far from here, Eddie told her, the headwaters of the Potomac River bubble up in a muddy ditch. They've come upon no rivers in their walk, only a few deep, girl-drowning creeks. Still, when she's quiet, she believes she can almost feel water moving beneath the stone.

"When I was about four years old, my mother carried me on her back all the way to Panther Gap," Eddie says. "The whole mountain was creamy white as if it had snowed. I can still make myself dizzy with the smell of all those chestnuts in bloom."

"What did they smell like?" Wallis asks, drying her hands on her skirt. Her father looks to Jasper.

"I'll tell you when you get to college," he says, scanning the horizon. "Look around. This used to be the chestnut graveyard."

Wallis stares out over the hemlock and deep basins of purple flowering laurel. She recognizes many of the trees from Cora's book but she sees nothing she can identify as chestnut.

"Loggers cleared out the carcasses during the war. Now all this has grown up in its place."

Jasper looks down over the running hollows that crisscross the ridge they climbed. A hawk catches an updraft through the lower branches, its glittering, inhuman eyes even with their own. It catches the current and funnels off, higher and higher, a blink, gone.

"I'm glad you made us get out here, Wallis," Eddie says. "Get a few houses huddled together and all our problems seem monumental. Come up here and you realize how inconsequential you really are."

"I feel invincible," Wallis says. "This high up."

"How does the eternal vastness strike you, Jasper?" Eddie asks.

"Like I don't want a tour guide to it," Jasper says.

Eddie nods and starts out again. "Keep your eyes down," he says. "This is where I used to find my best sang."

He steps down hard and breaks off a branch to use to prod the understory. They had been following what might have been a rudimentary path, but now Eddie veers off into denser growth. "Be careful," he says. "This is rattlesnake territory. They like to sun themselves on the flat rocks."

Her father walks ahead while they step cautiously behind. Wallis swings her hoe, trying not to look at Jasper. How can he act as if nothing happened? A kiss is supposed to be the beginning of something, but he is treating it like the end. She searches as if the thing that is missing between them could be found here on the ground. Real things, important things, can't be known by what isn't there. There is always farther to go and places you've yet to be.

"Are we ever going to talk about what's happening?" she asks.

"What do you mean?"

"I mean at the railroad tracks. The barn. This."

"What is *this*? This is you in a weird dress making me follow you into the woods."

Her father is far enough ahead not to hear them. She turns and touches his arm where a patch of pink rash has risen in the crease of his elbow. There were a few spots the jewelweed missed.

"Please, Jasper," she begs. "I don't want to fight anymore. I want us to be—you know. Nice to each other."

"I know what you want, Wallis," he says, angry now. "We live in the same house together. Where could anything possibly go between us? If people found out, I'd end up back on the street. I can't go back there. I'd die out there."

Jasper has been clearing his own way through the low trees and saplings, but now he pushes through a holly bush and lets the bough whip back behind him. Before she can react, its sharp leaves catch her just below the right eye in three razor-thin cuts.

"You did that on purpose," she cries.

"Don't crowd me," Jasper says. "I'm not going over the edge again."

Wallis stops as he walks ahead, catching up to her father. She touches her hand to her cheek, three drops of blood on her three fingers. Ahead is a sharp snagging dip of dead fire azalea choked with blackberry. Wallis plunges in, the brown blossoms rattling around her hips. To hell with them. When she was eight or nine years old, she had a recurring dream that snakes overran her bedroom floor; twining and restless, they trapped her between waking and sleep. Afraid to put foot to carpet, she felt safe only under the covers. Now she knows she will step on one and be bitten and die here alone in the forest without ever seeing her mother again. Wallis pulls and crushes, deadheading the azaleas as she walks, letting the dusty petals sift through her fingers. She half wishes she would find a snake just for the satisfaction of bringing the hoe down hard across its neck and watching its pieces slither away. The blackberry briars catch at her flesh and the hem of her dress but she reaches in anyway to take the warm, ripe fruit the birds missed. That kid paralysis, clutching the covers tight. How did all those snakes get into her bedroom in the first place?

Wallis jumps at the nearby crack of gunfire, feeling percussion inside her skull. Three, four loud retorts, then silence ringing off the rock. A dog bays, sharp as the shots, swallowing his last bark as if someone pulled up on his collar.

"It's hunting season already?" Jasper shouts. The three are spread out, barely in sight of each other. Her father answers.

"Try not to look like a deer."

Wallis has been scanning the ground but Jasper has been looking up and now he points to a ledge of green leaves overhead. She watches as Eddie makes up the distance between them, squinting, then nodding— yes, *yes*, that's it. She watches them, her throat tight. Jasper, on his side of the outcrop, finds his foothold, while Eddie, on the other side, does the same. He found it first. That boy in her house. She sees his face, lit with pleasure as she's rarely seen it. She turns away and leaves them up there, kneeling before their discovery, their fingers moving together in the leaf litter—she doesn't need to look to see it—counting the scars on the ginseng's neck, a notch for every year it pushed through hostile soil, nothing to show for the years in between. Her father is telling him not to pick it—it would be like shooting Bambi or tossing a fingerling fish into your bucket instead of throwing it back. No, her father is saying, plucking the red center cluster, staining his fingers. Take the berry like this, between your index and your thumb. Strip the pulp until you feel the hard seed inside. Work your finger in the soil, like this, and replant it deep, so you can come back after and have more root to harvest.

She stops her ears against them talking, marking their spot for later.

Up the slope, beneath the kaleidoscope of silver and olive pinion leaves, she is searching, but she has forgotten for what. She's lost the excitement of looking, left with only the dull fear of what she might find. Her red face holds the heat like the swollen berries held the sun. And then she sees it. The snake is coiled on the ground just in front of her and she freezes with a pang of primal fear. A hatchling, it must be, slinky and brown. No, she thinks. Something is not right. A wild rattler, even a baby, would have whipped away in terror by now. She inches closer, then kneels down, lifting the shoelace between her fingers, tugging it gently where it disappears into the leaves. Now she sees the metal eyelets, the hank of rotting leather. Yellow-green moss has preserved its shape and there is no mistaking what she'd flushed out. Not ginseng, nor a snake, but the remains of a grown man's shoe.

A second round of gunfire. Closer now. The hunting dog barks again. Why did she imagine they were all alone in these woods?

"*Wallis?*"

She starts at her father's voice, calling from far away. She rises, dangling the shoe from its string. She has walked farther than she thought, behind her is a high fence of trees.

"I've found something," she calls back.

"Where are you?" he shouts again. "Don't dig anything. Wait for me."

It's too late, she wants to say. She tugs the moss away and the tan leather underneath is cracked and dried like jerky. She turns it over, looking for a size, as if that will tell her what she needs to know about who wore it.

"Why did you run off like that?"

Jasper is behind him; now that he's had some success, he scans the ground like a bloodhound. He's not even paying attention to her. Wallis places the shoe in her father's hands.

"What's this?" Eddie asks.

"You tell me," she answers.

He turns it over, not answering, but she sees in his face that he recognizes it. "People dump all sorts of crap in these woods," he says.

"It's his, isn't it?" she asks.

"Wallis, stop playing around," Eddie says sternly. "Let's go."

"*Why does Jasper know things I don't know?*"

Eddie looks reproachfully at Jasper, who has stopped at the edge of the blackberry slope. Jasper looks down and kicks aside a tangle of briar.

"I don't know what you're talking about," her father protests.

"I found the other one," says Jasper.

She had passed right by it, but Jasper digs into a low mound of dirt and exhumes another leather oxford. This one is better preserved, the sole intact, the laces petrified in their original, tight double knot. Eddie takes a step toward Jasper then changes his mind and pushes past Wallis in the other direction, dropping the shoe at her feet.

"Where are you going?" she demands, stooping to pick it up. Her father doesn't answer. His eyes are fixed on the ground now, scanning what's left of the chestnut graveyard. He kicks aside loose stones and dry-rotted branches. The clearing of dead azalea is left behind as the forest closes in once more, casting cool shade over her arms and naked legs. She has never seen her father move so fast, like he knows exactly what he's looking for and where he'll find it. Without turning, she hears Jasper walking swiftly behind her.

Eddie is talking to them but talking to no one, restlessly moving forward, veering off uphill. She strains to hear him.

"I waited all those years," he is saying angrily. "For a postcard, a letter, anything. I walked these woods and dug up sang and waited for him like a goddamned idiot."

"Look," Wallis points to the right of her father, to a fall of eroded boulder that was once a part of the mountain above. Beneath the bottom layer, a filthy cuff peeks out, buttoned by a random acorn. Eddie lurches over and Jasper gains ground and together the three of them lift the stones away. Eddie rolls the heavy bottom off the chest, sending a web of pink earthworms squirming for cover. With her ginseng hoe, Wallis lifts the mud-caked, decomposed fabric, flinging it to the ground. The shirt is buttonless and shredded nearly to ribbons. She kneels before it, brushes away the dried mud, fingering its rust-colored tatters. A wild animal did this, she thinks. Only that sort of fierce hunger might rip a man to shreds.

"The kids started in on me at school after the sheriff came looking for him. He'd last been seen with my mother at the general store. They all knew the stories about the women of our family, and when I told her they were claiming she conjured a panther to kill him, she didn't deny it. She let everyone in the hollow think whatever they wanted to about her. I lay in bed, eight years old, wanting so hard not to believe it was true. If she did that to him, what would she do if I ever tried to go?"

"Eddie, over here," Jasper calls. He has jogged ahead, close up on the edge of a steep ravine. Trapped inside the fork of a chestnut stump that has cankered and died, resprouted and died once more, dangles a mauled pair of trousers to match the shirt. Jasper wraps his hands around the orange-stained linen as if to tug a sword from a stone. Wallis rushes up to help, slashing with her hoe at the gray fork of tree flesh around it, but weakened by time and weather the pant leg easily rips away in a cloud of shreds and spore.

"They never found a body," Eddie says, watching them. "He never wrote. I didn't know if I was living with a murderer or if I was nothing but a hit-and-run. And those kids kept saying, *Cora Alley tore him up.*"

Jasper holds the fabric, no longer recognizable as pants. The stitching of the pocket with its heavy cotton lining is intact, but nothing else. He reaches in and hands Eddie a dime, three wheat pennies, and a square of melted paper. Carefully unfolding it, Eddie traces the faded route of an old road map. Its writing is unreadable.

"You don't believe she did it," Jasper says.

"Fear made her famous in this hollow," Eddie says, "but that kind of fame is hell on a child."

Wallis walks a few yards beyond, to where the mountain drops away in vanishing tiers of dun-colored parabola. Great walls of fossil limestone, trilobite, and ammonite and the bleached, cemented skeletons of untold extinct creatures from when these mountains were beneath the sea. Far below, water carves through the gorge. Are his bones down there? Where else could he be? Across the way, the woods reel out, identical and dark, unreachable from here.

"There's a house," Wallis says. "Across the gap."

Eddie and Jasper join her at the edge, shading their eyes to see across the deep ravine. Half hidden in the shade of a tall, white-blossoming tree, it glows like a jeweled heart. Red, blue, green, amethyst. Someone had sunk chips of brilliant colored glass and gem in amber sap, worked into a pattern that completely covered the tiny cabin from roof to foundation, twisting and repeating, childlike and insane.

"My candy house," Jasper says. "That's the house I dreamed last night."

Around each window, the pattern continues in chestnuts, three rows deep. The door, too, has been covered in repeating rows of spiny chestnut burrs, like the plated back of a prehistoric animal.

"What's that?" Wallis asks, squinting at a metal hoop hung above the lintel. Sunlight filters through its tiny holes, casting a net across the yard.

"A winnowing sieve," Eddie answers. "To keep the witches away."

"He lives there," Jasper states. "He has to."

Wallis is still holding his shirt. She knows Jasper is right. "We should call the police," she says, looking across to her father. She wishes Mom were here to tell them what to do.

Eddie stares at the tiny, encrusted house, his eyes filling.

"I was such a dumb little kid," he says.

Back at the cabin, Wallis folds Tucker's ruined clothes and leaves them on the kitchen table. Better to have them in the house than strewn along a mountain path where they might rise up in the night. No one feels like eating and so they take their turns rinsing off in the spring before settling down to bed. Her father thought he was being considerate, giving her a room to herself, but she doesn't want to be alone tonight. She'll sleep anywhere they are—on the floor, on the porch, she'll invite them in to sleep across her grandmother's bed with her. The woods have moved closer to the flimsy house, she feels pressed in on every side.

Her father was silent and preoccupied on the walk back. Jasper asked questions. What was Tucker Hayes like? Was he a man who could live alone for decades deep in the woods? Was he a coward? Her father answered as best he could. He had a wife with him, who disappeared as well, Eddie said. It feels like I dreamed them both.

"Tuck me in?" Wallis asks him now. He nods, glad to have something to do, she thinks, and follows her into his mother's room. When she was little Mom would sometimes sit with her until she fell asleep, but rarely her dad. He was always working.

"Turn around," she orders him, taking the nightgown from its peg. She lets Cora's green dress fall to the floor and shivers when the thin white linen brushes her flesh. Before it was a relic, but now it feels like something alive, sending shoots into her own skin. She stretches her arms overhead and curls her fingers like claws.

"I wish you wouldn't wear her things," her father says to the wall.

"Tell me not to," she replies.

"Don't wear her things," Eddie answers.

"Too late," says Wallis, climbing into bed.

The moon is rising in the window, its light meandering around the room, touching the wooden leg of the dresser and her clothes on the floor. It misses her father when he sits next to her on the bed; he is nothing but a voice.

"When I didn't see you," Eddie says, "I was worried I'd lost you, too."

"That would have made Jasper happy. Then he could have you all to himself."

Her father strokes the hair from her eyes and tucks it behind her ear. He shakes his head.

"You're too hard on Jasper. He's alone, he wants a family."

"He can't have mine," she says. Eddie doesn't answer. He is too distracted to talk about Jasper or anything else. She can tell he is remembering.

"Why did you tell him before you told me?"

"I don't know," her father says. "Maybe I wanted him to know other kids didn't know the truth about their parents."

"So, what do you think?" she asks. "Did that man go AWOL or did your mother conjure a panther?"

"I think he dodged the draft and forgot all about us," Eddie says.

"I think she conjured the panther."

"You're young," says Eddie. "Think what excites you."

"Tell me a bedtime story?" she asks. She feels the sagging mattress in the hollow of her back and squirms to get comfortable. "One like she would have told you."

"Parents shouldn't be scary at bedtime," he says.

"Really, Captain Casket?"

He laughs because he would rather fright be forgiveness between them. In an odd way she thinks finding Tucker Hayes's clothes has been reassuring to her father, like watching *Psycho* a second time might help you feel less crazy for being so scared the first go-round. He sits silently for long enough that she is about to prod him again, but then he speaks.

"Once there was a woman of our family," he begins, putting on his storytelling voice, like the one he used down by the railroad tracks or trots out for his skits. She's learning where it comes from.

"Who had a beast of a husband and half a dozen beastly children."

"Is this a true story?" Wallis asks.

"My mother never told untrue stories," he says. "If she said every night this woman's husband came and took a deep gulp of her, and every morning her children suckled and sucked, until this woman's well ran dry, then that is how it happened. As my mother told it, this woman of her family found herself used up before her time. Her cheeks wrinkled, her heels cracked, the ends of her lustrous hair broke off. She looked in the mirror and instead of her fresh sweet self, she saw a wicked old witch. So, one night, while her whole family slept, she crept out into the woods by moonlight and threw three stones over her left shoulder. *Satan,* she whispered in the dark, *get up here, I need you.* The women of our family are hard to refuse, so the Dark Man roused himself and trotted up the woods near Panther Gap. *What can I do for you, sweetheart?* he asked, with honey in his mouth. *I want to fly,* she answered. *I want to fly away.*"

"I'm never getting married," Wallis says. Her father pats her hand and continues.

"*You don't need me to fly,* said the Dark Man. *Just unfasten that old skin of yours and hang it on a low branch where you can reach it again when you get back.*

"So she did. She stretched a bit to loosen it up, then stepped right out. Just for a spell. Just for a little rest from the troubles of home. Without it, she found she could take her wild, raw self wherever it was she pleased."

"She took her skin off?" Wallis asks.

"So the story goes."

"Did it hurt?"

"Maybe the first time," he answers. "But each time she shrugged it off, it got easier and easier to leave it behind. So while her husband snored beside her and her children thrust their feet in one another's faces, fighting over the few scraps of blanket, she took to tiptoeing through the dreams of all the men in the valley, trying out their unlocked doors, and when she'd found a man she fancied who'd laid down without turning his lock, she'd slip through his keyhole and whisper in his ear. *Come, let's ride,* she'd say. Mostly they were curious and mostly they would follow her. The minute they let her in, she'd leap upon their backs and ride 'em till they dropped."

"Where did she go?" Wallis asks.

"To have a destination would spoil it. It was for the thrill, to see what they might see. She rode all the men of her hollow, each in turn, as if they were her own private stable. Pretty soon all the other women were angry and discontent because they couldn't get any work or love out of their men. *I don't know what's got into me,* all these fine, strong husbands and sons would say. *I'm just wore out all the time.* She had the whole hollow anxious and upset, but no one could say quite why."

"If I had those powers," says Wallis, "I'd ride someone to a bank and steal enough money to live on for the rest of my life."

"This witch had trouble thinking past her own neighborhood. You, my modern little sorceress, have scope of vision."

Now it's Wallis's turn to laugh softly at the compliment. Telling this story he is forgetting his own troubles and that is what she'd hoped for them both. She doesn't want to think about the clothes or who lives across the gap. She doesn't want to think of Mom back home wondering whether she should call the police.

"One man she especially fancied," he continues, "she rode near to death coming through his keyhole every night, driving him farther and farther. He was all worn down to bone with just a few greasy tendons holding him upright. Got to where he couldn't think straight, started making bad business decisions, picked feuds with his kin. All he wanted was rest, but he was forced back into service night after night until, finally, he propped himself up behind the door, one bleary eye upon that keyhole, and when she slipped through, with his last bit of dying strength, he jumped her. Lord, it was sweet revenge, whipping and pushing as she'd pushed him. He rode her all the hours from midnight to sunrise, fast and furious, to teach her a lesson. Just because you're bursting full of wants and desires doesn't mean you get to slip out of your skin whenever you feel like it. He rode her till dawn, until at last she collapsed alongside him, nothing but sweat and bubbling white slather."

"And that's what finally stopped her?" Wallis asks.

"Stopped?" asks Eddie, bemused. "Then she wouldn't be a woman of our family."

Wallis mumbles in the dark. "That was more funny than scary."

"I used to think so, too."

He kisses her forehead and tucks the sheet under her chin. His face is spotlit by the moon for a brief instant before he passes again into darkness on his way to the door.

"Dad," she says, stopping him. "Look in the bottom drawer."

Eddie turns back and kneels before his mother's dresser; Wallis hears the slide of wood on wood. She can't see his face to know if he is surprised or mad that she kept the old projector a secret these past few days. He shouldn't be mad. It's just a movie, after all.

"It's not lost," she says. "Maybe he left it here for you."

The room is silver when she wakes, hours or maybe minutes later. She had only closed her eyes and she was back home showing her mother the clothes they found. Ann had taken them and stuffed them in the washing machine and when they came out of the dryer they were whole again and good as new. Wallis opened her eyes expecting to find her mother standing over her with the laundry basket—*You and your father, so melodramatic*—but she is alone, in Cora Alley's bedroom. Her eyes light on Jasper's thick black cable snaking under the windowsill up the wall to the bare-bulb ceiling fixture. It continues down the other side and through the wall to the front parlor where Eddie has made his bed. Low yellow lantern light leaks through the space above the floorboards.

He is awake in the next room. He shared this bed with his mother, he told her, when his father wasn't home, until he was ten or so. She can't imagine sleeping with her parents, unsure whether to snuggle close or cling to the edge, putting herself as far away from their heavy, hairy bodies as possible. Right now she can't imagine sleeping at all, her thoughts are galloping away from her, too insistent not to follow. She swings her feet to the ground and lets herself out of the stuffy room. The night has let go of the day's heat and outside in the breezeway it is dry and clear.

"Dad?" she taps softly on the door to the front parlor where the lamp is still lit. "I can't sleep."

She waits, but gets no answer. Could he have dozed off and left it burning? Quietly, she pushes open the door. Wallis hasn't been in this room since the first day, but her father has made up the antique sofa into a bed, with a quilt, and a rolled pair of trousers for a pillow. The room smells of wood smoke, but it must have been hours ago that they kindled the fire; only ruby coals remain in the hearth. She steps over four crushed beer cans and the uneaten crust of a sandwich. Two sharpened sticks with charred marshmallow tips. She didn't know he'd bought marshmallows at the store. Jasper had unpacked the groceries.

Wallis steps back into the breezeway, peers inside the dark kitchen with its faintly glowing, freshly painted walls. Skirting the woodpile, she knocks her shin on one of the leftover spools of cable Jasper used to wire the cabin. *Jasper, are you there?* she whispers. His sheet is spread across the planks, one corner flipped over by the breeze. They must be out front watching the stars, she tells herself. They wouldn't have left her here, alone on a mountaintop with a dead man's clothes and a panther on the loose. She walks around the house in the white light of the Milky Way, as fresh and close as the kitchen ceiling; the house seems less permanent than it is by day, its walls giving a little in each direction as if breathing. She had forgotten the Perseids, but now she sees the first falling star. She thinks of the poor citizens of Hamburg staring up into a sky full of floating aluminum strips. The falling stars make Wallis feel she is falling, too. Or maybe flying. Tonight they feel the same.

Turning the corner of the house, she sees blue light flickering through the gaps of the old barn boards. For a second, Wallis has the childish certainty that her father and Jasper are hiding a spaceship in there, secretly plotting their midnight escape. Then the feeling passes but the relief that should replace it—someone is clearly in there, she has not been left alone—doesn't come. There should be a word for this rapid cycling through, she thinks—the dread of the shadow on the wall, the sigh at discovering it was just the family cat, the swiftly following *of course,* when the ax connects to the back of the head just as you bend down to pet it. Wallis moves through the yard carried on this relief-dread, watching herself as she drifts through the musical strata of cricket and grinding bullfrog. She hears her father's voice, above the frog, below the clicking timbals of cicadas that cling to the forks of trees. Her hand is on the barn door when she hears the clack of film and the whir of the hand-cranked motor.

She puts her eye to the crack, below the hinge, and she has a clear view of the projector set on an upturned crate. Awash in blue, they kneel behind it, both sitting back on their long, thin calves, their cheeks almost touching. She and Jasper are kids and share their length in years, but Jasper and her father are alike in bodies. When you are learning to love, she thinks, which part of yourself are you trying to satisfy? Length? Width? Depth? How, she wonders, do we know how to fit ourselves together?

Jasper cranks too fast and her father places his hand over the boy's to slow him down. Like this, he says, showing him how it should be. Turn. Turn. Turn. Turn. Turn. The crate is placed too far from the wall and the picture is a little too wide and dreamy, as if being projected underwater. There is no screen to contain it and its borders seep into the cracks. Wallis has arrived at the end, the film is almost over. A pale man with dark circles painted around his eyes wrestles with the monster he's brought to life. They reach out to each other trapped on opposite sides of the mirror, and then the monster is gone, the fiancée rushes in. The movie is over and Jasper stops cranking. The bulb hiccups once and then the barn is dark. Bodies move, Wallis hears the rustle, but it's impossible to tell if they are moving closer together or quietly apart.

She shouldn't be here and slowly she turns to leave, taking the end of that movie inside her. Back through the night's soundtrack, across the yard, onto the porch, and to the bedroom, where she curls up on the bed, reaching for the comfort of dreams. She told her father where to find his Frankenstein, but she didn't believe he would show it. Not without her. She asked to have the future shown to her, but she cannot say what she saw. It was dark, it could have been anything.

It was dark. It could have been nothing.

II

Ann

1967

Just because she never made it to Europe doesn't mean Ann is uncultured. She keeps up. Old Masters. Impressionists. She wanders the halls of blinding white statuary, able to distinguish a Greek chiton from a Roman toga, the Archaic from the Hellenic period. She took art history in high school and knows how gaudily this pure white marble was painted back when those deities were all fetish and hung in dark rafters like cheap Puerto Rican saints, too pink and fleshy, with crystal eyes that watched all sorts of drunken orgiastic rites. She can say that word. Orgiastic. She's not afraid of it.

She didn't have to go to Europe because slowly, since the war, Europe has been coming to her. In the last two months she has eaten arugula *and* drunk Chianti, and she has visited this museum where they have the *Charioteer* on loan and other random godlets and shepherds, boys half dressed with hairless chests and rippled backs, and she studies them looking for clues to what makes them so desirable. She doesn't see it. She knows she should but she doesn't see what makes them so different from girls who are smooth and slim. Except. Of course.

The baby kicks in her belly and when she moves she sloshes like a wineskin. There is only one part of a man that swells, but she is all distortion these days, she doesn't even recognize herself. A fat, coarse face and thick middle, ankles as wide as her knees, breasts heavy and tender. Her fingers have swollen to the point that she can't remove her wedding ring, not that she would want to, except that it cuts into her finger where her flesh has closed over it like a barbed wire around a tree. She is hot and thirsty all the time. And pimply. A sculptor would never dare pock a boy's face, though surely they would have been covered in acne, wouldn't they? All those hormones. Maybe people didn't have hormones back then. Don't be stupid. Of course they did.

She would have made it to Europe. She had the route mapped out, beginning in Paris and following the path of Joan of Arc through Orléans and Tours and Poitiers, then overland to Spain and across the mountains along the Camino de Santiago de Compostela. She had no desire to see Greece and Italy, which were backward and dirty and full of perverts. The colorful brochures she had for small package tours focused on countryside churches and roadside shrines, tasteful inns in towns that had been untouched by the war. She would go on a clean bus with other women her age and be chaperoned but not oppressed and given enough room to shop a bit and haggle with the locals and feel herself *there*. She would send postcards home and collect dolls with different national outfits for the daughter she might one day have and flirt with a tour guide and maybe even kiss him one night by a hayrick, feeling the stalks press into the small of her back. She would have done those things.

There is an overpriced museum café with china and silverware and dainty teacups and she is very hungry but her doctor told her she'd gained too much weight already, she was only allowed two more pounds with four months still to go, and so she unwraps another stick of Juicy Fruit and tries not to think about food. She doesn't want to look at these boys anymore. She really doesn't understand it and when he tried it on her last night, claiming it was better for the baby not to go where they usually went but the other place, *there,* she tried to be modern. Of course he wouldn't want to look at this face, all swollen and grotesque. On her hands and knees it hurt so bad she bit her lip and she still feels the raw open skin like the slippery skin of the real place and he said it was his first time, too, but he seemed to know what he was doing and—STOP. Just stop.

When Eddie first showed up at the station they used to call him her stray. He followed her around like a puppy and brought her little presents, things he'd pawed out of the garbage because he didn't have any money—rimed Whitman samplers and bruised velvet roses. He made up songs for her, "Ann's Golden Hair," and "Ann, Won't You Ever Love Me?" that he played on the harmonica, the tune never quite set but meandering around a register both rueful and sad. She pled his case to her father like she pled the case of all the other strays that had wandered through their lives over the years. Please can we keep him? He won't be any bother. Her father, like he did with all the others, blustered and raged—you don't know the first thing about the mongrels you take in, then when they bite you, I have to foot the medical bills. She cried a bit and ran off and she scared him as she always did, and he gave in, as he always did, mentally calculating the weeks until he'd have to round up this boy like he rounded up the dogs and cats when the noise and chaos got to be too much and chuck him back into the world. *Eddie, you're in!* she'd shouted, racing to find him where he was helping to lay coaxial cable in anticipation of the new receiver that would give them a tristate range. *Go wash your hands. You get to come inside.*

Maybe he resented her for that. Maybe he hated being under obligation. Men don't like being beholden to women. Isn't that what her father always said?

The hallway between the classical statues and the café is hung with paintings from Iran on loan from the shah, which she passes by without a glance. Too many small turquoise and ruby figures, all that writing around the margins, she is forced to squint, which causes wrinkles. She passes a room of Chinese porcelain, vases and more vases, there is nothing here she wants to see. What she likes are the yearly Christmas card exhibits, lovely little squares of Currier & Ives, not the modern ones that are trying so hard, just lines and squiggles suggesting the holy family, a circle with a U for a cow, a reclining figure eight—infinity—for the Christ child. Why did everything these days have to be suggestion? Why did everything seem to mean something else? She should have gone to college. She should have gone to Europe. She had the brochures.

The museum will be closing soon and caterers in white aprons are spreading white tablecloths and setting out champagne flutes for a reception, everything is pure and white. She likes this absence of art, in fact, she realizes; she is always most comfortable in parts of the museum that are blank, that allow rest from all the things she is supposed to be there to look at. She thinks of the stack of snowy diapers she has in the closet in the nursery, how they'll never be that clean again no matter how hard she scrubs them. She thinks of the baby growing inside her, put there by a part of him that, all these years later, still feels like dirt under his fingernails. A Negro caterer bumps her with a platter of cheese cubes and strawberries and because she doesn't want him to think she thinks she's superior, she apologizes for being in the way and asks him what he's setting up for. It's a publishing party, he tells her. He nods to the small gallery behind him where Ann sees black and white photos hung on the wall and a stack of books on a table. There is a fountain pen set out and a crystal pitcher of water. The announcement has come over the public address system that the museum will be closing in ten minutes; they must all clear out, she knows, so that the important people might arrive. My husband is in TV, she says to no one, the caterer has set down his platter and disappeared. I am often welcome at parties like this.

Mothers are making their way to the exits, grasping the hands of school-age children. Why are they at a museum in the middle of the week? They shouldn't be on vacation at this time of year. Maybe they have stayed home sick and their mothers, to distract them, have brought them here, and then Ann feels a knot of anger in her stomach that any mother would dare bring an infectious child out to contaminate everyone else. She scans each one for a telltale rash, a flush of red scab. Measles. Chicken pox. Diseases that carry miscarriages and death.

Okay. She can't take it anymore.

Her hand darts out and she shoves a fistful of cheese into her mouth, washing it down with the juice of a frantically chewed strawberry. He won't know. I won't tell him, but whether she means Eddie or her doctor or the Negro caterer, she can't be sure. The people are streaming past her now, the whole museum emptying out through the main doors, and she ducks into the small gallery behind her to chew and chew and chew, looking down, concentrating on the crumb and sweet, and her mouth is so full, a bright red drop of saliva escapes her lips and before she can cup her hand to catch it, lands on the white marble floor as if it has dropped from between her legs, and she stares at it in horror and fascination until she realizes she's been staring for a very long time and then she smears it with the toe of her ballerina flat and looks up.

She is alone. No one has seen her and, emboldened, she moves to the crystal pitcher, pours herself a glass of water, and when she has drunk it all, wipes her lipstick from the rim and returns the glass to its place. She unwraps another stick of Juicy Fruit so that no one, should they get close, might smell the cheese on her breath. Now she might look at the photographs on the wall: originals, it seems, of those in the book on the table. Ann walks the semicircle of the exhibition, feeling the harsh spill of the spotlights pooling on her cheekbones. The wall text uses words like *prescient* and *muscular* and *kamikaze*. Ann stares at a dizzying color photograph of a building in napalm flames, two WWII fighter jets banking through the low clouds overhead. It was the presidential palace in Saigon, she reads, the failed coup of February 1962. On the floor of the living room, next to an undetonated bomb that spared the life of President Diem, lies the charred, smoke-damaged copy of the George Washington biography he was reading at the time. She moves to the next picture of taut-skinned North Korean women squatting over a roasting dog; she moves to the next—dazed men in wide stripes and yellow stars clinging to the fence of newly liberated Dachau. Ann realizes she is viewing the exhibit backward, moving slowly back in time rather than forward, and she should be noticing things about the artist's technique, a coarsening or youthful self-consciousness overcome in later work, but she doesn't. Every shot has the same intensity, dull eyes leveled at her like a howitzer, all that ugliness and brutality, degradation elevated to an art form. Then the war is over because it has not yet begun and the exhibit moves to the artist's Works Progress Administration period, photographs of the indigent she did for the government, before moving on to her earliest work—the Wall Street suicide that launched her, some very stylishly lit gloves on a table beside some fresh-cut tulips. The WPA photographs look oddly familiar. A stern mountain woman with feral eyes and a humorless mouth standing with a boy on a porch. A man, better dressed than the others, focused on something out of frame as he cranks an old-fashioned film projector in low light. Ann reads the caption: *In the autumn of 1940, Sonia Blakeman and playwright Tucker Hayes were mapping the mountains of Virginia for the state's first official*

WPA guide. Last seen in the impoverished community of Panther Gap, Hayes, pictured left, failed to report for duty at Fort Dix and was later declared permanently Absent Without Leave.

Ann nearly chokes on the gum in her mouth, spitting it into her palm as if she'd been chewing on a bit of gray mouse flesh. She opens her purse and wraps the gum in a corner of Kleenex, then shoves it deep down. The guards are locking up, but they hold the door for her as she scurries out, a woman in her condition.

Panther Gap

OCTOBER 1940

She was standing in the breezeway outside the parlor door in her thin white web of nightgown. Her hair floated around her shoulders, the moon cast a dark shadow between her legs. Cora was waiting for him, but he winced at the sight of her. Oh, no, you won't get me again, he thought. I know what I'm in for with you. Her face fell, she'd been looking forward to racing again. We had such a fine ride, didn't we? she seemed to say. Yes, it was hard, yes, it hurt, but when have you ever flown over the earth like that? Did you even know it was in you? She didn't speak, but he heard it all as if she'd said it aloud, and tried to stop his ears against it. He still had welts on his side from last time, he was just regaining his strength. Still she stood there, waiting. Look, I have a little something for you, she seemed to say, as she slowly extended her hand. Her fist relaxed and, shining like pure moonstone on her dry palm was a silvery, shimmering cube of sugar. Every facet etched, each grain in high relief. His mouth filled with desire, he licked his swollen lips. He was wary still, uncertain, but she was so beautiful and the sugar looked so sweet, like it would take all the bitterness of an entire life away, and he had to have it, he had to, and so he sidled over to her and touched his lips to her outstretched hand and as he tasted the sugar and her flesh together, he saw from her other hand, that which sneaked from behind her back, a bridle dangling, and before he could rear back, she had thrust the bit into his mouth, gagging him, and leaped upon his back. At his feet lay the nightgown and something slack and marrowless upon it. How did she slip out of her casings so quick?

They covered the distance of the first night in a matter of minutes. She wrapped her sinewy legs tight around his chest until he could barely gasp a breath, teaching him a new rhythm. His canter became a long undulating talus wave, sparking gold against the rock; he became once more all motion and desire and the desire for motion. But no sooner had he stretched out and found his stride than the whip came out. Frenzied, furious, he knew this went beyond the last time. There was no pretense of exploration or pleasure, merely the punishing ride to destination. He looked down over the curvature of earth and now they were nowhere on the mountain, they had entered a town, empty at that time of night, only a single traffic light spilling its light upon the pavement. He spooked at the blink from yellow to green, for how could he be seen like this, what *was* he? She struggled to hold him, wheeling him around to gallop for the cover of woods that followed the side of the road. In this way, they stalked the town until she found the route she was looking for and turned him out again, racing down a different street in a different part of town where what was man in him began to recognize storefronts and landmarks—the bank, the Esso station, the laundromat, the Woolworth's. She pulled him up short at the plate-glass window of a cramped office at the corner of Fifth and Plum, which he instantly knew, and felt himself—man and beast—balk again. What were they doing here? Why had she brought him to this place?

When she dismounted, tight red muscles of buttocks tapered down to legs streaked with fat and sinew. He was transfixed by her Achilles tendon, with its own pulse like that at the nape of her neck. He wanted to reach out and nick it, to hobble her and taste her and sink his teeth into something unyielding. She turned as if sensing his thoughts and grinned at him. They were all meat under the skin, animal and human alike. Stroking his mane, she reached her arms over her head, stretching along the length of herself like a bloody piece of taffy, reaching for the door of the draft board office, long and attenuated, coiling like a spring, stretching thin as a hair. She pierced the keyhole, twisting into darkness, feeding herself through until she was nothing but a pinprick of blood on the latch and was gone, swallowed up between inside and outside, in some interminable, intermediate place. Vanished. Then she was whole and laughing on the other side. He snorted with his muzzle against the glass, watching her pick her bloody way through the darkened room. Around the standard-issue metal chairs, around the metal desk, past the metal scale and cabinet of medical equipment, stethoscope, ophthalmoscope, reflex hammer, blood pressure cuff. She made her way to the battered file cabinet and rifled through it, smearing blood on the neat manila folders. What was she doing? He wanted to scream, but had no voice, could do nothing but pace the length of the building wildly, searching for a way in. He watched as she found a single white card, and held it up for him to see. His draft card, the document that identified him as having registered with the board and assigned him to his induction center. He saw the spark at the instant he saw the flame and the match between her bony red fingers and her touching it to the edge, he saw the whole thing go up and collapse into ash in her palm where before the sugar had rested, and he couldn't believe he was here, and he couldn't believe he was seeing this and he cried out in his mind, this is not real this is not real this is not real, but the bloody footprints on the linoleum of the draft office looked real enough and the blood on the keyhole as she wormed her way back through, less gracefully now, more like a grub, and the ash on her palm—how had she held it?—which she blew in his face and he coughed against it and his sneeze felt real and her breath as she leaned in with her hand still gentle on his mane and whispered in his twitching beastly ear, Now you are free. Now you are free.

"Mr. Hayes, please wake up." Eddie is kneeling over him, shaking him by the arm. It takes Tucker a moment to understand that he is still tangled in the sheets of his pallet on the parlor floor. Eddie is out of bed and dressed in stiff blue jeans, his red-checked shirt buttoned tightly at the cuffs and throat. His hair is wet and combed slick across his forehead. Tucker closes his eyes. Leave me alone to die.

"It's nearly lunchtime," the boy pleads. "Please don't go back to sleep."

His head is pounding, he feels worse than he did as a boy in the grip of the Spanish flu. The light is too bright and the morning heat makes Tucker feel like a specimen in a jar. He has no strength in his arms or legs, and he struggles to sit, leaning his weight against the back of the couch. He nearly falls over again but catches himself.

"Where's Sonia?" he croaks.

"She's outside. Mama asked her to take our picture. Something nice she could hang on the wall."

"You seem to be feeling better," Tucker says.

"If you were a bird," Eddie says, worriedly, "you'd get left behind. Mama says birds won't show their weakness even up to dying so that their flock won't fly off without them. You can never tell a bird is really sick till he drops out of the sky."

Tucker tries to piece together time. Two days ago he struck this boy with his car. Yesterday he walked into the woods and hunted ginseng. Last night, they came home tired but laughing. *Mr. Hayes found a root,* Cora Alley announced. *A four-prong.* Tucker had shown it off to Eddie and Sonia, counting the stress rings. *Beginner's luck,* he'd said, but didn't believe it. Cora had invited them to stay another night and, because it was late, he ignored Sonia's scowl and agreed. Touching her lips to Eddie's forehead, Cora felt for fever, but it seemed to Tucker her lips just needed to be pressed against something, anything at all.

"Well, I cannot be shown up by a bird," Tucker says. He pulls himself up and staggers to the window that overlooks the front yard. Wearing an apron over her black bombazine dress, Cora Alley is scattering feed to her hens. She has washed her face and legs and exchanged her braid for a soft bun at the nape of her neck. She sways as she walks, plump and juicy as one of her blue-black Silkies.

"Your mama seems different today," Tucker says.

Eddie follows his gaze. "She wants to look pretty for her picture."

Tucker tugs on his clothes, feeling some strength return the further he gets from the dream. He is not a man given to superstition and he is angered by the second night's ride, which can't help but suggest something more to him. Which is absurd. Eddie watches him, still nervous, and he doesn't want to scare the boy. He steps out onto the porch and, in the backyard, Sonia is fixing her box camera to its tripod. She must have been down to the car and back. They have all been awake for hours, while he suffered in his sleep.

"Why didn't you wake me?" he asks.

"I tried," she says. "You were a million miles away."

Sonia looks like she spent a rough night as well. She has pressed her cheeks with powder and put on some lipstick but the makeup can't disguise her pallor. Though she has set up her box camera for a long exposure, she still wears her Rolleiflex like a crucifix around her neck. Tucker thinks of that old story he heard as a child about a beautiful woman who always wore a crimson choker. One day her husband untied it and her head rolled off.

"I'm making a salt print," Sonia says with more enthusiasm, "like they did during the Civil War. Back then all you needed was a handful of chemicals and some sunlight. I hope it turns out."

"Everything you touch turns out," Tucker says. Sonia looks at him uncertainly, unsure if he's complimenting or criticizing. He doesn't know himself and he is too tired to care. Instead, he walks to the kitchen where a cold biscuit and a cup of ersatz coffee have been left for him. That's his problem, he thinks. He hasn't had a real cup of coffee in three damned days.

The coffee has no flavor and the biscuit tastes of sawdust. While he is choking it down, Cora comes in carrying the tin she used to feed her hens. The breakfast scraps had gone to them and now she taps out the smallest crumbs and runs it under the faucet. Tucker feels his stomach clench at her approach. He has to get control of himself, he thinks. It is ridiculous to be this afraid of a woman.

"I'm worried I tired you," Cora says with some concern.

He studies her face for mockery, but there is none. And yet she looks nothing like the worn-out, dusty creature of their first meeting. Maybe it's the novelty of having someone around besides a boy—a man to walk with and talk to. But how is he to know? He cannot ask any of the questions on his mind. Did you ride me into town last night? I have been dreaming of you, have you been dreaming of me?

"Mrs. Hayes asked if there was anything you all might do to help before you left," she says, to break the silence. "I'm running low on supplies and I could use a ride to the store. Would you be willing to drive when we're done?"

What he really wants to do is crawl back under the covers, but there's no safety there. He can hardly refuse her this one favor. "Of course," he says. "It would be a pleasure."

Sonia sticks her head through the door, finding them alone together in the kitchen. Tucker is eating his biscuit, Cora is washing out a pan, and yet he colors as if he's been caught at something.

"Are you ready, Mrs. Alley?" Sonia asks. Cora wipes her hands on her apron and hangs it over the back of a chair. She turns to Tucker.

"Do I look presentable?"

He pushes away the memory of her Achilles tendon quivering between his teeth.

"Very much so, Mrs. Alley," he says.

On the back porch, Sonia positions her next to Eddie while Tucker walks out to the camera. Is there a country boy anywhere in the world whose ears don't stick out? Tucker wonders. Mother and son stand stiffly together, shoulders just touching, both looking as if every crop failure and plague of locust must be represented in this one posed portrait. It has been his experience, traveling with Sonia, that women and children only smile when they are caught off guard.

"Hold very still," Sonia directs.

Eddie holds his eyes open wide to keep from blinking. Cora glances over at Tucker, trying to see what he sees. Sonia burrows under her drop cloth and as her ass moves higher into the air, his tired body is suddenly hit by a surge of desire. He feels emptied after last night, now all he wants is to fill himself back up.

"Eddie helped me this morning," Sonia is saying from under the cloth. "We brushed the paper with salt water, then some silver nitrate I had in my case—"

"When you're done, let's go," he interrupts her, leaning in so only she can hear. "I have to get out of here." Sonia surfaces briefly.

"I still need to develop the picture," she says.

"Send it to Washington like everything else."

"Then it will belong to the WPA. They'll never get it back."

His need to be away from this place, to be alone with Sonia is fresh and urgent. You don't understand, he wants to say, I need us to leave. Something terrible is happening to me.

"I'm sorry," she says indulgently, ducking back under the cloth. "It won't take long, then we'll go."

Tucker returns his attention to the pair on the porch: Eddie with his staring eyes and hair drying crisp and roosterish, Cora smooth and impenetrable. The two look like a wager between God and the Devil, he thinks, with Eddie fair and Cora dark. He slots himself in the frame between them—husband to that woman, father to that son. He could sit on this mountaintop and scratch out enough food to fill a belly and grow a boy. But no, that's not it, he thinks. He doesn't want to be *with* Cora, he wants to *be* Cora, living up here, needing nothing from anyone, waking every morning with the freedom to disappear.

"Done," says Sonia, releasing them. Cora and Eddie exhale, their shoulders and faces relax. Tucker turns to Sonia.

"Take a walk with me?"

She makes him wait while under the cloth she pulls out the piece of homemade salted paper and fits it against the negative. She slides the wood-and-glass plate out and sets it in the sun to expose. It will need to sit for ten minutes, so that's what she offers Tucker.

They walk out past the barn toward the drop-off behind the house. It is hot in the sun but cool in the shade where an east wind bows the red-orange treetops. Tucker aches to put his arm around Sonia, but she is annoyed at being interrupted and is letting him know.

"The blue of this sky should be reserved for the robes of consecrated virgins," he says. She nods. Yes, it should.

"Ansel Adams is out photographing the Sierra Nevadas, isn't he?"

"I think so," she says.

"The emptiness of landscape is so powerful."

Sonia studies him, wondering what he's driving at. "I never thought of landscape as empty."

"Not empty," he clarifies. "I guess I meant open to interpretation."

"I prefer faces," she replies.

"I'm sick of faces," he says.

"Rocks and trees aren't complicated," Sonia answers. "That's why you like them."

"Don't go to Europe, darling," Tucker says abruptly, taking her hands in his. "Why wallow in gore when we could wait out the war up here? I could do a little farming, you could photograph the mountains. You're twice as talented as Ansel Adams."

Sonia is surprised by his urgency. "Have you forgotten you've been drafted?"

"A person could vanish up here. Look around."

She casts her eyes over the bright autumn color of the hollow and beyond to identical, roadless ridges stretching on for days.

"Tucker, this isn't a game. If you don't show up for induction, they'll put you in jail."

"Not if they can't find me."

Before he dreamed it, he didn't even know he was thinking it. Now he's said it aloud and it's become possible. He continues, desperate for her to understand.

"So many points on the damned map, Sonia. We could keep going forever and ever and never find anything truer than right here. Why not stay? I could write a masterpiece up here. Where there's no *Rise and Sing* agitprop bullshit or Noël Coward faggots swilling champagne. I could write about real freedom."

Sonia interrupts. "What's gotten into you?"

"Something is happening to me here. I've been dreaming I can fly," he says, calming his voice because he can hear how crazy he's starting to sound. "That Cora took me—"

"You've been dreaming that Cora Alley can make you fly?"

"She tells these stories—"

"So you've said. The lovers and the panther. Why do you think she told you that story?"

"Because I asked her to."

"Tucker, there is no magic here," Sonia says. "Cora Alley is trying to seduce you. She shares just enough of herself to give you something to hang your desires on, and then she lets your imagination fill in the blanks. Look at her life—it's the only power she has. Cora Alley is no mystery to me. Where do you think I come from?"

"I have no idea where you come from," he says.

"Exactly," Sonia answers.

His head is pounding from lack of sleep and lack of coffee. He shouldn't have told her. He knew she wouldn't understand.

"I think this says more about you than it does about Cora Alley," Tucker replies coldly. "She asked me to take her to the store. I suppose we should get going." He turns back to the cabin and Sonia puts her hand on his arm, as she always does, wanting to stop him.

"We can talk about after. After you serve, after I get back—"

He turns, longing to stay. "Sonia, I wanted you from the minute you first slid into the front seat with that damn camera. But I don't want you to become one of those women who spend their lives chasing depravity and ruin. Life is about more than war and work. You don't have to dwell on human misery. It's not you."

"If you've already decided who I am," she throws at him, "what do you need me for?"

"Am I wrong?" he asks vehemently.

Sonia is staring over his shoulder and he turns to follow her gaze. Eddie has gone back into the house to change but Cora is still standing in her best dress, watching them. She doesn't look happy but she doesn't look concerned, either, as if she were expecting the scene before her. Could Sonia be right? Tucker has the swift and certain feeling they've been set up. It was Cora's plan all along to get Sonia excited about making this portrait, to provoke a fight, to have Tucker to herself. She is trying to divide them. Stop. He gives himself a shake.

"Cora is waiting for you," Sonia says.

"Are you coming with us?" he asks. But he knows her answer. She has already exposed the negative, she still has to develop the print, fix it and wash it and hang it up to dry. There's no stopping the process now that it has begun.

"Enjoy yourself," she says.

He leans in to kiss her. "Please, let's not fight. We have so little time left."

She looks as if she wants to say something more, her eyes are searching his face but he doesn't know what she wants from him.

"That's right," she says at last. "We have so little time."

Seeing the argument is over, Cora slowly advances toward them. She looks very proper in her bombazine and as Tucker joins her, he feels they could be any country couple walking to a Sunday meeting. There is nothing nefarious about him driving her to the store for chrissakes, yet he wishes Sonia would change her mind. He finds himself afraid to be alone with Cora Alley.

"Hey, wait up! Can I come?" Eddie calls. He has changed back into his work clothes and his shirt is unbuttoned and flapping as he races after them.

"Of course—" Tucker begins.

"We can't rightly leave our guest alone," Cora interrupts. She speaks carefully, like a lady from the city, in a voice he hasn't heard before. "Why don't you see if you can be of help since Mrs. Hayes so kindly took your picture?"

Sonia lifts the Rolleiflex around her neck and points it at them. Tucker feels caught in the crosshairs. But no, she thinks better of it, and swings the camera back to the hollow, turning her lens to the rocks and trees.

"Cora," he says, making bold use of her first name. "Which way?"

"Stay straight on this road," she answers.

"Do they sell coffee beans at this store?"

"They're expensive."

"Please," he says. "I want to get them for you. Let it be my treat."

Sonia rode with her camera pointed out the window but Cora rides leaning forward, her eyes gleaming like a child thrilled with the speed. The wind tugs at her bun and softens her face with a few stray tendrils, and it's not his imagination. She is growing prettier every day they have been here. Outside the window the shade is so green and the sky so blue, and all those familiar mountain signposts have become just something to move through, like a room full of strangers on the way to the woman you're desperate to meet. Cora throws her head back and smiles at him. They are driving to her familiar general store, but he knows he is taking her somewhere new.

"What's your first memory, Cora," he asks her. "The oldest thing in your head?"

"Why?" she asks.

"It's just a game I made up, a way to get to know each other."

"I don't remember my first memory."

He says, "It would be the first thing you haven't forgotten."

She sits in silence, thinking.

"Just anything," he says. "It's a game, it's supposed to be fun."

"My mother's hair on the pillow," she answers.

"That's a lovely image," he says, smiling over. "You've got the hang."

"But it was after they took her away," Cora says seriously. "One of her long, dark hairs was left behind. I remember wrapping it around my finger like a ring."

"I'm sorry," Tucker says. "I didn't mean to bring up something painful."

"I'm not sure it's the very first thing I remember," she says. "There could be something else."

"It's a stupid game," Tucker says. "Forget it." It was a game he made up for Sonia, to make certain she didn't confuse him with a lesser man, but Cora is too honest to understand the rules. They drive the remainder of the way silently and Tucker lets parking the car demand all of his attention.

The store's exterior plank walls are plated with signs for BC Powder and Nehi and Uneeda and Heinz. Boys on the wooden steps drink RC Colas while two pretty girls in turned-up jeans and pigtails jump rope by the gas pump, raising a cloud of dust. Twenty-three, twenty-four, twenty-five, twenty-six. He recognizes them as the kids who ran out on Eddie, leaving him for dead on the side of the road. The girls stop jumping as he cuts the engine of the car.

Tucker steps out and Cora waits for him to come around. He opens the door for her and the boys on the wooden steps sit stupidly with their drinks to their lips, forcing Tucker to step around them. He lets the screen door slam and hears the girls start up their jumping again. Twenty-seven, twenty-eight, twenty-nine, thirty. Eddie deserves better friends than this.

Tucker has been in and out of a hundred stores on the trip, and Cora's is much like all the others. He sees bunkers of oats and seed and flour, rows of tinned food arranged on metal shelves that sag where something heavier once weighted them down. As his eyes adjust, he sees a girl, not much older than those outside, sitting behind the register with her feet planted on the top rung of a high stool, her knees peeking above the counter, white and gleaming. Tucker takes in her soft cheeks, her thick head of brown hair that has been set with curlers and brushed out and pulled back from her forehead with a wide blue ribbon. She belongs behind the jewelry counter of a department store or on the arm of some young, handsome thing, boring him with raptures on astrology and the prophecies of Nostradamus.

From behind a bin of spark plugs, two boys watch them. In their plaid shirts and work boots they are almost men, though one's head seems too large for his spindly body. Tucker walks to the icebox, reaching past the paper bags of bloodworms and half-melted Creamsicles to retrieve Cokes for himself and Cora. He pries away the caps with his penknife, licking sweet brown foam from his hand. Cora takes one from him, matching her sips to his.

She strolls the tight aisles, casual in the way she glances at prices, they are nothing, they are everything. She nods to a bag of white sugar, she points to a wooden box of green coffee beans and Tucker carries them to the counter for her. The soda is helping and he is feeling a little stronger.

"What do you think of these?" Cora asks, holding up a pair of black boots like the big boys have on. "Do you think they'd fit Eddie?"

He likes being asked, and considers thoughtfully. "They seem a little big."

"You're right," she agrees, putting them back.

"He could wear an extra pair of socks," Tucker suggests. "They'll last more than one season."

"I'll get them," Cora says, throwing him a smile.

The big boys are laughing over the spark plugs. Cora glances at them and Tucker feels instinctively protective.

"I bet he'd like a new shirt for school," Tucker offers.

"That's quite thoughtful," Cora says. "I believe he would."

She hands him the boots and steps around him to the flour sacks. She can't afford fabric for fabric's sake, she needs the flour as much if not more than the shirt.

"That one, please," she says, pointing to the blue-checked sack before moving to the next aisle. A gray tabby mother cat sprawls on top of the sack, nursing four newborn kittens. Tucker looks down at the squirming balls of fur digging into their mother's belly, the mother dozing with her head thrown back. He squats down and scratches her behind her ear. Gently he nudges, but she doesn't stir.

"Come on, you," he says, laughing a little self-consciously.

The kittens go on sucking, the mother widens her gaze to include him in the languor of the midday meal. Cora's company in the woods and at the cabin had felt natural enough, but now he feels the strain of performing before strangers. Cora, the shopgirl, the two big boys, all are watching. He slips his hands under the mother cat, trying to lift gently, but her kittens drop off with tiny cries, their fat stomachs hitting the ground, too young for the cat trick of landing on all fours. The mother is soft and yielding in his hands like a dead thing and in disgust he drops her, too, watching as she stretches out her paws and yawns, then flops heavily upon her side. Without looking around to see where all the other eyes are, he lifts the sack and drops it on the counter, raising a cloud of white cat dandruff.

"This gentleman is here with the government," Cora explains to the girl behind the counter. "He's writing a book about Panther Gap."

"Well, Mrs. Alley—" he starts, torn between correcting and embarrassing her. "We're writing a travel guide. We're hoping Panther Gap will go on the map. It's not wholly our decision."

The shopgirl looks up, only mildly interested.

Cora has arranged her purchases neatly in front of her. The shopgirl rings her up and gives the total: $23. It takes Tucker a minute to notice the shopgirl is looking at him expectantly. Cora is suddenly preoccupied with a stain on the wooden floorboard.

Tucker has $30 left in his pocket, all that remains to get them back to the field office and New York. But what choice does he have? Slowly he peels off single dollar bills as Cora's smile from the car returns.

"And Jeanne, will you tell your grandpa I'd like to trade?"

"I'm sorry, Cora," says Tucker. "I'm not feeling very well. Will we be much longer?"

Cora looks over, worried. She'd been enjoying herself but now is troubled to see he is not.

"Just another minute," she says.

From the back, Tucker hears fumbling from a radio, volume turned up loud then down, and then the girl is replaced by her white-bearded grandfather. At least Tucker assumes it is her grandfather. There is little to say he and the girl are related except, Tucker sees through the tear in the old man's trousers, some small family resemblance of kneecap. The small surge of the Coke has left him and he leans against the counter. The clock on the wall says it's after three, only a few hours of daylight left. He wishes Sonia had agreed to leave when he asked her.

"You boys buying anything?" the old man asks the two big boys in the back. They have been fingering the same oily metal since Tucker and Cora walked in but now they head back out to join their friends. The boy with the big head smells of Lucky Strikes as he sidles past Tucker, his breath is hot as a south-facing ashtray. "Giddyup," he says, almost in Tucker's ear. "We're off." Tucker watches them go through the wire screen.

"Don't mind them," says Cora. "They're bad boys."

"What'cha got for me, sis?" the old man asks. Cora slides a white handkerchief across the counter. With shiny red arthritic fingers, he pries the knot.

Last night, when they came home dirty and tired from their hunt, Cora had gently washed the root he found under running water, careful not to damage a single twisted hair. Together they counted forty-two scars where it had pushed up through hard-packed soil, and the years it waited underground, she said, could easily be more than double that. The head branched out to rudimentary arms and legs, and from the notched crotch tiny tributaries wrapped back around its torso like a body evolving its own cage of barbed wire.

The old man lifts the root from its cloth, nodding. "He's a beaut."

"Got to be close to a hundred years old," Cora replies.

"Price is down from what it used to be," the shopkeeper reminds her.

"I know," Cora says.

"I'll give you ten," he says.

"You can't do more?" she asks.

The old man shakes his head. These are hard times for all.

Cora takes the ten-dollar bill, turning to Tucker as if she's struck a great bargain. He wants to be happy for her but he feels, irrationally, as if his pocket has been picked. She never explicitly said the ginseng root was his, but somehow he had assumed it was. He hefts the flour and stands against the screen of the porch door, looking out. The kids have left the front stoop to play on a red terrace up the hill. A dozen have gathered, big and little, faced off against each other in two long lines. He is too far away to hear what they are playing. Dodgeball with no ball? Red Rover, Red Rover? A shout goes up—*Watch out!*—then all the children scatter, shrieking, a tangle of arms and legs until they've exchanged places and one is left out. That's all he can tell of the rules of their game. The shopkeeper is asking if they need help carrying their purchases. No, says Cora. We have a car.

Tucker opens the trunk and drops her things on the floorboard. Cora hangs on to the black boots and settles in front, letting him close the door behind her. He starts the car without comment, leaving the old man behind, the kids flapping in the field above. Looking both ways, he pulls out onto the road, taking the curves back uphill.

"Is something wrong?" Cora asks at last.

"That was a very valuable root," he answers.

"It was a lucky find," she says. Luck, he thinks, had nothing to do with it.

"I don't know," he continues. "Maybe I misunderstood. I thought it belonged to me."

Cora seems surprised at the idea. "Do you want half of the money?" she asks.

"I don't care about the money," Tucker quickly dismisses the idea. "It's just that—" He struggles to articulate why it bothers him.

"You traded away something that we found together. I suppose I'd thought I would keep it, to remember—"

"Like a souvenir?" Cora asks. Tucker is embarrassed.

"Something like that," he says.

"I'm sorry," she says. "It should have meant the same to me."

Tucker feels sick all over again.

"Of course, you'll want things to take with you if you go away," she continues.

"It's not *if,* Cora, it's *when,*" says Tucker.

"I don't know, Mr. Hayes," she answers. "Something tells me the war won't touch you."

He can't ignore it anymore. Tucker pulls the car onto the shoulder of the road, coming to rest in a patch of low grass. Through the open window behind her head, he sees bees staggering fat and drunk against a bank of honeysuckle. He must be losing his mind.

"If anyone should know, it's you," he says.

She observes him silently, not denying, letting him think what he likes.

"I know what you are, Cora."

"What's that, Tucker?" she says, using his first name for the first time. "What do you think you know?"

Her face is so close and they are once again out of time together, locked in a car, high on a mountain road. Tucker takes her face between his two wide hands and kisses her, hotly and deeply, on the mouth. He parts her lips with his tongue and she tastes like a girl at a soda counter with whom he's innocently shared a float; but she is no girl, for Cora Alley is kissing him back, ferociously, and he doesn't taste anything then, just feels the relief surging through him that he wasn't imagining it, that this was exactly what she was expecting. He had to know he was right and now he knows, but the knowledge doesn't bring any particular comfort. His hand moves to her black church dress and the modest breast inside it. Cora pulls away and observes him uncertainly.

"I'm not sure what you mean by that, Mr. Hayes," she says. They are back to Mr. Hayes. "You are a married man."

"I don't rightly know, either, Mrs. Alley," he answers. "I suppose I'm just afraid to die and want to take as much life inside me as I can before I go."

"We're all going to die. That's a fine excuse to do just about anything you please."

She holds Eddie's boots in her lap as if to keep them from running away, and returns her attention to the window. She never would have bought those boots if it weren't for him, Tucker thinks. She would have had to wait until she could have afforded them herself.

"We should be heading back," she says.

Tucker starts the engine and returns to the road, driving the last miles without looking at her. He wonders if Sonia will know immediately that he has kissed another woman, and if she'll be mad or secretly pleased that she knew before he did. Cora is sober and distant and he thinks of all the other women he's kissed who are no longer with him, never where he set them down. They are even this minute moving and speaking and adding to themselves, bathing their children, making love with their husbands, while he is left with only the pain of where they used to be, laughing over chicken fried rice in a back alley of Chinatown or weeping together over the death of a pigeon on the sidewalk.

Tucker pulls the car into the clearing, parking in his old treads. Cora is out before he can open the door for her, and together they start up the path. She carries the coffee beans and the shoes and socks. He hefts the flour. Between them they have nearly an entire wardrobe for Eddie. He wishes now he'd insisted the boy come along. If Eddie had been with them, he wouldn't be feeling right now like he'd hit someone else with his car.

"Are you hurt?" Cora asks, noticing that he is limping like she is. He shakes his head but her concern gives him the courage to reach out his hand to help her up the steep path. Though they both know she's walked it alone for years, she takes it and lets herself lean on him, just a little. They pass the fallow tobacco field and follow the path up the incline of the creek bed. They crest the hill that leads to the yard and then—because why wouldn't it?—time leaps forward by decades, and Tucker hears Eddie laughing in the voice of a grown man come home to brag for his mama. Cora is ordering him about, almost flirtatiously, in the way women do with their grown sons, but no, Cora is standing silently beside him. Stepping into the yard, Tucker sees the laugh belongs to a man in a khaki uniform, leaning on the front porch pillar squinting into the lens of Sonia's box camera. Sonia has burrowed back under her drop cloth and her voice is muffled and husky as she commands him. *Freeze.* Cora's stiffening body tells Tucker all he needs to know.

"That would be Mr. Alley?" Tucker asks.

"That would be Mr. Alley," Cora replies.

*   *   *

"I'm ready for another," Sonia says and Eddie passes her a nail. She is standing on a crate in the darkest corner of the barn, behind the stall with the restless cow. With one hand, Sonia stretches her sparc drop-cloth, blocking the light that comes through the slats. With her other, she fixes a nail and hammers it. Eddie fetched water from the spring and she has mixed her stop bath in an old tray. She was feeling fine when she woke but as the morning wore on she began to notice the change. Light hurts her eyes; she feels faint from the vinegary smell of the chemicals, and the manure and mildew of the hay. Each month she marks an *X* in her leather date book, but she doesn't need to count back the days to recognize this feeling. It's not her first time. Or her second. Or even her third.

"Another," she says, and the boy reaches up. The corner is growing darker with each nail she drives.

It must have been down by the creek before they struck Eddie. Would she know this soon? Maybe it happened at that hotel with the pale blue chenille bedspread when all the knots dug into her back, leaving her looking like a factory punch card when she finally got up. Or maybe it was their very first time, the night he showed her the movie of mothers and dying sons. Whenever it was, she is angry at herself and angry at him. If they hadn't stayed so long here, she would already be back in the city where she could immediately do something about it. Now it would be next week at the earliest before they could get back to New York and she could see her doctor. Nearly a week to think about it and feel it growing. Alone with it for a week.

"Do you need another one?" Eddie asks, his palms full of nails. The hammer dangles from her hand and the cloth droops. She stretches the fabric as far as it will go and reaches down.

"Yes," she says. "This is the last one."

She holds the nail between her lips before she hammers. It is hot for October and the barn is hotter; her back is running with sweat and her cheeks are sagging and clammy.

Eddie is watching her closely. "Mr. Hayes is sick, too," he says.

Sonia leans her head against the slats and closes her eyes. It would feel so good never to have to move again. Women do it all the time. They sit still and raise families and make homes and make peace. It is done all over the world. And Tucker is a nice man, no better or worse than the rest of them; more romantic, maybe, more sentimental. She always imagined she'd marry someone useless, have a brilliant decorative husband she could admire but who was fragile so that she'd never be tempted to lean on him. Who puts weight on a china poodle or a failed playwright? A husband she could lean on would be the worst possible thing, because then she might be tempted to relax, to soften, and then she would be lost. Maybe Tucker Hayes is useless enough. He loves her, at least for now, as they all do, at least for now. What more is there ever to go on?

"Can we watch the movie again?" Eddie asks.

"It's Tucker's, not mine. I wouldn't feel comfortable," she finds the strength to answer.

"But when you're married, you share everything, right?" Eddie asks, and Sonia remembers, of course, *they're married.*

"I suppose," she says. "But it works better if you keep some things separate."

Eddie sits quietly in the dark.

"Do you ever get scared of things?" Eddie asks.

"Not too much," she says, swallowing the saliva that fills her mouth. She will not throw up, not here in front of this kid. "I sometimes get scared of the things I'll miss."

"Will you miss us?" Eddie asks.

"I meant the things I'll miss out on. Miss doing," Sonia clarifies.

"Oh," he says.

After the print is set, it will need to be washed for half an hour in running water and then she will be done and they can leave. "Let's check it," she says.

She carefully peels the salt paper from the negative, exposing the contact print. A sepia Cora and Eddie peer back, their pale tan skin etched into the paper, the shadows of their clothes and the porch deep chocolate.

"This is how they made pictures a hundred years ago," Sonia says, studying them. She almost got Eddie. The big ears and the wide, sham-innocent eyes. He's trying too hard, but he looks like a boy who tries too hard, and so it's right. But Cora is wrong. She must have moved at the last minute. Her eyes, instead of challenging, are downcast and glancing sideways, giving her a criminally secretive look. Sonia is disappointed. She won't be able to leave this portrait. Cora would never hang it on her wall.

"This is why I have to take so many pictures," Sonia tells Eddie. "Between what I want and what you're willing to give, it ends up a law of averages. I almost got you, but I missed with your mother."

Eddie is staring at the portrait. "No, you got her," he says.

Sonia drops the paper into the stop bath and moves it around with a pair of tongs she fashioned from two sticks. The soft motion of the print in the tray sounds like water dripping in a cave.

"You like taking pictures," he says.

"It's impossible to see everything," she says. "Trying is how God tricks us into staying alive."

"You don't sound like Mr. Hayes," Eddie says, grinning. "You sound different."

"Really?" Sonia asks.

"He sounds like he comes from here. Not right here, but nearby. No ladies around here talk Yankee like you do."

"I was born in New York," she says. "I've lived there all my life except when I've been on the road."

"How long've you been on the road?" he asks.

"Most of my life," she says, grinning back.

"If I lived in New York City," Eddie says, "I'd never leave it."

"You'd be surprised what you'd leave," Sonia says.

She lifts the print from the fixer, letting the last drips roll back into the tray. Eddie leans against the cow's stall, absently petting her bony back. She twitches her tail to shoo him away.

"We need to rinse off the chemicals. Take this to the spring—" Sonia begins, but breaks off. Cora Alley's face is too close to her own and her eyes are slyly observing Sonia's knotted belly. In the yard the hens can feel her distress. They set up squawking, their wings beating the dirt. The cow turns around awkwardly in her pen. Sonia swallows but it is too late—she makes the door of the barn just as the morning's grits and coffee come back up. It's humiliating to feel this wretched and weak. She hates him for putting this inside her, and her hatred must have summoned him for his shoes are there on the blasted grass before her, thick-soled and caked with mud. Why is he back so soon? Does he see what he's done to her? Looking up, the sun is behind him and his face is all in shadow.

"*Daddy!*"

From her hands and knees, Sonia looks up to see Eddie in the door of the barn, holding the wet print that has begun to curl at the edges. A slight but muscular man in a khaki uniform stands before them, a rucksack slung over his shoulder. He steps forward and now Sonia sees his eyes are the same color as his clothes, which are the same as the ground, and what she's just thrown up. Only his face is red with barely checked anger. Sonia starts to rise, to explain, but before she can move, Eddie has pushed past her, knocking her almost into her own puddle, before tearing off across the yard and down the path into the woods.

"*Eddie?*" his father shouts after him. Sonia watches him disappear, crashing through branches like a flushed rabbit. She is as surprised as his father at the boy's reaction and feels a swift pang of panic at being left alone with a man he would run from. Slowly, she reaches out for the portrait he dropped and picks off a stray chicken feather clinging to Cora's cheek. Mr. Alley stretches out his hand to help her to her feet. Sonia is not used to being off balance, especially in front of men.

"Beg pardon, ma'am, I don't know what got into that boy—" Eddie's father begins. He has the same flat accent as his son, only his voice is deeper and tightly leashed.

"I think you startled him. We weren't expecting—"

Mr. Alley shakes his head, staring into the woods. She doesn't know where to begin.

"I'm Sonia Blakeman," she says. "There was an accident and we wanted to make sure your son wasn't injured."

"Who is *we?*" asks Mr. Alley in some confusion. "Where's Cora?"

Sonia wipes her mouth with the back of her hand.

"Tucker," she says. "My husband. He's driven your wife to the store."

Mr. Alley takes this in. "And my son was here with you?"

"We have a car," Sonia tells him, and hears how weak it sounds. He looks her up and down, this woman who lets her husband go off with another woman while she is home vomiting in the barn. Sonia is suddenly as offended at being left behind as Mr. Alley is at arriving home to find them gone. He must be on leave, she thinks, studying his uniform. Not military but Civilian Conservation Corps. On his shirt sleeve, he wears a red and green chevron above two crossed hammers.

"Mechanic?" she asks, nodding at his badge.

"Assistant leader," he answers. "Been with the boys these last seven years. Here and there."

"I shot photos of Camp Nira in '33," Sonia tells him, "when the president came through. They staged a funeral for Old Man Depression, burned him in effigy. Some bugler started in with 'Happy Days Are Here Again.'"

"I was at Nira in '33," says Mr. Alley. "Old gimp FDR was shouting like a crazy kid, *That's right boys, burn him up!*"

"Maybe I took a picture of you," she says.

"Sister, you took a picture of me, you wouldn't forget it."

Sonia smiles and things are easier between them now. Mr. Alley drops his rucksack and turns to study the house.

"We thought we'd wake up and everything'd be different," he says.

"It was for a night," she says. "My camera's still set up."

Mr. Alley grins but hesitates. She sees his eyes go to her belly. "Starting a family of your own?" he asks.

"The water here doesn't agree," she answers.

He nods and loosens the top button of his heavy cotton work shirt to show a clean white crescent of T-shirt beneath. "Where do you want me?" he asks.

"On the porch," she says, handing him the picture of his wife and son. "Will you set this under the spring? I'll just be a second."

Fit and tan from working outside and eating three government meals a day, Mr. Alley saunters across his yard to the bathing hole. He sets the photograph under the gushing water, anchoring it with a stone. Sonia feels more like herself now that breakfast is gone. Maybe it is just the water. She steps back into the barn; with a yank, her drop cloth comes away from the nails with a dozen small tears. How stupid of Eddie to run away. He'll have to come home sometime, she thinks, and then it will be that much worse for him. Returning to the porch, she finds Mr. Alley waiting, his legs crossed at the ankle, his arms crossed across his chest.

"Mr. Alley, you're a natural," she says.

"Everyone calls me Bud," he answers. "Lady from the department store in town asked me to model once but I told her sorry, sister, that's for faggots."

"Okay, Bud," she says, throwing the cloth over her camera and ducking beneath. "Freeze."

Bud Alley shows two rows of sharp, white teeth and holds the smile like a stuffed cougar baring its fangs.

She opens the shutter and counts. One, two, three . . . Before she can count five, his eyes have shifted to the woods and she knows the picture is ruined. Eddie, she thinks, surfacing from under the cloth, but it is not Eddie. Tucker and Cora stand at the edge of the yard, each carrying an armload of bought goods. Sonia flushes, feeling caught at something, but then she sees by the way they are standing that they feel caught, too, and she knows something has passed between them.

Bud Alley doesn't move to help his wife, but waits for her to come to the porch and greet him. Cora crosses the yard to set down her things and lets herself be gathered into his arms. He kisses her so long and deep Sonia has to look away. When he lets her go, Bud picks up the pair of boy's black boots.

"What're these?" he asks.

"Mr. Hayes thought Eddie could use a few new things," Cora explains. Bud slides his eyes to Tucker, whose arms are full of more provisions.

"That's mighty generous of Mr. Hayes," says Bud, slowly.

Cora isn't listening. She has noticed the portrait of herself and Eddie Bud left to be rinsed by the pounding spring. She stoops to retrieve it before they are washed away forever.

* * *

His daddy is home.

When he pushed past Mrs. Hayes, he could almost feel his daddy's fist on his collar yanking him back—*What's wrong with you, boy?* Eddie's been asked that question so many times but he's still got no answer. He raced down the path to the road, then took the shortcut across the next ridge without stopping to rest. He has to reach them before they come home alone together.

Eddie, you ran all this way? Mr. Hayes will say. *With that hurt shoulder of yours?* And Eddie will say, *It's nothing, I didn't want you to be surprised.*

Bud always comes home with no warning. He was at Camp Nira for two years and when he came back the house felt stuffed like a large piece of furniture had been rolled in. A few months later, a thick-waisted woman showed up at their cabin, Mama got quiet, and he was gone again. Now he's on the Skyline Drive and comes home when it suits him. Eddie knows then to drag his own blanket off Cora's bed and onto the porch. When his father is away, Eddie pictures him astride a mountaintop, holding in his hands the slicing rays of the sun. When he is home, he imagines taking up a gun and pointing it at his chest.

Keep moving, he tells himself, though his shoulder aches from breathing hard. From the rise, he has a clear view down to the next switchback and a speck of road below it that leads to the store. He has run a long way and, looking back, feels he's seeing this mountain now as he might see it in the rearview of Mr. Hayes's shiny black '35 Ford—reclining, twisting the ashtray, enjoying the Centerpoise. What are the chances, he wonders, that out of all the boys in the entire world, their car should have struck *him*? Mr. Hayes believes he is destined for great things and Mr. Hayes has seen enough of the world to know. Eddie turns back to the road, letting all those other boys grow smaller in the rearview.

There is only the gully still to cross, the shortcut he always skirted as a younger boy, filled as it was with bright green fern his mother calls "rattlesnake." He runs alongside it now, remembering how he always imagined it thick with twined and slithering bodies. But no, *fool*, Cora told him. That fern's only called rattlesnake because its stems jut up tall and pointed in the heat of summer. It's autumn now, and all the rattles have died back, leaving a sea of skeletal fronds.

Cora taught him his colors by these woods. Red for bloodroot, blue for cohosh, green for just about anything else. But yellow was the color of money. And rattlesnake fern, he remembers now, like the crimson bird, is a ginseng pointer. Does he dare? Eddie glances over—not hunting sang, he tells himself, helping Tucker Hayes. But is there a difference? Is there ever a minute in a day he is not hunting sang? His eyes are always open for it, searching even under the pale blue crust of snow. Eddie looks up at the sun, which tells him it's getting late, then makes a swift decision. Veering off the path, he slips down into the hollow. Maybe he has a long-buried memory of his mama showing him where the plants were growing, maybe he is pulled along by instinct. Last time he came back empty-handed. But not again. Now Eddie has something he wants.

The golden leaves glow in the shade of a hemlock, exactly where he knew he'd find them. The plants are young, none bigger than a two-prong. Eddie watches the hill above him, as alert to unexpected company as he is when squatting to take a shit. His mother marked these plants for later—will she know her own son has poached? He doesn't want to see what his fingers are doing. The wind is in the waving fern when the first root goes in his pocket, small and underdone, still caked with dirt. Barely glancing down, he quickly digs the rest, each one a little easier to get out of the ground. How many make a ticket to New York? He searches the hill above him; there must be more.

Stop. He pictures Mr. Hayes helping his mother into the car and knows he has taken too much time already. Eddie jumps up and runs again, crashing through the gully, down through the woods until at last he reaches the terrace above the general store. He has come the back way to the clearing that serves as a parking lot, but even as he arrives, he sees the lot is empty, there are only tracks in the dirt where they had parked. He is too late.

Eddie rests his hands on his trembling knees and tries to catch his breath. Inside that magical building are cold bottles of Coke and RC, but he has no money to buy one. Then, from the hills behind the store, he hears a familiar chant go up. Oh no, he thinks. Friends. They come here to play, he's come often enough with them, but he doesn't want to see them now. In their dirty end-of-the-week clothes they race around the corner of the building to form two ragged lines, faced off against

each other. The witches on one side and the travelers on the other. Jim
and Calamus and Lou and DumbDon are traveling. Rosaleen and little
Ferris, the other Jim and Monty are witches. There are half a dozen
more—cousins and second cousins, barefoot and flushed. The parking
lot is the divide between them.

"*How many miles from here to Gal-il-ee?*" the travelers start the chant,
shouting across the gap.

"*Threescore and ten,*" the witches shout back.

"*Can I get there by candlelight?*"

"*Yes, if your legs are long as light.*"

Then they all yell in unison while everyone runs, swapping places
to no real purpose Eddie has ever been able to figure.

"*Watch out!*"

"*Mighty bad witches on the road tonight.*"

Rosaleen, a witch, spies him first and elbows Big Jim in the ribs.
Big Jim gestures for his travelers to stay put and they do, falling into
each other with the effort to stop. Eddie could try to run but Jim would
catch him. He stands his ground. The older boy strolls over to Eddie
and DumbDon breaks rank to follow, because DumbDon is so dumb
he gets to do whatever he wants.

"Your mama was just here," Jim says.

"With a man who weren't your daddy," DumbDon adds in his gar-
gling voice.

"Another one," says Jim.

The blood rushes to Eddie's face and he can hardly see for his fury.
He wants to tuck his head and ram straight into the big boy's chest,
but he knows Jim is just looking for an excuse to flatten him. He could
take Don but he's protected by all that water on the brain. That's his
hit-by-a-car luck. The bastard.

Rosaleen steps up, the knees of her jeans are grass-stained and her
shirt is unbuttoned one lower than she wears it at school. She is only a
year older than Eddie but she already feels far out of reach. DumbDon
and Jim are watching. Lou, Calamus, Monty, all the boys held back and
their random kin.

"Wanna play?" she asks.

Eddie doesn't want to play, but a beating's waiting at home and to save the beating here, he figures he probably should. He looks back into the woods and sighs.

"Which side am I on?" he asks.

Cora sets pigeon peas baked with pork and molasses on the table. With the flour she bought at the store, she rolled a dozen biscuits. She roasted and ground the coffee beans. They are drinking the strong brew with store-bought sugar and fresh cream. When she holds out her hands to say grace, she grips Tucker's as if to hold on forever.

He hadn't wanted to stay for supper. He took their suitcase and Sonia's cameras to the car but when he returned Cora was waiting for him. *You can't leave,* she'd said. *Not before Eddie's back.* I have to, Tucker insisted. They were speaking low in the kitchen while Bud milked the cow. Your husband is home. *It's getting too dark to drive,* she'd replied. Her eyes said, *Don't leave me here alone.*

At the dinner table, Sonia and Bud Alley are swapping latrine stories. What's the worst hole you've ever had to pee into?

"It was at the Hotel Metro in Leningrad," Sonia is saying. "Outdoors is fine, but a hotel invites certain expectations. The filth around that porcelain hole was five different shades of brownish green, and the smell—"

"Shiiiiiiiiit," says Bud appreciatively.

"Exactly."

Tucker watches them dully. It's bad enough Sonia has photographed celebrities and world leaders. He can understand her interest in them. But Bud Alley? His face is too small and regular, and with his proto-army haircut, he looks like backwoods Hitler Youth. The longer Tucker travels with Sonia the more he understands none of them are special to her. They are all just subjects that happen to catch her eye.

"You've met Reds?" Bud asks.

"I have lots of friends who are Red," Sonia says. "They don't believe Stalin is all about Stalin. Right now he's in bed with Hitler, tomorrow he may be in bed with us."

"Did you hear that, Cora? A lady who's been to Russia," Bud says, turning to his wife. "Cora here's never left the hollow."

"It's good to know where you belong," Tucker interjects. "I'd love to live here."

"I bet you would," says Bud.

While they were waiting for supper to cook, Bud had turned to Tucker. *Cora's firewood's running low. Help me with a few logs?* Together they walked to the barn. Along the back wall hung Bud's neatly organized tools. He owned planes for hewing and planes for smoothing, a polished wooden drill, a mowing scythe like Death himself would carry. He reached up and lifted his two-person crosscut saw from its nail. Behind the workbench, Tucker caught a gleam of wood in the shadows. A man-sized narrow box stood in the corner, which at first he mistook for a cabinet. Then Tucker understood he was led here not for the saw, but to see this and understand.

That got anyone's name on it? Tucker asked, trying for casual.

Bud reached out and stroked the coffin as he would the flank of a horse. It was no cheap pine box, but a buffed and oiled chestnut casket.

That's Cora's family's idea of practicality. Gave it to us on our wedding day.

A coffin for a wedding present?

That family has ways of keeping a man around, like it or not. I take my freedom where I can find it.

Bud took up his crosscut and gestured for Tucker to bring along the chains. He walked them a little ways into the woods, to where last time he was home he'd started on an ash that had been felled by lightning. Together they lifted the ash onto the sawbuck and Bud tightened it in place with the chain.

You done this before?

Can't be too hard.

You got to let go on your stroke. Let me pull. If you push you'll break the blade.

The weathered gray log was as thick around as the two men together. They dug into a deep scorched fissure to get started. Bud pulled hard and Tucker instinctively pushed.

You let your wife go around taking pictures wherever she wants?

I suppose we must trust our women.

I wouldn't trust Cora as far as the general store. Bud pulled the saw again and Tucker pushed, he pulled and Bud let go. Tucker was not thinking of his rhythm when Bud bent down and chucked a stone hard at his shoulder. It landed on his bicep hard enough to raise a bruise.

What the hell? Tucker dropped his grip and grabbed his arm. He felt like he'd been shot. Bud grinned to show it was all in good fun.

That's how I taught Eddie. Don't ride the saw.

Now in the kitchen, Cora rises to light the lamp and refill their coffee. Bud and Sonia laughing reminds Tucker of too many holiday meals spent in the company of loud distant relatives who, because they were all at the same table, he was supposed to consider close. The lantern light deepens a scene that electric would show to be perfectly banal. As Cora retakes her seat, her arm brushes his. *It's us against them, right?* the contact seems to say. Tucker pushes back from the table.

"I could use some applejack," he says. "Be right back."

Tucker steps out onto the back porch, breathing in the night air to clear his head. He finds the jug and takes a drink. God help me, Tucker thinks. Soon I will be living with hundreds of Bud Alleys and they will have to become the most important people in my life. Sonia will be gone and I will be sleeping in rows of single cots of Bud Alleys, eating on benches sandwiched between more Bud Alleys. Tucker had heard a rumor that other draftees who were against the war were planning to desert at the end of their year's term. OHIO they called it. Over the Hill in October.

He takes another deep draw of applejack. It's getting low and he can taste the sediment swirling up on the backwash. Across the breezeway, the door to Cora's bedroom—Cora and Bud's bedroom—is shut tight. Eddie is locked inside, the key in Bud's front pocket. Tucker rubs where the stone hit his bicep, the bruise has become a tiny seed like the pit of a stone fruit around which his flesh has grown. Back at the log, when Bud first winged him, he'd thought to rush the man, but then he'd caught a glimpse of red in the trees beyond him, large eyes watching them, and instead excused himself for a pee. He left Bud standing with the saw and walked deeper into the woods.

Why did you run off like that? he whispered.

I wanted to warn you he was here.

There's no emergency, chum. We're all fine.

Eddie was crouching in the leaves, digging in his pocket. In the center of his grubby palm were five underdeveloped roots, their pale tendrils tangled and complicated. If Eddie had presented him with five severed fingers, Tucker couldn't have been more irrationally disturbed.

You'll introduce me to the Yankees like you said, when I find enough of these?

Hold up, son, Tucker had stopped him. *It may be a while before I get back to New York. If I ever do. We don't know what's coming.*

I could wait with Mrs. Hayes.

I'm not sure Mrs. Hayes will be waiting.

What was he supposed to do? Let the boy hide in the woods his whole life? Bud had already turned to see what was taking him so long. He lifted Eddie by the arm and led him back to his father. You can't run away from your problems, he would have told Eddie, had Eddie not been struggling so. If there are never any consequences, a boy grows up believing nothing he does—even the good things—has any meaning at all.

Pick your switch, and meet me in the bedroom, Bud Alley had said, leaving his saw sunk in the wood.

Remembering it now, Tucker feels his mother's fingers digging into the meat of his own arm, her answer to his father's long and silent fishing trips and all the times she'd find her husband standing on the stairs, unable to recall if he was heading up or down.

"Tucker," Sonia calls from the kitchen. "You building a still out there? Where are you with that applejack?"

Tucker takes a final searing gulp and heads back in with the jug. Bud and Sonia sit close together, like old friends or war buddies. She knows how to make men like Bud feel important, and he will need to learn to do it, too. Cora hovers over the stove, avoiding them. Tucker pours shots into their empty coffee mugs then takes his seat next to Sonia. She leans his way now.

"Before this assignment, Tucker was a playwright," Sonia says, bringing him back into the conversation. "He had a play on Broadway."

Cora turns. "What was it about?"

"It was a Greek tragedy set in Harlem," answers Tucker, angry at Sonia for bringing it up. "It ran eight whole performances."

"Harlem?" Bud snorts, letting the word hang in the air. "Why'd the hell you write about that?"

"Because I was not a black man and didn't read Greek, so it seemed the perfect marriage of ignorance," Tucker explains dryly. "We all thought it was genius until the reviews came in. Then we understood it was *flawed*. *Flawed* is a very useful word, Mr. Alley—it means a little too much genius. Genius that's gone a bit ripe, like a soft, black banana."

Sonia puts her hand on his arm, but he shakes it off. Whose side are you on? he wonders.

"I've been living off the government ever since," concludes Tucker. "How long's it been for you?"

Bud narrows his eyes and Tucker can almost feel the punch connect. Go ahead, he thinks. Let's get it over with. Suddenly, any lingering ease in the room is gone. The women sit very still in their chairs.

"We started blasting at Mary's Mountain in thirty-four. Since then we've laid over ninety-seven miles of road, up to Jarman, then Big Meadows. When the niggers started showing up, we even built 'em their own picnic area on Lewis Mountain. It's as nice as ours."

"Always seemed to me the CCC camps were a good place to stash angry young men so there wouldn't be a socialist uprising," Tucker answers. "Keep you building scenic overlooks until it was time to kill Germans again."

"You got something against us joining the war?"

"Not at all," says Tucker, sick of playing games. "Cora tells me lots of men around these parts are hoping to get drafted. I suppose those of us going should consider ourselves lucky."

He's said it casually enough, but he knows it's landed.

"Your number came up?" Bud asks.

"I report to Fort Dix week after next," Tucker says. "So you see, we are not so different, Mr. Alley."

Tucker has silenced his host, but in doing so has shown himself to be an ungrateful guest, and he suffers for it. Cora glances at him reproachfully.

"Oh, no," says Sonia suddenly, breaking the silence. "Mr. Alley, we forgot about your print. I left you between glass in my camera. And now you are in the car."

"That's twice you've missed me," Bud says. "What you got against me, sister?"

"Not a thing in the world, Mr. Alley," Sonia replies. "We'll have to meet in seven years and try again."

Cora reaches over Tucker to collect his plate, her disappointment in him palatable. But what was he supposed to do? he thinks. Sit still and be humiliated?

"I've got one for your book, Mr. Hayes," Bud says, recovering. "A riddle we tell around camp."

"That's fine, Mr. Alley," says Sonia. "Tucker, write it down."

To appease them all, Tucker reaches back into the satchel he's left hanging over his chair and pulls out their Esso map. He hasn't unfolded it for a few days and is surprised to see how much he's written, nearly every inch of the way impenetrable with stories. He searches until he finds the Shenandoah Valley and the ridge of Skyline Drive, then he draws a line from it to a bit of white space and waits for Mr. Alley's joke. He sees the caption as he'll write it up and send it off: "The hardworking men forging Virginia's pristine new parkways relax after a long day with some wholesome joshing." Bud Alley waits until Tucker is ready to transcribe.

"What made the broke man sleep so sound?" Bud drawls, leaning back in his cane chair as if dispensing Solomonic wisdom. He continues with a low chuckle at Tucker. No, they are not so very different.

"'Cause he didn't have nothing when he first laid down."

"I wouldn't call that a riddle," says Cora. But Bud is done with these houseguests and rises from the table, stretching to work out the kinks from the long day's journey home.

"It's time for us to go to bed," he says. "If we miss you in the morning, have a good trip. Send us a copy of your book so we can read all about ourselves."

Cora hesitates, waiting for Tucker's reply.

"Say good night, Cora," Bud commands. "You can do the dishes in the morning."

"Good night," she says, slowly trailing her husband out the door. Tucker follows the back of her dress as she crosses the breezeway, the fabric bunching and wrinkled under her husband's firm hand. At the kitchen table, Sonia sits absorbing the echo of the man who just left the room. Until now, even with its dearth of possessions, the house hadn't felt empty, but now she has a sense of how Eddie and Cora must experience Bud's coming and going. When they are gone, Sonia turns to Tucker.

"He's exactly the sort of man I imagined Cora would have married," she says.

"Really?" asks Tucker. "I don't see the least bit of Eddie in him."

"Maybe Eddie's not his."

"Jesus, Sonia," swears Tucker. "Not every woman is like you."

Sonia chooses to ignore him, which only makes him more irritated. Her good mood has not been about him. His map is spread out on the table and he wants to be left alone to get back to work.

"I should go to bed, too," she says, rising from the table. "Are you coming?"

"I still have to write up my notes from the store," he replies.

"Don't stay up too late," Sonia says, putting her arms around his neck and kissing him more tenderly than she has in days. He is astounded at how quickly she can turn her attention from a stranger back to him, as if her desire were dependent on having both.

"Wouldn't it be something if I'd taken a picture of Eddie's father all those years ago?" she asks.

"That would be one more picture than you've taken of me," Tucker says. He meant it to be a bemused observation, but he hears the petulance in it. He really does have work to do, that's not a lie. So why does it feel like one? Sonia pulls back.

"I've taken many pictures of you," she says, leaving him alone at the table. "You just weren't looking."

He hears the parlor door open and shut. Across the breezeway, Cora's bedroom door opens and a bleary-eyed Eddie steps out in his nightshirt. The door closes behind him. He has been given a sheet and put out like a house cat to sleep on the porch. Disoriented, he turns his rumpled face toward the lantern light where Tucker sits at the kitchen table with his brandy and his map and his discontent. Under his injured arm, he is carrying the heavy wooden projector Tucker had left by the bed after he showed his *Frankenstein*.

"Daddy says, don't leave things behind in other men's bedrooms."

Tucker colors as he rises to take the projector from Eddie. He had taken the luggage to the car, yet forgotten what, only days before and for such a long time, had been so important to him. Eddie takes a staggering step, meeting Tucker in the breezeway. They stand together, those two, and both jump as Cora's body hits the closed door and the deep hungry growl comes through the keyhole, and if either of them were alone, either of them would place his eye to it, just to confirm, but they are together, alone outside, and so they hear but don't see Cora's answering sigh. They stand transfixed, not wanting to hear, not knowing how to pretend they don't.

"Can we watch the movie again?" Eddie asks.

Tucker nods. "Just don't let me fall asleep."

Sonia lies awake listening to them in the next room. At first there was such a violence to it, she thought Cora needed help, and she went to the inside of her own closed door and waited with her hand on the knob, ready to turn. She stood for perhaps five minutes as they ranged around the room, slamming into furniture and walls. She heard the crash of the white glass dish and bobby pins tinkling to the floor. Not long after that, it grew quiet, so quiet she realized it had become the game of Let's Be Quiet. She had played this game often enough herself, and then it became a game for her, too, to suspend her breathing long enough to catch a downbeat on the mattress or a stifled sigh. Her hand went to herself and rested there, but that's not what she wanted. She wanted Tucker to come to bed. But no, she didn't really want that, either. She wanted to be in that room with Bud Alley but whether she wanted to be slammed against the bed or the one doing the slamming, she didn't quite know.

Sonia returns to the pallet but she's not yet ready to lie down. She feels restless, trapped inside this room next to everyone else in the house. Cora and Bud in their bedroom, Tucker in the kitchen, Eddie asleep somewhere—he couldn't still be inside there, could he? She wishes now she'd skipped Cora's dinner. Her mother used to say that a pregnant woman should rejoice in her sickness, it meant the baby had taken hold. But the return of her nausea brings Sonia no comfort. For a few hours she managed to forget all about it. But here alone, it is with her again, and she knows it will stay with her every moment she's not otherwise occupied. She wants the baby to let go of its own free will so that she won't have to go through it all again. Her doctor in New York is not judgmental, in fact he's the opposite, a little too casual, in her opinion, as if he were an obliging Brooklyn butcher frenching the bones of a crown roast for a favorite customer. She wonders if she can make herself step into that office again, smell the chloroform and leather, make small talk with the other career women and the fat cloche-hatted mothers fiercely guarding their teenaged daughters. She thinks of her own stern, jowly mother and the first time they sat in that office together, when she was only a teenager herself. Her mother might have been sitting beside her in court, as straight and defiant, certain, somehow, Sonia would be acquitted. The last time Sonia was there, she sat next to a mother and daughter, immigrants from the Ukraine. The mother told her a gypsy said no child born to her daughter before October 1946 would be lucky. So here they were.

She opens the front window shutters and lets the moonlight stream in. It is bright enough to read by, and she takes up the book that has been her pillow the last few nights and flips through its pages. It's an old botanical identifying the plants of the Appalachian mountains, line drawings and medicinal uses and what to avoid. The drawings are delicate and finely observed, each hair and vein of leaf sketched in. You can admire these lovely illustrations and shut the book, or you can take these plants inside you and feel the full power of all they can do. She wonders if Tucker isn't right. Maybe she could work with wilderness.

She glances over at the empty pallet. Where is he? So many times over the past six weeks she'd woken alone to find Tucker sitting by the window of their hotel room, smoking into the night, his map in his lap, his hand wrapped around a bottle. She always liked him better at that distance, framed by a window, at work. She liked the intense concentration on his face, the way he grimaced and grunted a bit as he wrote, his hand flying over the page as if he were writing one long sentence that would never come to an end. First he would eat, then he would fuck, then he would drink, then he would let the day spill out as essential as the first three, trying to capture the essence, a person in that day, a passing expression in that day, that would evoke another person on another day who would have to go down on paper, too, until all his days and all their people became as one in his single sentence of understanding. She would watch him until her desire returned and then she'd stretch under the sheet and he'd look up and in doing so, it would be ruined because what she desired was the concentration and the flow and the instant he smiled and set down his pen to come to her it vanished. She could never have both at once, those two things she needed equally—closeness and distance. Sometimes love demanded one, sometimes the other. No matter what, there was loss.

She closes her eyes and when she opens them again the moon is setting. In the dark, she feels for his body, but she is still alone. Outside in the breezeway, she hears voices, footsteps, and motion. Tucker? But no, Bud Alley is coming around the corner of the house. With his rucksack over his shoulder, he is headed back down the mountain path, leaving as suddenly as he came. Watching him go, she feels sad he didn't say good-bye. She thought he had liked her.

She can't stand being in this room another minute.

The lantern still burns in the kitchen. Water hits tin, a pan held under the constantly running faucet; a match is struck. Cora, in her long white nightgown, is setting a kettle on the stove when she steps in. Tucker's map is spread across the long kitchen table, but he is nowhere to be seen.

"I'm having a cup of tea," says Cora, turning around. "Like one?"

"I would, thank you," Sonia replies.

"It'll just be a minute."

Sonia sits uncomfortably on the chair she took at dinner. They don't discuss the lateness of the hour or why they are both up. Earlier, the kitchen was full of people and light seemed to be carried on the flow of talk. Now the wick is dialed down low and the shadows turned up. Cora is lit by the flame of the stove, and with her hair loose and her body limber, she looks years younger than she did only hours ago in the presence of her husband. Lying with Bud, she's taken on some of his amplitude. She is graceful reaching for cups and saucers.

"Tucker seems to have disappeared," Sonia says.

"Men have a way of doing that," Cora answers.

Sonia picks up the map, touching the towns Tucker marked for their guidebook. His notes barely mention direction or lodging or anything given them by the chamber of commerce. Instead they trace the topography of steeples and dogs scratching their fleas and the peaks and valleys of women who believe they can fly. He has half a page about a blind teenaged waitress who served them in a Richmond diner. The cook was in love with her and every morning before the restaurant opened, he set out bowls of whipped cream, making her touch every chair and inch of counter to find them.

"Mr. Alley had to go so soon?" Sonia asks.

"He needs to make town by sunup if he's to get a ride back to camp."

"You must be sorry to have so little time with him."

"He brought his salary," she says, drawing down a wooden box from the shelf above the stove and setting it on the table before Sonia. It's a heavy, handmade cask with dovetailed joints and steel hinges, about the size and heft of Sonia's own chemical case. When Cora opens it, the room smells like the forest. The box is filled with silver-green bundles of dried plants, spiky purple flowers, seedpods, burrs, the leathery nubs of roots.

"I grew up in the city," Sonia says, peering inside. "I can barely tell the difference between a rose and a tulip."

"Sometimes it's near impossible, even those of us who've walked the woods all our lives. The mountain has a wicked sense of humor," Cora says, lifting two nearly identical feathery fernlike leaves from different sections of the box. "Take these two—this one is Queen Anne's lace, wild carrot," she holds up the one on the left. "This one," she lifts the right, "is poison hemlock. Chew a teaspoon of Queen Anne's seeds and it keeps babies from coming. Take a teaspoon of hemlock, and well, I don't have to tell you."

Sonia's mouth feels dry and she licks her lips. "I've noticed you are a rarity in the mountains, Mrs. Alley," she says, slowly. "Most women up this way have four, five, six children. You have only Eddie."

Cora passes the two plants to Sonia, each tied with identical black thread. "The Bible says for every illness God created, he placed its cure in nature." The dried and brittle leaves crumble in Sonia's fingers and flake across the pages of Tucker's work. She blows the pages clean and passes the herbs back to Cora.

"My stomach has been troubling me, primarily in the morning, for the past week or so. Do you think the tea you're brewing would settle it?" she asks, choosing her words carefully. Cora holds her eyes. Steam rises from the kettle over her shoulder.

"Bud told me they're not accepting men into the army who have children coming," Cora says. "Might not be the case if things heat up, but it is now. Bud really wants to go."

"I'd heard that, too," Sonia says.

"Baby coming is a good way to keep a man safe, if you're of a mind to."

Sonia nods. "Our water is boiling," she says.

Cora rises and takes the cask with her, strewing each cup with a handful of leaves and pouring in the hot water. "'Course you can get your man to give you a really good shaking one," she says. "That'll knock things loose in the early days, they say. And even if it doesn't get you where you're going, it's a fine way to be traveling."

Cora sets down the two mugs and takes the seat opposite. "I have some honey if you find it bitter," she says.

Sonia shakes her head no, and stares down into her inky cup. She doesn't know this woman, has no idea if she is wild carrot or poison hemlock. Cora lifts her cup and the steam curls between her lips just before the liquid touches them. Sonia understands now why Tucker would be attracted to her. She gives you so little, you can turn her into anything you need her to be.

"Do you love your husband, Mrs. Alley?" she asks.

"Do you love yours?" Cora asks in response.

"I'm worried I do."

"I'm sorry," she says. "Then it'll hurt to see him go."

Sonia nods. The wind through the door picks up and a cool breeze blows across the table, rustling Tucker's pages. Sonia lays down her hand to hold them until the breeze dies away.

Thank you, Cora, for making my choice tonight, for knowing when I don't. She thinks of that Bible always open in her parents' apartment, her father, so devout. *For an angel went down at a certain season into the pool, and troubled the water: whosoever then first after the troubling of the water stepped in was made whole.* A cool night and a warm drink and a good shaking one, what more can you ask of any given day? She blows upon the surface and watches the ripples lap the sides of the cup.

I know where we can go, Eddie said, wrapping the sheet around his arm. *Follow me.*

Carrying the projector, Tucker trailed behind Eddie. The yard was hushed and still as if snow had fallen and for the first time this season, there was the hint of winter in the thin, clear night. Tucker wonders if Eddie feels the weight, as Tucker used to, of being a boy leading a man. There is little to say at times like this, speaking feels too much like shouting down a tunnel for the distance it must travel.

"Where are you taking me?" he asks.

"To this place I know."

"Your mama showed me a little house in the woods yesterday."

"That's her old homeplace," Eddie tells him. "She says when she's gone, it'll be mine. But it's across the gap."

"Is that bad?" asks Tucker.

Eddie looks at him as if Tucker were not so bright. "You can't get there from here, you have to go all the way around."

They have walked along the high ridge of ravine and come to the tobacco field where the sky opens wide above them. Two parallel wooden frames for stacking the leaves still stand in the middle of the field though the crop has been taken in and sold at market. Tucker and Eddie crunch across the dried stalks, sinking into the softer matted grass beneath. When they reach the shoulder-high cradle, Eddie throws the sheet over it, creating a makeshift screen.

"Clever," Tucker says.

Eddie smooths out the wrinkles while Tucker unlatches the top of his projector and rewinds the film. On the backs of Eddie's spindly calves are three long red welts, perfectly diagonal and aligned as if an architectural draftsman had delivered the whipping. Eddie catches Tucker looking.

"Daddy is just trying to make a man out of me," he explains. "So that I can fight one day. Like you."

"Don't be fooled," Tucker says. "We're all still boys, we've just grown a little manhood around our edges. Twelve-year-old Eddie will hold eight-year-old Eddie who holds three-year-old Eddie who holds that little baby your mama used to hold, and eighty-year-old Eddie will hold them all long after we're dead."

Tucker is surprised to hear himself using the same words his mother had used with him the night his father dropped a glass in the kitchen. Tucker was supposed to sweep up, but he'd done a half-assed job and his father had cut his bare white foot on a missed shard and tracked blood all through the house.

Don't go, son, his mother had said, sobbing, her palms still pink from slapping Tucker's face, his shoulders, his legs, when she dragged him out of bed to see the stains his carelessness had caused. Don't ever go off to war because when a man takes a life, he doesn't just murder the man before him, he murders all those rings of self, past and future, that lived inside the one he's killed. And worst of all, he murders that piece of himself he's extended into the human tangle, that piece he puts in others when he tries to live by God's golden rule and love his neighbor as himself. You have to wrench your humanity back before you can kill, or yes, you are murdering yourself as you murder your brother. That is what happened to your father, boy, and why we must be so gentle with him now. He was ordered into self-murder just like all the others, and he's come home nothing but skin stretched over bones, there's no man left in there. They call it shell shock, but it's not from shells going off, it is because they sent us home the shells of our men, some fragile crust of a hollow pie.

Tucker doesn't tell Eddie what his mama said, sobbing that night. Her fury always ended in tears and crazy talk. He can't tell Eddie because he has yet to figure out how one is supposed to end violence by creating more of it.

"Let's watch the movie," says Eddie.

"You set the silent speed tonight, chum," Tucker replies. "I'm too drunk to crank."

Eddie aims the projector at the square of white sheet and slowly starts to turn. He is a natural, Tucker thinks, watching the look of concentration on the boy's face. Eddie cranks while Tucker reclines in the bed of felled tobacco stalks. Mole crickets restlessly chew in their burrows beneath his temples. His breath settles around him and he lies perfectly still imagining what it will be like to have his pockets picked and his fillings stripped, hands clasping his ankles and dragging him away.

"No one knows where we are," he says. "Doesn't it feel good to disappear?"

"My daddy disappears all the time. That's why Mama goes off, too, sometimes," Eddie says. "At night."

Tucker had thought all of the boy's attention was fixed on the old *Frankenstein*. But watching him, he sees the boy is watching the movie as if looking for the key to something else.

"Where does she go?" Tucker asks.

"Men around here say—" Eddie pauses. "She might be—"

Tucker waits, it is the first confirmation of what he's been dreaming, and yet he almost doesn't want Eddie to say it out loud because he doesn't want the boy feeling as crazy as he feels.

"Like the other women of our family," Eddie says at last.

"Tell me everything you know about witches, Eddie," Tucker says. "I've been thinking I might want to be one when I grow up."

Eddie glances away from the movie with anxious eyes.

"You don't want to be a witch," he says somberly. "They have to give themselves to the Devil."

"How do they do that?"

"Well, some murder a baby and drink its blood. Some plunge a silver knife into a stream at midnight when the moon is full. Some just talk—they call the Devil and he comes."

"Say I don't want to be a witch. How would I go about protecting myself from them, then?"

"You can pour salt under your window and they have to stop and count all the grains. Or you can hang a sieve over your door and they have to stop and count the holes. If you interrupt them, they get all frustrated and have to start over again."

The film has nearly played through but Tucker has decided if Eddie wants to watch it again, he'll let him. They are at the most boring part where the monster terrorizes Frankenstein in different rooms but always in the same way.

"But what if a witch is already inside?" Tucker asks, not bothering to joke.

"Well, Mama says, most important, you are never, never to loan a witch anything because if you do, they'll have complete power over you until you get it back. And you'll have no one to blame but yourself."

"That's a sound piece of advice," says Tucker.

Eddie cranks the movie to its bright white conclusion. The heat from the bulb lifts a small white cloud around the lens as if the projector was slowly smoldering inside. To Tucker's surprise, Eddie doesn't ask to see the movie again but walks to the tobacco cradle and takes down the screen. He is so different from Tucker as a boy, who could never get enough, but demanded *one more time* even with things he didn't care about. Maybe Eddie knows each time he sees it, he'll enjoy it a little less.

"I'm going to sleep out here tonight," Eddie says, spreading the sheet on the ground. "And in the morning hunt some more roots."

"You'll be okay out here alone?" asks Tucker. Eddie nods.

"You're not scared?"

"I'm never scared," Eddie says.

Tucker fits the top back on the projector and latches it tight. Eddie lies down in his clothes and boots, watching the sky. The cold doesn't seem to bother him. Tucker understands the desire not to return. He and Sonia will be leaving first thing in the morning and this might be the last time he sees Eddie. He takes in the boy's crazy cropped hair and his moon-bleached skin. The long, skinny shins ending in new black boots. The faraway, satisfied look, at eight years old, happy to sleep alone in a fallow field and dream of what he would be one day. This, thinks Tucker. You will always be this.

"Good night, Eddie," says Tucker, taking up the projector and turning back to the house.

"You don't really want to be a witch, do you?" Eddie asks. Tucker turns back briefly.

"I'm still trying to decide which way to go."

"Where have you been?" Sonia asks when he returns. She is sitting on the top step of the porch wrapped in his jacket. Her silver hair shines in the dark.

"I went for a walk with Eddie," he says. "He's camping out tonight."

"Did you tell him good-bye?"

"I did."

His map is folded in her lap; it seems a lifetime ago that she fed him a hard-boiled egg. Sitting down beside her, he takes her hand in his. Her black fingernails and tin wedding ring. He loves this hand.

"Where are we headed, Tucker?" Sonia asks. He knows she is not talking about the map. He's been thinking of nothing else.

"How can I ask you to wait for me when I don't know what I'll be when I get back?" he answers quietly. "My father left as one thing, he returned something else and we were trapped there with him. I would never want to do that to someone I loved."

"I wouldn't want to trap you, either," she says.

"Is there any other way?"

"I want there to be," she says.

He's gazed into these pensive silver gray eyes for such a short time but he can't imagine not seeing them every day, watching over his shoulder as he shaves in the morning, flashing at him when he says something stupid. He knows he is a man who needs to be in love. He needs it like food and water. The only time he knows where he is, is when he's inside a woman. It's the only dialogue he trusts, the giving and taking, timeless exchange of sex. All day, he thinks, we listen and wait our turn to talk, each of us talking to ourselves. But sex is rapt and utterly present conversation. Wasn't it Shakespeare's genius, to know this? What we remember are not the exchanges, but the soliloquy coupling of mutually exclusive choices. Man and woman. Here and there. To be or not to be? And afterward, in satiety and gratitude—to sleep. To sleep, perchance to dream.

He leans in and her mouth is on his and he cannot speak to tell her these things. She kisses him as if to steal all those words he's hoarding like nuts for winter, the ones he needs to write down before he forgets them. But it is such a relief to lay down the burden of being himself. Tucker wants no more violent rides, he wants only love.

"Come inside," she says, taking him by the hand and leading him to their room. Tucker wonders what it would have been like to ever have made love with her in their own bed.

*   *   *

He is dozing lightly beside her when Sonia rises and pulls on her trousers, rebuttons her blouse. She slips on her shoes and wraps herself in Tucker's jacket. *I'm going to wash up,* she whispers. *Come back soon,* he mumbles, kissing her ankle. Carefully, she steps over him and walks to the spring, where she takes it all off again.

The water crashes down, icy from the rock. She hadn't felt the cold before, but now she sees her breath against the sharp black sky. Her nipples are hard and swollen, her skin is gooseflesh as she turns around under the stream. With a trembling hand, she reaches between her legs to wash herself and, yes, it's as she suspected, the blood leaks warm into her palm. Was it the good shaking one? The tea? Can she absolve them all and say she just miscounted? The water washes the blood over the rocks back into the ground.

Tucker is awake. She has been gone a long time and now she sees the lamp from the parlor moving down the breezeway and filling the kitchen with light. He throws open the back door and is silhouetted in the frame, looking out into the dark, stretching, lighting a cigarette. She stands still, letting the blood flow. Closing her eyes, she waits for him to come out to find her. She imagines the things he'll say, the apologies back and forth. His clothes wet by her skin when he draws her to him. She waits for him to come, but when she opens her eyes again, he is sitting at Cora's kitchen table where he has left his notes. He has his jug and his chipped cup and his closely written map. He is as still as she; only his hand is moving. To raise the cigarette to his lips and to scratch his pen across the page.

Every one of their nights together, Sonia has felt his need to get it all down. When she is moved, she doesn't want to figure out what she feels or why she feels it. She wants only to capture the stark unadorned image of it and make love with a man about it. See the way that lamp flings shadows like heat? Make my body feel that way. See the way the mountain laurel flowers, see that dirty child washing in a splintered wooden basin? Put that inside me. I want to capture that instant, then I want you to feed it into me until in the explosion I can feel the big bang of it, everything in motion, traveling through us, taking flying bits of ourselves with it. This is why she needs a man around, not for himself, no, that self is always in the way. She needs him to stop her for a moment by fixing the beauty of the world inside her, even if it's only a pin through the wing of a still quivering butterfly.

Oh, Tucker, she thinks, why furiously strike out and rewrite? Why try to save the unsavable in frangible words, to keep a moment going by goading it to exhaustion? Only in the instant blink and the final thrust can we come close to fixing and placing the world's beauty, everything else is imprecise and perpetual.

The blood flows harder and she feels that old familiar cramping. She thinks of what had been growing inside her but is now lost, and she wishes so strongly that she could have it back, to go to him in his yellow light and say, Let's try. Maybe I could be like other women, maybe you could be like other men. He sits at the table, his mind ranging, and she knows that for her to work and love she must move to capture. If only they might go on traveling together, but love is always ruined by settling down. Don't men know if only they'd stay in motion, remain at war, she would trail after them with her lens and body forever trying to fix them in time and space, trying forever to fix herself?

She steps out of the spring and stuffs her underwear with a handful of leaves to contain what is still to come. She pulls her clothes back on and Tucker's jacket, where her hand finds the car keys he's left in the pocket.

What do women know of war? Tucker had flung at her the other day. You are never called upon to kill. Sonia slowly walks away from the small light of the kitchen, headed toward the car. No, we are never called upon, she thinks. We are merely conscripted at birth.

The sun will be coming up in a few hours and the quality of the night has changed. The moon is setting, and everything on the mountain is in its deepest sleep. He is so tired, he'll let Sonia drive so that he can doze beside her and pretend they'll go on forever, that their trip has not come to an end. For a single, blinding instant moving inside her, Tucker had thought he understood the entire human, heavenly, molecular struggle for balance, and what it cost the world when a witch slipped in. But when he tried to write it down, his brain stuttered and the paths went dark.

"You're still awake."

He looks up at the sound of Cora's voice.

Her hair is loose and hanging to her waist, her green eyes swallowed by pupil in the low light. She wears the thin nightgown of his dreams and beneath it he sees the pink flesh of her breasts, the long lines of her thighs as if she were wearing nothing at all. Remembering her husband, he glances nervously over her shoulder. Sonia, too, will be returning from the spring. He is suddenly conscious of his own bare chest.

"Eddie wasn't ready to come home," he says. "He's sleeping under the stars tonight."

"I'm glad," she says. "That you took care of him."

He wishes she would come inside the room. She stands, like the Unseen Guest hanging on her wall, watching him, expecting something.

"You've been too kind to us," he says. "It'll be hard to leave tomorrow."

"I don't think you'll be going tomorrow," she says.

"I'm sorry?" he asks.

"Your wife. She's left."

"What do you mean?"

"She killed your baby and she took your car."

Tucker looks out the back door but it's too dark to see the spring. He stares while he tries to make sense of what she's said. He laughs a little, absurdly, to keep from screaming. Cora sees him hesitate.

"Don't worry," she says. "Bud's gone, too."

Tucker doesn't answer but takes up the lamp and walks toward her. She steps aside and follows him down the breezeway to the parlor. Their pallet is still on the floor, the sheet tossed aside. That part of him that has been waiting for Sonia to leave him ever since he met her knows Cora is telling the truth. He looks around the room and sees his jacket with the car keys is missing.

"Did they leave together?" Tucker demands.

Cora shrugs. "Does it matter? She knew you wanted to stay."

Sonia knew Cora wanted to keep him here. She tried to tell him. This woman stole his dreams, burned his draft card. Why?

"I'm ready to hide you," she says. "Isn't that what you want?"

"I don't know what you're talking about," Tucker denies. He is dressing swiftly to quell his rising panic, retrieving his T-shirt and socks and shoes from where Sonia so recently stripped them off. He slips his suspenders from his shoulders and pulls on his oxford shirt, tucking it into the waistband of his trousers as if he were leaving for work.

"My old homeplace. It's hidden so deep, you'd be safe there. I could visit you. Later, when things calm down, we could go away together."

He stops. Cora has stepped inside the room and stands close enough to touch. She is more lovely than he has ever seen her, radiant and fresh as if newborn. She is offering him the opportunity to stay, not to go among other men and kill or be killed. Cora searches his face in confusion. Isn't this what he's asked for? Hasn't she heard him right?

"Up here," she says, "a kiss still means something. It's like a promise."

What have I done to you? Tucker thinks. You are a poor, beaten mountain woman who invited me into your house and I have turned you into something infernal. He wants to kiss her one last time to remember what the tipping point tasted like, he wants to make love with her slowly and carefully. A kiss, for him, too, is still a promise. But he knows once he starts kissing a woman like Cora Alley, he might never stop. The problem is never the war, he wants to tell her, it's how to live after the battle is over. It's never the kiss, it's how to live after the kiss.

"I'm sorry, Cora—Mrs. Alley," he says. "I think you've misunderstood. If I don't show up, they'll put me in jail."

"Where are you now?" she asks.

His hands shake as he folds the sheet upon which they slept, touching the sticky red stain that has soaked through to the cushion. He turns it over when he replaces it on the old sofa so that it doesn't show. He follows drops of blood on the chestnut planks to the door where there is the smear of a partial footprint. Walking to the kitchen, he folds the map he left on the table and shoves it into his pocket.

"You're going?" Cora asks.

"Please tell Eddie I'm sorry I missed him," he says, trying to find a self to sound like. "I'll write to him."

Cora nods, dumbly, stepping back to let him pass. He is on the porch reaching for his father's projector, which is the last thing remaining.

He'll be on foot until he catches up with Sonia and it is very heavy. He doesn't even want it anymore and can't remember why he's lugged it around so long.

"I'd like to leave this here with you. For Eddie."

Cora shakes her head. "No, it's yours," she says.

"Keep it for me, Cora," Tucker says. "I promise I'll come back when my time is up and get it from you. I'll even bring a camera, we'll make movies of our own."

"Take it with you, please," she says.

"Consider it a loan," he replies. "Just till I come back. Please, watch over it. For me."

He holds it out to her, needing her to believe he'll do what he says so that he may believe it himself. This family will not become one more memory rattling around inside him. Cora's hair covers her downcast face. He tries to meet her eyes to let her know he's true. Slowly, she stretches out her hands to take the box from him, their fingertips brush so gently. Tucker feels the current race up his arms, through his body, into his groin and aching heart like lightning in a jar. Cora raises her head, shakes it with a sad smile. This, too, she knew he would do. His hands twitch to take it back, but it's too late. She has him now and it is exactly as Eddie said. He has only himself to blame. In her face, he sees all he has given away to get away.

The cold front has come in and fog rises on the path through the hollow. He is following the still warm tracks of Sonia headed to the car. She has not really left him, she is waiting, surely, down below, for his apology and the reassurance that he will return if she will wait. After all, it was she who said, After. After I get back. After you serve, and sometimes men must learn to wait, it's a skill he's never mastered but perhaps it's time. He scrambles down the dry creek bed, skirting the ravine, and comes to the tobacco field he left only hours ago. In its center, Eddie lies sleeping on a clean white sheet.

The moon is nearly gone and the clearing is dark, but even without seeing, he feels the absence of the car. Here is where he knew he would find her, curled up asleep on the front seat. He would open the door and whisper, *Lift your head,* and he would place her head in his lap and she would look up at him with those troubled silvery eyes, and he would stroke her back to sleep. But, of course, the thing that could not be, is. She has killed their child and gone ahead without him. Tucker lifts his head and shouts.

"*Sonia Blakeman, where are you? We have a future!*"

Their future echos off the rock face, tumbling down stone and moonlight, and this, he'll think, is what calls the panther. She will find him, not by his scent of fear, but from the desire in his voice, calling another woman's name. Tucker's voice dies out and what comes back is an answering cry in the dark like a woman wailing in grief or childbirth, but it is clear to him this is no woman.

Even before she told him of the lovers and the panther, Tucker knew he would have to face his Devil down. He feels the circling prowl, her sniffing him out. The fool in Cora's story kept walking, telling himself it wasn't real, but Tucker knows it's real, what isn't real is the belief you can outrun it. He is proud of his understanding then worries that pride will be his undoing.

He waits. The woods wait. Early morning spiders are spinning their webs against dawn; in an hour, they will be weeping with dew. He had not thought beyond this moment. What if the panther doesn't come? Tucker takes a step but still hears nothing. He tells himself he's not disappointed, he is relieved to get away. No one wants the panther.

He reaches the road that leads to the store, knowing this is the only way Sonia could have gone. He wonders briefly if she has overtaken Bud Alley who, too, must be somewhere on this road, ahead of him. Who else is walking in the night besides Tucker and his lover and his enemy and his panther? The fool in Cora's story didn't know what was coming, he was blessed that way. But Tucker knows. Goddamn it, Cora, he thinks, get it over with. He walks another half a mile or so, and still no trouble. The waiting is so much worse.

And then, with no warning, it is on him. It must have been tracking along from limb to limb above his head and it drops down now upon his back, four great sets of claws hooking into his shoulders like an oversized parrot. Tucker feels the skin along his spine open up, but it is an almost delicious tear if only because at last the game is on, he doesn't have to wonder anymore. Now he can set his plan in motion, the one he'd been formulating since he left her house and knew his fate was sealed. Tucker drops to one knee, shaking the creature off as he tugs at his shoe. He hurls the shoe as hard as he can, deep into the woods. The fool before sought to distract, but Tucker plans to lure. He races ahead, plunging back into the forest, his thoughts are swift and focused, a strong man's thoughts. The panther is back at the shoe, licking and biting at the leather, tugging the laces with her wicked, sharp teeth, like a kitten. She can take her time, she knows she'll catch up. Do not play with me, Tucker thinks, tossing the second shoe. Here, kitty, kitty. Here, kitty, kit. The cat gives up the first, though really she is not done with it, and lunges for the next. Yes, this is it, he thinks, draw it on, feed her any new distraction and she will follow where you lead.

Through the chestnut graveyard he runs, leaping stumps as they did on their ginseng hunt. His belt comes off, a snake whizzing through the air. The panther leaps to catch it, she is having fun. They go this way nearly a mile as Tucker strips for her. Suspenders off and T-shirt off. Buttons flying as he loses his oxford shirt. He casts away his one, two socks, and then he has his goal in sight, the drop-off up ahead, the long dark fissure in the earth, a home for all the distractible demon panthers not looking where they're going. Without a stumble, Tucker Hayes unbuttons his fly and springs from his trousers, running starkly naked, full on toward it. He feels the glorious cold night air between his legs and beneath his armpits and inside the crack of his ass. His child is gone, his woman gone, his mother and father gone. There is nothing left to lose. He feels the panther's breath, hot against his ear. I have you now, Tucker thinks, the thrill of finally knowing gives him the extra push. He rushes top speed for the crack, they spring together, that man and beast, this is the end of love and fear, his wild chase through the woods. It's yours, he shouts, *Take it,* and instead of claws, his own nails dig into the flesh above his heart, and he feels the tearing, like that of silk. Once the first rip is made, the rest follows the grain, and it's not unpleasant, this feeling, it's almost like standing under the cleansing spring, letting some solid part stream away in the shape of you. Tucker soars with blood on his hands, his own, no one else's, and the question becomes not, What has she done to me, but,

What have I done to myself, and it is the pain and relief of that final knowledge, that all of our deepest wounds are self-inflicted, that lets him rip through that last final membrane, and then Jesus Christ, yes, he is free. The panther leaps, Devil and flesh fall away together, down to darkness, with a howl of rage and shock. He is soaring and in some echoing corridor he hears his own gallop and is conscious of not needing a rider, not needing to ride, which is perhaps the most terrifying thing of all, to be perfectly and utterly on his own.

He soars over the deep ravine in Panther Gap and comes down light on the other side, outside the lonely cottage where she grew up. She knew when she led him here that day of the hunt that this was where he longed to be. He couldn't see it at the time, any more than he could see the ginseng growing beside him, but now he's crossed the chasm and fear has cleared his eyes. All around the little shack, in the shade of the sole living chestnut tree, grow the waist-high golden leaves and ruby berries that mark the essence of man in the earth. He sets down in the clearing and by the first rays of the sun, he sees more treasure glowing on the ground, blue lapis and chips of amethyst, verdigris, and quartz. He walks to the timeless chestnut, where someone has carved a face and driven a nail; it is weeping sticky tears of sap. He touches his finger to it and picks up a stone and sets to work upon his pattern, creating something that will probably never be discovered or known by another living soul. But that's okay. It is his. Inside the open door, he sees a table and a chair and a bed, everything he needs. He walks to the window and cups his hands around his mouth and blows. Am I dead? No, it's there, the film on the glass. Beyond that reflected breath, the wars may rage and the bodies may rise in their pits and rains may wash the bones white and clean. There will always be men lining up to fight those wars. What he needs now he has, and the rest, he trusts, will come. He walks to the comfortless single bed and lays his head down and sleeps deeply for maybe the first time in his lifetime.

Eddie found no more ginseng the morning after Tucker Hayes went away. The sun was rising when he got home, and his mother was sitting in her rocking chair on the front porch, finishing the brandy Tucker had left. She didn't have to tell him they were gone. Her eyes were bright and glittering, excited and scared in a way he'd never seen them before. She said, Eddie, you will meet people who mean something and you know there is meaning but you don't know yet whether they are your ruin or salvation and they go underground and live inside you until they reappear maybe years, maybe decades later, but by then you have grown so much of your own skin around them, layer upon layer, you don't even recognize them anymore, and that's how you become your own ruin or salvation, that's the power of not knowing what's growing inside you, what you've lost for so long. She told him this as she drained the jug and nodded some to herself, as if finishing up a second different conversation. Then she rose and announced she was going to bed. He watched her go and after she did he took her place in the rocking chair, trying out what it felt like to be an adult, and it felt to him very lonely and sad. He sat with his empty hands in his lap, watching the sun rise, until he heard some rustling around in her bedroom, and then he knew that she was planning to visit Tucker Hayes, and she'd keep going back, as she had done with the other men she'd kept in the woods when his daddy was away. Over and over, night after night, until she was worn out and Eddie was completely forgotten. He snuck quietly down the breezeway and put his eye to her keyhole and sure enough, there on the floor was her beautiful ivory flesh, and he knew then what he must do to make it all stop. He went to the kitchen and fetched the salt cellar and quietly he lifted her latch. Her skin was heavy as he spread it out like a quilt and lifted the salt above it, pouring a long, high stream. He rubbed it in good like he was curing meat or killing garden slugs, and it was sticky and odd to be back inside his mother's body for the first time since he was an unborn. He tried to re-drape her skin, arranging the folds as she'd left them, so she wouldn't know he'd touched it. Then he hid behind the bed and waited for her return. He may have dozed off, for time was moving in slow waves. She didn't return until after dark the next night. Waking to footfalls on the wooden planks and the rattle of the latch, he saw that thing she was when she was away from him and he hated it. She put one foot into her casing and then the other and she tugged her skin over her shoulders, slipping her arms inside. But it didn't feel right, he could tell, and she had to tug very hard and pull and almost tear, and then her face was back on and it didn't look right anymore. It was pinched and tight and in that moment he was almost sad that he'd shrunk her, but she had driven Tucker away and if Eddie couldn't have him, she wouldn't either. Cora turned and looked around the room, searching out the thing that had done this to her, never suspecting it was he, though, really now, who else could it have been? After a while, she gave up, and sat hunched inside her skin, and maybe she knew then she'd never get it off again, or maybe she tried and failed many times later. That night, she crawled into bed and her shrunken skin pulled her tight into a fetal ball and all that excess salt seeped out in the form of tears. Hours and hours of them just rolling down her cheeks until the dawn. He felt kind of bad. But Cora Alley was a mother, after all. And it was about time she acted like one.

Ann

1967

Every time she turns her head to greet a guest, the hard spine of bobby pins digs into her scalp. The lowest one, especially, at the base of her skull, tugs at the roots, until finally she drops Eddie's hand long enough to twist it out and slip it into the pocket of her maternity dress. She had such a time finding a dress that would fit her figure in a fabric light enough for the season in a color dark enough for a funeral. She hadn't noticed until she needed something different how cheerful and scalloped and festooned all her smocks were. It was such a happy time in life, and to be pregnant in the summer should be the happiest of all, so no designer would want to spoil it with blacks and browns. She would have sewn something if she'd gotten the news earlier, but as it was, she barely had time to make it downtown to the department store before they had to leave. She chose a navy skirt and shirt with a sailor collar, and felt that to be somber enough. She didn't really care what people she'd never see again thought of her, but she wanted to leave them with the right impression.

She knew she had made the correct choice when she and Eddie arrived at the small Baptist church his mother had sometimes attended. A few older women wore black wool dresses but, of course, they weren't pregnant. Some of the younger women didn't bother to dress at all, just wore whatever they would have worn to work, as if it were any other day. The men had washed their faces, though many looked as if they'd stepped right out of the field, sweaty in dungarees and work boots. They clomped in and removed their hats and paid their respects to Cora Alley laid out in her open casket. Some of them stayed if their women were there and the rest of them left. Cars and trucks pulled in and out of the graveled parking lot all throughout the service.

From time to time, Ann glances over at the woman who could have been her second mother, would have been her child's grandmother. Laid out with her arms crossed over her sunken chest, she looks nothing like Ann had imagined. The corpse of Cora is heavyset with short grizzled hair, and the living Cora, judging by the memorial photo on the program, had worn a pair of translucent, gray, brow-line glasses like every other old lady Ann knew. There was nothing distinctive to mark her out that she can see. A moderate number of people have come to the service—not a huge showing, but certainly she was not without friends. Eddie shakes hands and introduces his wife, and Ann feels their appreciative eyes upon her. Eddie has done well for himself with a pretty bride and a child on the way. Her last-minute clothes are still far more stylish and expensive than anything else in the church, and it makes her feel proud to raise Eddie's status among these people he had left, so that he might confirm, simply with his arm around her waist, the correctness of his choice.

All the Baptist churches she's ever visited smelled of the same sweat and boredom. It is difficult to stand so still against the stench, but she will do it for Eddie. Squeezing her husband's hand, she sends him all the strength she has to give. Eddie had recently purchased a new suit for a hospital benefit and he stands beside her now, not exactly handsome, for that would be stretching the truth, but dignified and benign, his hair combed back from his forehead and his pink cheeks freshly shaven. He still has a little baby fat, just enough to keep him approachable, and more than anything she wants to lean in and kiss a soft cheek. It would embarrass him, though, in front of all these farm men. It is hard to imagine her sensitive, wry, goofy Eddie growing up among them. Thank God he'd found her and could finally be himself. There is nothing she wouldn't do for him, no burden of his she wouldn't bear. She was the one who answered the phone when the hospital called looking for next of kin. I am his wife, she had replied, and they had given her the news that Eddie's mother had been brought to the hospital with complications of diabetes from mellitus and had died earlier that morning of heart failure. She thought she should call him at the station but she didn't want to trouble him before the nightly weather, so she baked a pot roast and an apple pie and lit candles and put a record on the stereo, which was exactly how she'd delivered the news she was pregnant, and when he got home and she helped him out of his jacket and shoes, she could tell he was confused, knowing this dinner had to be about something, but now, seven months into it, it could not possibly be about what it was before, and Ann had waited until he finished his meal and ate his pie and drank his coffee, and perhaps it was not the best way to announce his mother's death, but she could think of no other. They borrowed her father's car for the trip up to Panther Gap because it was more reliable; it was such a lovely drive and only his silence kept it from feeling like a vacation. With so much silence she was left to her own thoughts most of the way, and she fell to wondering what Eddie's childhood home would look like and whether or not it would make an acceptable summer house once the baby was born. She hoped more than anything Eddie would not try to force the name Cora on her now if their child was a girl, when she had her heart set on Grace, her own mother's name; both mothers were dead now, she no longer had the upper hand in that matter, but, of course, everyone was telling her she carried straight out and high, and so it would probably be a boy, anyway.

The minister arrives and they sit through the sermon, which is mercifully brief because Eddie chose to forgo a eulogy. She keeps her hand in his until he rises to join the other pallbearers. She is not sure if she is to rise also—at her own mother's funeral she had been so distraught, an aunt had led her through the entirety of it and she remembers nothing. This is men's work and she can't trail behind them like a flower girl, so she waits until the coffin is safely out of the church and others have begun to rise before joining her husband outside. Cora Alley had wanted to be buried on her own land among her people, but the funeral home had been very clear that was not allowed anymore. She was laid in a new, midsized, nondenominational cemetery bounded by a chain-link fence. It was arid and treeless like something a sharecropper might get stuck farming, and because it was so new, Cora was only the third resident, the other two being veterans. Ann expected they might have spread things out a little and filled in over time, but instead of spacing out the graves, they were clumped up together in the far left corner, Once Upon a Time or In the Beginning, the first three words of a very predictable story. Many fewer people joined them at the cemetery. Just the pallbearers, really, and the minister. Poor Eddie was an orphan now. His father dead in Normandy (her father survived the same invasion, yet another bond between them), and she takes his hand again. He looks around the cemetery, just as he was looking around the church, and as he soon will be looking around the path leading up to Cora's house.

"Is there something wrong?" she asks. "You look like you're expecting someone."

"No," he says. "I've always been afraid to bring you here, but I'd like to show you where I grew up."

Ann's eyes well with tears. It would mean so much to her, after all the stories and all the years of wondering. It was hard to say exactly how it came between them, but she always felt it there. Not really a secret but a silence.

"Oh, Eddie," she says. "Nothing would make me happier."

"It's a little bit of a climb," he warns her, "but I'll help you, and we can always turn back if you get tired."

"I can make it," she says.

He helps her into her father's car and drives her up the mountain. She would like to look out of the window and take in everything about this place, but the sharp turns make her feel like she's flying over the edge and she is about to throw up from the heat and motion and the crowding baby. He parks the car in the shade of a clearing.

"It's just up this path," he says, taking her hand. "Be careful, though, there's poison ivy."

She draws closer to him, so close she nearly pushes him off the path. He helps her over fallen stones and up a dry creek bed. She is breathing hard against the weight of the baby and, in the pumps she wore for the funeral, has trouble finding purchase, even as he holds out his hand to support her. She is disappointing him, she can tell. She is not light on her feet and moving at his pace, she feels his impatience. The path is clouded with midsummer gnats, they brush her cheeks and stick in the moist corners of her eyes, but she will not complain.

"We're almost there," he says. "Hang in just a little longer."

She nods, winded, and keeps going. She climbs the last rise, stepping into the yard. He had told her stories of this place, painting a portrait of romance and mystery, a beautiful, uncanny mother who healed with roots and a childhood spent wandering the woods. But what he leads her to is a dark and parsimonious hovel, stuffed with rags around the window frames and roofed with rusted tin cans. It is nothing like the cottage in the laurels she pictured, set atop a sunny hill with a view of the valleys all around. It hunkers against the rock face defensively, like a cornered animal. The yard drops off steeply behind the barn and tumbles into sharp stone and briar. If a child toddled too close, it would fall to its death.

"What do you think?" Eddie asks, shyly. "This is home."

Ann turns to him with tears in her eyes. Her darling raised here? He had told her ghost stories but she never believed them. How could she? But seeing this place, for the first time Ann understands who she has married. This is what he brings her and without her, this is what he would slide back to. The weight feels so great.

"Oh, sweetheart, I'm so sorry," she says, embracing him. "I had no idea. You were so right to leave. We'll sell this place as soon as we get back and you'll never have to think of it again. We'll work hard and save for someplace bright and happy to raise our child. Never this, oh, God, darling, never this."

He has made a mistake bringing her here, she can tell that is what he's thinking. Better he had protected her from it. That is what he should have done. But she will not let his beginnings come between them. She is his future. Ann and his child. He puts his arm around her and kisses her cheek, but he is scanning the woods again. What could he possibly be missing when he has so much? A new career, a child on the way, and a woman who loves him well enough to forgive him every awful thing he is?

Eddie

New York City

4:50 a.m.

When I first got my diagnosis, Wallis, I thought a lot about death. I didn't talk much about it because every time I did, Charles would go shopping and come home with some new rare orchid we'd have to baby or matching sushi mats and Japanese cooking classes we'd need to attend. I didn't want to stay busy, I wanted to sit quietly, but I understood his need for activity, so I determined to study my own imminent demise in the Happenings section of *The New Yorker*—all those improbable, impossible lectures we moved here to attend. And, truly, every time I showed up at the red door of an Upper West Side stone church—for they were always held in the common rooms of churches or the crisp blue auditoriums of the JCC—it was to find a room full of old people exactly like myself, all smudged spectacles and broadcloth coats and fedoras and clutch handbags. We elderly, who needed magnifying glasses to read the tiny print of announcements, were lured to these lectures and documentaries and museum talks by some mysterious pheromone of the Afterlife. The aroma was as distinctive as mothballs and Vagisil, the dissonant perfume of resignation and a sharp New York need to understand.

Charles came with me to the first few and we sat close together in our folding metal chairs, sipping our coffee with its artificial creamer, silently praying to be stymied into revelation, believing if we sat among experts long enough and listened carefully and questioned and took our arguments home and slept on them and packed them along to the next lecture, something would shake loose and meaning would come before it was too late. He lasted about a month, but I continued to go to probably three lectures a week for close to a year, eating more Hungarian pastry than is good for a dying man, and every night when I came home Charles would refrain from quizzing me, knowing that there were no words for the things I was learning in those basements without him. Or rather there was only one word. Eschatology. The study of last things.

It was at one of these seminars, led by a rabbi—and, yes, I am a sucker for a long, white beard—that I heard the most cogent argument for a Creator. This delightful old rabbi told us God commanded His angels, "Make me a creature with the ability to say thank you." He didn't care how we got there, or how long it might take to arrive. But the ability to give thanks was the sole purpose of evolution, what separated reasoning Man from the animals, and it was predicated on one thing alone—the free will to accept or reject. This was the single truth I took away from all those talks on the funeral rites of the Arawak Indians and the marathon bare-bulb readings of Joyce's *The Dead*. We don't need a discussion or a balance sheet or an itemized list of all the transgressions big and small we've perpetrated against each other and ourselves. We need only for life to teach us the humility with which to give thanks. It takes many attempts and many more failures before we mortals can offer up those two simple words. Thank you. Some of us die never being able to do so. Some give lip service to our thanks, but most of us don't even know what we're grateful for. We throw our happiness away with both hands.

I didn't talk to Charles about that lecture, surprisingly enough. He's a very grateful sort, naturally, which is why everyone he meets instantly loves him. Instead I sat down and composed a letter to your mother. I wrote like a broken-down alcoholic from a twelve-step program, out to make amends. I am so sorry, I wrote. I wish I'd known enough to spare you all that hard work on all the wrong things. Men don't care about the artistry of everyday life, you see. We don't really like surprises because they make us feel inadequate and under obligation. We want someone who can hold steady, so that we can see ourselves, as if shaving in a mirror. If there is too much darting around, too much back and forth, the mirror shakes and our self-image is blurred and we are apt to cut ourselves. God must feel the same at the end of a long day. Stop trying to make Me happy with all that ritual up and down, all the good works and psychic genuflecting. All the good works in the world will not bring you any closer to Me. Stand still. Let Me look at you and find Myself reflected. Maybe for a brief moment, you thought it was about you, but surprise, Creation. It is all about Me. I wanted to write her: It's the same for you.

Wallis, we are the YHWHs of our own relationships, though we can't admit it, our names, like that of any jealous creator, must remain hidden, even to ourselves. It is too terrible to dispense with kismet and destiny; to accept that we are the sole inventors of our Edens, and with them, our perfectly personalized snakes. Only at the end of my life do I understand that *I* am the unpronounceable tetragrammaton containing past, present, and future of being, derived (I learned, this time from a mullah) from the Arabic *y-hawa*, which means not only "He who is," but "He who falls." Why did it take me this long to accept responsibility and with it find the humility to utter that singular incantation that makes everything else possible? Thank you. It's all He wants. It's all we want. And maybe a few memorable kisses over the decades. And maybe a grandchild. But those are our Elohim and our Adonai, a vowel or two added, different names for the same thing.

That night you showed me the projector hidden in my mother's bottom drawer, I took it to my room intending to hold a private screening for you and Jasper the next evening. I thought we'd pop corn and watch it a few times—if it wasn't ruined—before I donated it to a film museum or the Library of Congress or wherever it might belong. That's as far as I thought. When Jasper came in to offer me a sandwich and a beer and talk about the clothes we recovered, Tucker Hayes spread across the woods, it didn't occur to me not to tell him what you'd found. How we decided that tomorrow was too long to wait, I don't remember. I felt bad I wouldn't let him finish wiring the house. I felt bad about the poison ivy, about Captain Casket getting cancelled, about his father's suicide and his mother's death. What's the harm, I thought, in making him happy about this one small thing? How we came to watch it in the barn is also hard to recall, except I knew I didn't want to watch it with him in my bedroom. Maybe that should have told me something. We said it might be noisy and we didn't want to wake you, and after we ate and talked and drank some beer, we left the fire to burn down and walked across the yard together. Jasper pointed out the stars were falling through Perseus and I think I promised we'd come back in November to catch the Leonids.

We found the darkest corner of the barn and I balanced the projector on an old crate and we watched the short film all the way through. It was remarkably well preserved, considering. When it was over, we sat quietly breathing in the dark, neither of us moving, until I rose to light the lantern we'd brought to lead us there. I struck the match and raised the wick and when I turned around, he was pulling his T-shirt up over his flat stomach, just scraping the peaks of his pink, erect nipples. For a moment he was as headless as the conductor by the railroad tracks, nothing but gooseflesh of white torso and dimple of armpit. The backs of his arms were a constellation of freckles and then his shirt dropped to the floor and his eyes held mine, as still as mountain rock at dusk. He didn't take those cliff-side eyes off of me as he reached down and unzipped the fly of his jeans and wriggled out of them and his underwear at the same time. Women's clothes drop away, they are soft folds at the feet like a pool of water. Men's clothes are hard and sit up at angles and must be stepped out of gracelessly. He did, darling. The barn was wide and smelled of damp hay. The lantern flame leaped against his gorgeous penis high against his belly. It was large and perfect and reaching out for me. It knew, and mine knew, too, and it hurt so bad. I wanted that hurting to go on forever. In that moment he was neither a son nor a lover to me. He was like food. I wanted to eat him alive, I was so hungry. I didn't even know how starved I'd been until then. And yet to taste him would mean the end of everything. Your mother. You. Me as I had always been. Most of all, him.

If you could have just left him at the station, I wrote your mother all those years later, I could have handled it. But you invited him into our house. And you did it to please me when I was trying to protect you by keeping him away. Maybe, Ann, I owe you thanks after all for that, too, the fall of our family.

Tell me what I am, Eddie, he said. Tell me why you brought me home.

I glanced at the lantern, casting its soft light over his naked body. He was shivering uncontrollably, even as he tried to stand still. I thought I should warm him, I thought maybe it would be best to smash the lantern and let the flame catch up the barn and the barn catch up the night and burn us both alive. Better to burn now than later, I actually thought.

Instead, I told him he was confused and that he'd misunderstood my affection for him. I told him he missed his father and that the feelings he had toward me were just that, love he would have given to his father if his father had still been alive. I told him I loved him as my son and I would be so happy if he wanted to stay with us past the summer. I told him I knew you and he liked each other and that it was okay, these things happen between boys and girls, no harm done.

I turned and left, I couldn't look back to see those eyes. I didn't know how I could ever look into those eyes again, having lied so hard in telling the truth. I went to my room and shut the door and lay on the sofa, not daring to undress. The fire had died down to ruby coals and ash, the chill of the night had crept inside. For the next few hours I replayed every day of the last year, all the jokes and conversations and lunches, all the skits and odd jobs and backslaps. Most of all I replayed the day after Ann had led me to his room—the one she had prepared without my knowledge—when I stopped him in the hallway at the station. *I've noticed you haven't been going to school, you've been here almost every day,* I said. *I was on my own at your age, I know how hard it is. You're a special kid, I don't want to see anything bad happen to you. God, Eddie, you've given me so much already,* he said. And I couldn't think of a thing I'd done except take him out to lunch a few times and listen. And share my own story. I had begun a conversation I could not finish. He had misunderstood. He had understood better than I knew. He stood naked before me.

I closed my eyes to shut it out. I couldn't not see. I could never not see again as long as I lived. I squeezed them tighter. It's not my fault. I never. I wouldn't. I said all the words but I knew I had and I could. I opened my eyes.

The room was flooded with light.

I leaped from the sofa, flicked the switch he had wired. Off, on, off. You were up, too, the bare bulb in your room glaring. The kitchen, the porch, all the fixtures ablaze. You threw open your door as I raced past, shouting at you to stay where you were. I don't know if I'd ever even raised my voice at you before; you shrank back afraid. I ran across the porch to the backyard where, lucky for me, the light from the windows made the dark of the yard even darker and, not seeing, I tripped over the taut electric cable, falling hard on my face. I didn't have time to feel pain, I was so grateful I'd found the magic thread that would lead me to him. I groped along the ground, following the wire in and out of trees, through the crevices of rock, around blind corners of forest to the path we walked to and from the car. The hearse was still there, hunkering in the dark. Its back gate hung open and I climbed inside, certain I would find him curled up asleep in there as Ann sometimes took the couch after a nasty spat. The hearse was empty and I cursed myself, because in checking, I had lost the thread. Furiously, I felt along the ground, over roots and stone and dully glowing green mushroom, until at last my fingers tangled in it. The cable plunged back into the woods, weaving its way into the denser dark where the moon beat vainly upon the canopy. I went in after it, my fingers numb from running along its length, my back screaming from bending down tracing its path. It dropped off precipitously and from the rise above, I saw the road directly below, the spent spool, moonlight playing along the electrical wires overhead, snagging on the dangling jumper cables that he had taken from the hearse. Stray blue arcs still leaped between the makeshift circuit he'd used to complete the busted transformer. I shouted his name and crashed down the hill to where he lay, thrown from the pole with the shock of connection. I knew he must be dead when I pulled his limp body onto the shoulder of the road and cradled him in my lap.

Jasper, oh, God, Jasper, oh, God, oh . . .

His jeans, his shirt, everything back in place as if it never happened. Maybe it never did. Maybe he never happened. An orphaned boy at the station who appeared and disappeared, just a troubled dream in the middle of a long life. Did I want him to be over, like a nightmare I could forget? Was that why I had brought him here? To get rid of him once and for all? But with a long, deep shiver, like my mother used to say, someone walking across your grave, his chest moved beneath my hand. His lips parted, his eyes fluttered and opened. He looked up at me, shocked back into being a boy again, not that thing he'd been in the barn. He lowered his head so that I couldn't see his shame and I knew then he would live. I thought I had known gratitude when I was shown my first movie. I thought I knew it when I met my wife, when I received my Christmas bonuses, when I found you in the woods. Before that night I had never known the meaning of the word, it had been as empty to me as the word *fear* had been before I embraced the fear of letting myself love you, Wallis, my child.

"Did it work?" Jasper asked. I nodded over him, my tears wetting his hair.

On my life, Ann, I wrote your mother all those years later. That was the only time I held him.

Wallis

1980

All the lights are on at home when the hearse pulls into the carport. Through the sliding glass door, Wallis sees Mom sitting at the kitchen table in her buttercup quilted bathrobe, the one Wallis picked out and Eddie paid for last Mother's Day. By this time of night, Mom is usually nestled in bed with a library book. She keeps the television on in her bedroom and reads with the volume down until Eddie presents the weather and then, from her own bedroom, Wallis will hear her turn it up until her father is done, then turn it off. She has moved the television from her dresser in the bedroom to the kitchen counter. The volume must be turned up pretty loud for her not to hear the tires on the driveway. Or she hears and just doesn't want to turn around.

Eddie slides open the door and drags in the cooler packed with uneaten groceries. Wallis and Jasper linger in the car, gathering the fast-food wrappers and empty soda cans from the long trip, neither of them wanting to go in next. They haven't spoken about what happened. When her father disappeared into the woods after Jasper, Wallis waited alone in her grandmother's house for over an hour, wondering how much longer she would need to sit until someone came to tell her they were both dead, her mother was on her way. Finally Eddie staggered across the yard leading Jasper to the kitchen to wash the dirt from his knees and elbows. Jasper had a dazed, dreamy look about him as if he were sleepwalking through it all, and when Eddie sent him out to the spring to wash the leaves from his hair, Wallis thought she would get her explanation at last. About the barn and the movie, about the lights and their disappearance. But all her father had said after Jasper left was, *Pack your things. We're going home in the morning.*

In the kitchen, Mom tilts her cheek so that Dad can kiss it. She doesn't get up but looks over her shoulder to assure herself Wallis is there. Jasper is climbing out of the hearse with his rucksack and the old projector, and Wallis sees the flicker in her mother's eyes as if she'd hoped, somehow, Eddie had let him loose by the side of the road like one of those dogs they sometimes find at gas stations. Wallis slides her suitcase out of the back and follows Jasper inside.

"Your mail is on the counter," Mom is saying to Dad. An open envelope purposefully left on top of the pile is addressed: *Attention Shareholder.*

"I understand they're selling the station," she says.

"So it's done?" Eddie asks, trying to sound casual.

"Seems like."

"Things change, Ann," Eddie says. "It'll work out."

Mom nods but says nothing. Her father drags the cooler to the refrigerator. It sloshes with melted ice and he has to dry each item with a paper towel before he puts it away. Wallis watches him wipe down the mayonnaise, the two remaining cans of beer, wrapped ground beef. Water has gotten into the marshmallows and he throws them away. She glances at the program Mom has been watching. It's the news about the hostages in Iran that started coming on after the regular news.

"I'm going to bed," Jasper says.

"Good night," replies Ann politely.

"What time should we be up in the morning?" he asks Eddie.

Her father looks up from the cooler. "I'm going in alone tomorrow. I was going to ask Ann to register you for school. They'll need time to transfer your records."

"I told you I'm not going back to school," Jasper says reflexively. Wallis can't believe he would argue at a time like this. He can't even see how angry her mother is.

"Good night, son," Eddie says.

Jasper snatches up his duffel bag and pushes past Wallis. He stops at the bottom of the stairs and she thinks he is about to turn around to continue the fight, but he doesn't. He takes the stairs up to his bedroom as if his sack were full of boulders instead of a change of clothes.

"When you go in tomorrow," Mom says, "you should know I told them you had a ministroke and were ordered to rest. Those flowers on the windowsill are from John and the crew."

"You told them *what?*" Eddie asks.

Mom looks away from the television. "I told them that's why you were late for your party. That's why you were behaving so oddly and why you couldn't come to work."

Now her father is as angry as her mother. Wallis looks at the bouquet of roses and carnations that have started to go brown at the edges from the heat, and the big dopey Get Well card with its dozens of signatures.

"What did you do that for?" he snaps.

"I had to tell them something, didn't I? When you didn't show up? When they called the house? I had to lie and pretend I knew they were selling my own father's station when they said how sorry they were. You are my husband. *Why didn't you tell me?*"

Mom is on her feet in her bright yellow bathrobe. She looks like she hasn't slept in days or washed her hair or moved from this spot. Except that the kitchen is clean and the mail is sorted and all the plants in their beds outside are watered and weeded.

"I didn't want to hurt you," Eddie says at last.

"Bullshit," says Mom. "You're a goddamned coward."

They have both forgotten Wallis is there, and Wallis doesn't move. Her parents have always bickered so they wouldn't have to fight. But it is nearly impossible for her to remember what any of them used to do before Jasper came. On the small television, tinny theme music plays and that red-faced man with the big hair is saying it's Day 288 for the hostages and their families.

"Where did you even take them?" Mom demands.

"We went to the mountains," Eddie says.

"Not to that shack?"

"It wasn't so bad," Wallis breaks in. She can see her dad needs help. "Dad and Jasper are fixing it up. They're wiring it for electricity so we can all go back in the fall."

"Themselves?" Mom asks as if Eddie were not in the room. He lifts the cooler and dumps the dirty water down the sink. He turns it over to dry and wipes his hands carefully on a dish towel.

"It's been a long day," says Eddie calmly. "I'm going to bed, too. We'll talk more in the morning."

Dad doesn't try to kiss Mom again and she doesn't acknowledge his departure, but waits until she hears him on the stairs before speaking again.

"Did you at least have fun?" she asks grimly.

"I'm sorry we didn't call," Wallis says. "Dad went to town, I thought he would."

Mom sits back down and Wallis feels she should sit with her, she wants to be close to her now that she's felt what it's like to be so far away. Mom spreads her hands on the white Formica table as if trying to read a Ouija board.

"The first day you were gone, when I didn't hear from you," she says, "I unfolded all our driving maps and ran my fingers up and down the whole East Coast hoping they'd somehow know and stop where you were. I knew, in my gut, that he'd taken you there, but I told myself he wouldn't. He was responsible, a grown man. I almost got in my car and drove all the way to that old house. I didn't though. Even though I knew. I told myself he wouldn't."

"We didn't think you'd be worried," Wallis lies.

"I had the maps out," Mom continues. "So I made a list of all the smaller cities with network affiliates within three hundred miles of here. I wrote them down, see." She reaches for a list under the phone book on the counter. On it is a list of names inked in blue and beside them call letters. The list is not very long.

"There are almost no independent stations left and when I phoned them, I found out most of them were in the process of phasing out their weathermen anyway. They were looking for *meteorologists,* whatever those are, as if you needed to be a scientist to read the weather. I was so alone, I kept the TV on all the time just for company. And that man kept counting down the hostages' lives: Day 285, Day 286, 87, 88. You know, when the shah died a few weeks ago, I really thought they would release them. The reason for holding them was over. But no, they just found something else they wanted—the shah's assets, they said—and I thought, Ann, people will always find a reason to hold on to what they have until they find something they want more. Then they'll let go, just like that."

"I'm sorry," Wallis says, wanting to cry. "It's all my fault."

Mom looks up and sees her for the first time since she's come home. She opens her arms and Wallis buries her face in the quilted yellow satin that smells of margarine and pancake syrup.

"It's not your fault," Mom says, squeezing her too tight. "I wish I knew who to blame."

Wallis endures the prolonged hug and gently frees herself.

"It's late," says her mother. "You need to be in bed, too. If you want back-to-school clothes, we should go tomorrow while they're still on sale."

Wallis nods and takes up her suitcase that she left by the door. Her mother is not watching TV anymore but she makes no move to turn it off. Instead she pulls a vial of pills from her deep pocket, shakes two into her hand, and swallows them dry. Wallis has never seen her take anything stronger than vitamin C.

"Something to help me sleep," she says when she catches Wallis staring. "I got them on Day 287, which was my own Day 3."

Wallis takes the stairs to her room. Plenty of women need help, Mom's doctor would have reassured her, had Mom bothered to ask. If she hadn't driven miles out of her way to the new, bright, chain pharmacy so that the pharmacist she'd known all of her life wouldn't see she'd come to this. It's best Mom didn't ask. Wallis knows it would have made her feel worse, reduced to being like plenty of women.

The door to Jasper's room is closed but she hears voices, then the crash of glass breaking. Dad has not gone to bed, he is in there with Jasper, and they are arguing. Everything was easy before he came. She went to school and had friends and took piano lessons. Mom didn't swallow pills, Dad still loved them. Wallis knows whose fault all this is. The voices abruptly cease and she draws back. Her father throws open the door and behind him she sees Jasper standing by the bed, his clothes dumped out on the floor, the lamp overturned on the dresser. He is breathing hard. Eddie's face is set.

"That's right, Eddie, walk away," Jasper flings. "You're so scared, you're scary."

Mom left a brightly colored newspaper circular on the table by Wallis's cereal bowl. She put a check mark and a note next to a high, lace-collared shirt with pearl buttons. *Would look lovely on you.* For Jasper, she's checked a green and white baseball shirt and a pair of Lee jeans. *Jasper, darling, what size do you wear?* Though it is still the middle of August, summer is over. She has already put them on the school bus and waved good-bye. Wallis walks to the refrigerator for milk and shivers in the cold. She didn't use her air conditioner last night because after a week without it, it had felt like sleeping in a morgue.

"I've tripped over this damned thing twice," Mom says, coming inside with half a dozen ripe tomatoes and two fat zucchini. "What the hell is it?"

She lines up the tomatoes on the windowsill over the sink and pulls off her gloves. Her hands are swollen and pink, and though they aren't dirty she runs them under cold water anyway.

"It's an old projector that belonged to some guy Dad used to know," Wallis answers. His name was Tucker Hayes. She doesn't tell Mom that Dad's mother killed him and we found his clothes in the woods.

"It belongs in the attic," says Mom.

"Jasper says one of the movies is worth a fortune."

Mom sighs at the mention of Jasper's name. "I know what your father is going to say. We invited him into the house, now we're responsible for him. We can't just put him back on the street. But I don't know how we can afford to keep him."

"I still don't know why he's here," Wallis says. "We were happy before he came."

Her mother stares out the window over her yard and garden where she has had to re-stake her tomato plants against hungry deer. She has spent decades of her life getting this yard and garden exactly how she wants it. Wallis thinks of that trick where a magician grabs a tablecloth and yanks, leaving the cups and plates spinning in place. Mom shakes her head.

"No happy family would take a risk like this," Mom says. "That's how they stay happy families."

Wallis waits for more but more doesn't come. Instead her mother gives herself a shake. "It's after ten," she says, looking at the clock. "Who sleeps so late in someone else's house?"

It feels good to take action, so Mom marches up the steps to her sewing room and knocks sharply on the door. Wallis leaves her cereal melting in the bowl and follows.

"Jasper," Mom calls. "You need to get up. The school is expecting us before noon."

"What if he won't go back?" Wallis asks.

"He will if he plans to live in this house," Mom answers tightly, rapping again. They both wait for his sour, rumpled face to appear but a minute passes with no response. Inside, Wallis can hear the faint jabbering of the *Morning Zoo* over the clock radio. Traffic and weather. Always weather. Her mom wouldn't barge in but Wallis turns the knob and throws open the door.

"Mom said get up," she says roughly, stepping in.

The curtains are drawn and the room is dark. Mom flips the overhead light switch to reveal the empty daybed tightly made with sharp military corners. Jasper has picked up the overturned lamp and the room is meticulously tidy, nothing like her own room strewn with clothes and half-read books and half-eaten sandwiches, all the things she's picked up and discarded in the daily graze for pleasure. He still feels like a guest here; if he felt at home, he would have unpacked and moved in, trusted Mom with his mess and his jeans size and every other thing he's been withholding. By the bed, Mom sees his wastepaper basket overflowing with wadded Kleenex and shudders. This room used to smell like chalk and cloves from an orange pomander Wallis made one Christmas and hung from the doorknob. Mom had kept that clove-pierced orange until the fruit was shriveled and hard, because no matter how faint, she said, it smelled like a little girl's love. Now the wastebasket smells rank, like chestnuts in bloom.

"I've been up since six," Mom says. "He didn't leave with your father."

Wallis looks around the room and sees his duffel bag is gone.

"Maybe we should call the police?" she asks.

"We can't," Mom says swiftly. "They won't file a missing person's report until he's been gone twenty-four hours. He'll be back soon."

There is no note—he must be coming back. If he were running away he would leave a note. That's what people do. Wallis stands in the empty room, once filled with ribbons and thread and all the womanly things women no longer use but like to keep around. It smells so strongly of boy she can't even recognize it anymore. Her mother angrily snatches up the wastepaper basket and goes to dump it in the garbage outside.

"Well?" Mom says, when Eddie gets home from reading the eleven o'clock weather. She turned off the television and reheated the meatloaf and his hot supper is waiting for him on the kitchen table when he pulls up.

"They found a buyer," he answers, loosening his tie and undoing his top button. He hands Wallis his plaid jacket and she tosses it over the back of a chair. "Some guy from Atlanta with a superstation."

"What's that?" Mom asks. Eddie shrugs.

"We'll be watching a lot of Braves baseball and old movies."

"And the staff?"

"They want to keep the six and eleven. But they want kids. We're out."

Mom nods.

"Your show, too?"

"We tape the last promo tomorrow. *Frankenstein. As it was in the beginning, so shall it be in the end.*"

Her mother says nothing as she pours Eddie his glass of milk. She had been too calm all day, walking through the mall, letting Wallis buy whatever she liked. Only after they stopped for ice cream and Ann sat sipping her coffee for an hour had Wallis realized she was stalling; giving Jasper more time before they might have to return home and find him still missing. Her father takes a bite of his meatloaf.

"Jasper's gone to bed already?" he asks.

"I don't know," Mom answers. "He's not here."

Eddie looks from her to Wallis, but Wallis looks away. He pushes back from the table and starts up the stairs. "When?" he calls.

"Sometime last night?" Mom replies. "He didn't sleep in his bed."

"Why didn't you call me?"

"So that you could miss another day of work?"

Wallis hears her father leave Jasper's room and head down the hall to check the top drawer of his own dresser. All the credit cards are there, the checkbooks, the paper rolls of quarters and dimes waiting to go to the bank. Mom's rings and her grandmother's pearls. There was plenty he could have stolen but nothing is missing, they checked all that earlier. Eddie stalks past them downstairs and out the sliding door.

"Where are you going?" Mom asks, but Wallis already knows. She follows her father to the carport where his coffin rests on sawhorses waiting its retirement. He is looking for Jasper in the places Wallis hid as a little girl.

He opens the lid and the light of the bare bulb falls on the shallow heart carved in its underside.

"W + J?" he asks, searching her face.

Her hand the night she inscribed that heart had been moving in some other dimension where loving Jasper would be acceptable to everyone, cause no trouble, break no laws. Now that he has run away, she feels sick at the sight of it, as though she had awakened from a troubled fever dream.

Her mother steps out into the yard and stands at the edge of her peony beds. "Did Jasper hurt you?" she asks.

"Of course not," answers Eddie.

"I'm asking Wallis."

"Listen to yourself," Eddie turns on her. "He's just a confused kid who thinks nobody cares about him and it seems he's right."

"And yet," observes Mom, "we are not talking about finding you a new job, or where we might live if we have to move, or where Wallis will be going to school. We're talking about him. Even when he's not here, he's still the center of attention."

While they argue, Wallis leans against her father's box, remembering how peaceful it had felt to float. She wanted Jasper to kiss her and
he did. She wanted him to go away and now he's gone. She leaves them
in the yard and walks back to the house where Tucker Hayes's projector is sitting by the kitchen door like a pet waiting patiently to go out.
Wallis sets it on the table and flips the latches. The iron arms are naked
and the Edison short, as she knew it would be, is gone.

"He stole it," she says, when Eddie returns to the kitchen.

"It was his," he replies. "I gave it to him."

"Clearly he's going to pawn it," Mom says, stepping in.

He is a thief and runaway, Wallis thinks. He was my first kiss.

"I'm going to drive around," her father says.

"He's probably five states away by now," says Mom.

"I'll come with you," interrupts Wallis, following her dad to the
hearse. Her mother doesn't move.

"I guess I'll stay home," Ann says bitterly. "In case he comes scratching at the door."

Eddie throws the hearse into reverse and backs down the driveway
after Wallis climbs in. His high beams sweep the yard and soybean field,
penetrating into the woods where she buried and pissed on Jasper's
fingernail parings. I didn't do anything, she tells herself, it's not real,
but if she did nothing then there is nothing to undo, which makes it
worse. Eddie rolls down his window, reaches across her and rolls hers
down, too. He drives slowly as if searching out a dog struck and lying
dead on the side of the road.

"He can't keep running all his life," he says fiercely.

"There's a pawnshop downtown," Wallis offers. "I think it's open
all night."

"He wouldn't pawn that movie."

Still, he takes the back roads toward town. He doesn't have a plan,
but is moving to be moving so that he doesn't have to be at home with
Mom. They come to the intersection where trees and darkness swap out
for the neon of fast-food restaurants and doughnut shops, the strobing
of streetlights on the overpass. Eddie drifts straight through the green
lights at every intersection, past the three balls of the pawnshop with
their crackle and buzz of trapped red gas.

"It's not his fault," Wallis says quietly.

"Of course it's his fault," Eddie replies, his eyes still searching past the headlights. Maybe Jasper will dart across the street like a panicked deer. "If he didn't want to live with us, we could have found him somewhere safe."

"I put a spell on him," she says.

"What?" Eddie asks.

"I wanted him to like me, so I made up a spell and burned a lock of his hair. I stole his fingernail clippings and buried them. I'm like the other women of our family."

Her father looks over at her, annoyed. "Those were stupid ghost stories, Wallis. Made up by a bunch of ignorant women to feel important. Don't talk yourself into that shit like my goddamned mother. I can't take that right now."

"I mean it's not real," Wallis says, backtracking. "I know it's not real."

"Which is it? Do you want that much power over another person's life? It's fine to take the credit but do you want the blame?"

Wallis sinks down in the seat and looks up out the window. The sky over the city deepens from indigo, through violet, up to blindest black. The stars are falling here, too, as they were in the mountains, only the lights make everything harder to see.

"Look at it this way," Eddie says, realizing he's been too harsh. "Maybe you're not in control, either. Maybe someone has placed a spell on *you*."

She closes her eyes. It's a comforting thought.

Mom got the call two days later. She could have phoned Eddie but instead she and Wallis drove downtown to the Biograph alone. *Sit up and look straight ahead,* she instructed Wallis, hitting the power locks on her '78 Cutlass when they stopped at a light. *Don't make eye contact with anyone; even with the doors locked, a brick might come through the window. What have you done, Mom, to be so afraid? It's not me,* Mom assures her. *I'm the victim here, not being able to drive in whole sections of my own city. I mind my own business. I don't know what everyone is so angry about.*

The marquee of the Biograph still reads *The Cabinet of Dr. Caligari*, but it is daytime and so they are showing a movie called *Babylon Pink*, which makes Wallis think of plastic flamingos standing single-footed in yards. Two spots are open in front and Mom awkwardly parallel parks. A long line of men wait patiently for the feature to begin and Mom feeds the meter quickly, as if one of them might snatch the coins from her fingers.

"Hurry up, dear, they're waiting for us," Mom says more loudly than she needs, to let the men know she and Wallis are not alone down here; should something happen to them, they would be missed.

The manager who greets them inside the movie house wears a suit the same brown as Mom's Oldsmobile. He is pale enough to have crawled from beneath one of the cracked Islamic floor tiles.

"We found him in the alley," he says. "Sprawled out behind the Dumpster, looking like this. I tried to call the paramedics but he begged me not to. Said he didn't want to get Eddie in trouble. When he told me which Eddie, I said I'd call you instead. He didn't want that, either, but I couldn't leave him."

The manager leads them past the golden-cage ticket booth and the popcorn counter to a small door marked OFFICE. He'd locked it behind him, worried, Wallis guessed, that Jasper wouldn't be there when he got back. As he fits the key in the lock, Mom turns to her.

"You wait right here," she says. "Let me take care of it."

Wallis ignores her and pushes in past the manager. The room is even tighter than Eddie's dressing room at the station, with cheap teal carpet, a rust-colored velour love seat in the corner, more metal file cabinets, and framed, sun-faded movie posters. A window looks out onto the blank brick wall of the alley. Behind a desk overflowing with papers and books and stacked video cassettes sits Jasper.

"Damn it, Wallis," Mom says in exasperation.

Jasper looks up when they come in. His forehead is swollen over his brow and his right eye is a slit in purple flesh. His nose is bridgeless, as if it has been broken. The manager washed him up but he missed the dried blood crusted on his temple above his ear.

Mom doesn't rush to him as she would if it had been Wallis. This is a boy's beating, far beyond her experience.

"What happened?" Mom demands of the room. She doesn't care who answers but her tone says someone must. Wallis feels herself wanting to respond on Jasper's behalf. *I walked into a door.* Isn't that what battered wives say? His eyes—eye—has shifted back to the desk; he can't hold Mom's gaze. "We need to get you to the hospital," Mom says.

"I'm fine," Jasper cracks his fat lips and the words drop out.

"You are obviously not fine," Mom says, neither tenderly nor scolding, just speaking as neutrally as Wallis has ever heard her. Jasper rests his head on the desk and the manager steps in.

"Listen, this is a rough part of town. Kids can't wander the streets late at night. I should be calling the cops, but I know Eddie, and Jasper here says Eddie will get in trouble if I do. You guys need to work this out. I don't want to get in trouble for not reporting it."

"Do you have your things, Jasper?" Mom asks. He shakes his head.

"He was robbed," the manager says.

"Did you get a look at them?" Mom asks. Jasper shakes his head.

"I already asked him all this stuff," the manager says. "He doesn't know anything. He might have a concussion."

Mom has seen and heard enough. She thanks the manager, and in a completely unexpected gesture, reaches into her pocketbook. Is she going to tip him? Wallis wonders. Give him hush money? Mom takes out her checkbook, scribbling a figure and signature on it, and passes it to him. The manager isn't sure whether or not to take it—no one knows exactly what this transaction is for or about, only that somehow it makes sense for money to trade hands. Time. Effort. A donation. Call it what you like, the check implies. Jasper looks away.

"Thank you for your trouble," Mom says. She turns to Jasper.

"Let's go," she says.

Jasper shakes his head. No.

"Let's go," Mom repeats quietly. "Or I'll phone the police and let them sort it out."

Jasper rises then and trails behind them out of the manager's office. His jeans are torn and stained with mud. He walks with a limp, as though his hip has been knocked out of joint.

Mom steps out of the theater more confidently now, with a male beside them, a roughed-up male, like a spoil of war; she could be leading him by an invisible leash as a cautionary tale to all those men with their hands in their pockets waiting in lines for dark theaters on workdays. He is not one of you, she could be saying, he belongs to me. Whatever it is, she walks with her head held high, refusing to hurry now, though Jasper tucks his face and tries not to see. Across the street, sitting on the high marble steps of the beaux-arts post office, two black boys, skinnier even than he, sit smoking, appraising them.

"Take the backseat," Mom says, softer now, as she unlocks the car, "so you can lie down."

Jasper obeys, stretching out across the tan leather seats. For once Mom doesn't care about dirt or even blood. Closing his eyes, he is completely shut inside himself. Wallis hears his labored breathing.

"I'm going to give this forty-eight hours with ice and aspirin," Mom says. "If the swelling hasn't gone down by then, I'm taking you to the hospital no matter what you say."

Nothing from the back. Wallis has climbed into the front seat by her mother and turns around to look at him. Everyone knows this is what happens if you run away from home. She waits for the lecture she knows is coming, how he panicked them all with no regard for all they'd done for him, how having a home was a privilege and rules existed not to punish him but to keep him safe. But Mom sits behind the steering wheel without turning over the motor. She stares out over the crowd of milling men waiting for their porn movie to begin, and suddenly Wallis realizes what Mom has done. This was her chance to be done with Jasper. He left on his own, she could have told herself they'd done their best, let him be someone else's problem. But instead she reclaimed him like a piece of lost luggage, and now he is theirs. All those men outside the Biograph had mothers, too, good and bad, who let them go and hoped for happy endings. The men who were once boys shuffle into an orderly line just long enough to get through the door. Once inside, they'll spread out again, putting seats between them. Outside Wallis's window, a little red box flashes on the parking meter.

"We've expired," Wallis says, craning her head to look for the traffic cops. "Mom."

Ann doesn't speak or even glance at her, but turns the key in the ignition, backs up a little, and pulls around the car in front.

*   *   *

Jasper goes straight to his room and locks the door when they get home. Wallis didn't expect him to sit down and watch TV or want to go for a walk in the woods, but after several days alone on the street, she thought he might want to talk. Mom stands in the kitchen, watching him go. *He can lock us out,* she says, *but we can't lock him in. I don't know how we are going to live like this.*

Wallis putters around the kitchen while her mother makes telephone calls to all the doctors with whom they are friendly. *Put himself in harm's way. Very difficult life. Impossible to control.* Mom jots some notes and when she sets down the receiver, she looks relieved. "We have an appointment with Dr. Larson at two p.m. next Thursday," she announces. "He is supposed to be very, very good. If it weren't for him, Joanne's daughter would still be getting her stomach pumped every other weekend." She sets down her pen and pad and Wallis sees the figure $45/hour written next to his address.

"Children are such hard work, darling," Mom says with a sigh. "When your time comes, don't make the mistake I did and assume everything will turn out well. Plan for the worst and you won't be disappointed."

She opens the refrigerator and takes out a roast beef she's been thawing; it's sitting in a bath of its own blood. "I don't know whether to cook this or put it on his eye. Run ask Jasper if he feels up to joining us for dinner. Perhaps tonight he'd rather eat in his room."

Wallis leaves her mother in the kitchen and dutifully climbs the stairs to the bedrooms. While he was gone the house was tense with expectation and dread. Now he's back and the dread remains.

"What?" he asks when she knocks on his door.

"Mom wants to know if you want dinner."

"I'm not hungry," he says.

"Let me in."

"No."

"Come on," she insists. "Let me in."

After a minute, the door cracks open and Wallis pushes her way inside. The bed is still made, though the bedspread is wrinkled from lying down. Wallis doesn't know why she wanted to come in; she feels like she does at the zoo, curious and bored at the same time. She stares at Jasper, who stares back at her, and they both might as well start picking at lice and popping them into their mouths.

"What happened?" she asks. "I won't tell anyone. I promise."

"You heard. I got jumped, I didn't get a good look at them."

"Not that," Wallis says. "Tell me why you ran away in the first place. Was it because of what happened in the barn?"

Jasper is immediately on guard. "Nothing happened in the barn," he says. "I don't know what you're talking about."

"It doesn't matter. I'm not going to press charges," she says. "You know, for what you did."

"I should have known you'd turn it back to yourself," he says in disgust. "Other people don't really exist for you, do they? No matter what happens to them."

"Dad says you're not really in control of yourself because your parents died. Mom's made an appointment for you with a shrink. Maybe that'll help."

"I won't go."

"She'll make you."

"She can't. I'm bigger than she is."

"Threatening a woman? What will your shrink make of that?"

"Go away, Wallis," he says, rolling over to face the wall.

"We were worried about you, you know. You should think about other people before you run off and do something stupid. How do you think we would have felt if you ended up dead?"

"Relieved," says Jasper.

"If you stay we're miserable," says Wallis, "if you go, we're guilty. You win no matter what."

"I win? Even if I'm dead?" he asks. "Do you ever hear yourself?"

Every time she went to the zoo as a child, she'd pelt the monkey cage with peanuts. *Here's some food!* and the monkeys would wince and dodge, before cringing over and collecting it. Jasper brings his legs up to his chest and curls around himself and, thinking of those monkeys, for the first time she feels what it's like to live behind bars. No wonder they piss on everyone who walks by.

Wallis hears heavy footsteps in the hallway and a knock on the door. Her father doesn't wait for an answer but barges in.

"I got here as soon as I could," he says. Eddie kneels by the bed—*hey, son, hey, hey*—but nothing will convince Jasper to roll over and face him. He gently places his hand on the boy's shoulder.

"Did they hurt you?" Eddie whispers. Jasper squeezes his eyes tighter but he makes no answer. Eddie looks down at the filthy, ripped jeans, the blood in his hair.

"I'm taking you to the hospital."

"It's not the first time," Jasper says to the wall. "I'm okay."

"You're not okay," Eddie says, anguished.

At last Jasper rolls over and opens his swollen eyes on her father. Wallis sees something in his face she has never seen turned on herself—an honest desire to protect Eddie from the truth. He is as calm as Mom. Now is no time to get hysterical, his battered face says. What's done is done.

"The doctors will call the cops," Jasper says matter-of-factly. "The cops will throw me in foster care. And none of it will matter because I'll just run away again. I don't want another pretend family."

"It's not pretend, Jasper," Eddie says. "We want you."

Jasper holds her father's eyes until they falter. Eddie looks so helpless—he knows Jasper needs to go, he knows he won't. He reaches out to touch the boy's cheek but Jasper flinches away.

"Mom wants to know if you're coming down for dinner?" Wallis says, unable to watch any longer.

Jasper shakes his head.

"Come down," Eddie says, straightening. Wallis has reminded him that there is a life beyond the door to this room. "I bought something for you. For you both."

"What is it?" Wallis asks.

"Jasper, please," Eddie says, and slowly the boy rises from the bed, following him downstairs and through the patio door to where Eddie stops before the carport.

"I was going to wait until Christmas, but then I thought you two should be enjoying these last days before school starts—"

At first all Wallis sees is the hearse in the driveway. Then, inside the shadow of the carport, she spies the matching red and blue ten-speed bikes, propped on their kickstands. Frowning, Ann steps out of the kitchen to join them.

"I want you in our family, Jasper," Eddie says, putting his arm around Ann as if speaking for them both. "I thought you kids could use some freedom. You know, go riding together. It's what kids should be doing."

Wallis glances over at Jasper, the boy who has already run away, who is being given the means to keep going. But why is she being sent off with him? To guard him? To keep him company? Why does her father keep sending her and Jasper off alone together? Then the sickening answer comes to her. If it has to be one of us, he is saying with these bikes, better you than me.

Jasper is quiet, looking down at his high-tops. "You didn't need to do that," he says.

"Ann and I are working on my résumé," Eddie answers bluffly. "Something else will come along. We can afford these."

"You bought two boys' bikes," Wallis says.

Her dad glances at the straight crossbeams on both bicycles, different from the sloping Y of a girl's model. He watches Wallis as she struggles to stride it.

"I can take it back," he tells her.

"No," Wallis answers. "It's fine."

"Take them for a ride, kids, before it gets dark. Just don't go too far," Eddie says, but his voice belongs to someone else. Beside her, Jasper climbs dutifully onto his bike. Wallis finds her balance and pushes off, with Jasper close beside her. She doesn't look back until she explodes a cloud of dust at the edge of the dirt road. Her mother has gone inside but her dad is still watching from their driveway, a small and shrinking figure. She waits for Jasper to catch up, he, too, knows what Eddie wants and expects, and in that moment he is beside her and past her, racing ahead, raising a cloud inside the cloud.

They ride for miles without stopping. She wouldn't think Jasper could ride so hard, hurt as he is, but she works to keep up. He leads her on a long and winding route past the familiar fields of her childhood, the half-acre lots with their dingy ranch homes, plastic sliding boards in their front yards and busted trampolines in the back. Dogs run out to bark at them, they peddle faster. She keeps inside his cloud, coming close enough for the chips of gravel his back wheel throws up to nick her on the shin or cheek. He knows she's there, is dropping back on purpose, then surging forward when she gets too close. She doesn't know why she sticks by him, except that it's easier to have the goal of catching up than to strike off on her own.

The sun has nearly set when he slows his bike. Coasting along the shoulder of the road, their long, attenuated shadows fish out into the green crust of lily pads and the beaver-gnawed pencil points of trees. Jasper was right, the conductor's lantern was probably nothing more than gas from this swamp. Stories like that, no matter how much you'd like them to be, are never real. Cutting down a path that leads close to the water, Jasper climbs off his bike and parks it against a tree. Her legs shake as she climbs off, too, and she stumbles, coming down hard on the crossbeam of her boy's bike. Wallis swallows a cry of pain.

To her surprise, Jasper comes around to help her up, leaning her bike against his. They are salted with gravel dust, grimed at the neck, red-faced. He didn't seem to be winded but she can see now that he trembles like her. They leave the bikes and walk through the sedges of the swamp's rim where the sinking sun turns a line of dozing slider turtles on a log into an amber necklace. There are snappers in these swamps, tank-like, swimming just under the surface. Sometimes she sees their wake.

A fallen tree, its upended root collar splayed like a lizard's frill, juts into the water. Jasper steps out onto it as if it were a continuation of the land, walking until he reaches the broken branches of the end. Beneath his dangling foot a prehistoric beak opens and Wallis hears the snapping turtle's hiss of warning. Jasper looks down at it, his hot violet eyes erupting under the cooler flame of his orange afro. He is a Bunsen burner of a boy. Maybe he really is the mad scientist's experiment.

"It's peaceful out here," he says, turning back to her. "Come join me."

Jasper has never issued her an invitation that didn't hurt.

"You come back here to me," Wallis says.

"I'll take a step and you take a step and we'll meet in the middle," he says, taking a small step toward her to show good faith.

"I'll come out if you answer a question," she says, stepping onto the edge. She had expected her weight to raise him into the air like a child on a seesaw, but the wide tree is immovable in the water, waiting to rot there.

He is waiting.

"What happened in the mountains, the night the lights came on?"

Jasper takes another step and she can see he is trying to decide whether or not to tell her. "Take another step," he says. "So I know I can trust you."

She does and he is beside her now, with his bruised, beaten face. He leans in and for a second she thinks he plans to push her off, but instead he puts his arm around her waist and presses his swollen lips to hers, slipping his tongue inside her mouth.

He was her first and now he is her second. His hand reaches under her shirt, moves up her back, around and underneath the cup of her bra. He touches her differently this time, gently, with tenderness and desire. She can feel him hard inside the jeans he slept in on the street. He doesn't even have another pair to change into. His hip bone presses against her and something sharp pierces her leg. It's the coffin nail she slipped into her front pocket the night she carved their initials.

You are not kissing me, she thinks. You are kissing the man who sent you out here to kiss me. You are doing as he asked and you are punishing him as you do it, by giving him that impossible thing he wants, which is to find a way to keep you. If you can't have him and you can't live on the streets, I am all that is left.

"You didn't answer my question," she says. Jasper whispers into her mouth.

"I fucked your dad."

Her cheeks are wet, and when she pulls away, tears are streaming down his own. Hiding his face, Jasper squats on the fallen tree.

Wallis thrusts her fists deep in her pockets. What did Eddie say about all those dead chestnuts fallen in the woods? Their wood decomposed very slowly and fed the mountain streams, keeping dozens of other smaller species alive, but the oaks that replaced them choked the water with leaves that broke down into nothing. Wallis has learned a great deal since the night at the railroad tracks and the childish days spent wearing her grandmother's clothes as if they would impart magic. She read the walls of Cora's kitchen, she has seen the hostages on TV. History does not repeat itself directly, she understands. Real witchcraft doesn't follow a script. It's not something handed down like a recipe or a blood type but discovered and created anew in every generation. Someone else's curse, like the story of someone else's love affair, is meaningless and hollow. Only our own love has the power to damage.

Backlit by the sinking sun, the strands of Jasper's hair stand out like broken blood vessels in a crazed eyeball. Clouds slant, Venus is bright on the horizon. Wallis steps off the log onto soil so heavy with water it can't be called earth anymore. She feels it opening up beneath her feet and knows she could sink forever.

She steps to the tree where they parked their bikes, a swamp oak, nothing so rare as a chestnut. None of her spells are premeditated. They come as they come. She fishes out the coffin nail and carves a deep rough oval in the tree's bark. Two round eyes. A gash of mouth. A drop of amber sap wells up like spittle at the corner. Did she see this face across the divide at Panther Gap or did she create it, now, scoring the skin of the living tree? Jasper looks up, recognizing his own primitive features. She gives him a moment to take it in, thinking of the initials she'd carved into that lid, weeks before. W + J. Stupid, baby magic. Letters and hearts. She feels the humiliation of that little-girl desire, not to be able to think beyond a kiss.

"You were right," she says. "If you were dead, we'd all be so relieved."

She reaches down for a stone and with one sharp blow, hammers the nail directly between his eyes. Just below the surface at Jasper's feet, the turtle snaps its jaws. On the next log, awakened, the amber necklace slides away.

Wallis

NEW YORK CITY

5:00 a.m.

"You didn't kill him," Jeff says, leaning up on his elbow. "It was a picture. Some words."

"I was a selfish, vindictive kid and I drove him to it," Wallis argues. "Now I write the news—more pictures and words. They have so much power, Jeff."

Lying in his arms, Wallis sees he finally understands why she is here.

"You don't want to be comforted, do you?" he asks, sadly. "You'd rather be guilty. You know they made up the idea of original sin not to punish but to console us. When all the incomprehensible shit goes down, we can blame ourselves, it was something we did or didn't do. Without guilt, we are irrelevant. And that is so much worse."

"Who is They? Who is this mysterious They that makes up original sin?" Wallis asks. "I'm starting to believe what we call God is just enough people buying into an idea to form a force big enough to create the resistance to itself that can be called the Devil."

"This is why life evolved sex. So for a few minutes we can be separate and inside each other at the same time and forget about everything in between."

"Don't take my guilt away," she says, trying to smile. "It's all I have."

"I know what you're doing," he says, stroking her still-damp hair. "You're turning me into your confessor, the man you fucked for absolution on the anniversary of that boy's death. I can't give it to you. We had a lovely night together but my girlfriend is coming home this week and you are married. I stand behind the camera and I watch you, Wallis. You're a star, just like your dad. All the wars, trials, suspected biological attacks. The hunt for WMDs. You have a gift for keeping it going, hour after hour of nonnews, finding some new angle to keep us up all night, riding that rush. It's all just running and distraction from the one breaking story none of us can bear to face. If you don't want to be scared, stop telling ghost stories."

This stranger's face is so close to hers, more familiar than her own husband's. He has spent all night listening, but now his eyes are weary and closing and she knows she has worn him out. Wallis reaches over the edge of the bed for her skirt, pulls on her panties, and snaps her bra. She buttons her shirt and pulls on her pink tweed jacket.

"Thank you for having me," she says to Jeff.

"I'll walk you to the train."

He tugs on his own clothes, grabs an umbrella, and together they head out into the rain. Eddie loved to tell her how a young girl, just like her, had written a ghost story once, as part of a contest. All the men were much more celebrated writers, but hers was the story everyone remembers, the tale of a bad parent who created a monster he couldn't control that took its revenge by destroying everyone its parent loved. All Wallis ever wanted was the chance to tell the story. But to whom? Jeff? The insomniacs on the other side of the camera?

Mom and I watched your last show, Dad, from the living room at home, the length of the sofa between us. A week had passed since you sent Jasper and me off on our bikes. When I came home alone I told you Jasper had pulled ahead of me, that I lost track of him. I thought I should come back before it was too late, just like you'd told us. You pretended to believe me and I went to bed while you and Mom waited up. *Gone again,* I heard her say. *Maybe it's a blessing.* Sometime the next day you called the police, and Friday night they came to the door after midnight to tell us his body had been found in the swamp, his stomach full of sleeping pills. Oh, God, gasped Mom. *Mine.* Terrible shame you have to be mixed up in this, Eddie, they said. We know you tried to help, there's just no getting through to some kids.

All week the station ran farewell commercials for Captain Casket. They showed you climbing into your coffin while a disembodied hand nailed the lid shut. I wanted to come with you to do your makeup one last time, but you told me no, you didn't want to leave Mom alone again.

She made no popcorn or daiquiris that night, she was worn out from being on the phone all day making arrangements for Jasper's funeral. The opening credits rolled on the TV. The *Creepshow*'s dripping letters, and the Casketeers' warbling theme song. *I'll be so happy never to watch another horror movie again*, Mom said. I said nothing. It was the end of summer but the air conditioner was on and I was curled under a blanket.

The camera panned in on your coffin, center stage, and we waited for your hand to appear, raising the lid. We waited but the casket remained closed. The dry ice evaporated and the fog disappeared. In the dead air, Mom's body tensed beside me. Then, after what seemed an eternity, you stepped out from stage left carrying Tucker Hayes's old projector. You were not in costume or makeup, you wore your raw, fallen face and your weatherman's liver-colored leisure suit.

This is our last show, guys and ghouls, you said, *after twenty long years together. It's been an honor to thrill and dismay you, but all bad things come to an end.*

We heard nervous laughter offstage. None of the crew knew what you were doing. That Eddie, they were whispering to each other. You never know what's coming next.

In a few minutes, we're going to roll our feature—Boris Karloff's Frankenstein. *It was Captain Casket's first film. But Eddie Alley had his own first. A friend left it for me before he vanished. I thought it was lost and later I thought it was stolen. It came back to me in the mail today, a gift from beyond the grave.*

When you set down the projector, I saw you were holding a padded envelope. Jasper had written you so often over the years, goofy and sincere, starting from the age of nine. He sent you drawings of his pets and descriptions of his mother's hospital bed, and asked if you'd please write back. I imagined you walking into your dressing room before the show and finding that envelope propped against your makeup mirror. You would have instantly recognized the handwriting and the postmark. But for the first time, you would hesitate before you opened it. Jasper was a boy who played with fire and blew things up. Did he love you anymore? Did he want to hurt you?

Now, onstage, you unlatched the cover and threaded the film through the intricate mechanism of the projector.

It's not very scary, you said, *but firsts have a way of haunting you.*

You nodded for John the cameraman to dim the lights and you steadied the projector on the old family casket and began to turn the crank. John panned over to the wall above the news set that had been rolled aside and zoomed in so that he could capture the whole frame. I had only seen the end, that night through the slats of the barn, so I watched along with all your other fans, the silent comings and goings of the monster. I closed my eyes, but the creature was replaced by Jasper climbing the marble steps to the post office downtown. He turned and showed me the nail between his eyes. I opened mine again only when I heard ragged weeping beside me. Mom, on the far end of the sofa, was reading the last title card. *The Creation of an Evil Mind, Overcome by Love, Disappears.*

When John the cameraman panned back to you, the stage was empty. You were gone. Not knowing what else to do, after a brief, confused silence, John ran the feature.

Mom held out her arms and I crawled across the space between us.

"It's all over," she sobbed.

Eddie

NEW YORK CITY

DAWN

When Charles and I moved to New York you were here in college, squinting out at the city through the raccoon eyeliner you used to wear, your hair spiked blue, green, red, it was different every time. When we used to visit, you'd introduce us to your boyfriends—the tattoo artist, the skinhead, the Jew for Jesus you met on the subway, the drug addict. You liked trying to shock us with them as much as you liked trying to shock them with us—your gay dad, and Charles, so well brought up in his oxford cloth shirts and penny loafers, looking more like Dad's CPA than Dad's lover. We'd been up to see you a dozen times before we decided to move here ourselves, and I remember you were none too happy about it. I was crowding you, you said. In a city of eight million people. We took our first apartment on the Upper East Side over an Italian restaurant that became our living room, we entertained there so much. Those were heady times, just coming out, and I used to embarrass Charles by groping him in public just because I could. I would walk through the streets and smell burned pretzels and burned sugar and the clean laundry steam from pipes jutting up between taxis. Everything was new and clear.

One night, walking home from your apartment on the Lower East Side where you had made me sit at your folding card table eating vegan chicken and sprouts, listening to God-knows-what gamelan and chainsaw music you'd just discovered, trying to talk to your boyfriend without staring at his track marks, I left your building and passed a group of homeless men who had broken apart a school desk and were feeding the wooden top into a barrel. I looked down the median on Houston Street and I saw five or six more of those flaming barrels and men standing around them and such desire sprang up in me, Wallis, such shaking desire, the thought of going back to my third-floor walk-up where Charles would be waiting up, reading a military history, his white ankles crossed on the ottoman, a glass of wine on the side table by the chair, the apartment dark except for the spot of light under which he read—I thought, after all this time, I have finally accepted myself and I should be able to run amok like King Kong, shoving myself into the ass of every man I meet, sucking and stroking and exploding out into a million fragments of sex, and here I am at the moment of acceptance, for all purposes married again. I love that man, but I want to be down here, warming my hands over a flaming barrel, a man among men. I want to be broke. I want to be free.

What came next that night was the cold of the sidewalk through the soles of my shoes and my feet numb from standing and staring, and I turned away and got on the subway at Second Avenue and made my transfers and climbed the steps and found the lock with my quivering key. Charles was where I expected him to be, reading what I expected him to be reading, and smiled when I came in and made a joke about your awful boyfriend, and silently I blessed him for giving up everything and moving here with me so that I might have the freedom to imagine leaving him as many times as I needed to imagine it. I kissed him long and deep and was restored.

There is no past, my butcher told me. There is no future. There are only sirens on the avenue and the comforting knowledge I live at last in a city full of emergencies not of my own making. Somewhere far away, I hear pounding in the hallway and a distant shouting. I hear the splintering crack of a door broken wide and wonder how Charles will ever explain this to the co-op board.

Then there are capable hands and instruments and incantations and the painful, electric, convulsive reanimating of my corpse. I am lifted and transferred and am once again in motion. And somehow, Wallis, I know you have heard me.

Wallis

New York City

Dawn

Jeff waited with her on the cold elevated platform until the train's headlights swung down the track. The night had softened to a pigeon gray but she knew the rain would keep falling, as it had every day all summer. The train pulled away and Jeff, without a backward glance, took the steps down to the street.

Wallis leaned her head against the cold glass window behind her seat and felt an echo of the same crick she'd felt driving up the mountains the night of her father's anniversary party. Drawing her legs up under her pink skirt, she lay down on the triple bench and immediately felt more comfortable. Through the windows in the door, she could see neon advertisements for car parts, glowing boxes of low-end grocery stores, cascading traffic lights haloed in the fog. Rain ran down the panes but she couldn't hear it over the clack and crash of the train hurtling toward Manhattan. It was over an hour ago that she had called the ambulance from Jeff's bed, and surely it had arrived by now. The paramedics had broken down the door of his apartment, found his half-alive, barely breathing body, administered CPR, charcoal, hooked him up to tubes. She wondered if she did the right thing in calling them, if it wouldn't have been kinder, so near the end, to just let him have his way. But if he hadn't wanted her to try, he shouldn't have left her a message.

Let it go, she thought. I'll find what's there to be found. Sleepily, she thought of something her mother told her, trying to comfort her after Jasper's death. Some people are just too damaged to live. It's natural selection, sweetheart. I've never read Darwin, but I'm sure he would agree.

The train hurtles on and she is flying high above the city. She tucks her legs closer, pulls her damp pink jacket tight around her.

Dad, you pathetic drama queen, wherever you are between here and there, I love you.

The rhythm of the train is rocking her to sleep. She struggles to stay awake. She doesn't want to miss her stop.

Eddie

Wallis, my little girl. Love comes for us all. We run from it, we hide from it, but in the end it finds us where we are cowering. We creaky old monsters are returned to life. That's why all the best horror movies have a sequel.

It really wasn't necessary. Any of it. All of it.

But thank you.